GW00494425

THE HOLLOW HOUSE

THE HOLLOW HOUSE

CARLO DELLONTE

PICADOR

First published 2001 by Picador

an imprint of Pan Macmillan Limited
Pan Macmillan, 20 New Wharf Road, London N1 9RR
Basingstoke and Oxford
Associated companies throughout the world
www.panmacmillan.com

ISBN 0 330 48048 0

1 3 5 7 9 8 6 4 2

A CIP catalogue record for this book is available from
the British Library.

Phototypeset by Intype London Ltd
Printed and bound in Great Britain by
Mackays of Chatham plc, Chatham, Kent

To Mike Saphir, Richard Hogan and Paul Schreiber
who taught me the love for literature, and
in memory of my friend
Stefano

Acknowledgements

I'd like to thank my father, always my first enthusiastic but critical reader, Mattias Hulting and Erik Wollin for their honest and valuable critiques on my first draft, Anne Enright and Áine Miller for their precious suggestions and encouragement, and last but not least Fíona Ní Chinnéide, Mary Mount, Nicola Carpanelli and Christian Blencke.

I

Of my past before that day I will say nothing. I was racing away from it to the place where I would crush it. I couldn't stand the pain of having to look for directions, I had no patience, I had choked all clarity of mind with my desire to get to the Cliffs. I had left the city behind me, and I drove past small towns and through stretches of countryside that grew longer and emptier, while the rain and the darkness swallowed the land. By the time the Cliffs appeared on the road-signs, the villages had turned to small clusters of houses inhabited by lone porch-lights that shone over entrances and reflected in dark windows. These were soon gone too, and ahead only blackness remained under the assault of the weather. I had shuddered many times at the idea of this trip, before and after the road started rolling under me, but all I could think of now was the final stop, the gravel grinding to a halt beneath the car's wheels. It was so vivid and certain in my mind, but the pattering of the rain was all I would hear. I felt it meant something, not the rain but the distance of my imagination from how things were.

Still I went on. The road became a sallow, battered band in front of me. Tall grass brooded dark and drenched over its edges. I couldn't see much beyond, but I could feel the land rise and fall over hills that were a preamble to the Cliffs.

When I thought I had reached them the road dipped low

again and curved to the right. It skirted a group of houses lurid in the rain, a village too small or too forgotten to be on the map. I didn't even read its name on the road-sign.

Beyond a handful of roofs I thought I could see the black waves of the sea. The road ran parallel to it and up a steep slope. The cowardly thoughts I had kept at bay so far began to shout all at once, telling me I need not go any further, that I had gone far enough, but I was stuck in my seat, and my foot was on the accelerator. I couldn't turn round, I couldn't stop, I was moving forward with this dream or nightmare I was seeking, and hoping at the same time for a way out of it.

I realized I was not climbing the last stretch of land before the Cliffs, but another hill. At the top a house rose tall like the trunk of a gigantic tree. The boards of the façade were black and split like bark, but a spot of light lit a bed-and-breakfast sign, and the windows on the ground floor emitted a faint glow.

I lifted my foot off the accelerator. This house could be the answer to my hopes, or a pause, at least, before the Cliffs. Just a pause, I told myself, not the defeat of my plan. After all, it was too dark and stormy for me to go on now. I parked on a gravel lay-by to the right of the house. The handbrake clicked up and then there was no sound but the violent pattering on the metal roof. I hesitated, then flung open the door.

Rain and wind washed over me as I ran to the house and knocked. The door had a wooden frame and an inner rectangle of frosted glass through which I could see shadows. For a second one seemed to waver, then stilled. I knocked louder. The shadow wavered again, and slowly, with what might have been hesitation, it moved towards me.

The door opened a little way. A young woman peered out, a dark shape over the thin slice of the lit interior. She inspected me hesitantly. Then, her eyes opened wider in surprise.

'Hello,' I said, 'do you have a room available?'

'A room?'

'For the night. This is a bed-and-breakfast, isn't it?' I took a step back to look at the sign again.

'Well . . . yes.'

'May I come in? I'm getting soaked.'

She continued to look at me. The surprise in her eyes, if it had ever been there, was gone. The rain slapped at me. Had she not opened the door properly then, I would have run back to my car and everything would have been different. But she opened it, stepped aside, and I walked in.

A last claw of wind and rain reached after me, but only ruffled the girl's hair as she closed the door. Now in the light of the interior her dark shape had colour and substance. She was a few years younger than me, blonde and blue eyed, with a thin, supple body. She wore a white sleeveless top that hugged her, and ended just above a long, dark skirt. It let her abdomen appear and disappear as she moved. I wouldn't want to describe her physical beauty, for I felt something beyond the purely aesthetic pervading her figure, a pleasant disharmony of sorts, like the seraphic candour of her skin that seemed at odds with the abundance of her breasts and the pink burst of her lips.

'Right,' she said, looking down the narrow hallway and passing slender fingers behind an ear. She seemed to be re-directing her thoughts. She paid no attention to the wind and rain knocking at the door. I had been afraid that she might answer them by throwing me out. Instead she walked to a tiny reception desk further down the hallway. She knelt behind it and rooted around for something.

A door to the left led into a living room, the floor covered with carpets, the furniture old, its wood as sinuous and red as flesh in the light of lamps perched here and there. A metal one in the shape of a peacock stood on the reception desk, its tail folded and flat as support and its body arched around the dome of the light, which hung from its beak.

'Nice,' I said. 'Nice place.'

I heard her flutter some papers. 'I need to find the register,' she said.

The hallway ended in a flight of steps that ascended into darkness. 'Do you have any other guests at the moment?' I asked hesitantly.

'No.'

'So you have a room?'

'I can't find the register,' she said.

'Is . . . is it a problem?'

'I need to take down your name and address.'

'My name?' I asked, and I heard again the wind and rain at the door, and I could sense my car outside and the road I still had to travel to its end. 'Is my name so important?'

When I met her glare I made a hurried gesture towards the front door to change the subject, although I could only think about the end of my trip. 'The Cliffs I . . . I thought the Cliffs brought a lot of tourists.'

'They do, but why would anybody want to stay for more than a couple of hours? And hardly anybody takes this route to get there.'

'Strange.'

'Not really.'

She looked at me standing there awkwardly, and seemed to have forgotten the importance of the register. The peacock looked at me too, with reproachful metal eyes. Again the girl fumbled with some papers, but soon gave up and rested her elbows on the desk. She turned her head from left to right then sighed. 'Well, all right,' she said standing up. 'Just leave some form of identification so I can write down your details once I find the register.'

4

She pulled a key out of a drawer and held it on the reception desk under her hand. I fumbled for my driving licence and handed it to her. 'First floor,' she said, and pushed the key towards me. 'The door on the left.'

I managed brief thanks, but she had disappeared below the desk again.

The stairs were dark and I couldn't find the light switch. I looked back at my hostess, who was pulling out a leather-bound black book. It seemed too big for her not to have found it earlier. She glanced in my direction, but I pretended not to have noticed and continued upstairs in the dark, aware of nothing but the rain dripping from my hair, and the wind pressing hard against the windows.

I found my room and closed myself in, to place another barrier between me and my plan to leave. The window was a pale rectangle on the opposite wall, and the outside was staring in at me. My hand raced for the light switch. A trembling glow shone from the middle of the ceiling, the window turned into a black mirror, and the outside was gone under the image of a colourless room dotted with tired, old furniture. I was a miserable shape among them, the weak centre of a reflection shaken by gusts of wind and rain.

I pulled the curtains. I lay down on the bed, which was placed under the window, and looked up at the ceiling. I still felt the movement of the car under me, and I couldn't close my eyes without seeing the landscape change, towns and fields and scattered farms, and then that last stretch of empty land under the rain, rising and falling towards this place. I ran over the conversation I had had with my hostess and imagined it better. I shaped it into thirty seconds of perfect understanding, perfection between us, her initial animosity wiped out. No, I told myself, it was pointless to hope for something more than simple lodging, and I had to move on. My mind returned to the land undulating to the edge of the Cliffs. Still, I thought, there are no rules for how people are to come to-gether. It can begin in the worst ways. I tried to breathe deeply. The rain hit the window insistently. I felt an urge to leave or to see her again.

I walked to my door and opened it. A sound rang up into the darkness. A few more notes followed. It was not a melody, just bursts and trickles of notes, fast and slow, but I sensed impatience in them.

I followed the sounds to the threshold of the living room. A piano stood against the opposite wall, and the girl was sitting at it. One of her hands was caressing the keys. It moved back and forth over them, every now and then a finger pressing one. Her legs were crossed under her skirt. Through it I could see one thigh curving smoothly over the other. Next to me, under the reception desk where the girl had looked for the register, there were two shelves with a few papers on them. The peacock shone its light down on the leatherbound book she had taken out, and I thought its beak was smiling in mockery. My weight swayed, my feet unsure which direction to take. The floorboards squeaked under me and the girl turned round.

'Hi,' she said, and played a couple of high notes. 'Please come in. Sit down.'

I wasn't sure what to make of her smile but it glowed bright as sunshine after her previous unfriendliness. She pointed at a red armchair close to her. For a few seconds I wavered, then I pushed myself forward, afraid that her smile would disappear.

One of her hands was resting on her knee, my driving licence held between two fingers. 'Here you go,' she said, handing it to me. 'Your name is Charles.'

'Yes, it is.'

'Funny.'

6

'Funny?' I asked, then feared my question would spoil her mood. 'Oh, I don't mind. It's . . . it's interesting that you would find it so.'

'No, it's not your name that's funny. The whole situation is.'

'What do you mean?'

'I was thinking about another Charles when you arrived. It's as if thinking made things happen, isn't it?' She leaned forward, her arms resting on her thigh. Her cleavage rose under her top. She noticed me looking at it, but didn't seem to mind.

I was thrilled and embarrassed at the same time. 'Well,' I said quickly, 'I suppose it depends on how strong your thoughts are. You conjured up the wrong Charles, didn't you?'

'Yes, I did, didn't I?'

Silence flooded the room, pouring into nooks and corners of furniture, making it seem as alive as the belly of a whale, uncaring of the storm that raged outside. The girl seemed equally at ease, looking at me, waiting.

'To be honest,' I said, fumbling out words I thought might impress her, 'I think the only way to bring about something is by creating the right conditions for it. For example, I—'

'Depends what's within your reach,' she said, interrupting me.

'Then you need to stretch further,' I said, almost boldly, trying indirectly to exorcize my fear of the Cliffs. 'Sometimes literally, by travelling maybe. It might not seem like a good idea at first, or at any time, but it will lead you into something new.'

She looked at her lap and nodded, but I couldn't understand whether she was nodding at me or at some thought in her head.

'Are you superstitious?' I asked.

'Is that bad?'

'No, no, I'm just asking.'

'I'm not. But I have faith.'

'Faith in what?'

'Just faith.' She sat up straight. 'Not all the time, though.'

'So who's this Charles anyway?' I asked.

'Somebody I know,' she said, then shook her head. 'Doesn't matter now. Oh, by the way, I do apologize if I was rude to you earlier.'

'No, why? Nothing happened.'

'I mean, you're a nice guy.'

'Thanks.'

'Are you, Charles?'

'Am I what? A nice guy?'

She was waiting for an answer.

'I suppose so.'

Her eyes narrowed almost imperceptibly.

'Well, so, what's your name?' I asked.

'Amber.'

'That's a beautiful name.'

She leaned back against the piano. 'It doesn't mean anything. I'm named after old sap. If I had darker skin perhaps it would make sense.' She pulled a corner of her top above her stomach. 'You know what I mean.'

I stared at her skin glowing in the warm light of the room. 'Still,' I said, 'I think it's a beautiful name. Mine is very common.'

'Yours has a meaning. It defines something.'

'Well, I suppose you could interpret yours as well,' I said. 'Amber is like a precious stone really, and—'

'It's just a pretty toy. It's see-through and cheap. You're not the only one who thinks my name is beautiful.'

Her voice had altered and she looked away from me. She

pressed a key or two, then stretched a hand over the piano and stroked its smooth surface. I was afraid she was offended. I felt further away from her, but part of me was content and not worried because from this distance I could look at her with an easier desire.

'I don't know what my name means,' I said eventually.

'Funny.'

'Yes, I suppose this is.'

She smiled. We had moved closer again, just a bit, and I felt a touch of uneasiness again. I forced myself to ignore it. 'Do you live here alone?' I asked. She nodded. 'So we're alone now,' I said more to myself than to her. She nodded again. She seemed at ease with our isolation. 'And what do you do? I mean, apart from managing this place.'

'You know those houses down the road?' she asked, then paused, as if to choose her next words. 'I have some friends there. I spend some time with them. And then I read . . . I waste time, a lot of time . . .'

'You play the piano,' I suggested.

'What? No, I can't.'

'So how come you have one?'

She shrugged. 'It has always been here. I like the sound. And the way the keys respond to pressure.' She played a note and drifted away with it, then played a few more. She swung her foot gently. Grey woollen socks followed the sinuous lines of her feet and disappeared beneath her skirt. I moved in my seat, but she seemed to have forgotten me.

'I used to take piano lessons when I was a kid,' I said, with growing unease. 'I was pretty bad at it. My parents had to put stickers on the keys, pictures of cute animals or something funny so I would remember which one to strike. I think I can still remember a couple of tunes. I'll teach them to you.'

'What? No, no thanks.'

'They're very simple.' I said, moving to the edge of my seat. 'Kids' stuff.'

'No, really,' she said. I held myself on the edge of my armchair, still leaning forward in her direction. She didn't notice me. She was lost in her thoughts again. Her hand caressed the underside of her thigh. Her movements were thoughtless and pure, I felt, but they might have held an invitation. I was close to her and could smell a faint, pleasant fragrance. I inched forward.

'So you're a tourist, are you?' she asked.

'Am I a . . . no, not really.'

'But you're going to the Cliffs.'

I fell back in my seat. I didn't want to think about them. 'Not in this weather.'

She fixed a strand of hair behind her ear. 'Oh, the rain's not the problem,' she said. 'It's the wind that pushes people over.'

'I'm sorry?'

'Every year somebody goes right up to the edge and before they know it the wind has pushed them over. It comes when you least expect it. Remember that when you go there tomorrow.' She paused. 'We had an American last year.'

'Who fell over?'

'Yes. It's something you wouldn't expect. One moment everything's fine and the next he's over the edge.'

'Maybe he jumped,' I said.

She thought about it, tapping a finger against her plump lower lip. 'No, I mean the wind is what was unpredictable, not him. It was a sunny day, without a cloud in the sky. Of course, nothing would have happened if he hadn't stood right on the edge.'

She seemed to listen to her words dying around her then

drifted away again, into hidden thoughts. Through her words the weather had returned to me, and I found myself turning to look at the window. I saw my reflection and I thought of the American plunging six hundred feet to his death, a frothy wave moving fast to meet him. A simple mistake. I didn't want to think about it. My eyes glided along the glass to her reflection and looked at it for a long time. I couldn't have asked for anything more than just to look at her like this, to frame her image in my mind, but something in me growled at my passivity.

'So you rarely have guests here?' I said, turning back to her. She nodded.

'And you never get lonely?' I asked, nearly swallowing my own words with their implication.

'I don't mind,' she answered. 'And I do have guests now and again. I talk to them. I think only one or two stayed for more than a night, so I only scratch the surface when we talk, but it's enough to make me think. Most of them are from the city. I suppose you are too, aren't you?' I nodded. Her eyes seemed to find a new, but short-lived interest in me. 'I should say cities. They come from all over the place. Different places from here, though. It's nice, you see. The funny thing is that I like talking to them even if it unsettles me.'

'How come?'

She shrugged. 'You have to be in the right frame of mind when you talk to others. Listening without thinking about yourself.' She paused. 'Or something like that.'

'Well,' I said, 'I suppose I shouldn't bother you with my tales of city life.'

'Yes,' she said simply.

She pushed back her stool, then lowered her head slowly till her cheek rested on the piano keys. Several notes rang out at the same time. She held her hand in front of her face and continued her rarefied playing. I searched for words I didn't find. Her word had been final, but in a way I had led her to it. Frantically I looked back at my involvement, trying to understand how conscious it had been. The notes she was playing distracted me, but I found that the end of our conversation, of all interaction, had brought me a hint of relief.

Relief! The weather boomed back inside my head. This was the same kind of relief I had felt in delaying my trip to the Cliffs. It was not satisfaction, it was a feeling of having been spared. The only satisfaction I could feel was a lame enjoyment of her reflection in the window. I pushed myself out of my seat and walked out of the room.

'Goodnight, Charles,' I heard her say, once I was past the door.

I looked back. Her voice sounded a thousand times better than the weather outside.

'Goodnight,' I answered. I looked at the front door but I couldn't force myself to leave.

'I like your name,' she said, when I was already walking up the stairs.

I was going to return the compliment but I knew I couldn't, and I couldn't think of anything else to say.

In my room I drew the curtains, undressed and slipped under the blankets. The inane words we had exchanged rapped inside my head with the same evil insistence of the raindrops against the window. The curtains were no veil over the end of my trip, but they had to do for now. I was not looking for something to hold me back, I needed no help, but for something that would make me forget, for a while. The raindrops didn't grow fainter, and the words we had exchanged remained just as loud. Staying wasn't easy either. I turned in bed, repeatedly, mocked, I felt, by the sterile smell of the clean sheets. It was simple lodging that I was being offered, and I had no strength, no capacity to ask for more. And still I clung to thin words, to the lame conversation of that evening. The Cliffs, I had to get to the Cliffs, they would transform me, and afterwards I could come back, maybe . . .

I sank into sleep without realizing it, because nothing had changed. I dreamed of dark rooms where thoughts and images continued to echo about me, and she appeared, ripe and candid, to ask me what made her so attractive, and I thought her words were a proposal, but I said and did nothing about it. I gasped and coughed, my eyes opened, and my dream melted back into my room. Only she was still there.

The curtains had been opened and the rain had stopped. The weather had paused. It looked in, silently, with rays of moonlight. She was standing close to the wardrobe, her hands flat against it, flooded by that blue light from outside. Her hair was tied at the back of her head and it shone like marble, single strands running through it like carvings on its surface. Her face was more luminous and less defined, but her eyes were intense, and they were looking at me with an expression I couldn't interpret. She had noticed I was awake, and she stared at me for a long time.

When she moved she glided along the floor without a sound, and came to sit on the bed. I had lifted a hand instinctively, as if to protect myself. She looked at it in mid-air, and I looked at her looking at it, trying to peer beyond my rushing heartbeat and into her mind. Gently she bit her lower lip, her eyes gave into something, and she took my hand and placed it on her shoulder.

She guided my fingers between the strap of her top and that of her bra. I watched them pull the first strap past her shoulder. Her skin seemed to glow with heat as much as with light, or maybe it was my fingers growing cold.

The clarity of it! After the useless words we had exchanged, after my loser's dreams, our physical contact felt unreal and it ran through my arm and my body like ripples of vertigo. I was neither angry nor content any more, but afraid.

Under her guidance, my hand had reached her elbow. She let go of it, our contact was broken, and she stood up. My hand shook. Her eyes moved away from me, she grabbed the lower edge of her top and pulled slowly. Her stomach began to glow in the light from outside, but she stopped when the shadows of her breasts emerged. I looked at this pause with hope, I found myself clinging to the failure I had sensed earlier, to its safety, but she pulled her top over her head. She paused again, as if listening to an invisible voice, then she put her thumbs under the waistband of her skirt and slowly pushed it down.

Inside me I felt evolutions I didn't think possible. The more skin became visible, the more its light tore past my fears. I knew that the contact of a few moments earlier was about to be repeated, but I felt more ready for it. I was still removed, unsure, and I had the impression she was too, but in a different way, in her pauses and in her eyes, which shifted from me to some indefinite point inside her head.

She stepped out of her skirt. Her legs curved downwards with perfect lines to her woollen socks. She reached for the blanket and pulled it off me. I watched her hands slip under my T-shirt, and my breath choked, then eased a bit, and suddenly it was filled with the fragrance I had sensed in the living room. She stepped onto the bed, and with careful moves climbed on top of me. She reached for my hand and placed it on her cheek and ran it down over her body to her stomach, then moved it up again and held it over a breast, her eyelids closing for a few seconds.

The light of her body had burned through my fear. Our

contact, her softness under my hand, had flowed past its remnants, and I felt restored to a deep sense of comfort and security, and the house we were in appeared in my mind like a vision, solid like a tower, its interior untouched while time flattened the land around it into an interminable plain. I moved my other hand to her back, touched it gently, but she shuddered.

Her eyes shone in the light, looking past me. My hand went rigid. Like a wave coming back, my vision crumbled. My hands fell from her body like bricks. Several minutes passed, our closeness remained unchanged, frozen. She was tense, her eyes drying and not connecting, and the breath that descended to my face was weak. I waited without moving. I thought of saying something, but the words that came to me were banal, and I remained quiet.

Slowly her breathing grew strong again, almost like a sigh. She blinked once, twice, and her eyes saw me again. She pressed herself, tentatively, against me. I saw her eyes close as she brushed her cheek against mine, and I took courage and touched her back again. She opened her eyes and slowed her movements. She did not recoil from my touch, but her stare had become fixed on a point to the left of my head. I spoke her name and asked if she was all right.

Again she stopped moving. I kept my hands on her back, but I didn't dare to move them. Time passed, her body on mine, immobile and glowing like snow on a rock. There we were, so close and so perfect, and what could I do but wait, and find terrible comfort in the closeness I had feared? But I felt her skin cold, through my own cold fingers. I could hardly feel her breathing, and her scent was gone, as if it had retreated from me. I dug through myself for a word or a movement that might resolve our suffocating closeness and fix it in the silence and emptiness around us. I found nothing, and

15

nothing changed between us and nothing could change, and it was all going to end, and melt away, and I didn't know what to do about it.

She was the one to move. She pulled herself up, closed her eyes, pushed her head back, and that long sigh of earlier returned, more discouraged, almost a gasp. She ran a limp finger down my body, then stepped off the bed. She picked up her clothes. Her eyes were quick and focused.

'What's wrong?' I asked.

A shiver ran down her. 'Never mind,' she said, disturbed by the sound of her own voice. 'It's not you,' she said, as she left the room.

More than once I placed a foot on the floor only to retract it, and my thoughts were equally inconclusive. When I got out of bed I walked to the door and opened it. Beyond I found only darkness, and silence. I couldn't look for her as I felt that something greater than my passivity held me captive, and all I could do was cough to mark my presence. I felt hers somewhere, the darkness dense and impenetrable around us, held tight within the walls of the house.

I walked back into the room and sat on the bed. I thought I heard a knock at the door downstairs, but it was more like a memory than anything real. I went back to the landing anyway, but the sound didn't come again. I thought I heard a car too, but from my window I couldn't see lights in any direction, just the dark mass of the land I had crossed a few hours earlier, stretching empty towards other houses too far away to be seen or considered. I opened the window. The air still smelt of rain. Black clouds had returned and swallowed all moonlight, but for a moment their mass broke and a white beam touched a spot of land in the distance. The clouds closed, the beam raced back past them, and a sound came from the land, like a moan.

ii

Sleep came black and dreamless after hours of turmoil. When I woke up a pale light was shining through the window. It was already past midday but I didn't want to get up, nor did I want to open my door. I looked at it beyond the foot of my bed, encased in the wall, and I looked at the handle, a smudge of light on its metal surface.

She wasn't going to come back. I think I pretended to myself to be still asleep. In the silence of that room, in the loneliness that was not going to change, I imagined us culminating what we had started the night before, but how could I fool myself so few hours after her rejection? My wide-eyed fantasies drowned quickly in the reality of the facts. I remembered the Cliffs, heard them call to me, but I sat up in bed and my ears searched for other sounds.

Everything was silent. Unwillingly, I got dressed and ventured out onto the landing. I glanced briefly at the stairs and for a second I thought she was standing on them, mind and shadows casting an image that disappeared with a blink.

I hid in the bathroom, which I found behind one of two other doors on the landing. It was tiny with a small window that faced inland. The hills were deep green and wet, and the sun was concealed by a grey sky. I stood at the window a long time, but I realized that I couldn't hide there all day, that I had to see her again, at least once, to pay for the room. I gathered enough strength to walk downstairs towards the inevitable, and I did so with uneasy steps, the groaning of floorboards under my feet swallowed in the silence around me. The living room looked drab and tired in the weak daylight, and at the sight of it I felt something edging towards embarrassment. On a small table was a framed picture of my hostess that I hadn't noticed the previous night. She appeared in it alone in a field, wearing a blue dress patterned with white flowers. I told myself I had achieved enough the night before, but this thought was nothing but a second-rate attempt to banish my rampant sense of failure.

I continued my tour of the house while trying to ignore the promise of salvation the Cliffs continued to offer. Across the hallway was the dining room. Tables hid under droopy white cloths, and the slender, soft figures of the furniture were made heavy by the imperfect daylight. The dining room led into the kitchen, where not a pan or a plate was out, and the steel surface of the sink was clean and dry. The window here faced the last stretch of land before the sea. I leaned forward and looked to the right. With a tang of fear I searched for the Cliffs' crest, the sight of bare rock beyond the edge of the furthest hill, but I could see only green land, undulating into the distance.

I walked back to the bottom of the stairs. I forced myself to call her name, but there was no answer and I shivered at the thought of my voice travelling to rooms I had not seen. Behind me, the peacock ignored me with its light turned off. The register was still open on the desk, my name written down in slender handwriting. Next to it was the previous day's date followed by a dash, a bridge to the day of my departure, which wasn't there.

I knew I should have written it myself, left some money, d moved on to the Cliffs. But things had happened, I told myself, and at the end of that slim bridge of ink I didn't want to see a date.

I couldn't force myself to take a decision. Instead I wandered back into the kitchen and looked for food. I found some bread in a cupboard and butter and jam in the fridge. I left the fridge open and ate in front of it, ready to throw everything inside if I heard a sound. I grew cold, the fridge started to hum, but the house remained silent. I walked to one of the dining-room tables with a glass of milk and sipped it slowly. I expected to hear feet coming down the stairs, a key in the front door, I even expected her to appear, ghostlike and without a sound, staring at me from the hallway.

I finished my milk. The silence and solitude grew tense as time passed. There was only a clock that broke it, regularly, counting the hours from some unknown point in the house. I thought of doing something, but I only went back to the fridge to fill my glass again. I was passive. I waited for my destiny to be handed to me and I imagined it beautiful, but I felt this was my past creeping up on me and I couldn't ignore the promise of salvation and rebirth the Cliffs continued to offer. I knew it was going to be a horrifying rebirth, but I had convinced myself that it could be no other way.

Yet as I sat there, a ring of milk drying at the bottom of my glass, I clung viciously to another prospect, and I didn't care how meagre were the hopes on which it was based. I decided I wouldn't leave just yet. I wouldn't leave until I had met Amber again. I associated meeting her much more with her refusal than with her reconsideration, but I felt that whatever her choice would be it would lead me to a final resolve. After all, I had always relied on others to take decisions for me.

It was governed by a strong sense of doom that I set out to search the house. Under the aloof eyes of the peacock I found the key to the only other guest room. Back on the first floor I

19

opened the door opposite my room, but beyond it I found nobody, just the same furniture, washed out in the bleak light from outside.

I walked up to the second floor. The boards creaked under my feet, and I advanced with more cautious, slower steps, although I soon realized that my sneaking about would alarm anyone upstairs. I reached the landing with my arms held out between surrender and defence. There were three doors, arranged like those downstairs. The one above mine was closed. I peeked into the bathroom straight ahead of me and found it empty. A huge bottle of moisturizer stood on the edge of the bathtub and everything, including the soap, was bone-dry. The room on the right was used for storage, with furniture and boxes scattered about under a thin layer of dust. The window looked on to the sea and the higher position stretched my vision to it. An opaque surface of water was visible in the distance. I leaned out but I still couldn't see the Cliffs. When I looked at the ground two floors below, I felt giddy and weak.

I returned to the landing and stared at the last door of the house. For a long time I stood gripping the handle, my hand cold and sweaty. More than once I raised my hand to knock, only to return it to the handle. When I collected the courage to try the door I found it locked, and my knocking received no reply. Through the keyhole I saw a bit of the room beyond and a fat quilt pouring over the footboard of a bed. Maybe it was my eye pressed out of focus against the door, or some strange reflection that made the deep red of the quilt diffuse and soften in the air around it. Nothing else was visible, no matter how I moved my eye, but I remained there for a while, rapt in the sight of the quilt and its light pink haze.

I thought of approaching the locked room from a different angle. I went downstairs and outside and looked up past the dark walls at its window, but it only reflected the overcast sky. Around me empty grasslands stretched down the slopes of the hill on which the bed-and-breakfast was perched. On one side they plunged into the waters of the sea, and in all other directions they continued over more hills. The road I had travelled the previous night was a streak of grey through them that withered in the distance.

I stood there in the middle and nobody was in sight. She was gone.

I walked to my car and looked across its roof at the small village I had passed the previous night. It was at the foot of the hill, less than half a mile away. A long tongue of sea reached it between two rocky headlands. The water lapped a sickle-shaped beach, the sand clear, nearly white, dotted with the dark hulls of boats pulled on shore. The houses stretched from the beach inland, without getting very far. They were just a handful of desolate grey buildings with lichen-infested roofs. A steel slab of clouds advanced from the sea, and a cold wind followed or pushed it, forming green waves over the hills and ripples in the water by the beach. I was in the mood for nothing, but I felt ill rather than indifferent, and I continued to gaze at the waves breaking against the furthest headland.

I stood there for a long while with my arms crossed on the wet roof of the car, the sleeves of my jumper growing dank with water. I felt on the brink of the Cliffs, but I was looking in the opposite direction. More than once, though, I turned with the irrational fear that they were creeping up on me. I don't know what I would have done had I seen them earlier from a window, had they seen me.

I grew cold in the wind. It was almost six. The village was crawling with movement. Men trickled on to the beach. I thought I saw them stop, each one, to look up at me, but the

distance between us was too great for me to be sure. Soon
they were all in the boats, and I watched them row a short
stretch then turn on their engines. A faint hum reached me
and disappeared as the boats grew small past the rocky headlands.

Maybe somebody in the village knew where Amber was.
I searched inside my car for a piece of paper and a pen. I
scribbled that I had gone to town and that I would be back
soon. My hand shook and I made mistakes, but I blamed the
wind that flapped the paper. I scrapped the message and
rewrote it, then slipped the edge of the new note under the
front door and walked back to my car.

I drove down to the village to keep faith with my note more
than for any other reason. Trivial obligations were the only
ones I had ever managed to impose on myself. There was a
greyness in my spirit and in the air that grew thicker as I
descended the hill, but I told myself that going to the village
was like searching the house and not an excuse to drive in the
opposite direction to the Cliffs.

The only road in the village ran straight through it towards
the beach, slowly sinking under a layer of dirt and sand. Some
thirty derelict-looking houses lined up along its sides, their
windows looking at the road with resigned stares, like old
men looking at gravestones. The bed-and-breakfast was fierce
in comparison, and the air in the village felt murkier than on
the hill in the light of the hidden sun. A small van parked at
the top of the road was the only sign that the place was still
inhabited. At the other end of the road a small number of
sheds stood between the village and the beach. The last house
before them was a cross between a shop and a pub. Over the
door, golden letters on a green background read Knight in
Arms.

I parked and walked inside. A small shop was huddled next

to the windows looking on to the sea. Crates of vegetables littered the floor around a counter with an old till. Disordered cans and tins filled shelves behind it, mixed with cartons of long-life milk, boxes of sugar, tiny piles of soap and matches. Bags of potatoes were heaped against the wall next to a stack of petrol tanks that I suspected were for the boats.

The place was darker at the other end where frosted-glass windows blocked out the view of the village. Old tables and chairs hid among newer ones in front of a long, worn-out bar. Bottles filled shelves behind it. Dingy reflections of the shabby daylight reflected off their surface with the tints of different liqueurs.

The shape of a man slid between them and the bar. It moved my way, stopped behind a set of beer taps, and stared at me with eyes wide open. One of his hands climbed to a tap and hit it gently, releasing a brief jet of beer. He was a few years younger than I. A wave of orange hair spanned his head, and one of the flaps of his shirt collar curved out of his jumper in a similar motion and colour.

'Hello, yourself,' he said, after I'd greeted him. 'Can I help you?'

'Yes, I hope you can.'

He pointed at the door. 'OK. If you follow the road to the other end of the village,' he said and moved his hand away from him, 'continue straight to the second crossroads and turn left there, you'll be at the Cliffs in a few minutes. I mean, there was a big sign. You should have seen it.' He looked at me with restless eyes, his arm still held out.

'Why are you telling me this?'

'You asked for help, didn't you?'

'I didn't ask for directions.'

He blinked a few times. 'So what is it you want?'

I couldn't force myself to ask for Amber, and to have the

Cliffs mentioned by the barman didn't help. He continued to stare at me, his lips pressed tight.

I asked for a beer.

'Just thirsty?' he said to himself more than to me. 'A little drink on the way. Always good. Keeps you going.' He pulled a pint, but didn't seem happy with the speed of the flow, as if the glass was burning in his hand.

With similar impatience I looked at the beer settling in front of me. I rehearsed what I had to ask. Words welled in the back of my mouth like the foam at the top of my glass, but I had no courage to let them out.

'Well, what do you think?' he asked me.

'I'm sorry?'

'Do you like what you came to see? The Cliffs, isn't it? If you're not heading to the Cliffs it means you just came back from there. The road you took is hardly ever used. It's only taken by lost tourists coming or going to the Cliffs.'

Every time he pronounced that word I felt physically ill. 'I haven't been there yet,' I said.

'Oh, you still have to go?'

'That was the plan.'

He absently cleaned the shaft of a beer tap with a wet cloth. 'Well, it's a good plan,' he said. 'You can even do a tour of the Cliffs if you really want, walk along the edge for a couple of hours. It gets boring, though. It's just bare rock, and a lot of it.' He leaned forward, licking his lips, and continued in a whisper that grew louder and faster: 'Fact is, there's no reason for staying here any longer, because there's nothing here, really, just sand and water and a bunch of fishermen and their wives. Twenty-nine people in all, thirty if you count a shepherd who lives not far off, a man who they say bites the balls off his sheep to castrate them. That's the reputation he has, can you imagine? But the fishermen are no better, and the

24

fishing is not very eventful. They don't tend to pull much out of the water. I see you're a city person and you've seen things. The people here aren't used to city folk, they wouldn't be, mind you, no reason in particular, no, just a bit of distrust. They've never gone beyond this village. They don't know what TV is. They barely have fridges. Just think, there's one man who drives a van to the next town to sell their fish and they look at him as if he's some kind of man with no fear. And it's ten, fifteen miles from here, not a big place. You put one of these men in the city and he'll come straight back. Fear of catching some disease they can't be cured of.' He snorted. His words had embittered him more than they had urged me to leave.

I looked away from him. The old tables were more ruined than old. Their tanned surfaces had been slashed open and scratched off at the edges, as if rats had been chewing at them for the white, juicier pulp of the wood underneath. The new tables were almost intact. They seemed to nurse lonely cuts with optimism.

'Yes, take this pub,' continued the barman, as he saw me looking around. 'I had workers from out of town who came to renovate, to put in the frosted glass windows, new tables, and stuff like that. Well, do you see a finished job? The whole thing's annoying, of course, annoying for me, but that's the way things go. In certain circumstances people even give up easy work and money. It's just a question of fitting together well, with the people, with the place, and that just doesn't happen here. Of course, you can always escape. I'm surprised those workers lasted so long. And look at me, I'm twenty-six, twenty years younger than most people in this village. This place is slowly slipping into old age and what am I doing here? I'm saying all this to you for your own good. You might have thought, nice place, idyllic or whatever, but it's not like that. Look at this pub and you'll know what to do.'

My eyes had crept back to the tables. I became convinced that the new ones had some uncanny similarity with the furniture of the bed-and-breakfast. It looked like they had scurried down the hill and occupied the pub, like some strange invasion of headless animals.

The barman took a deep breath. I turned back to him. His anger seemed gone, and he looked eager, wanting to know if his oration had worked. 'So, you're going to the Cliffs today, aren't you?'

'Maybe,' I said.

'And then move on.'

I told him I was in no hurry, but drank my pint in long gulps. I decided I would ask about Amber before finishing it. The sight of the tables had amplified my memories of her.

The barman kept staring at me. I tried to ignore him by concentrating on my beer, but he was always there, in the corner of my eye. I thought I saw him squinting, as if to pry past an appearance that didn't satisfy him. He leaned closer, slowly, over the bar, as if he wanted to smell me too. I fidgeted in my pockets with something I didn't recognize that had the hard cold touch of metal. I pulled it out. It was the key to my room.

'That's Amber's,' the bartender blurted out. The other flap of his collar popped out of his jumper. 'It's Amber's. You've been up at the bed-and-breakfast.'

'Yes,' I said, taken aback. 'I got here last night.'

'You didn't say that,' he protested. 'I thought you'd just arrived.'

'Well, does it matter?'

For a moment he just gazed at me, his hand a few inches from one of the beer taps. 'No, no,' he said and hit the tap, freeing drools of beer that dropped on to the tray below. 'Of course not. I'm just surprised you decided to stay for so long around here. There's no reason, I told you. I mean, the Cliffs are something you can tour in a few minutes, maybe an hour if you really want to have a walk along the edge. I mean, you are going there, aren't you?'

'I'm looking for Amber,' I said, with half of my beer still in the glass. I felt good.

'You are?'

'I was wondering if she was here in town.'

'She's not up at the bed-and-breakfast?'

'No, that's why I'm here. She doesn't have a car, does she?'

'There's only Jim's van in the village,' he said, and stood with his mouth and eyes wide open. 'Are you sure she's not up there?'

'I don't think so. I looked.'

'You looked, eh? And she was home last night?'

'Yes, she was.'

'And . . . how was she?'

'How was she what?'

'I don't know. Was she fine?'

'I think so.'

'You talked to her?'

'Yes. We talked a bit.'

'She does that, doesn't she?' He looked at me a moment longer, then hit the tap again. Spurts of beer hit the tray. 'You didn't . . . upset her, did you?'

'No, not at all. We just talked and—'

'And?'

'And nothing.'

'But you're leaving?'

'I didn't say I wanted to stay.'

'Right.'

'It's not nice of me to leave before she comes back, though. I need to sort out a few things.'

'Which are?'

'What do you think?' I said, surprised at the arrogance in my voice. 'I'm a guest at a bed-and-breakfast.'

My new attitude made him more nervous, but it wasn't enough to hold back his prying. 'Of course,' he said, 'of course. A guest, I understand. So you *are* a tourist, aren't you?'

His insistence made me evasive, and suddenly curious. 'Can I be anything else?' I asked.

'What does that mean?'

'Is there any other reason why I would be here?'

More beer hit the tray. 'No, there isn't, is there?' he said, almost cheerfully, fixing his collar back under his jumper. With it gone I realized his hair had also fallen out of place while we were speaking. 'No other reason,' he added.

I sipped my pint. The barman rubbed his forehead just above his eyebrows. He seemed absorbed now, oblivious to my presence.

'Is there anywhere else she could be?' I asked.

'Anywhere else? What, down here?'

'Maybe she came to town to see somebody.'

'See who? The men are out at sea, the women are locked up somewhere, grumbling about their husbands.' I didn't seem to concern him any longer, but I still felt my presence disturbed him. 'Well,' he said, 'maybe she left for a few days. She does that, you know. She has things to do or I don't know what.' He really didn't seem to know. 'You don't need to wait for her. Just leave the money on the reception desk and go to see your Cliffs.'

I wanted to move on, but not as far as the barman wanted me to. I liked to think he was right when he claimed that

Amber wasn't in the village, just as I was almost sure she wasn't in her house. The image of the quilt had returned to me, annoying and inviting like an itch.

I stayed a while longer. I hadn't finished my pint and maybe I would learn more. The barman retreated further back behind the bar, but his eyes were still on me and grew whiter as the light began to fail. They made me nervous, but I was secretly pleased with the attention I was attracting.

'It's a nice place,' I said. 'The bed-and-breakfast. Perched on the hill like that. It's like an ancient temple overlooking its city.'

'We have a church up the road, you know.'

'I'm sure. I was just saying.'

'Just saying,' he repeated without taking his eyes off me, but then his attention was drawn to something beyond the windows facing the sea. 'Well, you'd better finish your pint and go to the Cliffs,' he said in a different tone.

The boats I had seen leave were approaching the beach. They were old, with bulky black hulls. The modern engines looked like appendices from another world. 'They're an odd bunch,' said the barman, when the boats touched the sand and the fishermen disembarked. There were a dozen of them, of similar appearance, faces carved by wind and water, dark caps and mended clothes, and they were all in their late forties or early fifties. Apprehensive, I looked for anything odd, but all I could pinpoint was an unusual vigour as they thrust their boats out of the water.

Then one fisherman glanced carelessly up the road, and his eyes remained fixed there. He spoke, and the others looked too. They all saw my car.

They returned to their job, but seemed distracted. They shuffled things I couldn't see inside their boats, then stretched opaque sheets of plastic over whatever they were handling, and walked to the pub. The barman welcomed them with an excess of cheerfulness. They raised hands in his direction to order beers more than to greet him. They saw me immediately, but pretended not to. 'They're an odd bunch,' the barman repeated to me, and his cheerfulness was gone. 'Odd, odd, odd,' he whispered.

I ignored him. A strange scratching noise was making me more uneasy than his words. I turned in my seat so I could keep a discreet eye on everyone in the pub. The fishermen had sat down at the newer tables, and some were scratching their edges with thumbs curved like hooks. They spoke little to each other, I couldn't make out what they were saying. I tried not to pay any attention to them, but showed an unlikely interest in the floor by the crates where red and grey blotches patched the wood, as if somebody had been grinding tomatoes into the boards. When the barman went over to serve the beers, the fishermen asked him questions while pointing furtive fingers at me. He put down the glasses on the table, two per person I noticed, and gabbled into their ears.

I forced my attention back to my pint. One last mouthful stared at me from the bottom of the glass, while the foam clinging to the sides was drying. I didn't want to finish drinking, I wasn't sure what to do afterwards. The fishermen were now more openly engrossed in their study of me. Their conversations were subsiding. I caught some comment on the weather that was left unanswered. The scratching had died down as well – they were holding their beers now, one in each hand. On the beach only one man remained, long-limbed and dressed in darker clothes than the others. He seemed to brood over his boat, his back curved and his hands pulling and rolling an ancient rope as if he was weaving it.

The barman gravitated around my glass, but I wouldn't drink up. He moved away from me and headed for the beer taps as the last fisherman walked into the pub past the tables and to the bar.

He sat down two chairs away from me and rubbed his face with a hand. 'Who's that?' he asked the barman, uncoiling a finger in my direction.

'He's staying up at the bed-and-breakfast.'

The man seemed to think about this before speaking again. 'Tom, I asked you who he is.'

'You ask him,' said Tom, shoving a pint under his face.

The man looked at it without drinking and turned my way. He studied me with glacial eyes then spoke. His voice seemed too deep for his body, and maybe because of this it didn't boom but broke in a raucous inflection. 'Not many people stop at the bed-and-breakfast,' he said.

'I've been told it's a bit off the main routes,' I said.

He continued as if I hadn't spoken. 'Not many people go there without a reason or some kind of purpose.'

'It's a place to stay for the night.'

'We hardly know when anyone's there,' he said, raising his voice slightly, 'those few times when there is somebody.' The men at the tables seemed even more curious than they already had been. The fisherman at the bar seemed to take this into consideration before resuming. 'Few guests', he continued stressing the second word, 'come down here.'

'He's looking for Amber to pay for the room,' said Tom.

'Did I ask you?' snapped the fisherman.

All this attention made me bold. 'You didn't ask anybody anything,' I said. I was sweating. 'If you intended to ask a question,' I said, 'then yes, I'm here to look for Amber, as your friend said. She wasn't at the bed-and-breakfast when I got up.'

'She wasn't,' the fisherman repeated.

I nodded. 'And I don't think it's good manners for me to

31

leave like this. I'm in no hurry, really. I suppose you haven't seen her either today, have you?'

'What's that supposed to mean?' he barked. 'I've been pulling and throwing nets in and out of the water all day. Can't you smell?' He stretched out a hand towards me, and the stench of fish wafted to my face. The question asked for an apology not an answer, but I hurried a mixture of both. The fisherman looked at me for a while longer, then turned back to his pint. I was shaken by his frostiness, but I had been made curious by the silences and whispers caused by my presence in the bar. I spun my glass, the liquid at the bottom melting some of the dried foam. I thought I heard Tom say to the man, 'Ask his name,' but I wasn't sure and the man didn't reply.

'I've heard that sometimes she goes off for a few days,' I said.

'She does?'

'He told me,' I said, pointing at Tom, who froze on the spot.

'What are you telling people?' said the man to him. 'What would you know?'

Tom retreated behind the beer taps and began to fill glasses, maybe a new round for the men at the tables, who were now looking at me openly, as if they had been awakened by the advancing dusk. Their hands had crawled back to the edge of the tables. The man at the bar tried to ignore me, but he looked ahead at bottles and shelves, at the fading reflections he saw there and that I began to notice myself, my own image in his eyes, distorted between labels. Something hid in the air, for me and for all of them, and it became more present and yet more subtle as the light continued to fail.

When the pub door swung open everybody turned, almost with relief. A plump woman walked in and headed for the shop. She was looking our way, though, and tripped over a crate of cabbages.

'Dora, what the hell are you doing?' said the man at the bar.

With a hand she checked that her hair was in order, then straightened her skirt with a couple of slaps. She approached slowly, peeking at me past him.

'Eamonn, we need to buy some . . . for dinner . . . I saw the car outside . . . Who . . .'

'It's nobody, Dora,' said Eamonn. 'Just a tourist staying at the bed-and-breakfast.'

Dora swallowed visibly. 'A tourist?' The shadow of a grimace came over her face but was gone as quickly as it had arrived. 'And where's Amber?' she asked.

'She's not around,' I said. 'That's why I'm here. I'm looking for her.'

'You saw her last night?'

I nodded.

She seemed surprised, upset even. 'And . . . how was your night?'

'Dora,' said Eamonn, suddenly defending me, 'will you leave him alone?'

'How was my night?' I enquired.

She stuttered a bit. 'Yes, I mean, slept well? Comfortable bed?'

'Everything was good,' I said.

'And she's gone now,' she said, and then glanced at my pint. 'Drinking . . .' she muttered trying to make it sound disparaging, but she was clearly dissatisfied with her effort. 'Just a tourist . . .' She looked me over, while Eamonn had got up and was trying to make her leave.

I watched them move towards the door. In my head the quilt waved like a flag over the chaos of a battlefield. 'She's a nice girl,' I said, loud and fast. Everybody in the pub looked at me. Everybody was silent, no words, no scratching. They waited for more. 'I think Amber's a nice girl,' I said again, but I felt I had weakened my initial statement.

'Yes, she is, isn't she?' said Dora. Something either tender or angry governed her voice, but whatever it was she seemed to fight it.

Eamonn pushed her out and left with her.

'I thought she was supposed to buy something,' I said, almost to myself.

'Grumbling women,' said Tom, running a hand over his forehead. 'I told you, didn't I?' He leaned forward. Perspiration framed his forehead there where his hand hadn't touched. 'And damn inquisitive too. What questions! Comfortable bed! They just hassle people, and they do it to me too. Trust me, you'd better move on. To the Cliffs. You get this advice for free and the beer's on the house. Just don't talk to the women on your way out. They're all mad here.' He paused. 'Not Amber,' he added, 'I don't mean her. I mean the ones down here in the village.' He nodded vigorously at his own argument, as if trying to get me to do the same.

I looked at the last sip in my pint, then at the fishermen who had returned to their sparse conversations. The quilt was still waving in my mind, bright red. I wanted to get back to it. I drained my glass and pushed it towards the barman, who took it gladly. 'Might see you again, Tom,' I said, and I saw my words were not happily received. I tried to say something similar to the others, but I only managed a nod, which was answered by a last few scratches.

I got into my car and drove up the deserted road with my window down, letting in the cold air. I heard voices as I passed in front of a dark alley. Faces stood in the shadows, middle-aged female faces, pressed close to each other, looking at me. I thought I had imagined them, but the mouth of another alley appeared soon after, and more faces were there. Dora was among them, I was sure, her face rounder than the others, and an arm was outstretched to point at me, and it was hers. I drove on, up the hill, while in my head echoed what I heard coming from those alleys, my name whispered by innumerable voices, my name that only Amber knew.

iii

My hopes and fears had always hammered my understanding into their own image, but this time they failed to give shape to what I had seen and heard. They tried, but the villagers' words and moods swirled in my head, and I wouldn't let them stop. I liked them as they were, vague but with me at their centre. I felt myself grow large and multiform, the red quilt moving in and out of focus, and I had the impression that if I remained in the village I was fated to do great and terrible things.

But it wasn't that simple. The Cliffs wouldn't leave me alone. They were still in my head and at the end of the road, and they called me, telling me I was being sidetracked, and for what? I had felt good in saying that I was looking for Amber, I had even felt that the villagers' attention gave me some claim on her, but what claim? I couldn't forget the abrupt ending of our encounter the night before, the way she had walked out of my room. It had been decisive. It had been certain. It had made me feel inadequate, and I still felt that, and my transparent hope for a change of heart in her had almost vanished. I believed that her return could only mean my departure.

The bed-and-breakfast was dark and silent, the B-and-B sign turned off. I waited with the engine running for a light or a figure to appear in one of the windows, but they all remained blank, staring indifferently ahead. I parked. I held my breath and walked into the house. The message I had left was still on the hallway floor. I moved wearily through all the rooms, checking behind every item of furniture, lifting tablecloths and bedsheets with trembling fingers to look under them.

Nothing had changed from when I had left. Nobody was in the house except me and the solid presence of the locked room.

Through the keyhole I saw what I had seen earlier, and I abandoned myself to it. The sight comforted me and I struggled to see more as if my desires could undo the limitations of the keyhole. Reluctantly I settled for the edge of the overflowing quilt, but the daylight was almost gone and soon it decayed completely. Everything turned to vague shapes and even the quilt lost its brilliance. I stood up, resigned, and caressed the metal frame around the keyhole.

I was getting used to the silence, and the solitude. I started to think that my past was already severed from me and that because of this the Cliffs could ask nothing of me. I could hear my own thoughts ease in the empty environment: they looked for comfort on the sofas, fulfilment in the beds. They were drawn by the memory of Amber that persisted there, but they were still tentative, still frustrated by what had happened between us.

I sensed her scent and traced it to the bathroom, to the bottle of moisturizer. It looked at me, white, almost bright with expectation in the darkness that had engulfed everything else. I uncapped it, smelt her scent and didn't know how to react to it. If this was the smell of her memory, then, after trimming what I remembered of the previous night, I would have filled my lungs with it, but if it was the smell of her return I didn't know what to do.

I walked downstairs into the living room. I stood in front

of her framed picture and looked at it. It filled me with similar emotions. The abrupt ending of our encounter was nowhere to be seen in it. I could cling to these marginal things. They gave me a new kind of hope, and they didn't frighten me with the threat of rejection.

I brought the picture with me into the dining room and put it on a table. I left it there while I prepared some dinner. The scent of the moisturizer that had lingered in my nostrils was replaced by the smell of meat as I started to fry some lamb cutlets I had found in the fridge. I ate dinner sitting in front of the picture. I hadn't expected this to be a self-catering place, I thought, my chuckle ringing in the empty room. No other sound filled it, apart from the clinking of cutlery against the plate and the sliding of the fork between my teeth. I was nervous, though. If Amber had gone for the day she would be back any time now.

I waited, my appetite turning to nausea. I was afraid of hearing a noise that wasn't mine. I thought I could prevent it by being noisier myself. I coughed, I moved in my seat, I almost dropped the fork against the plate after each mouthful, but I began to imagine Amber in that locked room upstairs, pressed against the door, head thrown back, about to laugh at my foolishness.

I looked at her picture for reassurance, but I was still sober enough to understand that I couldn't expect much from it. I grew quiet again. Time passed slowly. I gave up eating when I realized that if I continued the food would all come back up. Only the wine I was drinking continued to go down. Amber looked more and more amiable in the picture, unlike what had become in my drunken mind her repudiating, almost fiendish, three-dimensional self.

That clock I still hadn't located was chiming midnight. It was probably too late for her to come back now. My mind eased a bit. I finished the bottle of wine and walked to the living room with the picture. On the way, the peacock gave me a look I ignored. I turned on the lamps of the previous night. I put the picture on the piano stool, placing it at the angle at which Amber had been sitting. I sat in the red armchair I had occupied. We looked at each other in silence. I remembered the conversations in the pub. 'They said things about you,' I remarked.

I felt stupid. I looked around to make sure I was alone. It was just me and the picture.

'They said things about me too,' I added. The picture was listening. We both thought of the vagueness of the villagers' allusions. I pressed a few piano keys, as if the picture was pressing them. I moved next to it on the stool. I laid my head on the keys as Amber had the evening before. The keys were like a black and white road in front of my eyes. My red armchair was just to the right, on the horizon. She must have seen me even when she was like this, I thought.

I stayed there, sleep beckoning but still distant. My foot hit the piano pedals by mistake. Without thought I pressed one and heard a faint metallic sound. I leaned forward and, with trembling hands, I felt the pedals. Around one was a string with two keys tied to it.

I scrambled up to the last floor. One of the keys slipped into the locked door like a tadpole in a pond. I was tense and excited, and when I finally decided to open the door and the lock clicked I was impelled to run away, but I walked in with squeezed eyes, afraid of what, of who, I might see.

The light from the stairs sliced the floor in two and lit fully what I had already seen through the keyhole. I advanced, walking on the band of light. The quilt stretched from the footboard over an empty double bed and disappeared under huge pillows. On the other side of the room stood a chest of drawers almost as tall as me. It was newer than the furniture on the ground floor, but of a rougher make, cruel, I felt, and the knobs of the drawers looked like teats of a huge udder, or like protruding blind eyes. I didn't touch them, but stepped off the band of light into the other half of the room, and rested my eyes on the more pleasant sight of the bed. I ran my hands along the cool surface of the quilt, and as I did so my body followed. I lay on my stomach, my hands curving around the huge pillows, and I plunged my head between them.

I dreamed of the faces I had seen the previous day, the village, the waves gliding towards the beach in the dim light of the leaden sky, and I dreamed of the empty bed-and-breakfast and the land around it that seemed to know neither end nor contamination. I saw them vitrify and I saw my reflection in them grow larger as they raced towards me. Or was it me hurling myself towards them?

I woke up and jumped out of Amber's bed. It took me some time to grasp that nobody else was in it and that the floor was solid under my feet. The quilt was rising, inhaling new air. I sat back on the bed, searched for the parts of it that were still warm, recoiled from the cold areas of the pillows. I returned to the space I had left, but with what little confidence I lay there! I curled up, invading areas of cold but hoping to keep my heat less dispersed, while my eyes and ears fearfully probed my surroundings. They paused at the gloomy surface of the chest of drawers and at a sound I heard coming from it, a multitude, termites eating wood or remembered words from the same voice.

I got up. The house was unchanged from the night before. I looked at the picture downstairs with embarrassment, and put it back where it belonged. The frolics of the previous evening felt bleak and shameful in the light of day and in the prospect of Amber's return. I felt that my past had found me and had crept inside me again: here was the continuation of the immaterial loser's past that I had intended to leave behind.

I didn't want to think about it. I told myself instead that I had felt different since I had reached the bed-and-breakfast. I was on the edge of a new beginning, this I was sure of, and at this stage I wasn't certain any longer that the edge had to be the Cliffs.

I spent hours at the dining-room windows, looking down at the village, while the day grew behind the clouds. Inside the house shadows were undefined, but a general, disturbing sombreness grew more certain and intense. The village remained unchanged. I saw no movement, it looked expectant, as if waiting for me.

With the passing of those bleak hours, the hope that Amber would reconsider me vanished completely, but what surprised me was that I was no longer resigned to the idea.

I decided I was going to find out where she was. I had begun to cling to new hopes. They had bloomed secretly since I had found her picture. For the first time, despite the warmth I harboured for her, I hoped to find Amber too far away for her to be able to return.

I walked down to the village. I was still afraid of the potential of the car, of where it could take me. The mass of clouds was still dragging silently overhead and the grassland stretched thick and uniform down the hill. The windows of the houses were blank eyes, but as I approached they awakened with a surreptitious fluttering of curtains.

I almost ran the last stretch and hid in a humid black alley held tight between two buildings. I could feel the windows search for me from their immovable faces. I forced myself down the short stretch of the alley and onto the main road.

Down by the beach some fishermen were pushing their boats into the water. I walked towards the other end of the village. I told myself I would stop to talk to anyone coming my way and demand to know where Amber was.

A few fishermen came out of their houses, but only when I had passed. Their timing felt deliberate. All of them looked at me over their shoulders. The windows of the houses continued to show me the same oblique interest, but I never caught anything more than the vague movement of yellowed curtains.

Soon the road swelled in front of the village church. A balding fisherman was hurrying from it in the direction of the beach. A look of surprise escaped him when he saw me, but he lowered his head to put on a cap and kept it low till he had walked past me. He also looked back at the church, briefly, at the only window of the façade, a round eye above the entrance door that seemed more interested in him than in me.

I didn't speak to him. His evasion and the church's apparent disregard for me redirected my own attention. I thought that maybe the local priest might help.

I walked over to the church. Inside, faint beams of light touched spots at random, and I thought I could hear lost words echo under the wooden vaulting. The walls of the nave were of rough stone and the windows were tall but narrow on both sides. A bulky confessional of black wood stood against the right wall. The altar was an irregular slab of rock lit electrically from above, and beyond the cone of light and against the far wall was the crucifix. I walked down the aisle, but stopped after a few steps.

I wasn't alone. In the shadows between the altar and the confessional booth stood a towering figure. I raised a trembling hand and tried to utter words that choked in my throat. I was looking at Amber. She didn't move, pretending not to have noticed me. My senses raced back to her looks, her scent, her feel, but these were not intercessions or bonds that could protect me, but illicit captives of my memory. Yes, this was the level of my confidence in front of that dark figure: I didn't notice that she was much taller than I re-membered her – I actually thought I was shrinking. All I could do was stagger closer, recklessly, ready to wail out some excuse for sleeping in her bed, and for her picture.

A couple more steps and I saw that I was about to speak to a wooden statue. I blinked, I breathed. It wasn't even that tall, but simply placed on a pedestal that raised it a couple of feet off the ground. The hands of the woman were closed in prayer over her breast, and she wore a long dress with confused, restless folds roughly chiselled in the dark wood. Over her head was a small halo of a lighter colour that looked like a wooden plate. I moved closer, but my legs were still trembling when my face turned up to look into hers.

'Does it feel strange to kneel in front of your hostess?' said an echoing voice. I looked round and saw nobody, but found that one of my knees had sunk to the stone floor. I rose quickly. 'Just a joke,' the voice continued, 'a joke I make with some resignation and a touch of blasphemy, but I believe you are the guest at the B-and-B and I'm quite sure you've noticed the similarity that runs between this statue and your hostess.'

Silence followed. Then I heard the sound of a curtain being pulled, and from the shadows of the confessional booth the head of an old priest emerged. He had a sharp face framed by grey hair that seemed too long and messy for his profession.

I took a few steps towards him. 'I was looking for . . .'

'And found a statue,' he said, not moving from where he was. 'Well, maybe you can blame me. After all, it was made to my commission. I was walking in the fields with my bre-viary one day when I saw our shepherd William sitting on a stone carving a sheep out of a piece of wood, and immediately my thoughts went to our little church here, and to its sculptural deficiencies.' He seemed to ask for my approval, although he didn't look at me.

'Yes, it's—'

'We had a beautiful crucifix,' he resumed, cutting me short, 'but nothing else, you see? So I thought he could attempt a depiction of the Virgin. William told me he needed a model, and Amber is the only young girl in the village, and she agreed to pose. I suppose that in a big city you might never meet the model for a statue, so you can dissociate the two, but here several people look at this statue and recall the model. Which is quite deplorable. I thought of asking William to chisel the face into a different shape, but I'm afraid he might ruin it.' He paused for a moment. 'Well, I added the halo. I nailed it to her head.' One of his hands had appeared over the knee-high door of the booth. It held a glass and was rotating it as if to swirl its contents, but it was empty. He looked down at it, absorbed in thought, and his nostrils flared. He looked back up, and searched for the statue, which I had blocked from his view. He seemed to see me for the first time.

'Well, I suspect you're here in church for a reason,' he said. 'Maybe to confess?' He stopped rotating the glass. 'You've been told I hear confessions in the afternoon.'

'No, I wasn't here for that,' I said. He cut me short, before I could ask him about Amber.

'I understand,' he said. 'Well, that's good.' He rotated the glass again. 'If I'm allowed the following comment, confession is my least favourite sacrament. It lays bare my failings as a spiritual leader more than it reveals the people's repentance and desire to improve their lives. But then again, you're not from here, so maybe it wouldn't be so taxing on me. Maybe interesting . . .' His eyes were inquisitive now. 'It's not

44

every day that we have visitors from afar. The sight of a foreigner here is such a rare event. Those who pass by never stop for more than a few hours. They move on and quickly forget ever having been here, I'm sure. But I've been told you decided to stay longer. Here people talk, you see. The villagers are a suspicious lot, and I'm sure you found them inquisitive, but you have to understand that a two-day permanence like yours can give birth to strange beliefs.' He smiled and leaned forward, but nothing more than his head and hands appeared from the booth.

'I . . . From what I could understand they seemed worried about Amber. What I thought of her, and—'

'What you thought of her. Yes, I've heard. There was some commotion in the pub yesterday. You quarrelled with some-body.'

'No,' I protested. 'I wouldn't say so at all. We talked . . .'

'Maybe I've heard wrong. Or somebody interpreted the event wrongly for me. You have to forgive them, if that's the case. This village is no idyll, and when people live on a shaky balance they always try to guard themselves against those who can make them fall. A lot of people have been holding their breath recently, and for them the sight of a new face is like a punch in the stomach.'

'Am I that exciting? Who do they think I am?'

'Not who you really are, I'm sure. You'll find everybody here is fixed in their fears and delusions. It's the easiness of it that is so disconcerting. They're lost sheep, but it hasn't always been like this.' He held his glass to his lips and, eyes closed, he sipped some air, or maybe a drop of something left at the bottom.

'But who do they think I am?' I repeated.

He didn't seem to hear me. He held out his glass and looked into it. 'You see,' he said, 'I don't believe in the idea of good and bad paths. I find it more realistic to think of us in a precarious balance on the steep slope of a mountain. How shall we move? Can we decide? We have no reason to do anything at first, but we're not left alone for long. A wind will pass to push us over, or a beam will illuminate the snows on the mountaintop and make us turn our heads. Just turn our heads, because to climb is hard, while to fall is so easy. There's no momentum in climbing, and the beam might be tiring to the eyes after a while. But the wind will keep on passing renewed each time, refreshing, inviting, even if you've decided to climb. And the fall promises to be sweet and intense, just a leap away.'

I had visions of the Cliffs and of the hill with the bed-and-breakfast. They fought viciously within me.

'I'm sorry?' said the priest.

'What?'

'You said something.'

'No, nothing.'

'Maybe you have something to confess?' he asked again.

The nothingness I've filled my life with. 'I . . . I was looking for Amber,' I said.

'Ah, of course, Amber! Our beloved bed-and-breakfast hostess!' He retreated into the depth of the booth. I leaned forward, afraid he would disappear. I heard him sip some air.

'I was wondering whether you've seen her,' I asked.

'Have I seen her?'

'I don't know, for confession maybe.'

'Confession?' A vague outline of his body stirred inside the booth. 'She doesn't even come to church for mass. As if she was already here.' An accusatory finger emerged into the light. It pointed past me at the statue and withered back into the darkness. 'She lives a very isolated life up at the B-and-B. It's not as if I can drag her down here.' His head appeared again. 'She came to confess once,' he resumed. 'Once. How about that? Once in the two years she's been here.'

'Amber's not from the village?'

'Never been one of my flock. Not now and not before.' He smiled a rusty smile that waned quickly. 'No, she's not from the village. She arrived two years ago, with some inheritance papers, and turned the house on the hill into a B-and-B. Which, among its merits,' he grunted, 'has had the honour of bringing another half-pagan to town to serve us at the pub.'

'Tom?'

'Yes, Tom. Fatal coincidences. He was staying at the B-and-B a year ago, just when our old barman died.'

'But what about Amber?' I pressed him. 'Where did she come from?'

'For me she might have fallen down from the sky one night. Appeared one morning with her inheritance papers.'

'Maybe she's gone back home then.'

'Not unless one of the men gave her a ride in his boat. She's from an island off the coast. But I wouldn't know. I told you I hardly ever see her. Doesn't come to mass.' He shook his head. 'Such a sweet girl she seemed, though.' His mouth twisted as if he had just drunk something he didn't like. It reminded him of his glass. He sipped some air from it and kept its edge against his lips. 'Yes,' he continued, 'she gave the impression of being too pure for a weekly communion with God.'

'Hence the statue?' I asked.

'What? Oh, our Holy Mother. No, of course not!' he almost shouted. 'You think I've done this on purpose?' He seemed angry and ready to leap out at me, like a spider from his hole. His anger continued to echo in the church.

'But you're sure you don't know where she could be now?' I had to ask again.

He kicked open the door of the booth and stepped out. 'Do I have to keep telling you that I don't see her that often? All this interest . . .' He slammed the door shut, but hung on to it. 'Well, I'm going now,' he said, more composed. 'I have to say my evening prayers. I'm sure you'll understand.'

'I just came for her,' I said meekly, as he was walking away.

He stopped. I was afraid he was going to chase me out of his church, but instead he swung round and stared at me open-mouthed. 'I'm sorry, I think I haven't been listening properly. You came for her, here? To the village?'

'She's been away now for more than a day.'

He moved forward into a beam of light. 'And you came for her.'

'Yes.'

His face was glowing. 'From the capital?'

'I'm from the capital, yes.'

'And your name is?'

'Charles,' I said, and I felt strange saying it, as if suddenly I was the true proprietor of my identity.

The priest's eyes almost fell out of their orbits. 'Ah!' he burst out. 'And I was told that you were a tourist! Just a damn tourist!' He barked a laugh. 'I thought you would never come, that you didn't even exist. What a faithless man I am.' He tried to control himself. 'Don't mind me, there's nothing funny, nothing at all. I'm just . . . surprised . . . I . . . I should have asked your name earlier. My mind – my mind's not lucid.'

'Nobody has asked my name so far.'

'Nobody expected you to stay. Why ask the name of a stranger? If he is a stranger. People here are inquisitive, but they're afraid of what they might find out. It's normal when—' He stopped. Something behind me had caught his attention. I turned round.

48

Tom was standing next to the entrance door. He clearly hadn't expected me to be there. 'Am I disturbing you?' he spluttered. 'Are you confessing?'

'Confessing?' said the priest. 'Now? Why have you people started to pester me at all hours? It's late, and it's time for me to say my prayers. I'm sure you can wait another day, whatever you've done. You've already waited so many.' He pointed a finger at me. 'By the way, let me present Charles to you. This is Charles. He told me now his name's Charles.'

In the weak light of the church I wasn't sure if Tom's face had grown pale. I walked towards him. I wanted to know – I wanted to know who they all thought I was.

'Your name's Charles,' I heard the priest say behind me. 'Everybody will know now,' he promised. 'Everybody.' I heard him clink his glass against something and slurp the air left in it, and when I turned round he was gone.

I stood with Tom by the church door. After a short dance of favours I preceded him outside. Across the road, over the roofs of the houses I could see the bed-and-breakfast perched on top of the hill. I felt hope clamour inside me only to hush with a sense of anticipation, as fantasy and reality seemed to kiss, tentatively, for the first time.

'I'm Charles,' I said, turning to Tom.

Spasms tugged a huge smile across his face. 'Hi, Charles,' he said. 'It's good . . . good to see you again.' He looked around at the blank houses. 'I was in a rotten mood yesterday, and maybe I was a bit rude. I mean, with the Cliffs and all. I hope you don't think badly of me.' He continued to smile. 'I offered you a beer,' he added. I waited. His eyes drew paths on the ground as if his head was kept low by a leaden hood. He searched for something else to say. 'Did you see William's statue?' he said.

I told him I had.

'Yes, nice statue,' he said with genuine pleasure, then stumbled into a few appreciative words on the priest, but corrected himself quickly when I suggested I had found him strange. 'Yes, strange,' he repeated. 'They say he was more . . . normal, years ago.'

The fluttering of curtains was expectant, like hands ready to clap. We drifted down the road, and I waited for something that would reveal who they all thought I was. Tom, though, seemed more eager to show himself useful and friendly. When we got to the beach he waved back at the village and told me he would show me around, that I had to tell him if I had any problems with anything. Beads of sweat shone on his forehead.

Maybe I could lead him on to what I wanted to hear. 'You're not from the village, are you?' I asked him.

'How do you know?'

'Amber told me.' I looked around, afraid that something would happen, but nothing did. The village was quiet, the narrow bay stretched before us, and the fishermen's boats were dots on the dark horizon. The tracks they had left in the sand were still visible around us, disappearing under the waves lapping the beach. Tom redirected his steps to kick a couple of lonely pebbles, lifting clouds of sand.

'I told Amber I was sure you were a great man,' he said. 'You know, no offence. We talked, we talked a lot. I was a close friend of hers, I should say. I've often brought her food and stuff up these months. She hasn't been coming down to the village that often this past year. Hardly ever.'

'She lives a lonely life up at the bed-and-breakfast,' I stated. 'She told me she doesn't even come down for mass, since she got here two years ago from her island.' I waved a hand in the direction of the sea. Still everything calm.

Tom was nodding. He looked out to sea too.

'Did you notice this village at all when you first came here?' he asked.

'When I first came here?'

He nodded. 'Yes, not this time. Six months ago . . .'

'No. No, I didn't.'

'Neither did I. Small place, you know, but good people.'

'Yes, I'm sure. Amber spoke about some friends she had here. That first time, six months ago.'

'Did she mention any? By name?'

'I'm sure she did.'

He laughed nervously. 'And what did she say about me?'

'I can't recall.'

'You said she told you about me.'

'She said you were not from here.'

He seemed displeased. 'Well, maybe you don't remember everything she said.'

'Could be,' I answered. I sat down on the sand. The beach stretched on both sides of me, its outermost points as thin and sharp as blades. 'You forget things over six months.'

'I'm sure she mentioned me,' said Tom. 'She likes me. In a friendly way, of course.' His eyes met mine with a malevolence that sobered me. It was just a quick glance, before he looked out to sea. He walked towards the water and picked up a large shell from the flotsam and jetsam that the fishermen must have cleaned off their nets since time immemorial and that had piled and sunk into the sand by the shore. He flung it hard in the direction of the fishermen, with a quick, violent swing that put him off balance. The shell moved fast at first, then it caught the air and flew down towards the water, disappearing silently into it. 'Eamonn!' he shouted. 'Amber's boyfriend's here!'

iv

I rose in answer. Nobody saw me; the boats were too far away, nobody leaned out of the village windows, and Tom was still bent forward facing the sea. Nobody saw the smile or grimace that spread across my face, that barely contained eruption of what I felt inside.

I wouldn't have felt any different if Amber had declared her love for me.

Tom walked back and forth along the shore. He tried to kick a shell, but his foot sank into the wet sand. In the distance, behind the clouds, the sun's outline was becoming progressively more visible as it moved towards the horizon. 'They're late today,' he said, looking out to sea.

We watched the approaching sunset with different emotions. He seemed restless. I was violently happy. I was not myself. Irrational happiness, irrational thoughts, but I couldn't, wouldn't, hold them back. I stopped worrying about meeting Amber. Our confrontation was already resolved, surpassed in what Tom had said. I didn't believe, if I met her again, that she would see me with the same mistaken eyes as Tom had, but my happiness was too fresh and too strong for me to bother with such thoughts. Surely even impostors must be carried away by the pleasure of their new identity from time to time, forgetting the dangers that always threaten their act.

'Well, yesterday I really thought you were a tourist,' said Tom, as if wrapping up a long speech he had been delivering.

'I didn't know whether Amber had told you about me,' I said, without feeling the need to look round for anybody who might contradict this new lie.

'She didn't tell us much.'

I asked him what she had told them. He needed no encouragement to speak: he wanted to show himself knowledgeable and friendly, and there was something in the air, the delay of the fishermen or the sunset to burn in the distance, that made him impatient.

Six months earlier, he told me, a certain Charles from the capital had lost himself on his way to the Cliffs and had stopped at the bed-and-breakfast. He never reached the Cliffs. Amber had said it was love at first sight, for her and for him. Like nothing before. Their secluded love story had bloomed for a few days, before Charles had had to return to the capital. He wanted to settle what tied him there, or something like that, then come back. It might take a while, he had said, but his was a sacred promise, and Amber waited impatiently for his return.

Nobody in the village had seen him. Only Amber knew what he looked like.

The sun was turning orange behind the clouds. I romanticized about Amber and me. In my head I made up the perfect past she had lived with somebody else. I could see it. We had been so happy.

'Can you imagine,' I asked, 'what I would have missed had I continued to the Cliffs?' I tried to imagine it myself. I looked at the visible world around me. Behind us, in the orange light, the houses had grown fleshy, vibrant. They sent my eye up to the bed-and-breakfast, and my

53

mind back to that first evening in her living room. The Cliffs were distant now, and I thought of them as I would have thought of a childish dream that maturity had dismissed as a nightmare. 'Now I'm Amber's boyfriend,' I said.

Tom didn't respond. His hair was trembling in the sea-breeze, orange like the sunset.

I wanted to tell everybody that I was Amber's boyfriend, to solidify the notion in my mind, to enjoy it. I wanted rowdi-ness and physicality, not the mute silence that hung heavy all around me. The village, I felt, was eager to be introduced to me in its unusual but growing sunset splendour. 'You were supposed to show me around,' I said to Tom. 'Maybe you can introduce me to the village.'

He turned round and looked at the houses, but he wouldn't move a step. His friendliness had dried up or grown lazy, but in its name or in the name of consistency he forced himself to give me a brief description of the place. He stated that the village had been shrivelling up, due to deaths and departures. Half of the houses were empty. Without moving, he pointed up the road at the others and droned on about couples who resembled each other in everything but their names. All the women were housewives. All the men were fishermen, with the exception of the priest, Jim the van-driver, and William the shepherd, who wasn't married and lived alone in a house in the fields. Otherwise it was all middle-aged couples, plus Amber on the hill and him in the pub. He said the pub was his main connection with the villagers. He saw the women when they came to buy food. He saw the men around seven in the morning after they had pulled up their nets, then twice in the evenings, after they had cast them back into the sea, and a couple of hours later, after dinner. On Sunday mornings, he concluded, he improvised as the village barber, a service he had introduced, with good will but little success, to the unkempt fishermen.

His voice was impatient. It struggled to convey the routine of the village life. 'Are you planning to stay?' he asked.

'You decided to stay,' I said to him, 'and I have my reasons to stay too, don't you think?'

'I was looking for work,' he said, almost as an excuse. 'I was touring around here. I stopped and I asked myself, Why not? You know, some people like it quiet.'

A buzzing noise made us turn round. The boats were escaping the conflagration over the horizon. Tom seemed upset at this intrusion in the peace he had spoken about. He didn't look as if he wanted to shout out my identity again, but fidgeted with his shirt collar instead, pulling its purple flaps out from under his sweater then putting them back inside. He turned to me. 'Well, I hope we'll be friends,' he said. He attempted a smile. He seemed puzzled by his own friendliness.

I smiled back genuinely. He cast a last glance out to sea and ran up to his pub.

I waited for the fishermen with my hands in my pockets, shifting about impatiently. I wondered if Tom's shout had slid over the waters to them. I couldn't tell. They were ashen, indistinct figures in their charcoal boats, bobbing out of the sunset fire. When they were close they turned off their engines. Each one stood alone in his boat, rowing the last stretch with an oar. They were looking at me, I could determine that much, and I looked back while the oars plunged and dripped rhythmically. I was sure they were waiting for an explanation of my presence there, and I was unbearably eager to give it to them.

'I'm Charles,' I said, when the boats hit the sand. 'I'm Amber's boyfriend.'

They blinked and looked at each other. Some fishermen

asked what I had said. I repeated my name, happily. 'Yesterday I didn't know whether to mention it,' I said. 'I didn't know if Amber had told you about me. But she has told you about me, hasn't she?'

The noses of their boats were in the sand, their tails swayed gently in the water. The fishermen nodded. I even rescued mumbled but undeniable yesses from the noise they made as they disembarked. Nobody spoke of another Charles.

I hopped back and forth as they pulled their boats on shore, almost dancing in my happiness, surfing close to them and trying not to get run over. I tried to calm down. I didn't want my presence to be unpleasant, I didn't want to interfere with their job, lest they should, by some unknown means, erase the clear honesty of their acknowledgement.

I stood aside. They pulled their boats with heavy grunts. They raised, folded and threw rags beside their engines. Some hacked at barnacles that clung to the hulls with the blades of their oars, then threw the oars inside their boats like cutlery onto a plate after a bad meal.

I didn't pay much attention to their mood. I was too lost in mine. I looked at them, though, with a curiosity that searched for more recognition. They looked at me rarely, and briefly when they did. They would force their eyes back to their work, or glance up at the village. Their weathered faces were still moulding in the furnace of the sunset or in the light of my revelation. It made them uneasy. It was like an invasion, maybe of my own good mood, a surface of paint over their real expression that had run for cover in the crevices of their features.

They kept it hidden there. I didn't disturb it. I waited for something more to be offered, and when they left they granted me short, sharp waves suspended on their way to the pub, and nods that plunged their heads deeper and kept them there, submerged in the shadows, out of the reach of the red brush of the sun.

I would have liked felicitations at my new-found life, favourable comments on Amber who was there with me, in my excitement, on the crest of words I had not yet spoken. I received no felicitations, no comments, but in the lukewarm response they had given me I saw their incapacity to contradict my new identity, and it was enough.

Eamonn was the last to leave the beach. His face was like that of all the others, the same contours, the same dark crevices, but his eyes were fixed when they looked at me. 'So Amber was waiting for you?' he asked sitting on the edge of his boat.

'All this time,' I answered, with a smile.

'Yes. A long time.'

'I had a few things to fix in the city.'

'And where is she now?'

'She's away,' I said. 'I shouldn't think she's gone for long. She probably left me a message, and I haven't looked carefully enough for it. I think she had a few things to fix herself.'

He opened his mouth to say something, but gaped and seemed to take in some of the darkness lingering around him. He looked at the pub. Darkness invaded his face: he seemed to have summoned it or breathed it out of his mouth. 'I'm going to get a pint,' he said, and left.

I drifted after him like a scrap of paper in the wake of a train. Like a love letter, I thought in that thick, warm sunset.

I didn't go into the pub but flapped happily up the road of the village. Clouds were moving in the same direction. They lost their red tints as they were swallowed by the night ahead. My past – I allowed myself a brief but dutiful last look at it –

was out there, already swallowed, already dismembered. I was imbued with the red, expectant present of the world around me. The village was like gold and fire. The dullness of the previous evening's dusk was gone under this blossoming of colour. An odour of dinner wafted from the houses, a scent of cooked vegetables and of meat still rare, roasting.

Curtains fluttered again more focused this time, then doors opened on both sides of me, spaced out, intermittent, almost choreographed. A woman stepped out of each. They stood in their doorways, a handful of them, smiling, their hands one in the other in front of them, their long skirts rippling gently in the evening breeze. The sunset blushed their middle-aged faces. Their expressions weren't struggling in that light as the men's had been, instead their smiles moved up their cheeks slowly, as if screws were pulling and tightening them at their edges. I felt they relished looking at me. The smell of dinner swelled in the evening air.

'Hello, Charles,' said one woman.

'You're Amber's boyfriend,' said another.

Tom's shout must have rung this way as well. Other women repeated the same greetings. I smiled back, I said my name myself, I thanked them for I don't know what. Their acknowledgement was unanimous, homogeneous, as the fishermen's hurried one had been. Once more I clung to the recognition and thought of nothing else. Those red cheeks inflamed by the sunset could only make me think of the fleshy interior of the bed-and-breakfast.

I smiled at the pleasure of my new identity. It felt like homecoming, to a home that felt mine but that I had never known.

'I'm going up to the bed-and-breakfast,' I said. Up to the quilt, the moisturizer, that picture of her. 'To see if Amber's back,' I said.

I plunged into one of the short, dark alleys that led to the hill. I took eager steps along it. I could sense the whiteness of my smile glitter in the darkness.

Then my gait faltered and my smile disappeared. Had I just said 'to see if Amber's back'?

Reality struck me. I could have invented something about Amber and me, about our love, and my heart and soul would have clung to it. After all, what do words have to do with truth if not help to create it? But the truth I had begun to craft was still no more than a mask I was balancing on my nose, and if Amber was back she would rip it off in front of everybody. What would it matter if I told her I had done it out of my feelings for her? What did she care about my feelings when she had already refused me?

I walked down the alley and onto the fields with dread in my heart, afraid to lift my eyes to the bed-and-breakfast and see the light of her return.

I didn't have to look that far up. Behind, I had left that village of shy blushes, and right in front of me I saw that colour intensified, angry. I stared into a huge, fluttering red square. It was Amber, I thought, holding her quilt in front of her, asking for explanations, as if my sleeping on it had left traces she had found.

I felt dizzy. I had enough lucidity left in me to realize that it wasn't Amber, and it wasn't a quilt. It was a thinner, poorer version of it, just a sheet hung parallel to the village on a high clothes-line, and it wasn't red, but a discoloured pink that blushed into a darker tint in the light of the sunset. For a moment I relaxed, then the wind pushed it away from me and on its surface emerged the fleeting shape of a person.

I don't know how I advanced, but I did. After a few steps I saw that another sheet hung behind the first on a parallel clothes-line and in the gap between the two I saw her.

She leaped for me. She grabbed me by an arm I had half raised to protect myself and with a quick jerk pulled me into the space between the sheets.

Their redness had already turned into the colour of my own blood when I realized that fear had fooled me a second time. I was not looking at Amber, but at a shorter woman with cracked traces of youthful beauty on her face and a disconcerting vitality in her grip. It was Dora.

I tried to free my hand. I retreated out of the narrow enclosure of the sheets, but she traded my hand for my waist and pulled me back in. I struggled, I managed to slip out of the grip of a few fingers, but she adjusted her hold, panting, and moved closer to me, followed by a damp smell of ironed trousers. I stopped resisting, hoping that once I was back between the sheets she would let me go.

She did, and I gave her an instinctive shove to speed up the process. She seemed to accept my violence, even lowered her head in apology, but soon she was looking at me again, and she was close, and I was sure that this time she would hug me.

'What do you want?' I nearly shouted.

'You're Charles,' she said.

I stood between her and the sunset. I thought her eyes grew slightly red as if rays had snaked past me or had dripped from the sheets. It gave to her vigour a touch of sadness, as if she was about to deliver me to a wretched fate. I was expecting nothing else. I was convinced that Amber was back, that she stood behind the sheets listening in, waiting to lay bare my lies.

'I'm Amber's boyfriend,' I said with some last, shrill defiance in my voice.

'You are,' she said. Mockingly, I was sure. 'We've all been waiting for you. A few months that have felt like an eternity. Charles . . . may I call you Charles? It feels like I've known you for ages, and I'm happy you're here. We're all happy for you and Amber. Amber's a nice girl, smart . . . respectable. But never mind that. She's beautiful, young, ripe in her figure.' She ran her hands over her body, eyes closed, remembering curves she had long lost.

'Ripe,' I whined, tantalized. Dora's eyes opened in answer. I pushed away the sheets for air, to check whether Amber was listening in, to escape. I had a brief glimpse of empty grasslands, then Dora grabbed my hands with her moist ones, and the sheets billowed freely in the wind. She danced darkly, left and right, not to touch them. She wanted me to do the same.

I stood immobile, slapped by the sheets. I could not dance at my demise. I asked her to tell me where Amber was.

'I don't know,' she said, 'I really don't know.' She looked past the sheet facing the village. I tried to do the same but she held me back. 'I don't know,' she claimed, for a third time. 'Amber's special. I cared for her like a daughter, but I didn't see her that often, although she has always been here – I mean there at the bed-and-breakfast. But you're not thinking of leaving, are you?'

I was, but I couldn't help hoping that I would locate Amber far from there. 'If you don't know where she is,' I said, 'then somebody else might. Maybe your friends, the other women . . .'

'No, no, I know what they know, and they don't know where she is. Amber has lived an isolated life, I told you, especially this last year. We've mainly seen lights on at the bed-and-breakfast.' A grain of bitterness scratched her voice, but it was quickly gone. 'That's as much as most of us have seen of her recently. We saw you, we'd like to think that we saw you six months ago in those lights, even if we found out you had been there only after you had left. But we don't want you to leave again so suddenly. Not now that we've finally met. You shouldn't worry about Amber. You would be the first and only one to be told if we knew were she was.'

I began to move with her, not touching the sheets. 'Maybe your husband might know?' I asked.

'No, you can leave Eamonn alone. He wouldn't know. He saw Amber when I saw her. Nobody—'

'The other men then? Somebody else?' I pressed. 'Amber said she had friends here. So maybe—'

'No, no, you say friends, but I wouldn't call them that and you shouldn't either. Sometimes I think they believe she doesn't even exist. As a person I mean. They'd never admit it, of course, and I'd never ask them. They say they don't mean any harm, and I say that's hypocrisy.' She held out her hands and caressed the sheets, which had suddenly stilled. We paused too. 'It's not . . . like this, you know.'

'So nobody—'

'Yes, why would anybody know?' she said, as she peeped beyond the sheet that faced the village. 'Of course, this is no reason for you to leave. This is a good place to wait. Maybe not friendly at first, but you have to understand that we're not like you. We're country people. You have to be patient with us. You are patient, aren't you? You look like you're in no hurry. So be patient. And be careful what you believe. Things have happened, but it's rumours, just rumours, so they shouldn't bother you. I'm just warning you now, in case you find them out, and in case they might push you to leave. They shouldn't. They're harmless rumours, that's all they are. And that's the past, you know.'

I didn't care about the past. All I had been asking was for somebody who knew where Amber was, and from what I could grasp nobody did, or Dora didn't want to tell me. I was beginning to feel, though, that in the answers she was providing, she was weaving in something else, some other information for which I had to be prepared with brief glimpses. And in those glimpses I saw myself settled in at the bed-and-breakfast, looking out of windows for an arrival that would never happen.

The colour of the sheets started to feel like a warm, pleasant haze. 'But she'll come back,' I asked, 'won't she? Wherever she is.'

Dora took a false step and was gone in the crimson fold of a sheet. She stepped out of it with a grave expression. 'She will be away for quite a while.'

She waited, fearful of my reaction, and I fought to curb an upsurge of joy, and force on my features some of the disappointment she was expecting to see.

And a tremendous effort it was because I fully, passionately believed her. For me Amber's return had already changed from a bloody onslaught to a shower of rose petals. How easy it was to tip the scale in my head! That time I was surprised myself, but no possibility of salvation can ever be too small a lifeboat even for the most giant of hopes.

And, after all, Dora seemed terribly honest. 'Quite a while,' I repeated anyway, to solidify this conviction.

'She will be back eventually,' she assured me. 'after some time, but she will be back. Of course she will. For you.'

'And I can trust you on this.'

'You have to trust me.'

'Quite a while,' I crooned. By this time I was dancing left and right with Dora, better than Dora, in harmony with the ever-changing play of the sheets.

She was still afraid she couldn't leave me like that. 'Oh, son, does it worry you?' she asked. 'I'm afraid it's worrying you. It shouldn't. You know, I would have thought she was gone a long time ago, if it hadn't been for those lights that kept appearing at her windows at night. Like ghosts. She just lived an isolated life. And those lights were always there.' Her lips had curled in a slight look of disgust.

'I'm OK with quite a while,' I said.

'I'm happy, I'm happy. You look like you're the patient type. You won't leave, I'm sure, even if you have to wait for more than a while.'

'More . . .'

'Maybe she will be away for a long while.' Again that serious expression. 'Not too long, of course.'

'And nobody knows where she is.' I was thrilled.

She nodded gravely.

'Maybe I should investigate.'

'No, no,' she said. 'There's no need for you to do that. You don't need to worry and you shouldn't leave.'

Again I curbed my enthusiasm. She hadn't noticed it anyway. Her anxiety must have projected its own distressed reflection on my face. 'I won't leave,' I stated. 'And I'm not worried. I'm her boyfriend. *I* am Charles.'

She peeped beyond the edge of the sheet facing the village, and I craved to return to the bed-and-breakfast. 'I have to go now,' she said. 'Just remember what I told you.' She held out her arms for the hug she had not managed earlier, but I kept her at a distance. She nodded understandingly. 'Let's keep all of this a secret,' she said. 'Nobody needs to know, and heaven forbid if my husband catches us here.' She reached out to pat my arm and was gone.

The night continued to advance, but I didn't notice it. I could only see the flapping sheets and think of the fat, carnal thickness of Amber's quilt. I moved past them and walked up the hill. I felt the village behind, growing louder although I heard no voices, just faint echoes of the fishermen coming home. Ahead of me the bed-and-breakfast was empty and I didn't even have to look to be sure. Over the horizon clouds were tearing, shreds glowing white-hot and fading into magmas of pink and cream, inflamed by a sunset that was becoming visible, a slice of sun that I felt was rising and not setting, just above the sea, blood red.

V

Tall and glorious, the bed-and-breakfast bathed in the last blaze of the day. I found it empty, as I had left it, and I called out Amber's name and said who I was, and heard the calm sound of silence answering me.

How much I felt for Amber at that moment! I hastened to the living room, picked up her picture and held it close to me. I went upstairs with it, floated, I should say, for the anticipation was wonderful, and I didn't want it to end too soon. Her door was ajar, as I had left it, and again I saw that quilt, and in its redness I saw the blushing of my cheeks, the timid shame of my approach. I took in the sight of the bed, I caressed the quilt, I took the picture out of its frame and ran it over the quilt. Then I moved away from the bed, and I leaned against the wall, and my eyes rolled back, and closed. For a long time I nodded and smiled to myself, her picture held against my chest.

Later, I don't know when, I walked to the bathroom to pick up the bottle of moisturizer and brought it to the bed. I had smelt its fragrance since I had walked into the house, but now I uncapped it, let the scent explode, and felt hopelessly drugged by it. I laid her picture in front of me, and looked at it without saying or thinking a word. I contemplated the duality that pervaded her and that was her nature, present and absent. How I loved her body and each element that made it so perfect, her slender bone structure, her lean muscles, the fat so wisely distributed, and that vulnerable yet reproachful look I saw in her eyes as she stared at me.

I lay in bed with her picture, and time passed, and the feeling that almost crushed my chest grew stronger. I compared her size in the picture with mine, but breathed in the smell of the moisturizer, and the difference seemed less. With my eyes I followed the contours of her body, their perfection that nearly burst through her clothes, and I inhaled the smell of her, which made them seem closer. I ran a finger along the back of the picture, marking and trailing her body as if pressing it out. And so it was happening, and nothing else, but total joy; and sleep. I woke up feeling happy and wet. I found I had turned onto the bottle and squeezed out some of the moisturizer. Then I looked up, and watched her eyes open to see mine.

My laughter, of joy and disbelief, rang in the room and hers rang like the echo of mine. She laughed, she moved. The contours of her white body were bright against the redness of the quilt. Without having to ask we knew that we had both dreamed of each other, dreamed of finishing what we had left incomplete two nights earlier, and to emulate our dream we made love again, or for the first time.

I marvelled at the vision, I loved her scent, her voice, her touch, that already knew me so well. This was my Amber. After we had made love we watched our perspiring bodies, watched them cool, warmed them up again. We lay in bed for hours. There was nothing else we wanted to do. The room was our realm, but there was no boundary to what I felt for her.

By the time I got up it was already afternoon. I took a quick shower. The water, the steam, the sight of a room that wasn't hers breezed over me like a veil. Afterwards I took my time over drying myself with a towel that could only have been hers. I went downstairs with it tied round my waist and stood, hands on hips, on the front step looking at the land that stretched into the distance. Clear, vaporous clouds covered most of the sky. Beams of light shone down between them. The grassland was brilliant and full with the rain of a couple of days earlier. I barely noticed the village. Even the road I had travelled seemed harmless, a wound healing, or a snake sinking under green waves. I felt that nothing and nobody could cross that sea. I shivered in the cold air, but I took the towel away from my waist and draped it over the B-and-B sign, covering it carefully.

I went back inside and prepared breakfast with what I found in the fridge and the cupboards. I placed everything on a tray, two cups of coffee, two glasses of juice, rolls, fruit, everything in pairs, then brought the tray up to our bedroom. Amber woke and was surprised and grateful to see the food. How beautiful it is to see things that are born without request nor plan, from neither argument or confrontation! Our appetite grew in our expression, we saw it bloom on the face of the other. We ate with joy, fed each other, tempted our mouths and laughed, pleased with our splendid isolation. We joked about crumbs in the bed, and we chased them away across the irregular shapes of sunshine that rose and fell over the folds of the quilt.

Even now, from a distance, it is painful to remember that perfect first day, and I have to get up from time to time to search for a breath not plagued by that feeling. I get up, walk around, I look for my breath of fresh air, but before I find it I've returned to my seat. That first day was Amber, and me, and a future already lived. Our love was life held in a thought.

68

And so, maybe because of this, when we noticed that the rectangles of light cast by the window were crawling up the boards of the wall and fading in intensity, we saw them as coronation and elegy, but still I couldn't quell a disappointment that was almost horror. 'The end, the end,' I think I whispered, but the sunset burned again somewhere outside the house, and she caressed away my fears, and in the darkness of night we searched for our consolation.

The second day we woke early. The house rested on a cloud of morning mist. The world was cut off, at a standstill, maybe gone. Nothing lay beyond our house and there was nobody who could reach us. Amber's skin was tense and cool in the morning air, her inner thighs a rose of heat. I loved her wild eyes, her fair nipples, the lean feel of her back, the way my name emerged from her lips as an exhalation of hot pleasure when we made love.

Her name was always on mine. When she rested in my arms I lulled her to sleep, repeating it softly. I loved to watch her sleep, and at times my eyes wandered around to look at the pleasant simplicity of our room, our big bed, the bare warm walls and the low ceiling, the wide window and the suffused light that filtered past its drawn curtains.

But perfection was not complete. The chest of drawers broke the harmony of the environment. It was a bulky, intrusive mass. Once, when Amber was sleeping, I walked up to it to inspect its drawers. The various knobs had looked at me with such insistence, stretched out like snail eyes, that I had to know what hid behind them.

Pulling out the drawers felt like pulling memories from somebody's head. I didn't find anything of great interest, although I didn't dare to dig deep under the upper layer of each drawer. I found clothes neatly folded, two leather belts, a collection of handkerchiefs, a sewing kit, a pair of black boots placed in a sixty-nine position, a mixed array of white underwear that sprang out and that I took my time to press back in.

Overall the experience gave me little solace. Afterwards, the knobs looked at me with evil pleasure, as if I had only skimmed the surface of what they hid. I wandered around the house to clear my head, but I felt something preceding me. It hid in the boxes of the storage room, it curled dog ears in the register, it left a pale, greasy stain of a hand on a window. I saw only traces. I couldn't locate the source. The only presence on which I could put my hands was the peacock lamp: it had observed my prowling with an air of expectation, I felt, rather than with its usual snobbery. I looked outside. The day was the colour of steel.

I searched for comfort back in Amber's arms but afterwards, when we were finished and nothing remained but our calm breathing, my eyes found their way to that imperfection in our room, that looming hulk of rough wood. Amber paid no attention to it, nor did she seem to hear sounds rising from distant points of the house, a moaning of floor-boards, like a dilated, crackling laughter.

I tried to dismiss these perceptions, but when I went downstairs to prepare dinner I stopped to inspect random points of the house. I found them all quiet, but I couldn't relax, and I prepared the food grimly, my eyes fixed on what fried and boiled.

When the food was ready and the table set Amber arrived. I took the peacock lamp and placed it on a cupboard next to the table. It shone down a soft, warm cone of light that enveloped only Amber and me, and I felt it did so almost with tangible pleasure. I wanted to bathe in that sensation, but I was uneasy. I ate silently, as if I was digesting all that had happened since our isolation, as if this was a farewell, our last dinner, as if Amber's presence, there, in that room, would fade quickly, leaving behind just glaring, untouchable memories. For a moment I looked past her as if she was truly gone, and I saw myself in the window-pane, which had become a black mirror. I gazed at my face, angst on it, a muscle twitching at my temple as I chewed, and the trace of my skull, there, behind my skin.

I tried to joke with Amber to cheer myself up. I threw breadcrumbs at the peacock, pretending to feed it. Amber watched them bounce off its metal surface and drop to the floor. She didn't say a word and I felt misunderstood, but then I saw that she was letting her gown fall open as she ate.

When she got up I walked after her decisively, leaving my dirty plate on the table, throwing down my napkin next to it. She walked into the living room and played a few languid notes on the piano. They floated in the air, but hung like fog between us.

All of a sudden everything seemed to take substance. Those notes teased me with a past that wasn't mine! I grabbed Amber and held her against the gaping, black mouth of the fireplace. We knew our present, we knew our future, but what about our past, I asked her, was it not something to forsake?

She answered that our past was what had moulded us into the matching souls we were. I told her that if that was so then the past had done its job, and that now it shouldn't interfere with what it had created.

She was unsure. I led her upstairs into the storage room. I pointed at the boxes that cluttered the floor. I told her she didn't need any of this, we didn't need it. We didn't need all those papers, objects, even diaries that she kept in those boxes and which were from a world and a time I didn't know, from a world and a time she didn't have to care about anymore. And what about all that stuff she kept in the chest of drawers in our room? What did it have to do with me?

She was beginning to understand. I got her to help me bring the boxes downstairs from the storage room, and we piled them in front of the fireplace. I wanted to bring down the chest of drawers, because I felt that emptying it wouldn't be enough. For a foolish moment I even thought of dismembering it, but I couldn't suppress a fearful reverence for it, and so, in the end, I limited myself to throwing a sheet over it, and left its contents untouched.

I had no qualms about the rest of the stuff I had brought down, and I could see that Amber felt the same. I ripped out the pages of the register that had been filled in, and lit them with the matches I found on the mantelpiece, using them to start a fire. The flames struggled at first, but we shovelled stuff into the fireplace, like coal into the furnace of a steam train, and soon they blazed beautifully.

I burned clues that might have helped me later on. Those pages of the register, for example, what names had they contained, what transactions? I hadn't even looked at them, and I had paid equal neglect to everything I threw into the flames. I wonder now if it would have made a difference to the way things went. Back then I was beyond caution and foresight, I wanted to cut all bridges to our past, and with mine already gone and hers going in a swirling of hot flames and billowing smoke, all I could do was lay her down in front of the fireplace and love her anew.

Only one thing disturbed me at the time: the key I had found tied round the piano pedal with the one for Amber's bedroom. It looked like the key for a room, but it didn't fit any of the locks in the house. I had thrown it into the fire, but when the flames subsided it remained, a dark question mark in the glowing ash.

The third day was to be the last of our isolation, but I didn't know that when I woke up. I had forgotten about the key, and instead I basked in the same promise of happiness I had felt on the previous two mornings. Time passed and we felt it move, but we kept no track of it, and it was all laid out now, past, present and future, not a moment that we didn't inhabit together.

From time to time I toured the house. That clock I couldn't locate counted the hours. Outside the sky had grown dark again, pregnant with rain that wouldn't fall. A steel light trespassed it, painting no shadows. Green hills, a leaden sea. Between grass and water stood the village, with its sickle-shaped white beach. I had paid minimal attention to it in the past two days. I tried to ignore it now and relax in the comfort of my home, but I found myself drifting over to the windows that faced it, and I did so fearfully, tiptoeing as if my weight would tilt the house and make it tumble down the hill.

I wasn't sure what to make of that village. From a distance it looked like a sore on the land. At intervals it crawled with minuscule life. At certain hours boats left it like spores, but they returned, as if pushed back by the sea. Once I saw the van that took the fish to the next town return from its delivery, drawing a thin, thin line from the outside world. Was the village an outpost of that world, a camp that laid patient siege to my hill? No, I thought, maybe that village was my feifdom and I was a too lenient feudal lord, allowing my subjects to ignore my recent romantic accomplishment.

At a distance the village granted me no clear answer, but

stimulated all my suppositions. Desires I couldn't quell took
shape within me, the wish to speak of my love and my happiness, and subtler cravings for revenge and glory. I felt that my
love was ever changing and ever wanting to grow. And I felt
suddenly impatient, as if something was moving towards me
to cut short my bliss.

I told Amber that the village, whether it was the extension
of our world or the invasion of another, was a land of pagans
where we had to preach the good news of our union. I told
her it had to be done because something had changed.
Something was creeping in with the cruel light of cloudy days.
Had she not noticed it? She had not. She thought the world
did not have to concern us, that it could only strengthen
our union through our isolation from it. Yes, I said, the
world *could* strengthen our union, but isolation was not
the way. Interaction was going to make it more complete. It
was the next step to take in our relationship, the next
renewal.

She tried to dissuade me. 'How come every day something
new bothers you?' she asked me. Wasn't our isolation, there
on our hilltop, all I desired? Wasn't she all I needed?

I didn't answer. I told her I loved her. I told her to forgive
me if my love made me a fool at times. She smiled. I felt dizzy.
I thought I could die for that smile. I could kill for it.

That fading afternoon her lovemaking was more intense
than ever, as if to show me that this was all we needed. I
sought fulfilment, and found it, but afterwards I was prey to
a strange restlessness, even as I lay with my naked flesh resting so comfortably against hers. I didn't think that it could
end, this idyll with Amber, but I wanted it to be more perfect.
My heart was pure but filled past the brim, and I felt I
wanted to share this joy, or others to envy it.

And so when night advanced over the land, I got up to be

alone with thoughts that had never left me. From the dining-room window I watched the village, a dark patch of black broken by few lights, and as night grew thick I saw in the window-pane my own image imposed over it.

vi

That clock I couldn't place counted the hours with its lazy chiming as if it was the slow heartbeat of the house. At eleven I could no longer resist the desire to go down to the village. I went into our room to pick up my clothes, silently, so as not to wake Amber, but then I stopped and asked myself why I was leaving her, even for a moment, her gentle soul, her moonlight skin.

Outside the air was fresh. The irregular whooshing of my feet through the tall grass was the only sound as I half-walked, half-tripped down the hill. Hardly any light filtered though the clouds and the landscape was a canvas of different shades of black. I walked without looking at the ground, but with my eyes set on the village lights, and my arms stretched out to encompass them all. The lit windows were bright squares that dotted irregularly the upper floors of the houses. Fleeting shapes moved behind them. The walls merged with the shadows, making each sharp roof stand on what looked like an oblique, madly drawn structure.

I reached the mouth of one of the short alleys and made my way to the other end. Up the main road, the fishermen were coming home from the pub. I watched one being swallowed by his house. I felt elation at noticing another before a lit window, looking across the street and up the hill in the direction of the bed-and-breakfast, where I had left lights burning for all to see. I wondered if he could make them out with the light on in his own house. After a minute or so, when he moved away, his wife came to stand in the same spot and cupped her hands around her face, as if to pry more meticulously into the night.

A few lights turned off elsewhere. A fisherman entered a house two doors down, and I leaped to it through the shadows. A window was lit on the ground floor and I could see a living room beyond its lace curtains. The night breeze flapped them at intervals, antagonized by an outward breathing of the house, like a musty burping of the evening's dinner. The man appeared at the living-room doorway. He swayed, close to leaning against the jamb but never quite touching it. He looked around slowly, then walked back past the doorway, turning off the light. Darkness poured into the house. I was about to turn and go when I heard a noise. I crouched down just as I saw a dark shape reach the window and close it. It was a woman who had appeared from I don't know where, and once the window had been closed and I looked back inside I thought I could see her glide out of the room, after the man.

Down the road two or three fishermen were wandering home. I plunged into the alley closest to me and scurried around the back of the buildings in the opposite direction from the men. I felt like an explorer, and the little gems of light and movement felt like moths I wanted to capture but that, for now, I could only look at.

The alley that flanked the pub was lit by the scarce glow of the frosted-glass windows. I could hear the door opening and closing onto the main road and a few voices emerging and sinking into the night with quick words I didn't catch. Then silence. Maybe all the men were gone. I reached the end of the alley and looked beyond the edge. Further down, past the door of the pub, the normal windows cast rectangles of light on the sandy surface of the road and of the beach. The door opened and drew a new beam of light with confused shadows moving inside it. A long-limbed man I recognized stepped out and demanded composure from his swaying body. By the time he had secured his ground another, younger man had appeared. The door closed behind them, making Eamonn and Tom dark outlines over the rectangles of light further away. 'At last you're all out,' said Tom, with a voice not more sober than the other man's walk. With some imprecision Eamonn pointed a finger at him. 'Don't group me with the others, and be happy if anybody even talks to you. I wouldn't if you weren't standing behind those beer taps.' 'Why are you angry with *me*?' protested the other, rapping his head with a fist. 'It's not like I made this happen. Do you think I like this situation?' Neither seemed to like it. A vigorous but low argument broke out. I stretched an ear, but heard nothing except grunts; only at the end, a quick 'shut up' rang twice, like an echo.

The two men remained immobile, surprised by their reciprocal anger. They looked at each other as if they were staring into a mirror. Tom ran a hand through his hair, raising it like a cockerel's crest. 'Don't you have to go home?' he asked. Eamonn didn't seem keen to leave. He said something about Dora being restless. Tom found nothing unusual in this. 'Not with me,' I gathered from Eamonn's grumbled answer, ' . . . restless, like when her sister died.' Tom scratched his head. 'Do you think it's because of Amber's . . .?' Eamonn looked at him, considering that broken question. 'What would she know?' he said.

He took a few steps in my direction and Tom followed him. I pressed myself against the wall to be less visible. As they got closer their contours glowed in the light from the frosted-glass windows. They were speaking more quietly, something about not asking a name. 'I was afraid,' said Tom. 'But I was sure he was a tourist. He said he was.' With a foot he searched for the road under the sand. 'I imagined him differently,' he continued. 'I didn't imagine him,' said Eamonn, 'and now I can't say I like him. That arrogance! Coming here as if he owned the place, as if he owned . . .' 'Who knows?' said Tom. 'Maybe he's just a tourist, thinking he can have a cheap laugh.' A short pause followed, or words were whispered. I pressed myself harder against the wall. Could they see me? 'No,' said Tom, 'it must be him. Maybe he pretended to be a tourist. Maybe she told him something or he's suspicious and wants to find out.' Eamonn chuckled. 'Find out what? Something about you maybe.'

At these words Tom lifted his arms in exasperation and headed towards the beach. Eamonn stumbled after him. From round the corner I looked at them bathing in the light of the pub's last window. I saw Eamonn speak and claw handfuls of air while Tom stood in front of him, waving away his designs. I grasped little of Eamonn's accusations. His raucous voice made his words sound like a disturbance in the air. At the end I caught something. 'For heaven's sake,' I heard, 'you moved into Frank's house during his wake! She kicked you out from up there, didn't she?' Tom became more animated than he already was. He stopped waving away Eamonn's designs and began drawing his own. The roles were slowly reversed. Now Eamonn was trying to dismiss whatever Tom was waving at him. His words were clearer than Eamonn's, but I couldn't make sense of them. Loose ones reached me – shoe, dinners, hands, something about a 'leg incident' – but I couldn't piece them together. 'Damn it, Tom,' I finally heard Eamonn say, 'she's young enough to be my daughter. I was just helping her take off her shoes.'

Both were quiet and still. They had moved slowly into the darkness. Two napes and a strange archipelago of irregular folds of jumpers and trousers floated into the light. I heard voices again, two voices that became one, but their words were not much louder than the waves lapping the beach, and I only heard Amber's name, once, and something melancholic in their tone, praise and passion for that which couldn't answer, a confused lamentation that seemed to rise from the sea. I leaned as far forward as I could, hanging on to the corner of the pub. Both men sank fully into the darkness, but one of Tom's arms surfaced into the light: it drew shapes and curves that remained like the ones a torch leaves when swirled in darkness. In them I seemed to see Amber, gentle, bright, ever-changing, and I was happy that Tom could only evoke shapes in the air, while I could make mine true.

I lost my grip on the corner of the pub and fell face down. I hadn't made much noise, but Eamonn and Tom were walking in my direction. 'In any case,' Eamonn was saying as I crawled backwards into the alley, 'I don't want to talk about her with you and you know that.' Two red outlines appeared in front of me and I was sure they had seen me, but they stopped just above my prostrate body, oblivious to it, dark shapes leaning against each other, arms dangling, one of Tom's shoes a few inches from my face. Their eyes shone and were not looking at me, but straight ahead, down the alley.

In an instant my fears of discovery disappeared. I was filled with the uncanny confidence only madmen and conquerors must possess. Without having to turn round, I knew they were looking up the hill, at the ghostly lights I had left on, there at the top. I was sure I could have rolled around on the ground, coughed, sneezed, and they would not have noticed me. I was almost tempted to try it.

'Damn the Cliffs,' said Eamonn. 'Of all the coast available, they had to be here.' Again they were silent, as if to meditate on the weirdness of chance. 'No need to worry any more, is there?' said the other. 'From when she told us about him . . . like trickling away . . . and now she's gone.' There was a silence I wanted to fill. I swallowed, but they didn't hear me. 'And what shall we do with him?' Tom asked. 'Do with him?' Eamonn repeated, but didn't add anything. The figures swayed above me like scarecrows in the wind. I cleared my throat. Still they didn't notice me. 'Not the classy man she told us about,' said Tom eventually, 'with that messy hair and that stubble. Let him come for a shave tomorrow. Barber Tom will take care of everything,' and as he spoke he raised a finger and ran it across his throat from ear to ear. Eamonn looked at him and Tom searched for approval in the older man's expression, but Eamonn turned away.

By now I was charmed. I wanted to laugh, I wanted to get up and hug them for thinking about Amber and me with such intensity. I held back my laughter and I didn't get up, but I couldn't hold back a desire to kiss the shoe in front of my face, and I pouted as much as I could, trying to fill the short but impossible distance between it and my lips.

The men drifted away, cutting short my attempts. Tom reached the pub door and put a hand against it, but didn't push it open. 'I went there,' he said, with his back turned to Eamonn. 'To the Cliffs, I mean. When I was staying at the bed-and-breakfast. Maybe I shouldn't have gone. Like him.' He seemed absorbed in himself, rather than as if he was waiting for an answer. Perhaps the other man had not heard. 'I remember when I went to pick her up on the island,' he said, and pointed straight out of the bay. 'She stood there barefoot with all her things and her boxes, her hands in front of her one in the other, like a schoolgirl. I told her to take a step back and not get her feet wet because winter was coming and the water was getting cold. But she said she had just come out of the water . . . The sun lit everything about her . . . like a mirage . . .'

'And now she's gone,' Tom said again. 'For good, hasn't she?'

Eamonn didn't comment. 'I feel old today,' he said instead. The door of the pub opened and Tom went inside. Eamonn lurched up the road and into the darkness. The light past the pub windows disappeared. I waited a few minutes. My excitement was turning into calm. The peace of the night had seeped into me. When I stood up I brushed the sand off my clothes and walked to the beach, through the shapes and curves that George had drawn. They lingered about me like rings of smoke that I had changed and stretched.

Brittle ribs of moonlight glowed where the clouds had thinned. They burst open, and I watched the moon evaporate the thinnest threads and make the larger ones incandescent with its white light. And as I watched this, my lungs filled with a new, fresh breath, and the waves were calm, and the sand was soft under my feet, the heavy hulls of the boats slumbering around me. I closed my eyes and I imagined myself casting a net up into the sky, its threads appearing out of the village, out of each house, and the net caught the moon and I pulled it down, freed it and held it in my hands, and as it glowed fiercely the people of the village came out, pulled by the threads, and they all saw me.

vii

I wanted to see what they would do. I was eager for our next encounter. Amber was still sleeping peacefully when I returned to bed. My popular girl! How much they thought of her down at the village, how much they thought of us, and I was sure that I had only heard the beginning of it.

I sprang out of bed when the first light of dawn crept into the room. I felt good, wonderful even. I had dozed for a few hours, and had become obsessed with a dream that was more like a vision, and in it I saw myself surrounded by people complimenting me, sincerely and insincerely, and I couldn't hold them back but had to accept all with shy thanks.

Presently I had to worry about looking good for my meeting with the villagers. I gathered it was Sunday from what Tom had said the night before about shaving, and I wanted to dress in my best, but I didn't have a change of clothes. I collected the ones I had and went in search of an iron. I found a rudimentary one in the kitchen and used it on my sweater, shirt and trousers. Everything needed to be washed, but I didn't want to wait for it to dry. Still, I was not going to wear filthy underwear and socks, so I washed and scrubbed them in the kitchen sink to have them ready for the next day. I could do without them now. I had grown accustomed to walking around the house naked, and I doubted that the invisible absence of underwear and socks in public would bother me.

I prepared breakfast and brought it up to bed. Amber woke, but her smile faltered when she saw I was dressed, and my hair had been combed carefully with my hands. Suddenly I lacked the courage to tell her I wanted to go to town, but it was clear that she had already guessed. We ate in silence, but her thoughts were as tangible and noisy as the food I was chewing. 'But I want to go,' I burst out eventually. 'I want to meet the people at the village again. I have to tell them all about us.'

For a while she did not reply, but then her voice crept up on me like a bad conscience. 'What has happened to our wonderful solitude?' it asked.

I looked at her. She was bright and expectant, asking for an answer that required no words. My clothes were a thin barrier I had raised between us, and her charm had begun to work against it. No, I would not desist! She had to understand that I was doing this for both of us. 'Our solitude was our first step,' I told her. 'I'm not bored with it, if that's what you think. It's just that there are many more steps we have to take. Our love wants to grow, can't you see that?'

Eventually she walked me downstairs with the quilt wrapped under her armpits. She kissed me goodbye as if I was off to work, and she hugged me tight. 'Look, I have to go,' I said to her, as she continued to hold me. 'We're also running out of food.'

Outside the air was cutting, and an early sun hid behind smudged grey clouds. The cold was invigorating. It froze the view of the village as if to preserve it forever, and the land and sea around it were like a huge, endless frame. I walked down the hill, and the fresh grass sneaked between shoes and trousers to tickle my sockless ankles. Maybe it was what I had seen and heard the previous night, and my insistent vision of the morning that made me feel nothing could go wrong that day. I felt I was more than a simple boyfriend in a simple couple, because I was sure that everybody in the village had an interest in Amber and me that went beyond peeping curiosity. Somehow, though, I doubted anybody would tell the true nature of their interest, and I didn't want to sound too ignorant about Amber's past with transparent questions. For the first time I regretted having burned her diaries, but I was sure that what had been destroyed could be retrieved in some other way. I was almost convinced that Tom, edgy, newcomer Tom, could be provoked into some kind of revelation about the village and Amber's past.

I ran my hand under my chin and felt my stubble. I even had an excuse to visit him. I hadn't forgotten the threat he had uttered in the darkness the previous night, but I didn't feel frightened – rather, intrigued. I saw it as killing two birds with one stone rather than presenting my throat to a guy I was going to provoke.

As I approached the village I was spotted. Curtains here and there fluttered behind closed windows. I felt pleased, but I pretended not to see them, and I continued to the pub. I found Tom standing in the middle of it with a broom in his hand. 'Tom,' I said, soothingly, as I walked up to him. I laid my hand on his shoulder and ran it over his back to the other. I squeezed him to me. 'Tom, my friend, how are you? Have you missed me? Have the others?'

He stood there, limp, looking at me with disbelief. He was confused by my vigour, as confused as I was surprised and pleased with its spontaneity. His friendliness of a few days earlier seemed gone, or maybe I had given him no time to prepare it. 'How are you?' he managed to ask. 'You're . . . here.'

'Of course I am. I took possession of the bed-and-breakfast. Didn't you see the lights?'

'Yes,' he mumbled, 'I've seen them. A . . . a lot of people thought Amber was back.'

'Well,' I said letting him go, 'it seems that all eyes in this village are pointed at the bed-and-breakfast! Maybe you wanted me to leave,' I said jokingly. 'But never mind. Today is Sunday, isn't it? And I want to go to mass, but I've got stubble to shed before I show everybody I'm still here. You told me you shave on Sunday mornings, so . . .'

He aimed a couple of pointless broom strokes at the floor, hesitated, then pulled out a chair for me. I sat down. Tentatively he found his way round the bar. He tossed a towel over his shoulder then shuttled to the table next to me, carrying a bowl of soap, an old-fashioned razor, a brush, and a small towel floating in a tiny basin of steamy water. The razorblade was a bright rectangle of light in the dull morning.

'Where is everybody?' I asked.

'I doubt anybody will come,' he said.

'I'm early?'

He dipped the small towel into the basin, rhythmically. 'It's not that,' he said. 'I told you they hardly ever come. They've stopped caring about looking good for mass.'

'Well, better this way. I don't have to wait, and we won't be disturbed.'

'Yes,' he said. The towel dipped into and out of the water. 'You sound cheerful today.' He submerged the towel one last time in the basin, then took the dry one from his shoulder and secured it around my neck.

'Well, I'm trying to sound cheerful,' I said.

'Trying?' He shot me a glance that stayed on me for an unusually long time. He seemed to realize this because he shook his head then patted his pockets in search of something. He found a pair of round turtle-framed glasses, formless from staying too long in his pockets, and bent them back into shape.

'Cheerful people often have something to hide,' I said. 'They put on a mask to hide what they really think or feel.'

'You have something to hide?' he asked, absently using the brush to whip the soap into lather.

'I do . . . By the way, I didn't know you wore glasses.'

'I stopped.'

'It's not like a bad habit, you know. I mean if you need them . . .'

'Well, I don't always.'

'It's not like they don't suit you,' I lied.

'Yes, well . . . you were talking about hiding something.'

'I don't know if I should tell you,' I said, and observed his reactions closely. He was about to apply the lather, then remembered the small towel in the basin. 'I'm hiding how I really feel,' I said. 'And it has to do with Amber. Staying these days in her house waiting for her . . . She's not back although it's as if she was. I'm there with her past, and then I think about what I heard from you, and about the way people re-acted to my arrival . . . There are a lot of question marks in my head, mysteries about her . . . mysteries I think I'm start-ing to understand.'

He squeezed the towel then flung it over my neck and face. An intense burning sensation ran from under my nose to my throat. I enjoyed it, for its suddenness, and for the pearls of sweat that had appeared on Tom's forehead. He fiddled with his collar, then pointed at the towel. 'It's to soften the hairs,' he said, almost as an apology.

'I know,' I said, from under it, and waited. The burning sensation subsided and the towel rapidly grew tepid. Behind

Tom the windows looked onto an empty beach and an absent sky, and a faint wind whistled past a crack in the wall.

He peeled the towel off my face, regretfully I thought, and began to apply the lather with imprecise strokes of the brush that sent particles of foam flying about.

'I think I've discovered something,' I resumed. 'It was inevitable, I guess, sitting alone with her past in that house, with her belongings, with her old diaries.'

'You . . . read her diaries?'

'God, no, of course not. What a question! I don't read other people's diaries, not even hers. Especially hers. I'd rather burn them.' I smiled to myself. 'In any case,' I continued, 'I wouldn't read them in case I didn't like what I found. But wandering around the bed-and-breakfast made me remember stuff Amber had said to me, and stuff she didn't want to talk about. Which has made me think of the last time I was here at the pub.' Tom was becoming more frantic with the brush. The taste of lather slowly filled my mouth. 'I thought about the way the fishermen looked at me,' I said, spitting out foam, 'and about the way even you looked at me, and how you said they were odd, as if they were about to say something, maybe against you. I suppose this is just an impression I got, but I'm sure *something* was hiding in the air.'

He held up the razor. Perspiration covered his forehead, his lips were pressed tight, and an unnatural darkness had descended upon his face. Behind him the beach was still empty. The clouds were the colour of ice. With a finger, he tried to raise my chin and expose my throat.

'It's too soon for that,' I said. 'I've got very sensitive skin there. It's better if you let the lather soak in for a while.' He hesitated. 'Please don't misunderstand me,' I said. 'I'm not trying to teach you your job.' Slowly he moved the razor to

88

my sideburn, and I heard it crackle down my cheek. 'I think I have to apologize,' I said, between razor strokes. 'How can I say stuff like this to you? I don't mean about my skin, but how can I think badly of you when you were so friendly the other day? I should be ashamed of doubting your intentions. But just now I was acting cheerful but feeling quite the opposite. Appearances, you know. Were you also trying to hide something the other day? Even those glasses of yours make me wonder. Why don't you usually wear them?'

'I can do without them, if you like,' he said, and with lathery hands he folded them and pushed them back into his pocket.

'I'm sorry,' I said. 'It's that house, the solitude of it. The mind wanders when you're alone. But that's enough! I don't want to think about it anymore.' My cheeks were clean-shaven. The razor strokes had become heavier and less controlled and I wondered how much was to be blamed on the absence of the glasses. He finished my chin, pushed it back and leaned close to my throat.

'It's really quiet this morning,' I said. 'It seems I'm going to be your only customer. I made sure not to be seen when I came down here. I want to surprise everybody, show up at mass, and afterwards introduce myself properly to the village.' From my Adam's apple the razor moved up, dragging my skin along, letting it go with regret. It also dragged new words into my mouth, provocative bubbles that I had not intended should shoot out so quickly. 'I don't think everybody knows who I am. Maybe people still think I'm a passing tourist pretending to be somebody else to have a cheap laugh at their expense. Especially if you say they think I'm gone.' The razor dragged again. For a moment I didn't want to find out about Amber's past. I was prey to the glittering of the razor, to the silence and solitude I felt in the pub and beyond, and to a kind of desertscape I sensed past a paper door that had flapped open inside my soul. I wanted to feel the blood gushing out of me, and a game of cold and hot between blade and blood. 'I think I'm going to talk to Eamonn,' I continued recklessly. 'I felt he had something to tell me the other day. I thought it might be about you.' Tom's razor travelled over tensed muscles, and I almost pushed my throat against the blade, but the impulse was a last grain of something I had cleansed from me: it lasted just a second, and my blood didn't gush out, but provoked a different reaction.

Suddenly I became aware of the absence of my underwear. My trousers seemed connected to the razor by an invisible string, for I felt them rise each time the blade moved up my throat. Later that day I understood why, but then and there I felt only that it related to Tom's struggle to control the instrument. 'I want to meet all the villagers,' I insisted, animated by this new thrill. 'I'm sure their company will cheer me up, and that they can clear away my awful doubts.' I continued to look at Tom. He was tense, almost in a trance. His hair and his collar seemed to stand on end, raised by some inner wildness. He had begun to whip the foam from the razor onto the floor. Modesty made me place my hands on my rising lap. 'But then again,' I continued, 'maybe it's all useless. Why bother making their acquaintance?' The razor eased a bit. 'I might leave with Amber once she comes back. I don't think this is a place for either of us.'

With a last burning drag, the razor finished its job. George stood there panting, searching eagerly for places he had neglected. I raised one hand from my lap and felt my face. 'Great,' I said.

Unwillingly he pulled the towel away from my neck and buried his face in it. When it re-emerged it seemed to belong to him more.

I had calmed down a bit as well. 'Do you have some after-shave?' I asked.

He remembered he had. Limp towel in a limp hand, he went behind the counter to look for some. He came back with a dubious bottle and poured some of its contents on to his hands. The smell was as dubious as the bottle – I was sure I detected whisky – but he patted my face very carefully, as if he wanted to slap me but couldn't let himself. 'You've got a couple of cuts,' he said feebly. 'You were talking as I was shaving.'

'It's great,' I said again. 'Thank you.' I was trying to figure out how to get up. I needed a minute for my trousers to cool down.

Tom didn't seem to notice my problem. He was ruffling his hair and struggling with something he wanted to say. 'So you're going to leave with her?' he finally blurted out.

'I like the city more,' I said, resuming my roundabout prying, 'and I'm sure Amber will too.' I looked at him looking at me. 'No, that's not it,' I said. 'I can see you don't believe me. It has to do with what I told you earlier, with my suspicions. I don't even know how I opened up to you like that, but I felt I could tell you, that we can relate. But on the other hand . . . I know what goes through the mind of someone our age. And you actually moved here. To this village! And those glasses . . . I think you decided not to wear them to look better.' He was clearly growing frantic, and that gave new impetus to my words. 'Amber told me you moved to the village during the barman's wake. Only now I started to wonder why you would do something like that. The villagers must have taken it badly – they were unfriendly towards you the other day. Eamonn in particular. He looks like he could—'

'Eamonn should be quiet,' he finally cracked. 'He's the one

who brought her to town, and he thinks everybody has to answer to him when dealing with her.'

'When . . . dealing with her.'

'You said it. You're wrong about me – you shouldn't suspect me. Do I have to hide that I'm on good terms with Amber? I say it openly: I'm on good terms with Amber. Eamonn is not.'

'How can he be so protective if he's not even on good terms with her?'

'Exactly. Ask him. Straight after she moved here she used to go and have dinner at his house. He and Dora wanted her to settle in, he said. Then all of a sudden she stopped going.'

'She had settled in,' I suggested.

'Dora had found him with his hands on her legs.'

'With his hands on her legs?'

Tom glanced briefly at me to see how I was taking it. I tried to hide my interest behind a frown of distress. He continued, and I could see the tale genuinely upset him: 'He had his hands on her legs,' he said, miming this. 'Dora caught him like that. Amber had just arrived for dinner, and he claimed he was helping her remove her shoes. She had sprained her back moving her belongings to the house. That's what he said. That's what Amber said. But your hands don't need to be that far up a leg to pull off a shoe. So she had dinner there that night. Dora didn't say a word, but she was never invited again.'

'Well, all of this happened before she even knew me,' I said, as I got up. 'And if this happened right after Amber arrived, that's a year before you moved here. The story had probably been blown out of proportion by the time it reached you.'

'Word runs fast and true here,' he said. 'Especially about Amber.'

'Well, then, I suppose this incident was an exception. Eamonn looks like an exception.'

'An exception?' he blurted out. 'He might be the worst of the lot, but he's no exception.'

'I don't understand,' I said, encouragingly.

Tom leaned closer. 'There are a lot of rumours going around, but there's a history of violence in this village. I suppose nobody has shown you the Black Mirror?'

'The Black Mirror?'

'I'm not surprised nobody has. Well, come, you have to see for yourself.' He gestured for me to follow him.

We left the pub in a hurry. 'You're not locking it?' I asked.

'Nobody locks doors in this village but the dead.'

We walked up the main road, keeping to one side, as if the middle was too exposed. He was half a step ahead of me, trying to make me speed up. I saw it made him anxious to walk slowly. 'Pretend nothing is happening,' he whispered to me.

Nothing was happening anywhere. Even the usual fluttering of curtains seemed at rest. We reached the church and he walked to the right-hand corner of the façade. 'This is it,' he said. 'The Black Mirror.'

I looked at it. It was a crooked, black rectangle nailed to the wall. 'Well?' I asked, with some trepidation.

'Now you've seen it,' he said, 'let's move away from here.' He didn't speak again till we had reached the other side of the church. 'It's a village legend,' he said, still uncomfortable. He looked around repeatedly as he went on, 'Now it's burned, but it used to be a mirror – I'm not sure how long ago, but when this village was bigger and not so isolated . . . Are you listening to me?'

I was looking around. There was no movement anywhere, but I had the impression that invisible ears were eavesdropping on our conversation. I asked Tom to go on.

'It was in the days when a certain saint or holy man lived here, and maybe he was holy because he lived among terrible sinners, but that's my opinion. The women of the village doubted their men's fidelity, and they asked the saint whether their fears had any basis in truth. The saint produced this mirror and nailed it to the wall of the church. Every woman who looked into it would see what her husband was doing at that precise moment. Do you understand?' He leaned closer. 'As you saw, the mirror is black. It was burned because it caused too much trouble. Nobody knows who burned it. The legend mentions a mob of men, angry that their wives were meddling in their private affairs. Some even claim that it was women who burned it. Makes sense – if the men betrayed their wives they did it with other women. Or maybe it was the saint himself who burned it. Who knows?'

'And?' I asked.

'What do you mean?'

'I mean, what does it have to do with anything? It happened a long time ago, didn't it?'

'It did, but it's not that simple. It's part of the history of the village, you see.'

'It's not even history,' I said. 'It's a legend.'

'But the mirror's still here,' he insisted. 'I've seen the priest stare into it, right into it. I asked him what it was and he told me the story I just told you. And then he had a go at the saint and said that his methods had been all wrong.'

'Yes,' I said. 'I was under the impression that he thought highly of his own ideas.'

'Who? Father Terence? Yes, I would say so. Fact is, nothing much improved after the mirror was burned. I think things probably got worse. I mean, Father Terence spoke of it as if it was a current thing.'

'So the men and women here are still . . .'

'I don't want to say any more,' he said. 'But you shouldn't believe what they say about me. They're an odd bunch and I'm an easy target.'

I apologized for my earlier suspicions. I felt a touch of guilt for having pressed him so much, and I was glad to see him relieved. 'And what about Amber's involvement in all of this?' I asked.

He opened his mouth but closed it again. He must have remembered to whom he was talking. To tell or not to tell her boyfriend? Would I see rumours, legends and truth as if they were the same thing? Would I leave Amber, or take her away to the city?

'I don't know about Amber,' he said.

I went back to the Black Mirror and looked at it, fascinated. In it I saw an opaque, almost invisible reflection of myself, but I thought I could discern something beyond it although the mirror had no depth – something riotous, raging in unnatural silence. Yes, it must have been worse after the mirror had been burned. There's nothing as consuming as suspicion or the presence of something that might provide answers but never will.

My brief encounters with the villagers made sense now. I was sure the women still looked into the blackness of that mirror and saw their husbands laying secret siege to the bed-and-breakfast, but I was equally sure I had changed all that. I had appeared, an obstacle between the men and Amber, and the women loved me for it and would never let me go, while the men could do nothing against me for fear of fuelling their wives' suspicions.

Tom was beckoning me. I went to him calmly. I must say, I felt a sense of revulsion at the thought of Amber's involvement in this, but I didn't know how much was speculation and how much was truth. The women's suspicions, the men's desires – none of them necessarily had any connection with the way things really happened. In any case, it was her past that repelled me, and maybe, as Amber had told me, it was that past that had made her into the woman I loved. I realized it didn't matter whether she had had affairs to divert herself from the sorrow of an emotional void that only I could fill, or whether she had waited and saved herself for me. They were both signs of love, and I loved her. And I can't deny that I was grateful. How I looked forward to declaring my love to the village! How important Amber had made us in our little world!

Behind me the church bells began to ring. Doors opened on to the main road, and silent couples walked out in dusty, Sunday clothes. My presence changed faces and made steps falter, and I raised a hand to reassure them, to change that initial surprise into understanding.

viii

'Put the shave on my account,' I said to Tom, 'or open one, if you haven't done so already.' He seemed surprised by the change in subject after all he had revealed. 'Well, who knows?' I added. 'I might even close it soon, considering all you told me. Really, I think they're just rumours. I'll have to see. Find out.'

He said nothing, but watched the villagers approach. He was unsure what to do. 'Don't tell anybody what I told you,' he said, 'but remember . . .' He waved a discreet warning finger at me.

He made for the door of the church and stumbled inside. I walked up to it too, but waited, hands behind my back, for the rest of the villagers to arrive. I held the door for each couple and greeted then politely, adding 'I'm Charles.' The women smiled and thanked me. The men limited themselves to grunts and aloof glances. I saw the same two faces re-appear, couple after couple, and the same reactions. By the time Eamonn and Dora arrived I was so into my routine that I introduced myself to them as well. 'We know who you are,' Eamonn growled.

I waited until the road was deserted before I walked into the church. The faint chanting I could hear from outside came more clearly when I opened the door. I made the sign of the cross and knelt briefly. The hymn wavered as everybody turned to look at me. The women's voices returned quickly to the melody, and after a few elbows had been poked into their husbands' sides, the men resumed singing too.

It was beautiful. The women's voices seemed to have drifted higher, the men's to have sunk. The priest looked refreshed, hair combed, and pleased to see me. I had the impression he winked at me as I walked down the aisle. Everybody looked at me as I did. I made the sign of the cross again, elated as I was, and looked for a place to sit. The pews were only half full. Gaps in the congregation gave the impression that people had been plucked and removed from above. The first pew on the left was empty. It was perfect. Everybody could see me there.

Mass began. I paid little attention to the ceremony, and I didn't seem to be the only one. The priest looked at me most of the time. The people behind me must have stared at me even more. I felt dozens of eyes on the back of my head. More than once I turned round with the excuse of looking for a hymnbook I never found, and I saw those eyes dart from me like flies waved off a cake. Outwardly I was a mask of peacefulness, but inside I hid a physical thrill that now and again pitched my voice as I recited some prayer with the others, or as I hummed hymns to which I didn't know the words. The statue of the Virgin Mary heightened my state even more. 'Amber, I'm here for you,' I said to myself.

Mass was drawing to an end. The priest finished the wine, dried the edge of the chalice with a cloth, then brought it back to his lips for some last, obstinate drop he struggled to capture. Everybody waited, somebody coughed. The priest sat down for a moment of reflection. When he stood up he gazed down at his flock from behind the lectern. Everybody had stood up, waiting for a blessing that he didn't seem to want to give just yet. 'My children,' he said eventually, 'words are spoken uselessly all the time and too often I realize that I'm throwing more and more of them into the chasm. Christ was even put on a cross for words He had spoken. Fools said that He was given a chance to prove what He preached then and there on the cross, because if He was the Son of God then He would come down from there, and everybody would believe. But He didn't come down from the cross, and people thought that the world He promised was nowhere beyond His words, that it was a make-believe designed for people who weren't capable of snatching enough now, in this world.

'It's normal that we're dissatisfied with our lives,' he continued, and his voice rose slowly. 'And it's inevitable that we look around for something better. But snatching and getting fairly are not the same thing. And nothing is obtained fairly if it is at the expense of others. How many times have I told you that we're not deprived children, that we do not need to find easy ways out of our imperfect lives, but that we need to accept them and mend them parsimoniously? How many times have I told you that real purity comes from honest actions, while real crime is but a thought away? Not all that shines like gold here will be gold after we die. Because now we know better than those fools two thousand years ago, and we know that there will be justice one day.' He coughed. I looked round briefly. His words had caused a stir. Some people were straightening their collars or sleeves, others frowned, while I was attentive, sensing the direction of his thought. He cleared his throat. 'Our life has its course and we need to accept what happens around it. It's not every day that somebody moves here to our village, but it's time that we started to deal with it appropriately, not with . . .' and here he waved his arms frantically in the air ' . . . confusion. We should all be happy that our friend Charles has come here, and we should hope that he will stay.'

'I will, I will,' I said, jumping out of my pew. 'Thank you,

Father, thank you, thank you,' I said, and walked towards him, as if he was on a stage and about to hand me a prize. 'I'm so glad that you remembered me and my recent arrival. I would have liked to come sooner!' He stood unimpressed where he was, maybe a bit surprised, then took half a step back. I moved into the space between him and the lectern and looked onto a gaping audience. 'I really wanted to come sooner,' I said, 'but I had some stuff to do in the city . . . you know . . . before returning . . . but I'm happy, because I wouldn't be here if it wasn't for Amber. I owe it all to her, who unfortunately isn't here today.' I turned, almost gestured towards the statue of the Virgin Mary, peacefully immobile and present. I allowed a brief moment of silence to pass, and then I went on. I managed to cram a lot of broken, emotional sentences into the space of no more than a minute. I spoke of my happiness, of Amber's, of ours, I thanked Fate for leading me to her, then corrected myself and thanked God instead. I continued mumbling something even I didn't understand, and I ended up thanking them all, for surely, I said, with a touch of subtle but unintended irony, they had been good neighbours to her. 'I'm so looking forward to getting to know you,' I added and searched for something to top off my speech. 'I'm already considering moving to this village permanently,' I said. 'I guess I have to wait for Amber to come back and see what she thinks. Ask her where she wants to marry. Why not here, in this church?'

The silence of a funeral had descended on the congregation. The people in front of me had been no more than flames feeding my passion and the fast, furious flow of my voice. I looked at them, attentively now. A few smiles dawned here and there. Some women were smiling – many women were smiling. Most of the men were frowning. Eamonn seemed unaffected. Tom, sitting at the back, was whispering to a corpulent, white-bearded man, who wasn't paying much attention to him. I thought it had to be William the shepherd, as I had not seen him before.

I didn't care who he was. I think I waited for applause or a general welcoming, although I was already happy with the simple silence I received and the turmoil that I felt was hiding behind it.

I felt a tap on my shoulder. It was the priest. I let him back into his place and returned to mine. My steps resounded in the church as I walked back to my pew. I knelt, pretending to pray but in fact concentrating on the emotions that surrounded me.

In my past life I had always feared attention, feared being judged, feared failing in front of others. I had hidden in the shadows and told myself that my withdrawal meant no failure, but the absence of defeat left me with no victory, just a vague, traitorous feeling that I had been spared. Everything was different that morning at mass. I was the centre of attention but I had no fear. I felt the villagers' happiness and jealousy around me, and I wanted to jump out of my pew to hug everybody or to step on a pedestal for all to see me better.

Maybe I was getting carried away.

'Mass is over,' I heard the priest say. 'Go in peace.'

I tried to calm down and, with my eyes shut, waited for them all to leave the church. When I got up Father Terence was standing by the door. A few strands of grey hair cut across his forehead like a scar. 'Not a nice speech,' he said, 'and I shouldn't have allowed you to barge in like that, but I'm happy you spoke.' His breath smelt of the wine he had drunk, and he was scraping his lips with his teeth. He opened the door a bit, producing a slit of light. 'You'd better be good for this village,' he added. There was a gravity in his expression that I had not seen before, almost a pathetic sadness. At the time I thought little of it as I wanted to tackle the villagers again, so once he opened the door for me I left with only a brief goodbye.

Outside, the wind carried the sound of the last front doors closing. How could they have gone so quickly? I was disappointed. Only a man and a woman still walked along the road, arm in arm towards the beach. It was Eamonn and Dora. She held him tightly, her arm locked around his. When they turned back in my direction, I saw pain on Eamonn's face, pain at the clutching that held him captive, and I thought I saw him look up briefly at the sky. Dora wouldn't let go, but I felt she depended on Eamonn to hold her up.

I had never been good at reading people as I had tended to be too busy with my own unease, but that day I burst out of my cocoon with such speed that I was almost blinded by the clarity of each new perception. People weren't inscrutable judges any longer but open books, and I saw their desires and their fears so close and real that I could touch them, and do it with pleasure.

I walked towards Eamonn and Dora with a sure step and a smiling face. Dora seemed to look forward to our meeting, but Eamonn used her grip on him to steer her away. My smile wavered as they moved from the middle of the road to a house, and before I could intercept them they had disappeared past its door.

That was no way to behave, I thought. Not after my warm speech, and not after my offer to settle in their grimy little village. I stood where our encounter would have occurred and licked my lips.

I walked up to the door behind which Eamonn and Dora had disappeared and tried the handle. The door opened and tugged me forward. Eamonn had pulled it from the inside.

'Hi,' I said, with a demented smile. I never intended to look too good in his eyes.

'What do you want?' he asked.

Another voice came from within. 'Is it him?'

'It's Charles,' I shouted.

'And?' said Eamonn.

'And, well . . . I wanted to pay you a visit.'

He didn't seem too impressed.

'It's not an inconvenience, is it?' I asked.

'Not at all, Charles,' said Dora, who had appeared from behind Eamonn. 'Please, come in.'

I followed them down a dark hallway and into a bleak living room papered in faded green flower patterns. The walls and the ceiling had lost their sharp corners and straight lines as if the whole house was gradually collapsing. The furniture looked resigned to its fate. There was no sign of modernity, not a radio or a television. Dora seemed at ease, Edgar less so, a miserable look on his face, as if he was embarrassed by me seeing him there.

I felt honest pity for him. 'I don't want to stay too long,' I said, 'I just felt it would be nice to . . . spend some time together.'

Eamonn had moved closer to me and had stretched his head in my direction like a tortoise. 'Are you drunk?' he asked with disgust.

'It's my aftershave,' I said, and took a step away from him. 'It's a new brand.'

'Maybe you'd like to stay for lunch?' Dora asked.

'I don't want to impose.'

'You're not imposing, Charles,' said Dora. 'I always cook too much for us. We're inviting you.'

'*You* are inviting him,' said Eamonn. 'He should go back to the bed-and-breakfast in case Amber returns.'

Fear gripped me at the thought of it. 'She should be away for a while longer,' I said tentatively, and looked at Dora for a sign of confirmation. She nodded discreetly, without Eamonn seeing her.

'Will you stay, then?' she asked.

Her face was hopeful, lips and eyebrows lifted and tensed. Eamonn had lost all trace of embarrassment and that made me feel better, because I still had pity for humiliation. Hostility was all I could read on his face, and that inspired me. 'I think I can stay,' I said cheerfully. 'Especially if I'm offered such kind hospitality. As for Amber, I'm sure she left me a note, and I've been too careless to find it.'

'She's a nice girl,' said Dora, out of context.

'She's a wonderful girl,' I said, and sat down at what I judged to be the dining table.

Dora looked happy.

Eamonn looked at her. 'Well, go on,' he told her.

'Right,' she said, breaking out of her state of contemplation. 'I have to . . .' she said, pointing at the kitchen and disappearing into it.

Eamonn sat down opposite me and stared at me. I let my gaze wander from him to the room to nowhere in particular. I kept a smile to show my benevolence, and sometimes I tried to force one out of him when our eyes met.

Dora returned to set the table. She made a comment on how quiet we were, but neither of us replied. I offered her the same smile I had used with her husband. She smiled back, then brought the food.

For lunch there was roast beef with cabbage, mashed and roasted potatoes. Eamonn turned his attention to the food and stabbed at it quietly. He pretended to have forgotten me, but I could see my presence weighed on him as he lowered his head painfully to snatch the mouthfuls from his fork. Dora was made happy by my presence, she said as much, and she looked at her husband's bad mood with suspicious eyes.

That meal, the silent beginning of it, Eamonn viciously tearing his bread, Dora offering me water, felt like the moment when I had knelt in church. I could have spoken words of praise about Amber, and I tried a couple of times, but gave in to silence, said nothing, savoured everything. Eamonn and Dora were quiet too, because what could Eamonn say in front of his wife, and how grateful could she be without betraying why? I was the cause of hate and love, but I faced neither threat nor commitment, and I asked for nothing more than that dancing of moods in front of me, food stabbed and drink gulped on one side, absent nibbling and readiness to serve on the other.

Eventually Dora asked me vague questions about my past, trying tactfully to find out whether I had the means to back up my decision to stay. I reassured her that not only had I cut off my relations with the outside world, but that I had enough money for a long autonomy, in case I failed to find a job somewhere close to the village. She seemed pleased, but also concerned for having been nosy about money. She moved on quickly and asked me about the first time I had been at the bed-and-breakfast and about an even more remote past. I spoke a few vague words about the former and indulged even less in the latter. 'Yes, I'm a good man,' I said, to round up the little I had said.

'Oh, Charles, I wouldn't think otherwise,' said Dora.

'I know, I know. Would Amber have chosen differently?'

'That's a good question,' said Eamonn, lifting his head for the first time. 'I ask myself that.'

'What do you mean?'

'Nothing,' he said, before returning his attention to his plate.

Dora looked as surprised as I was, but she recovered more quickly. 'You know,' she said, with a burst of forced vitality, 'your arrival in church today reminded me of Amber when she first came to mass.'

I was still looking at Eamonn, but he had lost interest in me. Slowly I turned to her. 'I didn't think she'd be so dramatic,' I said.

'No, not as dramatic, but more . . . solemn, I would say. We were all in church when she walked in. It looked like she wanted to smile at everybody, but I thought she was too shy and she only glanced quickly here and there. She walked down the aisle so slowly. And she sat on the first bench like you. Had she walked down the aisle after you today you would have looked like a couple ready to get married.' She smiled. 'Well, I hope you do. I think you would make a nice couple. Getting married here . . . it would be romantic.' She continued to talk. I envisaged the wedding I had spoken about. I saw the world of the village distorted as if by a lens, my Amber and me at its centre, untouched, in focus. ' . . . she introduced herself *after* mass,' Dora was saying, 'outside the church. Oh, and did you see the statue? It's nice, isn't it? It's funny because by the time William had finished it Amber had started to come down here less often.'

'I don't think the statue is very good,' said Eamonn. 'Amber is much nicer.'

'A nicer girl,' said Dora.

'What did I say?' said Eamonn.

A tense silence filled the room. Eamonn grabbed his glass and poured its contents down his throat.

Dora found her way back to her story. 'Well, that first day when she presented herself, some of our neighbours almost took a step away from her, as if she was God knows what. You see, Charles, we're not used to change. We're used to seeing the same faces and only those. At most we see people leave. So everybody was surprised by her arrival. Somebody thought that she was the girlfriend of somebody's son come to look for him.'

'Somebody's son?' I asked. 'I haven't seen any around.'

'The children of this village have left,' said Dora. 'Even before Amber arrived. There's not much for them here. Some are too far away even to visit.'

'And do *you* have children?' I asked.

Dora seemed embarrassed. Eamonn crawled out of his silence and spoke. 'We have no children,' he said.

'I didn't mean to be intrusive,' I said, 'even if I guess that's hard to believe after I invited myself here for lunch today.'

'Yes,' said Eamonn.

He was making me nervous. 'Actually, one of the reasons Amber likes me', I continued, 'is because I don't hassle her too much. I like to think of myself as a nice guy.'

'Oh, she likes nice guys,' he said sarcastically.

'Sometimes it pays off to be a nice guy,' I insisted.

'I'm sure it does.'

'Eamonn!' said Dora. 'You're being very rude.' For a long time they stared at each other across the table. There was a hardness in Dora's eyes I hadn't seen before.

'From the little Amber had said about him I imagined him differently,' he said at last.

'That's just your imagination,' I said. 'I'm Charles.'

'It's a common name. We have a nephew called Charles.'

'Eamonn!' Dora insisted.

'Oh, don't worry,' I said. 'It's all right.'

'You're being very nice,' he said.

He was staring at me with eyes that knew too much. Or were trying to find out too much. I searched for some infor- mation that might prove my identity, that might show who I really was. I thought of the conversation I had overheard the night before between Eamonn and Tom. 'Yes,' I said, turning to Dora, 'well, Amber has told me a lot about you. She said something about your sister who died. I was sorry to hear that.'

'Oh, thank you,' said Dora. She looked a bit shaken. 'That was . . . that was quite a while ago now.'

Eamonn looked at me with even greater suspicion. I looked at Dora for help, but she seemed absorbed now, a forkful of food frozen half-way up to her mouth.

'That was even before Amber got here,' he said.

Suddenly I felt transparent in his eyes. I felt he saw things in me that I had forgotten. Was my joy to be so short-lived, was I going to be ousted from my place so easily? Again I ransacked that overheard conversation, and I also rummaged through all Tom had told me for something else I could use, for a weapon this time more than for proof of my identity. 'Did Amber stop coming to dinner here because of this attitude of yours?' I said, remembering the leg incident of which Tom had spoken. 'I know about your dinners,' I said, leaning forward in my chair.

The fork in Dora's hand, still half raised, trembled. 'Did Amber tell you?' she asked.

'Who else?'

'She came here just a few times,' she said.

'Unfortunately just a few times,' Eamonn added. Dora shot him a look. He sustained it for a while then returned his attention to the food left on his plate. Slowly I returned to mine. The atmosphere was bleak and tense, and they seemed busy with thoughts I had stirred up. The confrontation had moved between them, but while I felt safer, I was also annoyed at Edgar's suspicions, and the more I thought about it the more irritated I became.

'My husband's a nice man,' said Dora, 'even if he can be a bit grumpy sometimes. You have to excuse him if he's a bit rude now.'

'I remember Amber spoke highly of you,' I said, keeping the 'you' vague. 'But still she stopped coming.'

'Well, I think she just needed to settle in,' said Dora.

'Right,' I said.

Silence returned, broken by the sound of cutlery against plates and teeth. Dora was tense. She shot angry looks at Eamonn, and then quick ones at me to make sure I had not seen them. I pretended I hadn't. I reached over for more bread and she touched the edge of the bread-board pointlessly to make herself look helpful. Eamonn looked at his empty plate, collecting some leftover gravy with his fork. I wondered whether he was studying his next move. I could see that his moroseness fuelled Dora's suspicions and that she was trying to make sure it wouldn't fuel mine too.

But I didn't want her protection. I was ready for any attack. 'So, why did she stop coming?' I asked.

Eamonn looked at me obliquely. 'Didn't you just ask that question?'

I shrugged. 'I don't remember. I mean, I hope there was no falling out. I know she can be a bit tricky sometimes. She can . . . you know, give out the wrong signals.' I waited for them to speak. Dora looked at Eamonn. He said nothing.

'I don't remember,' Dora said, turning to me. 'I think she just stopped coming. Maybe she had a lot to do with the bed-and-breakfast. She opened it a couple of weeks after her last visit here, you know.'

'A lot to do for very few guests,' I said.

'Whatever,' said Eamonn, throwing down his knife and fork. He stood up. 'I'm going now. I've got some work to do on my boat.'

I wasn't finished with him. 'You're going out to sea?'

'I said I have some work to do on the boat. We rest on Sundays, and I never go out unless I have to fish.'

'What about when you picked up Amber from her island?'

He gave me a vicious look, and I held it. 'I was asked to help somebody move to the house on the hill,' he said slowly, 'and that's what I did.'

'Yes,' I said. 'Well, I'm sorry, I understand that you don't like me, but I ask myself why you were so polite to Amber and you have to be so rude to her boyfriend. It makes me think. You don't even wait for me to finish my meal before getting up, while I bet you would have tied Amber's shoelaces if she asked you to.'

Slowly he leaned on the table and sat down again. I could see that he had taken my example for an allusion. Dora tried to say something, but I continued before she could. 'I don't know,' I said, 'maybe I'm not the most amiable of people, maybe I'm not the best of company, but I'm still Amber's boyfriend and if you had so much respect for her it should follow that you have respect for the person she chose to be with.'

'Yes, there's something wrong somewhere,' he said to me. 'I respect her, and her judgement, so why do I have this gut feeling about you? Maybe there's something else. I seem to remember you were on your way to the Cliffs and were looking for Amber to pay for a room.'

'Going to the Cliffs?' I burst out. 'I'm even afraid of heights! As for paying for a room, I think that's what Tom said to you. I didn't contradict him because I didn't want to present myself straight away as Amber's boyfriend. I don't think it would have been fair on her if she hadn't told you about me. I just wanted to study my position a bit. And yours, for that matter.'

He got up again and pushed in his chair. 'Well, we didn't know what Charles looked like.'

'Handsome and smart, like me,' I said jokingly, and laughed a bit. Eamonn had no proof against me. He was recalcitrant but he was getting nowhere, while I was enjoying strengthening my position. 'Tom recognized me all right,' I added.

'Ah, Tom,' said Eamonn, unimpressed.

'Yes, Tom,' said Dora, hoping to help the conversation veer away from Amber.

'I thought you and Tom got along well,' I said.

'Tom', said Eamonn, 'moved to town during our old barman's wake. He came down from the bed-and-breakfast with his suitcase asking if he could move in. And we were sitting around drinking in Frank's memory! It's not that he had run out of money. He had been kicked out.'

'He's not that bad,' said Dora.

'He's a fool.'

'Because of the way he moved to town?' I asked.

'Because of a lot of things.'

'Well, you were hospitable towards him,' I said.

'Hospitable! I suppose he was more arrogant than you, and took advantage of us even more. Started mourning with us and handed out the drinks, and before we knew it he was doing the same downstairs behind the bar. As you can see he stayed, so he got our hospitality all right.' He didn't seem too happy about it, but he was angry with himself, not Tom. 'And, you know,' he said, 'he went after his stuff, the stuff he had left at home, wherever his home is, a month after he had moved in. A month.'

'I suppose he was afraid you might stop being so welcoming.'

'He's a suspicious brat,' he said. 'Well, now I'm really going.'

I got up and said to Dora that I was going too. I thanked her while she apologized for her husband. I followed Eamonn out of the living room and down the dark hallway. Dora rushed after us.

'Maybe we can carry on our conversation some other time,' I said. 'I can invite you up to the bed-and-breakfast one day.'

'I've never been up there,' said Dora, with an enthusiasm that didn't sound genuine.

'I'm sure your husband told you about it,' I said, 'when he helped Amber move her stuff. And it must have been quite a job, considering all the stuff she had.'

Eamonn opened the door then shut it again. He turned round, and I was sure he was going to hit me. Instead he walked past me and up the stairs, taking off his suit jacket. When he was gone, Dora gestured after him. 'He's getting changed,' she said, before returning to her apologies.

I told her there was nothing to apologize for. 'I'm just a bit nervous about Amber being away for such a long time,' I said. 'Maybe that's what puts me in such a confrontational mood.'

'I'm certain she will be back,' she said. Her face was in the dark and I missed the subtleties of her expression, but her tone was unsure and I was comforted by it.

I left. Outside, the air was still cold under the same sky, in the same empty road. There was no sound, no movement anywhere, but when I began to walk towards the beach I sensed something move behind curtains at the edges of my vision. I still couldn't distinguish the inhabited houses from the empty ones. It's as if they were shuffled when I wasn't looking or as if the villagers scuttled invisibly between them. I slowed down, full of expectation. For a moment I thought the houses would turn inside out like gloves and spill their inner life all over me.

Nothing of the kind happened. Nothing even got close to it. I kept seeing the same vague movement I had seen since I had got to the village.

Soon the beach opened up in front of me and I went to sit on the shore. The scenery wasn't much to look at. The sky was dreary, the water too. It looked animated by something that wasn't life. The grass at the edges of the beach weakened in colour as it approached the rocky headlands.

I began to doubt that mass had changed anything. I feared that the men were already resigned, the women feeling secure. Maybe everybody had found their way back to their lives where I didn't exist.

I was absorbed in such thoughts when I heard Eamonn arrive. I didn't turn round but continued to look ahead of me. My confrontation with him and the one with Tom earlier that morning were two bright spots in my melancholic recollections.

'Did you come here for any particular reason?' I heard him ask, after a few minutes.

I got up and turned round. He was standing by his boat, his Sunday clothes replaced with a pair of faded black trousers and a black jumper. 'Just thinking,' I said.

Eamonn didn't seem convinced. I walked up to him, drawn towards him. I sat on the edge of his boat and lay back on one of the benches. We were alone. The silence was unreal. His face was still tense from our earlier conversation. He had been working on a net that he was now amassing at the bottom of his boat. Without taking his eyes off me, he picked up a bag, pulled out some large fish-hooks and began to clean them with a cloth. He cleaned them with his right hand and, to avoid putting them back in the bag with the dirty ones, he placed them between two fingers of his left hand. Almost instinctively I patted my stomach, rubbed it, then left it exposed, locking my hands behind my head. 'It was a good lunch,' I said. 'I really enjoyed it. You're lucky to have such a good wife. You must have been very happy when you were young and freshly in love, when nobody else seemed to exist.' The hooks glimmered unnaturally in the faint light of the overcast sky. 'I feel like that now with Amber. But I know I have to grow. As you must have done. You cannot ignore others, they will always be there. Maybe I used the wrong approach earlier today, flaunting my relationship in front of you in church. Maybe that was immature.'

Eamonn began to nod then stopped as if he deemed me unworthy of the effort. It was clear to me, though, that my presence made him uncomfortable. He knew I suspected him of having desires but what could he do? He continued to clean the hooks. That's all he did. He cleaned them until they shone with all the light they could collect on such a drab day.

'You know I have doubts about you,' he said eventually.

'And I about you,' I answered.

He didn't reply. His face was impassive, his expression grey like his hair. From somewhere darkness collected around his features, and he continued to clean those hooks. They jingled eagerly in the bag when he fished for another, and they stuck out like claws from his left hand, but the threat he tried to convey with them was just frustration, and I was sure it could never be anything else.

My body's peculiar reaction to Tom's razor began to make sense. Eamonn's hooks were having the same effect on me now. I swung my arms forward and pulled myself up to try to hide it.

'I'm finished,' he said, shaking the hooks from his hand back into the bag. 'I'm going home. Can you please get away from my boat?'

He waited for me to take a few steps back. I did so with

my hands clasped in front of me. He looked at my stance obliquely, then dismissed me with a gesture of his hand and was gone.

I turned to the sea and went to sit by the shore. I stretched out a hand to feel the water and it was cold. The waves lapped the beach rhythmically, like breathing. My trousers cooled. My initial childlike enthusiasm was reaching maturity. I was acquiring new vision. I saw what was needed. I was planning ahead. I thought of how I could do everything I had done that noon at Eamonn and Dora's house but on a larger scale. Attention was short lived, but emotions . . . Everything they felt, I wanted it all out, I wanted total dedication, in love and hate.

ix

I wanted to tell everything to my Amber. In a hurry, I bought some food at Tom's shop. He served me reluctantly, still puzzled by my good mood. I think he wanted to remind me about the Black Mirror, but I gave him no time to say anything.

I ran up the hill, and the sight of the bed-and-breakfast brought a change to my features. 'Honey, I'm home!' I shouted, once the front door had closed behind me. Her quilt was lying at the bottom of the stairs where she had kissed me goodbye that morning. I picked it up and went to our room half wrapped in it, wading through memories of us as through a fog that got thicker as I ascended. I found her at the centre of it, a hazy glow, and for a moment nothing else existed, my senses were filled to the brim, my soul went out to her and I was a shell, resonating with the memories of that first perfect day we had spent together. But that was just the beginning, I told myself, our love had developed and its prospects had increased. Amber asked me about my day, and I told her. I told her about Tom's silly rumours, about the frowns and smiles in church, about lunch at Eamonn and Dora's.

She enveloped me in her misty arms when I finished talking. I stayed there in bliss, almost in oblivion, for a long time. 'We're the perfect couple,' I whispered to her. 'I was so happy to tell everybody about us . . .'

When evening came we went downstairs and prepared the food I had bought. We ate, we drank, we toasted under the peacock lamp. The bird seemed pleased to shed its glow on our dinner. At the end of it Amber stood in front of the window and I behind her, my chin on her shoulder, my arms around her waist, and we spoke to each other's reflections in the glass. I could see that something was on her mind. Upon my enquiring she asked me if I was not afraid of the men's jealousy. 'Why? Were you of the women's? I'm sure they were jealous of you. I know that maybe it was childish of me to tell the villagers about us. I should have expected that they would react like they did. Great people cause great reactions, not just great emotions. The way Eamonn attacked me! It seems that if they can't have perfection they don't want anybody else to have it.' Amber seemed worried still, but she said nothing. I had plans, *I had plans*, but I didn't want to enter into explanations. 'And in any case,' I said, 'what can the men with their jealousy do to me? Can they hurt me in any way?'

Night came and grew thick, and we felt the tiredness of our bodies. I had slept little the night before. Our conversation became an unconscious murmuring; I heard myself talk of the village beyond the glass, about the men, the women, and I was telling Amber to look more closely, at the lights, at the movement; somebody was looking up at us. I told her our lit window was like a star to them. Then all talk subsided, it grew dark as if darkness itself had crept into the house and had flicked off the light, and I felt my legs grow weak, then catch me again, and I found myself pressed against the window, a cloud of breath on it. The light was on and that clock I had always heard but never seen was marking the last hour of the day. It was soon after that she spoke. 'When will you tell everybody I'm here?' she asked. 'Maybe soon they'll get suspicious, and they'll think . . .'

I felt the cold surface of the glass against my forehead. I didn't know what to answer. I looked for Amber but she was gone. I was alone, and not a word of reply came to me. Thoughts I could not reconcile, I could not even name any more, buzzed in my brain without ever settling. Dora came back to mind, her face in the shadows of her hallway, promising Amber's return. Her unsure tone had withered away, only her promise remained, and her face, which hovered in the darkness above the buzzing. It grew blacker each time I tried to look at it, more illegible, like the pages of a book burning slowly. I tried to dismiss it. I considered going to bed.

With time, though, I found myself wandering down the hill. My path was lit by filtered moonlight. The village was silent and dark, not a sound, not a movement, not even as I walked past the houses. A faint smell of fish breezed up from the beach.

I found my way to it. For a while I wandered around the boats, with the dreaminess of a sleepwalker and the dread of a child afraid of the dark, then I took courage and felt the cold surface of an engine. My fingers ran along it tentatively, and converged around the thin, rigid frame of a key sticking out. All the other boats I checked had one too. I chose Eamonn's, pushed it into the water and hauled myself in. I lowered the oars and started to row towards the end of the bay. The rocky headlands were far away, and I couldn't see more than a few docile waves in front of the bow that grew slowly in size and temper as my arms began to ache. When I could row no longer, I turned on the engine and sped into the darkness. I went on for a long time, lifting and slamming on the waves. They appeared for a second, silently chasing each other, before disappearing under me, and I wondered, in a kind of stupor, whether next I would see stagnant rocks instead, feel the keel crush against them and fling me against the jagged coastline of the island.

The clouds tightened, all light went, my journey became a fall into a chasm, wind cutting my face, my wet feet frozen, my ears filled with the scream of the engine. On a bit more, I told myself, and on I went for at least an hour.

When I stopped the engine, I listened for a sound that was not the slapping of waves against the keel, for another, more violent or gentler sound of a shore, and I looked for a lit port, a lighthouse, the glimmer of just one window in the distance, ahead of me, to the right or to the left, but the sea stretched on unhindered, its smell deepening across the vastness of the ocean, towards another coast too far off to contemplate.

The waves had calmed and were entreating me back towards the beach and the village, and when I did the moon parted two clouds and spied on me past a film of mist, and I saw the path I had marked lit in front of me, the froth and the flatness left in my wake, a road among waters onto which I turned back, gliding as on a blank slate.

I slept long and well through the night and into the following day. At times I surfaced out of sleep, or I dreamed. Amber's bedroom appeared to me, a hazy light, a warm environment, luminous moments that disappeared as I pulled over me the red edge of the quilt. And ghosts. Did I dream of ghosts moving around my bed? I don't remember. When I woke up it was almost dark. I jumped out of bed. I realized that the light of day had come and was almost gone. It was about eight in the evening. The bed-and-breakfast was silent, the clouds outside were racing away from the approaching night. Amber was still sleeping when I left.

I ran down the hill sneezing. I must have caught a bit of a cold the evening before. I didn't care. I was more eager to nurse the desires I felt than my physical health. And I had plans. I wanted to meet the village men, and I didn't want to be late for that. In my mind Eamonn's affront had become the affront of all the fishermen, and I wanted to put them back into their place.

I sneaked to the pub. Once again I found Tom alone, cleaning. He was mopping the floor with an intent look. A smell of acrid lemons hung in the air. When he saw me he started. 'Oh, hello,' he said. 'I . . . I . . .' He pointed at the floor.

'You keep the place very clean, I can see that.' In reality there was not much to clean. The floor's griminess resided deep within the boards, in those grey and red blotches I had already noticed and that the wet mop seemed only to darken in colour. 'Where are the men?' I asked. 'Are they having dinner?'

He nodded.

'But they *will* come back, won't they? You told me they come after dinner.'

He nodded again. He resumed his cleaning, but he had lost concentration. He plunged the mop into a bucket and took them both behind the bar. 'Is Amber back?' he asked.

'No,' I answered. 'But I found the note she had left me. She should be back any day now.'

'A note?'

I didn't answer but asked for a beer. He brought it over. Night was approaching below the clouds. Tom turned on a few lights, and I sat at a new table in the middle of the pub. I ran my fingers over the cuts on the edge of the wood. With difficulty Tom found chores to do. He cleaned glasses, he rearranged bottles. He wiped the bar with a wet cloth. He gave up, moved behind the beer taps and started hitting them with his fingers. 'There's not much to do here,' he said, almost as an apology.

'That's the impression I get. And that's why I was telling you that I'd like to take Amber to the city.'

'Oh well, I don't think she hates it here. And look at me,' he corrected himself, 'I might complain, but I'm still here. Maybe I should just get myself a television. I miss it.'

'I don't. I don't feel the need for it. It breeds . . .'

'Breeds what?'

'Nothing,' I said, after a while.

'I loved it.'

'Yes, I did too,' I said. I was drumming my fingers on the table and slapped my hand down, to stop myself. 'Well, you've got your Black Mirror here. Not very entertaining though. You never know what's on.'

He tried to smile at my joke but couldn't. 'I heard you had lunch at Eamonn and Dora's,' he said.

'Yesterday,' I answered. 'It's good to get to know the locals. They spoke a lot. Even about you.'

'I suppose your ideas about me have only got worse.'

'I can make up my own mind about things. I felt they were a bit much.'

'There, you see? It's not me. I don't like them, any of them. OK, I get along with the women, relatively. But the men . . .'

Yes, the men. Where were they? I was growing impatient and excited. I began to add chairs around my table.

'What are you doing?' he asked.

'Just setting the scene. I'd like to socialize with everybody.'

He didn't seem too pleased. He asked me if I was going to talk about Amber and about the note she had left. 'I have no plan,' I said. 'I just want to chat.' He tried to remind me of what he had told me the day before in front of the Black Mirror, but I waved him away, telling him I remembered. He retreated behind the bar, pulled himself a pint and drank it in long gulps. He felt awkward in his own pub. If he wasn't drinking or hitting the beer taps he was fiddling with his or his collar, and I felt he was doing this to make himself more presentable to me. I thought that even his revelations of the day before could be seen as a gesture of friendship but still I could see he expected something, as if he had lost a race to me but still hoped for some kind of concession or recognition.

When the fishermen began to come in I asked them to sit at my table. They hesitated, but before they could refuse I told Tom to get them beers and put them on my account. Most men who sat down were attracted by the offer rather than the desire to sit with me. I could see that many soon reconsidered and wanted to get up as soon as I had made them sit down, but by then I was in charge. Some sneaked off to isolated places while I was luring others, but I rounded up the fugitives. It was enough to look them in the eye, I soon discovered, to throw off balance their intention to refuse.

They were an odd bunch, homogeneous in their weather-beaten looks and clothing, and in their attitude towards me. They were eleven in all, not counting Eamonn, who had not yet arrived, and not one seemed comfortable in my presence although they didn't look like shy men. Some were scratching the edge of the table as if discreetly searching for a way out of my company. I drank my beer, long, healthy gulps, and I exhorted them to drink too. 'We have to get to know each other,' I said, 'especially as we will be neighbours.' They drank as an excuse not to talk. I ordered a second round before the first was finished. Eamonn still had not arrived, and I missed his presence. These other men were more introvert-ed, even if equally sceptical of my ways. I could see they glanced at me dubiously when I pretended not to look at them, but I was being amiable. I asked questions only about weather, work, favourite drinks. I paid little attention to their answers, and I forgot their names as soon as they spoke them, but I was slowly creating the right mood and winning from them a limited confidence.

The third round of beers found them decently relaxed. They began an almost proper, fluid conversation, and they asked me a few tentative questions.

'What I did before coming here', I answered them, 'doesn't matter much, or does it? The past has passed and there's no need to dig it up. Anyway, I did a job you probably wouldn't be interested in. But I'd had enough of it.'

The pub grew quiet. I had nipped their questions in the bud.

'Well, I was an actor,' I said. 'Yes an actor,' I stressed, beginning even to convince myself. 'Actually I started with modelling then went into acting. I was good, got very involved . . .' I paused. I had no doubt they knew what a model was after Amber had posed for the statue, but around me there was silence and blinking.

'An actor, you know?' I said, 'Like in the movies . . . at the theatre . . .' A few nods answered me.

'So you left?' somebody asked.

'I'm living my real life now,' I said, and laughed.

Eamonn arrived. He went straight to the bar, and only at a second glance did he see us all sitting there. A look of disgust contorted his face.

A fisherman with a black beard turned to him. 'Eamonn, you know he was an actor?' he asked him.

Eamonn didn't answer. I decided to change topic. 'That's my past,' I said. 'It's all back there, gone now. Here's to the present.'

Eamonn's eyes were still on me, his body immobile, one elbow leaning on the bar. 'Did you go anywhere close to my boat last night?' he asked.

'Close to your boat?' I said, with my glass still raised. 'Well, I was there with you . . .'

'After that.'

'No. Why?'

'It's as if somebody took it out at sea. It was wetter this morning than last night.'

'Rain?' I suggested.

He didn't answer. I heard a few fishermen talk, and I caught words about clouds that wouldn't release rain and about dry boats. I tried to understand whether they were considering Eamonn's suspicions or whether they saw no reason to doubt the innocence of my answers. Tom flicked between the two, his eyes darting between Eamonn and me, but I wasn't sure about the others. It was clear, though, that Eamonn had broken the unity of my audience. Two fishermen had escaped to the bar to get beer, although the glasses I had bought them were still half full. A few others had retreated into a whispered conversation, and I felt they were looking at me a bit too inquisitively. I invited Eamonn over to the table, but he seemed content to sit at the bar and cast filthy looks at me every now and then. Tom had moved in front of him whispering, but Eamonn chased him away with a few harsh words, and he retreated behind the beer taps, hitting them nervously with his fingers.

I managed to pick up the conversation again, and reclaim some kind of general attention, but the talk continued along infertile lines. As I had already asked about their lives and had dismissed my past, there was little left to talk about.

'Amber is a great girl,' I said at last. 'Great girl. I'm proud of her, can I say that? It took a bit to conquer her, but it was worth it. The first night I was over, the first time I was here, I talked to her in her living room, just normal talk, nothing more. I already knew then that she was the woman I was meant to be with forever. She found out my name, and I was eager for her to find out everything else about me, but instead of asking me more questions she said I reminded her of somebody else called Charles.'

I looked around and felt my spine chill. Questioning eyes, silence in the pub, and a pitch-black night outside. I was remembering, I was inventing; I wasn't sure. I wasthrilled, though, and I went on: 'Can you imagine how hurt I felt? Nearly betrayed. Could I be so possessive towards a woman I had just met? But it was a sign, don't you think? And I took it as nothing but that. I told her I was going to bed early, to make sure that she would be downstairs for a while longer. When I got up to my room I threw myself out of the window.' I waited for enough eyebrows to be raised around the table. 'I mean I jumped, but I broke a hand on landing. I didn't care about that. I had a little act to put on. I knocked on the door, and when she opened I pretended to be the other person she knew, to show her how much she meant to me. And that is when she fell in love.'

Was mine a tenuous story? Maybe it was, and still it worked. The frowns persisted, but I was sure I saw the men silently contemplating the foolishness that had helped take Amber away from them. Only a few seemed to be directed more at my enthusiasm for Amber than at my story.

'From what you say you seem pretty damn protective,' said Eamonn, from the bar.

'I can be,' I answered. 'But I need a reason to be protective.' Tom looked at me as if I was stupid, but I had never told him I understood that Black Mirror talk he had given me.

'Well, if you're so damn protective,' Eamonn continued, 'why are you sitting here when Amber has been away for almost a week?'

Everybody looked at me.

'I found her note' I explained.

'Really, you found it?' he said, failing to sound aggressive in his surprise.

'Yes. She should be back quite soon, so I'm not worried.'

'A note,' he repeated. He turned back to his pint, more absorbed than angry.

I felt relieved that I had pushed back his attack, but not entirely at ease. He had distracted the other fishermen. In their eyes, in their movements, I saw a reflection of his suspicions, and this I wasn't sure I could control. But I was not going to give up now. Somebody asked about the note, but I pretended not to hear him. 'One thing is certain,' I said, 'I don't want to be so protective that she cannot keep her old friendships. I don't see why I should. Her happiness is mine, don't you think?'

A few instinctive yesses came from around the table, and a few fishermen adjusted themselves on their chairs. I was quite sure that an air of cautious happiness had spread around me. 'So don't worry about my presence here in the village. There might still be some connections with the city I'll have to deal with. I might have to go away for long periods of time. I don't think I can find a job here in town so I'll probably have to look for one in a city close by. I don't think my credentials are much use here. No offence taken, I hope.'

I hoped well. They told me to do what I had to do.

'Thank you,' I answered. 'I know I can count on you guys to look after Amber when I'm away.'

'We hoped you wouldn't take her from us,' said a bald man with bushy eyebrows.

'Do I have any reason to?' I said casually.

Tom had arrived with a tray of beer, but he had difficulty placing it on the table. Nobody helped him or seemed to notice him.

I gave him a hand. 'Well, maybe I could find a job here after all. Become an assistant barman.'

'Like Amber was,' said the fisherman with the black beard.

'Oh, she helped out here, did she?' This was my chance to bring the men out into the open, although I could only marvel at the inextinguishable past Amber had in the village. 'You didn't tell me she served here, Tom.'

He grimaced at me and lifted the empty tray, showing me he had to take it back. Some of the men watched him retreat to the bar. The fisherman with the black beard leaned close to me. 'She worked here after he had taken over the pub. Then he fired her a month later, when he began the renovation.'

'Which he never finished,' said somebody, louder.

'That story again,' Tom burst out. 'Will you lay off? I've told you a thousand times those damn workers asked for too much money.'

'You told me they left,' I said.

'He *made* them leave,' said the man with bushy eyebrows.

'Oh, *I* did? Maybe they had a problem with *you*, not me. In any case, as I said, they asked for too much money.'

'Amber invited them to stay at the bed-and-breakfast for a small sum,' I was told by a fisherman with sharp features. 'Just to have some work herself.'

'I wasn't going to pay for their lodging,' said Tom, 'if that's what they thought.'

'I don't think they wanted you to.'

'Well, for some reason they raised their price ridiculously, and I wasn't going to pay.'

Silence returned for a while. Tom regained some control. He was looking around, making sure nobody was going to start again.

'But you fired Amber too?' I asked.

'I don't think *she* asked for that much money,' added the fisherman with the sharp features.

'I didn't fire her! She was tired of working here.' He was losing it again. I deliberately moved out of the conversation and pushed myself back in my chair.

'Tired of working here!' somebody was saying. 'She accepted your offer because she was bored up at the bed-and-breakfast.'

'Well, then, she didn't like it. Maybe she had a problem with the customers slapping her arse.'

'We didn't slap her arse.'

'She never complained.'

'You're a bunch of liars. What about the times she sat on your laps?'

'She did it herself.'

'You can say what you like, but I didn't fire her.'

'Now who's the liar?'

'She enjoyed serving.'

'Maybe she had a problem with her boss,' continued one of the fishermen, 'not with the customers. She hardly ever came to the village after that, thanks to you.'

Tom looked like he needed a day's sleep to recover from this. I remained as still and quiet as possible. In the heat of the argument they had forgotten me and I didn't want to interfere before the conversation had developed further. Only Eamonn was still aware of my presence and of what was happening, and he glanced at me and at the fishermen while he curved himself protectively over his drink. He was shaking his head slowly.

'And what was that thing about the name of the pub?' asked the fisherman with the black beard.

'You got it up there, before you fired the workers.'

'You meant it for her, isn't that right?'

'And what did she tell you? That it should be Knight at Arms and not Knight in Arms.'

Laughter broke out. I screeched my chair along the floor and it died at once. Suddenly everybody was aware of my presence again. I spoke in a soft, shocked voice. 'I didn't even know she worked here. And now I find out about arse-slapping and what-have-you. I understand why she didn't tell me. And why you were afraid I would take her away from you.'

'I think you misunderstand,' said the bald man with the bushy eyebrows.

'I have difficulty believing that,' I said. Tom seemed to enjoy this. 'And you, Tom,' I said, not to leave him out, 'I remember you saying that the workers had left because of something here in the village, not because you didn't have enough money to pay them. And the name of the pub . . . I don't know who's worse.'

They were all quiet and tense. Some fishermen were scratching the edge of the table as if trying to dig their way out of the situation. Only Eamonn seemed to find the distress on my face a reason to become angry.

Somebody stirred and a glass fell from the table and broke. We all looked at the pieces. Some fishermen leaned down and picked up sharp blades of glass.

'I don't know,' I said, 'I spoke to you tonight without expecting any of this.'

'We were just being friendly,' said the man with the black beard.

'Towards me or towards Amber?'

'I don't think you can come here and accuse us like that,' said the man with the sharp features, and he was holding a long, glittering piece of glass.

'Why? Do you want to accuse me for being Amber's boyfriend? Are you going to stab me with that glass, maybe?'

129

He looked at it, but did nothing. Somebody blamed Tom, then others' voices did. He jumped back and tried to wave away the accusations.

'In any case,' I said 'I doubt Tom can be blamed for everything.'

Eamonn broke his silence. 'I can't believe Amber got together with a man as rude as you.'

'Rude?' I said with some pleasure, for this time I could strike back. 'So she should prefer being slapped on the arse by you lot than being with a guy who defends her, rudely as he might do it?'

'Now, listen . . .' said the fisherman with the black beard, but didn't add anything. I listened to his silence with pleasure. I looked at the glass he was holding. It stuck out of his hand like a knife. Other fishermen were scratching the edge of the table with the bits of glass they had picked up. Somebody cut himself.

'You tell me I should listen,' I said. 'Well, what do I have to listen to?'

Silence. Again silence. Light trembled on the bits of glass. My eyes saw nothing else, glimmers like fireflies in the night. I was thrilled. I was mentally, physically thrilled.

'And your wives know about all this?' I asked.

Somebody stabbed the table from below. Somebody else cut himself.

'Now, listen!' I heard. It was Eamonn this time, his raucous voice blaring loudly. 'You're jumping to conclusions. You're making a lot of stuff up in your own head. And there are still things you've got to explain. Like why Amber left the very day you arrived.'

'It's easy for you to change the subject now. It doesn't rub out what I've heard tonight.'

'But this was a year ago,' somebody said.

'And if Amber was friendly . . .'

'Yes, and if she sat on somebody's knee . . .'

'Oh, so she did?' I said. 'And, of course, it's not your fault. Well, I'm not going to think that Amber is like that. I suppose you'd like me to run away disgusted and leave her here to you, but if I'm going I'll take her with me. Poor Amber, what did you do to her?'

Many faces turned away. They searched for relief in spots on the floor or ceiling. A couple looked at me as if they wanted to speak, but they didn't. I know they saw me as a competitor, but also as the voice of their conscience, and they could do nothing about it.

Behind the bar Tom was tense, expecting some new jab. Eamonn was livid. 'You're lowering us to your level of thinking,' he hissed.

I didn't care what he said. There was silence again, and those pieces of glass. Many fishermen threw them on the table, surrendering them into a small, glittering pile.

I asked for nothing more. I wanted to jump with delight, but I limited myself to getting up slowly, absorbing the atmosphere, filling up like a balloon. 'Well, I'm going now,' I said. I waded past them and they did nothing to stop me. Outside the air was beautifully fresh. I shook the distressed look from my face and breathed deeply. All that impotent hatred in the pub made me feel good. I knew that those slaps had been just the expression of a greater desire, and they knew I knew. But what *could* they do, how could they take out their guilt on me for their own illegitimate thoughts and actions? I didn't have to turn round to see that nobody had followed me out. All they could do was grant me their jealous, hate-filled recognition.

I wanted to go home, to my bed-and-breakfast, but a lit window up the road attracted my attention. A man stood in the light it cast, leaning over the van's open bonnet.

It had to be Jim, the 'man with no fear', as Tom had described him, who kept the connection with the outside world. He looked insignificant, rather plump, and maybe because of this he looked a bit younger than the fishermen. He lacked speed in his movements, as if he considered each one before committing himself to it. It was so when he lifted his head after I greeted him. 'Good evening,' he said, and waited with an oil-can in his hand for what I had to say.

'Good evening,' I said. 'I think you know who I am, but I'm not sure. I don't remember whether you were in church yesterday morning.'

'Everybody is in church on Sunday morning,' he said.

'Well, then, you must know me. And I guess you know Amber.'

'Yes.'

'Nice girl, isn't she?'

'She is.'

I couldn't understand the economy of his answers. 'Pity you weren't in the pub just now,' I said. 'It was a good evening. I got to know the other men. Everyone was there but you.'

'And William.'

'Oh, yes, the shepherd. Well, I'm sure we'll have a lot more chances in the future to meet and talk, won't we?'

'Yes, probably.'

He was making me nervous with his easygoing attitude. 'A problem with the van?' I asked.

'Just some maintenance that needs to be done,' he said, looking back under the bonnet.

'You're a . . . pioneer of technology in this village. Aren't you?'

'I deliver the fish and bring back the things for Tom's shop.'

'Yes, I know, but you're the proprietor of the only modern vehicle in town.'

'It's not the only one. Tom has a car.'

'Really? I haven't seen it.'

'He never uses it. It's rusting in one of the sheds by the beach.'

'I see. But you . . . Amber must have liked you with the van and all.'

'I took her for a ride a couple of times,' he said.

The innocence of his answer disturbed me, as if he was a man with nothing to hide. He held the oil-can as if it was a teapot and he was ready to serve me a cup. We stood in silence in the light from the window. A woman was moving beyond it, in a living room.

'Your wife?' I asked.

He nodded.

'So you took Amber for a ride,' I said. 'Where to?'

'To the next village. She kept me company a couple of times on my deliveries.'

'Recently?'

'Two or three months ago.'

'I thought she never came down to the village.'

'I wouldn't know. I picked her up on the road, past William's house. She goes for walks probably.'

'And she had no other reason to come with you?'

'Maybe just to look around.'

The woman past the window had moved to some other room. 'I'm Amber's boyfriend,' I said.

'I know,' he said. 'I'm Jim.'

Silence again. We looked at each other, or rather, I looked at him, at the void, calm expression on his face. I blamed the light. It cast too many shadows for me to read him correctly.

'Well,' I said, 'maybe I should go. I'm happy to be your new neighbour so to speak. And your new competitor.' I waited for his expression to change and it did, but into puzzlement. 'I mean, I also have a car,' I said eventually. I stood where I was for a while longer, idly kicking some sand from the roads towards him. I said goodnight and before I walked on he had returned his attention to the cylinders and valves of his van, and I felt that there always has to be somebody who spoils the fun just when it reaches its height.

✗

Jim had given me an aftertaste that stung like poison. I felt sicker and sicker as I went up the hill to the bed-and-breakfast. How naïve I had been the previous morning when I ironed my clothes to make them neat, when I delivered my message of joy to the village. How thin the line is between success and failure! My happiness was so close to completion yet I could feel the whole structure crack and collapse. Had my new life been so short-lived? Was I already being pushed away from it?

The hallway of the bed-and-breakfast felt different. It did not smell the same: it smelt like a place I had never been in, and still it had a terrible familiarity. I advanced with unsure steps past the dining-room door. From the height of its cupboard the peacock looked at me with an indifferent, mocking expression. That house! Was it toying with me?

Amber was coming down the stairs. I didn't want to look at her with my vision tainted by my recent thoughts. She came to me and held my head, searched for my downcast eyes. She said she wanted to celebrate. 'Celebrate what?' I asked. It had been a week since my arrival, she told me, since the day of my return. I didn't say anything. I hoped that my state of mind would be evident without me having to speak but all that seeped through was that I was being ill at ease. I was fine, I said, I really was, maybe just a bit too tired to celebrate. I had talked with the villagers all day, with the men, you know. And with Jim. Not a look of alarm on her face. Was she hiding it well or was it candour? I told her I had a headache. She believed me. Was she pretending? I was, and I couldn't keep it up. I couldn't mask my spiritual turmoil, I was no actor, and I realized the impossibility of her brushing away with proof the doubts I would not voice. So I found myself tangled up in explanations I couldn't sustain about the physical nature of my illness, and I became frantic after each word, while she, poor soul, acted with such concern and understanding, twisted by the insane fabrications of my mind. How could I doubt her when she was caressing my hair and hoping her anxiety could give her fingers healing powers? I tried to look at her appearance that had once charmed me, but the purity in my thoughts was gone and each of her features had lost its perfection, tempting me into interpretations I couldn't face. How could I see her failure in the past as an affront to a present when she was exclusively mine? What was it about the past that so obsessed me? *What was it?*

I told her to go upstairs, that I would catch up with her. She left, I was alone. Or was I? I heard muffled noises around me. Was the house tricking me again? At first the ground floor seemed empty, the past mopped up and flushed out. Yet slowly, first at the edge of my vision, then crawling forward till I could see them fully, I saw figures, fishermen walking about like frightening puppets with their arms stretched upwards as if to catch moonlight, or seated on the sofas, resting and speaking their post-coital praises.

The sight of it! I walked around them, I recognized all the faces, I counted almost a dozen. I leaned against a table, then pulled back as if I had touched a rotting tree stump. When I went upstairs I found other men in the guest beds – Tom was there and the workers he had fired, all crammed in, their eyes fixed on the ceiling, their bodies eager. And I went further up, and I was drawn into the storage room by a rank stench. Those boxes we had emptied so lovingly just a few days earlier now stank of fish and seaweed, but the smell seemed to reek more from a shadow that roamed around them, jingling fish-hooks in a bag, so close to the threshold of her room.

Did I need more proof than this? I went into her room, a bent hulk, walking with heavy steps towards the chest of drawers I had so often shunned. I looked back at her over my shoulder, my face contorted by fresh stubble, grating teeth and murky eyes. I ripped the sheet off the chest of drawers, and my shadow engulfed it instead, and inside the drawers it poured over her personal belongings. When did she wear those black boots? For whom did she wear all that white underwear? Where had she got all those handkerchiefs? And I dug deeper than I had the first time, and to the surface came objects that had been gifts, surely, hidden there because they were more intimately hers, objects that couldn't lie to me and that could only have come from the village men, a bunch of fishing-flies, and a chisel even, clothes for barmaiding, and on them stains of beer, many stains, as if she had been rolling around on the floor behind the counter, a leg falling bare through a slit in her skirt, and up against the walls of the houses in the darkness of night, her breasts pressed, lips swollen, her body turgid.

I took it out on her. I demanded to know what that pestilence of seaweed was, and those stains on her clothes, those objects, that chisel. She stared at me wide-eyed, eyes that had spoken to me of a soul I had so tenderly and innocently loved. 'Why don't you speak?' I shouted. I opened the handkerchief drawer and saw initials on one, then another, and I began to throw them on the bed, sure to count twelve like the fishermen in the pub that night, twelve and not one more, but I lost count and wept, and the handkerchiefs flapped open in the air and fell one on another in a jumble of colours. Amber grew frightened and tried to fold them up. 'No, no,' I wept, 'you don't understand. They're beautiful, so beautiful.'

Those tears that filled her eyes . . . She lay down in bed, her back facing me, naked and graceful, heaving with sobs. I saw no sin in her beauty. I felt that it was wrong of me to think differently, but life is more complicated than what we can see and touch, and the simplicity of perfection even harder to achieve. I lay down too, turned off the light. She tried to quell her sobbing, not to have me hear it, but I had to put a pillow over my head to sleep.

When I look back, I can't make fun of the way I was, of what I believed in, even if I try. I translate what happened in words but I can't joke about it, I see no self-irony. Maybe my eyes sparkle as I report my past. I can't say. Maybe a certain type of grimness is its own joke.

I spent that night in anguish and only after several hours did I manage to persuade myself that Jim was just a glitch in my perfect world, and that it was not going to be less perfect because of him. I was sure that all the other men liked Amber, so I tried to concentrate on that, and I wondered what they had told their wives about our quarrel at the pub. I doubted they had said anything.

Dawn began to creep under an overcast sky, and slowly my mind cleared and saw the new step to take, the next turn of the screw.

When I got up Amber was sleeping, or pretending to sleep. I decided not to talk to her until I had spoken to the village women. I waited at the top of the hill for the men to leave with their boats. In the faint light of early morning I saw them get to the beach like dim, slow ants, and I was sure, despite the distance, that many hesitated and stopped to look up at me. Most of them didn't seem too keen on going out to sea with me balanced precariously at the top of the hill, but from such a distance I couldn't be sure. Maybe they were just preparing their boats, maybe they were being no slower than on other days, but eventually they were all gone, moving out of the bay.

I drove down to the village. I was sure my car had been watched from the moment it left the bed-and-breakfast, and fearful eyes must have questioned its descent at such an early hour, afraid it would not stop at the village but go on, away, into the distance. I could feel eyes on me as I parked at the top of the road and as I walked down it, and saw shapes behind curtains.

It was then that I started my lamentation, wailing loudly, with intermissions made of a stream of words that bubbled up and sank back into a monotone. I was not screaming, but my voice boomed in the silence and my demeanour heightened my show of misery as I swayed from side to side, as if I was about to fall, weak legs under me, arms dangling helplessly.

Curtains were drawn back and faces peeped out. Then voices. I contained mine a little as I passed in front of the church. I didn't want to catch the priest's attention. For a moment my eyes fell on the Black Mirror, but at a distance it seemed like a hole in the church façade. When I looked away from it I saw that women had appeared on doorsteps and that Dora had left her house and was walking up to me.

'What's the matter?' she asked me.

'Oh, everything's the matter. I don't think I want to talk about it though. It would upset you too. Let me go down to the beach to get a breath of fresh air.'

I tried to walk on but Dora stepped in front of me. 'No, no, wait. Is it something about Amber?'

I nodded. 'It's her past.'

'Surely it's nothing to worry about. You're not thinking of leaving, are you?'

'Oh, I don't know. Maybe.' Other women had moved closer to us. Several were in dressing-gowns, their hair in curlers. All were shivering in the morning breeze. Dora gave them a nod and paid no attention to their questions. It seemed many had heard something about my leaving, or they had thought it for themselves. They kept at a distance from me, but I had the impression that if I had tried to break out of their circle they would have jumped on me to keep me there. Dora wasted no time: she took my arm and walked me towards her house. I leaned on her and she held me up determinedly, as if her balance and security depended on me standing.

We walked down her corridor to her bleak, papered living room. Eamonn's absence gave a different feel to the place: there was no creeping suspicion in the air, but a different kind of tension, a silent anxiety that I saw move under the features of the women who had poured in after us, in their worried expressions, in the reverence with which they stood around me. They resembled each other, only their perfumes distinguished them, almost arrogantly, but in the small living room they blended, and the result was an almost nauseating stench.

'Why did you bring me here?' I asked Dora. 'I will say things nobody will like, and I don't want to give you any trouble with things I'm not sure of myself.'

'So you're not sure?' she asked. The other women were waiting as well, in religious silence. Some had sat down and one was pulling out a chair, slowly so as not to make any noise.

'Do you ever go to the pub?' I asked.

The woman pulling the chair furrowed her brow, as if the action was taking all her concentration. Somebody said that they went there to shop.

'I see, I see,' I said. 'Well, never mind. I want you to know that I love Amber.'

'We know it already,' said Dora.

'Love plays strange tricks on the mind.'

'What do you mean?'

'It sets in motion all kinds of bad thoughts. What I want to say is that her presence is an anchor in my mind, but with her absence . . . These days without her, I've spent them alone with what I've heard here in the village. It made me think a lot about her past. And instead of feeling reassured I felt threatened. I can understand that it might seem strange that Amber leaves the day after I arrive, but what can I say?'

Dora had sat down in front of me, leaning forward on her elbows. One of her hands moved from her knee to mine, as if to reassure me, or to hold back my words.

I carried on regardless. 'Your husbands were so suspicious of me last night,' I said. 'It was useless to tell them that I found a note Amber left me, useless. They are suspicious of me, and what they said . . .'

'Amber left you a note?' asked Dora.

I nodded. 'She wrote that she'd be back soon,' I said vaguely.

Dora's hand remained on my knee. A woman in a red dressing-gown told me they all believed I was Amber's boyfriend. Other women confirmed it. There was genuine honesty in their voices, almost surprise at the idea that my identity could be questioned. A woman was tugging rashly at her curlers rather than unrolling them. 'So our husbands doubt you?' she asked.

'Yes, I talked to them last night at the pub and then to Jim . . .' I asked if his wife was there. She wasn't. I felt angry with myself for even having thought of him. He had to stay out of my life. 'Anyway,' I managed to continue, 'they were all very suspicious. Maybe they wanted to scare me into leaving. And I don't know whether they did it intentionally, but they said things that fuelled the bad thoughts I was telling you about. I found out that Amber came to dinner here, that she served at the pub for a month or so . . . Even a statue was made of her. You see, Amber seemed to be part of the life of this village in a big way, and then suddenly . . .'

Faces looked at me, waiting, fearful. The woman removing the curlers was holding one a few inches from her head, a strand of hair, fully stretched, clinging to it.

'I'm not worried about her serving at the pub,' I continued, 'or about her coming to dinner here. That's all fine. I'm worried about why she stopped. Something was going on that ended all these things.' The women looked at Dora, waiting for her to speak. 'What went on?' I asked, turning away from her to demand an answer from them. The woman with the red dressing gown was fixing the belt around it. The woman with the curlers was looking for a last one that she couldn't find. The others did nothing except avoid looking at me.

'Nothing went on,' said Dora. 'She just stopped coming down.'

'But why?'

'She probably preferred being alone. We didn't know her well enough to explain it. She came down sometimes to get her groceries.'

'I thought Tom took them up to her house.'

'Not all the time.'

'Groceries. And that's all?'

'She would stop for a chat.'

'But never came down for one.'

Silence.

'Sometimes,' said Dora.

'Sometimes,' the others echoed.

'Well, I don't see her coming here for tea and biscuits. I remember her saying that she didn't get along with the women of this village. Or maybe she never said that. Maybe there was something that made me think that the whole thing would be explained if you had had a fight with Amber.'

'We never quarrelled with her,' said Dora. The chorus kicked in again.

'I sense that you all like me, and I'm grateful for it.' Some smiles appeared. 'But I still get the impression that you don't like Amber.' The smiles died. 'You like me because you don't like her, isn't it so? Just as your husbands don't seem to like me but like her. This means something, surely.'

Dora's hand remained on my knee. Nobody spoke. Absently I searched in my pockets, pulled out one of Amber's handkerchiefs and blew my nose violently. I crumpled the handkerchief into my palm, but a large puff of it escaped. Several eyes had fallen on it. They looked at the handkerchief as if they were staring into the eyes of a beast that had appeared out of nowhere.

I looked at the handkerchief with an absent stare. 'Where did Amber get this?' I said to myself. 'It's got initials on it, but they're not hers.' A few hands jutted out, with promises to have a look at it, but casually I ignored them. 'Oh, you see? I'm letting my imagination take over again. I don't want to say anything bad. I don't want to be suspicious like some people are towards me. But please understand, I have doubts and I have started to think that maybe it's better for me to go back to where I came from and leave Amber behind. If she's the girl I dread she is . . . in that bed-and-breakfast that is more like a bed-and-broth—'

'No – why leave?' said Dora, pressing her hand on my knee. The chorus of women asked the same.

'Please, then, tell me it's not so, tell me that you sincerely like Amber. If what I believe is true, you should hate her, but if you don't, if you like her . . . nothing must have happened, right?' They all looked at each other, feeling the pressure of their own silence. I waited. I wanted this confession. I wanted them to lie, I wanted them to lie about their past. I think I wanted them to hand it over to me, revised.

Dora was the first to satisfy my desires. 'I like Amber,' she said. 'I've always liked her.' Other women bandwagoned, trying to let Dora's words do the work for them. 'Oh, but really? Are you sure?' I asked around, wanting a longer reply.

They looked for things to do, for curlers to free, robes to fix. I blew my nose again. 'I guess, you don't like her, then?' I suggested. They said it wasn't so.

'We do,' said Dora.

'Why shouldn't we?' said somebody else.

'She's a nice girl.'

'A nice young girl.'

'She reminds us of when we were young ourselves.'

'But still we do like her.'

They blurted out more jumbled words of praise, failing to instil them with sincerity and failing to hold back a few transparent bolts of hatred, mere intonations or silences it was not difficult to interpret. For a moment, though, I had the impression that the way they talked hid something I couldn't grasp, maybe something to do with Amber's disappearance, but the impression was gone as quickly as it came and I could only feel gratified by their efforts. And hard efforts they were, I could feel that, for them to lie about their true feelings. I felt treasured, welcomed. I put the handkerchief back into my pocket. I adjusted myself on my chair a couple of times, and each time I watched their sudden anxiety with fascination, as if they feared that I was getting up to leave. Nothing seemed to scare them more.

'Oh, but how can I stay after I've insinuated such terrible things?' I said.

They were taken aback. At first they didn't know what to say, then they began to wave aside my earlier words, saying that mistakes can be forgiven.

'But I've alluded to . . . I can't even say it. Really, I'm so embarrassed, I feel so bad, I'd like to leave.'

Dora got up faster than I could and placed a hand on my shoulder to keep me seated. 'No need to leave,' she said, 'no need to apologize. It's just a misunderstanding. Why don't you stay for a cup of tea?' She waited for my shy nod before she disappeared into the kitchen. A few other women wondered whether they could bring something over, then ran off to see what they could find in their cupboards. Guided by a dozen hands I moved to a sofa where I might be more comfortable. I said how nice it was to have a girlfriend that women liked, it was such a guarantee of her worth, wasn't it? They agreed.

It was beautiful. I felt I loved Amber even more. Absently I sipped the tea Dora brought me, and nibbled at a few biscuits. The women who had left were coming back. From my sofa I could see past the hallway to where they were standing by the door, whispering. I could hear no words, just their abrupt tone. They hushed when they returned to the living room.

I was offered more biscuits and cake. Some women ate a token biscuit with me and tried to chat among themselves. Most kept looking over at me and, slowly, all were becoming restless: I had been there almost an hour and their husbands would soon be back.

'I think it's time for me to leave,' I said. 'I don't know how to thank you all for being so nice to me.' They said I didn't have to worry. They all got up as I did. 'But I need to repay your hospitality, and I won't take no for an answer. How about this very night? Yes, let's do it tonight. I can prepare a buffet at the bed-and-breakfast. Shall we say around eight?' Somebody was a bit unsure, somebody asked what a buffet was. I explained it and then I repeated that I wouldn't take no for an answer. 'I count on your presence,' I said. 'Your husbands too, of course. Please, give them my apologies for my moodiness last night. It was unreasonable. And please let Jim and his wife know. I would be terribly offended if anybody from the village didn't come.'

The women had no time to object. I saw they wanted to get home. Dora was trying to return the food they had brought. She held a cake in her hands, one slice snatched from its perfect shape, but the woman to whom she was offering it wouldn't take it. 'You keep it,' she said, 'otherwise if . . .' I didn't catch the end of it.

All the women left. Dora saw me to the door. I had a glimpse of the same face that had looked at me the previous day from the shadows, but I didn't want to linger. I was sure, though, that this time I saw teeth, although I couldn't say whether it was a smile or a forced grin. She said she was happy that I had found Amber's note. I said I was happy too, and added a quick goodbye, reminding her of the evening's buffet.

The other women were being sucked into their respective houses. I drove down to Tom's shop to buy food for the evening. Once again he was surprised by my joviality, considering my dramatic exit of the previous night. I told him

146

that sometimes my moods had the best of me, but that all was forgotten now, that he should offer my apologies to the fishermen too. I invited him to my buffet and told him to put what I had bought on my account. He was growing worried by its size, but I told him he had no reason to. 'I'll pay for it,' I said. 'It's not like I'm running off.'

In the distance the boats were approaching. I didn't want to meet the fishermen before my buffet, so I shuttled my shopping to my car and drove off, but I slowed down to wave and smile at some women who were looking at me from their windows. Dora was on her doorstep and silently watched me go past. I waved at her, but she looked at me without responding.

She retreated into her house, and I returned my eyes to the road. I was passing in front of the church, a dull façade with a black rectangle in a corner and a long, black brushstroke next to it. I stopped but kept the engine running.

'Father Terence,' I said, stepping out of the car.

He had an unhealthy look on his face and was scratching the palm of one hand with the fingers of the other. 'What are you doing here?' he asked.

'I'm here to stay, like I said in church.'

'I'm talking about today,' he said. 'I heard you cry earlier and now you're cheerful.'

'Well, I'm happy I capture everybody's attention,' I said. 'I came down because I had some bad thoughts about Amber, and the women helped me get rid of them. They spoke so highly of her.'

His eyes opened wide. 'Excuse me?'

'Yes, they were all very nice.'

He was now scratching his other hand. I could see the mouth of a glass emerging from one of the pockets of his cassock.

From the sea a buzzing of boats reached us. 'Well,' I said,

in a hurry, 'I'm having a buffet at my house tonight and I invited the whole village, so if you'd like to come . . .'

'I don't think so. I go to bed early.'

'I'm sorry,' I said, 'I thought you approved of me.'

'I think you should leave with Amber as soon as she comes back,' he said.

'Why?'

'I thought you would be good for the village, but I'm changing my mind. I fear you're putting things in motion that I don't like. I was . . . walking around last night . . .'

The buzzing was already dying out. Some of the boats had touched land. 'You were walking around last night and . . .?' I pressed him.

He gnawed at his lips. 'I was walking around last night and I did a bit of thinking. Maybe you should never have come here.'

The fishermen were disembarking. 'But honestly,' I said, 'I'm trying to bond with the people here. That's why I'm organizing this thing. It would be nice if you could come. Are you sure you—'

'Yes!' he snapped. 'I've been up there once already, and it was enough.'

'What? You've been up to the bed-and-breakfast?'

'Months ago. But I'm going back to church now,' he said, walking to the door.

I felt a surge of anger at how he turned his back to me. 'Well, maybe you should watch my buffet in your mirror tonight,' I said.

He turned around slowly.

'The mirror nailed up there,' I continued. 'I thought the priest could look into it to get a peep into his flock's life.'

He didn't seem amused. He turned round and staggered inside the church. The fishermen's voices breathed up the road. I got back into my car and drove off. I decided to ignore the priest's mood. I had an evening to prepare for, and a good evening it was going to be. I was on a roll, things were going great, and nothing had to upset this wonderful balance. I was also looking forward to spending some time with Amber beforehand, to make up for the fight of the previous night. I was almost glad that we had quarrelled. Our relationship would hardly have been serious if it hadn't experienced at least one hiccup. I knew she would forgive me. We had no pride that could restrain our love, we would do anything to make it better. Almost everybody around us was making such efforts for it to be perfect.

xi

By evening I was ready. I was pleased with my appearance even if I was still wearing the same clothes and had been brushing my teeth with a finger for a week. My reconciliation with Amber had been sweet, and I told her that the evening's buffet would make our love invincible. She had to trust me, I said, and let me do the work. When the light outside began to fail, I asked her to hide under our bed, because I didn't want the villagers to see her. She agreed without complaint. She didn't want to impede the new, stronger balance we were about to find.

Everything else was ready. In the afternoon I had cleaned the house, and I had prepared the food: sandwiches, potato salad, sliced vegetables and other stuff that would require no more attention from me once my guests had arrived. I had lit a fire and turned on lamps, and the ground floor of the bed-and-breakfast seemed to dance with the flames and glow with pleasure in the soft lights.

Enough food to warm bodies, and an atmosphere to soothe souls. It was the promise of the evening, but only I was going to call it true. How many dinners, how many social gatherings of all kinds had I attended and found that the food filled a cramped stomach, and that the most cosy atmosphere was full of tension, but tension that the laughter of others had told me was only mine? And then there were the backs of people that had often turned my way or had drifted between me and others, unintentionally most of the time, and the false promises in the curves of a woman who would not even look at me. My youth swallowed by my fears and inhibitions. Too many years had flown by during which I had contemplated my hidden potential from afar, while I romanticized that the free will of man could have everything within its reach with the right effort and the right sacrifice.

In my room I unfolded the map I had used to get to the bed-and-breakfast. I gazed at all that labelled land, that world that had disappeared but that I felt was condensed in a green area of the coast, the village unmarked, and a dark blue stretch of sea in front of it, without an island, not even a small one, between the coast and the edge of the map.

'What are you doing?' asked Amber, from under the bed.

I started, crumpling the map. 'Nothing, nothing,' I replied, shoving the map into the chest of drawers and walking out of the room. Nothing had to disturb me that night. It was to be my night, the completion of my rebirth. I only hoped I hadn't rushed it.

I walked downstairs and along the hall, straightened a painting that didn't need straightening, smoothed the edge of a carpet with my foot, then opened the front door. A long shaft of light lost itself down the slope. With a couple of steps I was out of it and the gravel of the road was grinding pleasantly under my shoes.

Sunset was still fighting its inevitable plunge into the sea. Lights were being turned off at the bottom of the hill, one by one. A silent procession of shadows was trickling out of the village and moving up the road. They seemed to separate, the tall ones on one side, the short on the other. As they got closer I tried to make out the villagers from their walk and speed. I wondered whether I should have tried to learn all their names. I shrugged. For now it was enough for them to know mine.

I walked back and stood in the doorway, feet wide apart, chest out between firm shoulders, and the light from within enhancing my pose. Soon shadows emerged into the shaft of light, took substance, and the groups rearranged. The women went in search of their husbands, then pulled them along to show me they had brought them as I had wished. I walked backwards to the bottom of the stairs. When a couple stood on the threshold I drew them to me with a smile and a curling of fingers as a magician does when summoning a hypnotized subject. I helped the women take off their grimy coats, and I answered the dusty silence of their husbands with amiable words of welcome and quick apologies for my behaviour of the previous night, which they accepted with forced words.

I asked them to go into the living room. The women moved slowly, scanning their environment. Their eyes were stern, almost threatening, as if they could wring out of their surroundings some kind of confession. I could see they searched for alcoves, recesses where life might have burned intensely, where lascivious things might have happened, and I could see they searched for something, maybe a smell, or an object out of place, or a reflection in the windows, that spoke of those past times. They searched, but the bed-and-breakfast yielded nothing.

They turned to look into their husbands' faces. I did too. I was sure to see the expressions I had imagined the night before in the bed-and-breakfast, but there was a clash between the men I had imagined and the ones I saw now. These men looked heavier, more unpredictable in the ways they moved. Where was the contentment I had imagined? Did they recognize anything? Did they see glimpses of their past in these places? I tried to see if memories surfaced behind their eyes, but I was not sure what I saw. Clearly something was going on inside their heads. Maybe nothing on the ground floor called to mind anything vivid enough.

The place had filled with noise and voices, and all telling looks had perished in the confusion. I was increasingly dazed by all of this. I was pleased by the looks the men gave me, and by the effort the women showed in dragging me into their conversations, but I couldn't be comfortable with it. I stumbled upon the piano and banged a few notes. Dora's head appeared from behind another woman and asked me to play something. Others asked too. 'I . . . Amber plays,' I said.

'I didn't know Amber played,' said Dora. 'I thought she said you did.'

'Well, yes,' I managed to say. 'She doesn't know how to play properly. She just strikes notes at random, but it's the sweetest of melodies.'

Dora and a few others watched me as I moved away from their questioning with a wan smile. I drifted on through this invasion I had welcomed and that strained me. The women still tried to draw me into their small talk. 'Why not have a tour of the house first?' I said to everyone. 'I'd like to show you the place where Amber and I will live.' With no effort I persuaded a bunch of women and Tom to follow me to the bottom of the stairs. A few men joined the group as if they had drifted into it by mistake. All the others, I said, could come up later.

I showed them the first floor and introduced it as the place where our guests would lodge. Tom recognized it, he said as much before he saw the guest room opposite the one I had occupied, and he described it as if the place's existence depended on him remembering it. I looked at the other men, but nobody showed as much knowledge as he had.

I led everyone to the second floor. My heart was beating fast. Nobody seemed interested in the storage room and I didn't expect them to be. The bedroom was a different matter. 'This is Amber's bed,' I said, 'our nuptial bed to be.' I half reclined on it with a thrill, thinking of her hiding under it. Some of the women gasped silently at the sight of it, at the redness of the quilt. The men looked at it with closed mouths and wide eyes. Frantically I tried to see what they were seeing. Whatever it was, they hid it by pushing their gaze to the rest of the room, but each attempt was short-lived and their eyes felt again the drawing power of the quilt. Tom brushed against it courageously. Some of the women were running their hands over the chest of drawers, clearly not appreciating its crudity.

I needed more clues. I hurried everyone downstairs so I could take up the others. I asked Dora to convince Eamonn to come with the second batch, and I had to persuade a few others. I felt that the more reluctant ones might be hiding the most. Indeed, Eamonn's eyes showed recollection all the way to the storage room, where he absently touched a box with a foot, and there was a strange look in his eyes when we got to the bedroom, but it was mostly directed at me. The other men behaved like those I had brought up earlier. I saw an effort in them to contain something and hide it from my scrutiny and that of their wives.

All of a sudden I understood. It wasn't memories they were trying to hide, but the wish for them. There was no languidness in their eyes, no melancholy, just eagerness. What I was seeing were minds working forward rather than back, creating memories they would never have.

All those men had desired her from a distance, and their desire had grown until the whole bed-and-breakfast was imbued with it. All I had heard made sense now, Eamonn's trembling hands on her legs, Tom's jealousy in the pub at the sight of her talking with other men, the gifts that they had made to her, offers, sacrifices that evoked nothing and bridged no distance, lost in the depth of the drawers of her past. The desire for her had even forced the priest up the hill, up the wrong slope, towards a divinity that had pushed him back down. I was convinced that nothing had ever happened, but I could still see the men stretching their claws towards her, hoping for something to reach and dig into. The women hadn't understood how wistful their husbands were: they were too close to them, and too irrational to understand. And now I knew the men had sought escape and had found no release, while their wives thought they had, and were struggling to win back their devotion. Oh, I knew there was nothing greater than envy for something that one has never tasted, or the craving for something that one has long lost!

It was time to get things rolling. I had surrendered enough to keep alive the men's fantasies and the women's nightmares. I asked them to return downstairs. 'Time to eat,' I said.

I let them go in front of me. I lingered behind, just a minute, and when everyone was out of sight, I slipped under the bed. The sound of my guests had faded down the stairs and for a moment I was alone with my Amber. I hugged her, I kissed her. I couldn't put words to my happiness. I could only tell her to stay where she was and that we would see each other later when everything was finished and settled.

I slid from under the bed, stood in the doorway and turned off the light. There it was another beam of night that lit that bed, empty, colourless, but solid and invincible in my mind, now as it was then, in the swirling images of the past. She blew me a kiss, and I didn't see her but she was there, sweet and absent and total, her kiss rising towards me, just then, before everything changed. I stood on the threshold between her and my guests downstairs, my needs branching out like the legs of a spider.

Maybe I'm romanticizing now. I hurried down the stairs. The living room was filled to overflowing. I was no longer disturbed by the heavy, noisy presence of the people there, and I felt in tune with the silent, warm expectation of the bed-and-breakfast. I asked my guests to move into the dining room. I had aligned the tables against the far wall and on them I had laid out the food. The drinks were plentiful but not excessively so – I didn't want my guests to escape me by getting drunk. 'Please,' I said, 'help yourselves. I'm afraid I don't have plates for everybody, so the last ones to the food will have to use bowls instead. Hope you'll enjoy everything.'

I began to eat. Food had never tasted so good, had never satiated such an honest and heartfelt hunger. The atmosphere was perfect, and I moved around my guests with ease, collecting compliments from the women, grunts from the men, on the food and my hospitality. More than ever I felt the men's angry stares, while the women smiled at me with almost motherly pride. 'Ah, if only Amber were here,' I said, pretending not to see her in everybody's mind, where I really wanted her.

With time and a bit of effort, especially by drifting in front of people to cut groups in a surgical fashion, I separated the men from the women. It was relatively easy as I had already seen that the women preferred to talk to each other, even more so after the tour of the house, and although they didn't want to lose sight of their husbands, neither were they disposed to be too close to them. I managed to get them bottlenecked in the corridor but they wouldn't go any further. I felt like ramming them into the living room, but instead I ex-horted them politely to go in, claiming that the sofas next to the fire would be a better place for them to sit and talk. 'Don't worry,' I said jokingly, 'I'll keep a sharp eye on your husbands.'

I had the two groups completely separated. I could hardly believe it went so well. I left the living room like a sheepdog that had safely secured its charges.

No, there were two escapees, sitting on the stairs at the end of the corridor. 'Jim,' I muttered to myself, as I approached him and his wife. For the first time I looked at her closely, and searched for something to distinguish her from the other women, but could find nothing. She wore the same old clothes, she had the same barely individual features. She sat there with her husband, both of them eating potato salad from bowls, as relaxed as if they were in their own home. I had been so pleased with my other guests that I felt unsettled by these two. I wasn't even sure whether they had participated in the tour of the house. 'What are you doing here?' I asked them, pointing at the stairs.

'There was nowhere else to sit,' said Jim's wife.

'Are you sure? I bet we can find a place for you in the living room. And, Jim, maybe you want to talk to the men over here.'

'I'm fine,' he said.

'But your lady wife . . . what's her name?'

'Mary.'

'But Mary must be uncomfortable. As host I can't allow that. Surely a sofa in the living room would be much better than the stairs.'

'I'm fine,' she said, 'really.'

I scratched the back of my head and looked at them. I might have thought they were behaving like kids trying to annoy me, but they sat there with a transparent innocence. Jim's wife had looked at the stairs almost with surprise when I had indicated them. No, I told myself, I was not going to let them ruin my evening. I was not going to chase them away from where they sat at the expense of my peace.

I had to concentrate my efforts elsewhere. A whole school of fishermen was waiting for me in the dining room, which was calling me with its welcoming lights. I looked for Tom and found him closest to the door, furthest from everybody. I put an arm around his shoulders and pushed my way with him into the limelight.

'So, Tom, did you tell them?' I asked loudly.

He looked at me, not understanding.

'That I was a bit upset last night when I shouldn't have been.'

'Oh, yes, yes. I told some . . .'

'Then I can tell everyone now. I asked Tom to give you my apologies for my moodiness yesterday. I was upset but, as you can see, I'm all right now. I had a talk with your wives to clear a few things up.'

'I'm sure you've been delicate about it,' said Eamonn, who was leaning against a wall with his arms crossed.

'I think I was. Some things have to be treated with tact, I know that.' I looked back at the door and continued in a whisper, 'And I didn't expect your wives to know too much.'

Nobody said anything. A lot of men looked at the door too. Those who were eating were chewing slowly now.

'It all started with the workers' incident we spoke about last night,' I said. I let go of Tom, put my hands in my pockets and glanced at the floor. 'It set in motion a whole train of thought. When you get to know a woman in a very few days there's only so much you can find out about her. And she may be unwilling to reveal her past. But I'm happy about everything now, I think I've sorted out what I had to sort out. But to think that I suspected Amber had betrayed me. Imagine! *Her* betraying *me*!' I laughed.

They tried to laugh along.

'Betrayed me, and with whom?' I said. 'There's only you guys here.' Those who were still eating stopped and put their plates down, with great care. I reached the tables with the food. I plunged a carrot into a bowl of dip and bit off its tip. 'I had to have a talk with your wives about this whole affair and they put me straight.'

'What the hell?' the man with the black beard burst out. 'What are you saying?'

I paused before answering, a hand in front of my mouth, pretending I had to finish chewing. Secretly I bathed in the anger and in the anxiety my silence produced. A woman appeared in the doorway of the dining room. A man strode up to her and, after a brief exchange, made her return to the living room. He remained by the door as if on guard.

'I'm saying,' I resumed, 'that I can't imagine how I could have suspected you. I was pretty upset last night, but finally I realized that the only people who might give me reason to worry were the workers, who stayed here at the bed-and-breakfast. But I'm sure Amber didn't give in to them if they thought they could get more than simple hospitality. And I didn't need to voice my suspicions for your wives to convince me of this. I didn't even have to mention the workers.'

Faces began to relax. Some plates were picked up again. The man with the black beard combed his hair with a hand and coughed away his earlier anger.

'My dear guests,' I said, 'are we to quarrel when we are united in this beautiful evening? My honest intention was to invite you here to apologize for any *other* assumptions I might have made last night. I must say that I'm truly, truly sorry about them.'

Muffled words of acceptance rose here and there from the untidy mass of fishermen. Somebody, to downplay my assumptions even more, suggested there was nothing for which I had to apologize. Only Eamonn seemed unaffected, as always. 'And what did Amber write on that note she left you?' he asked.

I had written the note myself that afternoon, with some unease but with more foresight, as a possible fallback in case something went wrong. I had written on it 'I've gone you know where' and nothing else, and placed it under one of the pillows of our bed. 'She wrote that she will be back soon,' I said to Eamonn. 'I'm glad you mentioned the note. You see, I was so impatient before I found it. I admit that waiting made me jealous. But how could I not be jealous of Amber? How can one not be jealous of perfection when one has it? But this evening my mind is at peace. This is a great place, this house, full of memories already, and full of promises for my future, don't you think?' I gazed around, and the warm wood of the bed-and-breakfast seemed to glow at my words. 'And it's a relief when you come from an unhappy place where everything has become so familiar and so empty.'

Evil looks flared at me. I was pleased by the reaction, but I pretended I had been misunderstood. 'I'm talking about myself, of course.' The evil looks turned to questioning frowns. I finished my dripping carrot. 'You see, yesterday you wanted to know about my past. Well, the first time I came here I was very depressed. I told myself that I was young, that I had plenty of time ahead of me, so many things to taste and see, so many women to love to satisfy my curiosity, and make sure I would be faithful once I was married. But I told myself these things in a voice I didn't believe. I didn't want experiences, I wanted certainties. I wanted love, a relationship, but it had to be absolute. But what can you do when you find that nothing is forever? How many marriages rot with time, like the faces of the people in the relationship? How many men constantly wonder whether their marriage is all they could really wish for?'

I had kept my voice low, but I could see how far my words reached. A couple of fishermen were trying to talk between themselves but couldn't concentrate as I spoke. A bit further away a man was poking about potato and egg slices on his plate, without eating them, and the man next to him seemed to be burning silently under the peacock lamp, which dominated the scene from the top of its cupboard. Even Eamonn was changing. His arms were still crossed, but a couple of fingers had begun to scratch his elbow. 'Aren't you a bit young to come up with all of this?' he asked me.

I smiled. 'You're right, but unfortunately I have a keen eye. In the city, wherever I turned I saw the desperation of others. I felt something like it myself once, and since then I have always seen my own future in the failed lives of older people. I couldn't imagine that I might be different. All those unhappy faces, all those ruined relationships . . . But what can you do if you find yourself in one?'

'Yeah, what can you do?' snapped the man with the sharp features. I was sure this question had been thrown at me to shut me up, but I had the impression that, despite all their anger, everyone was leaning closer involuntarily, as if they didn't want me to stop talking, but to provide an answer in which they could believe.

'There's not much you can do,' I said. 'Be lucky from the start. Find the right person. Of course, you're country people, and wise, but so many men in the city don't share your wisdom. I've seen their pathetic attempts at cheating on their wives, their unrealistic desires for a beautiful model or their neighbour's daughter.' I paused to pour myself a glass of wine, and pretended not to notice the tension in the room. I kept my eyes on the bottle, heard the wine gurgle out.

'But what can they do?' I continued. 'How do you forget fantasy and accept reality? In any case, why am I asking? My fantasy and reality have merged into one. I imagine my life and live it at the same time. But I've been lucky. I've found the right person. What if I had met Amber and found her in love with another man? Imagine the horror I would have felt at having her so close and knowing that she was beyond reach. Imagine what I would have felt at the thought of going back to my dreary life.'

The silence welled up. It grew and grew like a tidal wave about to come crashing down, frothing with rage, but I was confident it wouldn't. I spoke true to the fishermen's hearts, but I had not spoken about them, and they knew I couldn't be blamed for the way they felt. I turned to the table and threw a sliced potato into my mouth. In the window in front of me was the reflection of the room, bright in every nook, and dotted with tired old shapes. I turned round. The men's evil expressions had caved in, and now their eyes seemed to be looking at something inside themselves. 'Why are you telling us this?' asked the man burning under the peacock lamp.

'Well, I wanted to apologize. I realized I was treating you like city people, dissatisfied, frustrated by their neighbour's achievement, you know, what I said before. But this is not a city, so why should I treat you like that? A week ago Tom was telling me how life here is different.'

Tom, who had retreated into a corner, took a step forward and nodded, happy to contribute to the easing of tension, but nobody noticed him.

I turned round for another piece of potato. Silent shadows remained still on the window-pane, immobile even. 'Well, I wanted to apologize,' I said, cheerfully 'not make you so pensive. There's more to drink here,' I said, pointing at a modest number of bottles, 'so help yourselves. I'm just going to check on my other guests.'

I was excited that everything was going so well. I grabbed a box of biscuits and left, sure that nobody would follow me, but something disturbed me on my way to the living room. Jim and his wife were still sitting on the stairs. 'Not going anywhere?' I asked them.

'We're fine,' he said.

'Sure nothing's wrong?'

'Nothing, thanks,' she said.

Nothing, thanks. I couldn't hope to ruin everybody's evening. I forced myself to walk on. No point in wasting time with the party rejects.

A low bustle of voices declined as I walked into the living room. I breathed a more intense mixture of perfumes than the one I had smelt that morning. The women were spread out evenly and they sat solidly in their seats hanging on to their armrests as if trying to appropriate them, and the living room seemed to accommodate this dull invasion.

'We were admiring your house,' said Dora, looking up at me from a sofa.

'Yes,' I said, 'but you should congratulate Amber. I'm only keeping it in order.'

'You have to take care of it all by yourself?' asked a woman with porcelain earrings.

'You're being neglected,' said the one sitting next to her.

'But she will be back,' Dora said to them, before turning to me with a pleased smile. 'You spoke about a note today.'

'Yes, where did she go?' asked the woman who thought I was being neglected.

What *was* this obsession with the note? 'She just wrote that she'll be away for a while,' I said, dismissively. 'But she will be back soon. Quite soon. Who knows? Maybe she'll come back tonight!' I looked around, smiling. 'Yes, maybe tonight!' I repeated. A few women frowned. It didn't look as though I had come across convincingly, and suddenly I felt unsettled under the weight of what I had said.

'It's nice of you to be so relaxed about her,' said the woman with the porcelain earrings.

'Maybe a bit too relaxed?' suggested a tiny lady from the depths of a sofa.

'With her so far away . . .'

'It sounds like a long way from here,' came the voice from the sofa. 'For us at least. Even when our men go out at sea, they feel so far beyond our control.'

They looked at me in silence. The benevolence in their eyes wasn't gone, but there was a touch of doubt in their brows. 'You don't have to worry,' I said to myself more than to them. 'I'm not worried about where she went. I mean, should I worry? I don't mind waiting a day, a week or a year.'

'It's good to know you won't leave,' somebody said.

Others agreed. They all agreed. Maybe they didn't believe the story of the note, maybe they even had doubts about my identity, but it didn't seem to matter. I smiled. Slowly, they smiled back at me, to please me I felt. Yes, they'd rather have a fake Charles than no Charles at all.

I offered the biscuits around. They took them amiably. Everything was back to where I wanted it to be. I made some comment on the weather. They were keen to talk about it, but I was ready to do to them what I had done to their husbands. Yes, the weather was improving, I agreed, but that morning I had *really* been intending to leave, even if there had been a storm raging.

'Now, I know it was unfair to project on your village the vices of the city,' I said, 'but I was so used to such terrible stories there, about . . . you know . . .'

164

Nobody said anything. When I turned to them some women looked at their biscuits. Many patted their armrests, unsure whether to cling to them or push themselves up. I leaned against the mantelpiece. The fire was crackling behind me. I threw in one more log.

'Yes all those stories,' I said, and gave examples. I spoke of traitorous men and easy women, of successful affairs and disastrous marriages. I spoke lightly, as if I was telling anecdotes we could all laugh at, but there was no laughter in the room and even the polite smiles that bloomed were quickly gone. I went on with ease while a lot of eyes grew wide and fixed. I looked regularly at the living-room door, mindful that some of the men might creep up on my speech, but none did. 'I understand men,' I concluded, after the sixth or seventh example, 'and I can understand the tremendous appeal of something new and young, but to do something . . . that's shameful and dishonest. Love is not just feelings, it's devotion as well, and we swear to good and bad times when we take the big step, don't we?'

All eyes were on me as I finished my monologue, their humid surface vibrating with the crackling of the fire. I moved away from it, but their eyes were fixed. My footsteps sounded heavy on the floor, and after a while some heads turned to look absently at my shoes. Nobody said anything. I was ecstatic. This silence was even more complete than the one their husbands had granted me. 'Anyway,' I said in a hurry, 'I'll let you get back to your talk. I'll see your husbands for a while. And for those of you who are wondering, they're all behaving well.'

I noticed Jim and his wife laughing as I rushed past them. Were they laughing at me? No, I didn't want to think about them. Everything else was going so smoothly. I was thrilled and impatient to find myself just a step away from perfection.

In the dining room most of the men had recovered. They had blinked away those void stares with which I had left them and had found a new, keen interest in a pair who were turning bottles upside down into glasses. One after the other they all proved empty. 'I'm afraid I don't have any more drink,' I said. 'And I hope this dinner didn't disrupt your schedules too much. Did you skip the fishing tonight?'

'We went earlier,' said a man.

'We can't skip a night,' said another.

They were eager to talk about trivialities. I forced myself to join in, and they seemed relieved that I had. I felt impatient, but I laughed and joked enough to regain some of their confidence. The man who had been standing under the peacock lamp had retreated into a shadowy corner, and I moved over to stand under the cone of light.

'I'm sorry to have changed your plans,' I said, 'but who knows? Maybe it's good that I did. I know how routine can get boring.'

'It's work,' said Eamonn, impassive, with fidgety Tom at his side.

'It's work, but sometimes when work is routine everything else around it becomes the same. Same job, same things to do in one's free time . . . Maybe there's nothing wrong with that, if thoughts and feelings don't become just as familiar and boring.'

I was hit by a hail of glances. The couple who had been talking earlier resumed their conversation, but it hobbled forward spiritlessly. Others tried to exchange remarks among themselves so that they didn't have to listen to me. I could see they feared that I would start talking about them again indirectly, but I was not going to. 'Amber's a world of novelty,' I said. 'Oh, all the stuff I can tell you about her!'

Their conversations ceased. The guy in the shadows

shivered, while somebody was still shaking bottles, violently this time, for a last drop.

I looked around languidly. 'Ah, you have no idea what these walls have seen, what this room has seen! Our bodies wanted to meet and we couldn't hold them back. And this room! How these lights make her skin glow, all her skin, how they heighten her curves, how her face glimmered with simple pleasure and the desire to satisfy me!' I continued to talk about her beauty, about what we had done. The dining room itself incited me: each nook fought to offer a better story. The looks I had received from the fishermen slowly caved in again. I saw the men struggle, not with me, because I was sure I had become a voice without a body, but with themselves, and I saw them blink uncomfortably but the room gave them no relief. Only Eamonn still seemed to resist me with an impatient snort.

And so I went on and on, repeating myself, embellishing my tale. I spoke of things I had done with Amber in a virtuoso play of *double-entendres* and scorching detail, and I would ask, 'Do you know what I mean?' and then I would explain it even if they nodded because I wanted them to face the beauty of it. Even Eamonn lost his composure and began to swing slowly from side to side, as if to look for a way out.

At the end I was out of breath, although I was sure I had been speaking calmly. I thought I heard my name, and questions being asked, but not of me. I looked at everybody. Everybody was looking back. Their image was foggy, as if I had just woken up. I realized that the buzzing of conversations had returned, but they reached me as if from a vast distance.

I slid out of the room, I was feverish, and I nearly managed not to notice Jim and his wife on my way to the living room. I was almost there, I thought, almost there.

The women were still sitting where I had left them, but their grip on the armrests had withered, and the bed-and-breakfast seemed to have grown between them like vegetation. 'Ah, you have no idea what these walls have seen,' I said, without preamble, 'what this room has seen! Our souls wanted to meet and we couldn't hold them back. How these lights made her eyes sparkle and her face glimmer with tenderness. How she played her random tunes on the piano . . .'

'Will you play us something now?' asked Dora.

'Yes, play us something,' somebody agreed.

'No, no,' I said, shocked by the interruption. 'I want to talk about Amber now. About us. You must understand.' And so I went on and on to them as well, speaking candidly about Amber and me and about a loftier, less carnal relationship than the one I had described to the men. And, from beyond my words, I caught glimpses of the women, and I saw how each additional word tickled their fancy and brought them up into my higher world of romance, and in the rarefied air I would shoot another subtle, poisoned reference to their husbands to remind them of how far they were from their reality.

I went on, finding new breath and disarming calm, until a man appeared at the living room door. I wrapped up my speech, then almost withdrew, perspiring expectantly. More men arrived. I was sure I saw a sparkle in their eyes, a stolen but rotten reflection of what must have been in mine when I spoke to them about Amber.

Couples formed again. He approached her, she tried to move away. I walked around pretending to look for the box of biscuits, while I listened in to several conversations. They all sounded like each other, in one way or another.

'Shall we go home?' he said.

'Are you in a hurry?' she answered.

'I'm tired.'

'You usually come home later than this,' she said to that. 'From the pub.'

Silence.

'I don't believe you're tired,' she added.

'And what should I be?'

Pause.

'I know what you are,' she said.

End of conversation.

There was a tang of sweat in the room, eager sweat, and a trace of musty but still proud perfumes that asked for nothing but respect for lost dreams. The rift I had opened! He thirsting for flesh that wasn't hers, and she for virtue and a capacity for romance that he had long lost. I could see the scene that would be enacted later that night, him trying it on in bed with her, the lights turned off or his eyes closed, and she refusing, pushing him away. He would get up in a hot sweat, exasperated, and he would look out of the window. My house would be there, in his eyes and in the mind of his wife, who was still in bed, turned away from him, tearful maybe. Didn't that uniform carpet of grass that rose up the hill give the distinct impression of growing thicker, greener towards the house in the clear glow of moonlight?

'And he told you about what he got up to?'

The hair stood up on the back of my neck. I turned round. It was Eamonn talking to Dora. I wasn't expecting the men and women to share with each other what I had told them. I had been sure that their respective guilt and grief would keep them quiet.

'Yes, he did,' she whispered. 'He's very moral.'

'Moral?' asked Eamonn.

In a leap I was next to them. 'Everything OK?' I asked, hands clasped reverentially in front of me.

'What have you been telling her?' asked Eamonn.

'I told your wife and your lady friends what I told you.'

'What you told us?'

'In different terms, obviously. You always have to take into account your audience before you speak, don't you think?'

'Indecent,' he answered, 'and all those insinuations.'

On hearing his words some men had turned to me. 'I said nothing indecent,' I replied. 'And what insinuations? If I spoke about private things I did it because I trust you as good friends, not for you to criticize them. I'm happy, then, that I haven't said a word about the love letters we used to write when I was away.'

'Oh, really?' said Eamonn lifting himself on his toes a couple of times. 'How interesting. You wrote each other love letters.' He called to Jim, without taking his eyes off me. 'Did Amber ever give you letters to post?' he asked, when Jim appeared on the threshold.

Jim shook his head.

'There's no postbox here,' said Eamonn to me. 'Jim takes all our post to the next village.'

He was triumphant. The men around us stirred with un-expected excitement, and for a moment I felt all was lost. But it couldn't be, it just couldn't. 'We didn't go through Jim,' I said. 'I have a friend who works at the Cliffs. I sent the letters to him and he brought them here to her. I'd rather trust my friend, if you don't mind.'

'A friend at the Cliffs? There are no houses there, you know.'

'I didn't say he lives there. He works there, in a souvenir shop.'

'We never saw him.'

'He came nowhere near the village,' I said, growing angry

and raising my voice. 'Or am I to believe that you know all that goes on in this house?'

Our conversation had attracted a lot of attention. At the beginning Eammon had raised his voice, but I had raised mine more.

'His name is Chris,' I added, as he remained quiet.

Somebody seemed to remember a Chris.

'There, you see?' I said, although I didn't know what they meant. 'You can all check. I even spoke to him on the phone just a few days ago, before coming here.'

'And what's her surname?' a voice asked from behind me.

I turned round and saw Tom, shaky but convinced of the power of his enquiry. '*His* surname?' I asked.

'Not his. Amber's. If you knew her bra size, you must know her surname too.'

'Her bra size?' asked Dora.

'Nothing, nothing,' I whispered to her. 'I was stupid enough to answer one of their questions.' I turned back to my attacker, who was still shaky but clinging to his whiplash. 'Tom, what is it with you?'

'If you wrote to her,' he said, 'you must have put an address on the envelope.'

Everybody was looking at me. I had the impression they were drawing closer, slowly, like animals surrounding a prey. I had read Amber's surname on some of the papers I had burnt, but I had not thought about it then and I couldn't remember it now. I began to sweat and I had the impression the beads of perspiration on my face were shining in the light for everyone to see.

I thought I heard the voice of a woman asking me to play a tune for them. I wasn't sure whether she was attacking me as well, or whether she was trying to help me get out of my corner.

I tried to laugh. 'I guess you weren't listening properly,' I said to Tom. 'I sent my mail to *my friend*. I put my friend's address on the envelopes. I didn't know Amber's surname and I still don't know it. It's deplorable, you might think, but our relationship is not bogged down in detail. We know each other for who we are, not for names or circumstances we didn't choose and had no power over. She told me she doesn't even like her *first* name. As for her surname, she didn't want to tell it to me, but she will soon have mine and that's all that matters. Maybe she wants me to think of her as always having been mine. Well, I don't know, I spoke innocently to you tonight, and I guess that if there was innocence in you, you would have been happy for me.'

There was silence again, from both the men and the women. The fire crackled unperturbed in the background.

Dora was the first to recover. 'Eamonn, you should be ashamed of treating him like this,' she said. 'And it's not the first time. And you too, Tom.'

'No, don't worry, let them attract everybody's attention,' I said, loudly enough for everyone to hear. 'Let them ask away. As if I had something to hide. Amber told me about those two, how they are. I didn't want to say it before, but I can't hold myself back now. She didn't like either of them, and if she made you believe otherwise,' I said turning to them, 'if she made you believe that she did, even a tiny bit, then it was for politeness's sake only.' They didn't reply. I looked for one more nail to hammer into the coffin, one more detail that would make her feel even closer but further out of reach to the men, and even more suspicious in the eyes of the women. 'If you really want to know,' I said, 'she had a particular sympathy for your old barman Frank. You might be surprised, but she can hide these things well. I barely managed to find out myself. I'm sure that she didn't want to upset our love with the memory of an infatuation. And, of course, Frank's dead, and that kind of infatuation won't happen again.' Maybe I had taken a step too far into unknown territory, but nobody seemed to find what I had said strange. There was silence from all quarters. 'Any more questions?' I asked.

Eamonn began to mutter some protest, but Dora gave him a look that stopped him. I hated having produced this diversion in my guests: I was afraid I had distracted them from their previous moods, but as I looked around I saw that the women viewed their husbands with fresh suspicion, while the men looked at Eamonn and Tom, at their defeated faces, and saw their own.

The evening was rushing towards its end. The men wanted to go, but the women didn't, even if staying had become unbearable to them too. I was sure the men were still hungry and eager, the women suspicious and disillusioned. Ah, the night that would follow! Amber and I in perfect union, and contorted bodies down in the village that would find no harmony, no contact that was not painful, not a word or a move that would resolve their suffocating closeness.

I was about to propose a toast to myself when somebody tapped my shoulder.

'We're leaving now,' said a voice behind me.

'Oh, yes, I'm not holding you back,' I said, turning round. 'Oh, it's you, Jim.'

'We had a good time, thank you,' said his wife.

'You didn't mingle much.'

'We enjoyed the evening, anyway.'

'Well, I mean . . . I tried to talk to you.'

'Really, it's no problem,' she said.

I think they had even missed my argument with Eamonn and Tom. I forced a smile and dismissed them. The others would soon follow. I returned to my feelings, and looked at myself in the window to see the pleasure on my face.

But just beyond the window-pane another face was staring in at me.

My God, was it her?

It was just a glimpse, a nose floating out of the darkness, pressed against the window, and the brief sparkle of two eyes, but I was sure it was *Amber. It was Amber!* I had said to the women that she would be back that night and she was! What had I done? She had walked to the window first to find out what was going on in her house, and she had looked at me while I stood there, as if in a fishbowl, naked and unmasked. How long had she been there without me noticing? How long would it take her to get to the door? I had no way out. It would have been easier to shed my skin than to save myself. I pictured *my* Amber upstairs, hiding under the bed, and I was sure I could hear her deflating suddenly like a balloon.

For a moment I saw who I was and I saw the sham of my life and of this situation I had created, and imagined how infinitely more pleasant it would have been with her there and us truly together, among strangers or people we knew, looking up from different conversations to find each other, faces radiant and secret, an uncomplicated and complete bond in a crowd far beyond our interest . . .

'Are you all right?' I heard a voice ask me.

I searched for its owner. It was Dora. 'Uh?'

'I asked if you were all right, you've turned pale.'

'Must have poisoned himself with his own lies,' said another voice.

'Eamonn!' said his wife.

Nobody dared to say anything more. I looked at this world I had conquered, and at the hopelessness of my victory. I was sure I had heard a dull knocking at the door. My last week flashed before my eyes as I plunged towards a reality I had forgotten. And what was there left to do?

I lashed out at Eamonn. 'Yes, Eamonn,' I said, 'why do you have to hassle me like that? What have I done to you? Do you think I have something to hide? What about you?' I stamped my foot with indignation, to cover the sound of another knock at the door. I was sure that nobody had heard it, but how could I expect Amber to give up and go away? Still I talked and accused Eamonn of abusing my hospitality, and I continued to stamp my foot, but that knocking came again, stronger, and this time I wasn't the only one to hear it. I thought all was lost, but nobody made for the door.

Maybe everybody feared what was outside. I was frightened that Amber would expose me, but maybe the men feared she would unmask them, and perhaps the women feared both. In a last moment of panic I told everyone to leave. 'I'm offended,' I said. 'What kind of thanks is this for my hospitality! This is Amber at the door and I don't want you to say a word to her. I don't want her to suffer like you made me suffer now.' My voice became stronger but not louder: I did not want *her* to hear me. My mouth was filling with foam, bubbling as I hissed, and my neck ached. I was convinced of a new folly, that if I kicked everyone out before Amber could stop one and ask what was happening, perhaps I could reason with her, convince her – of what, though, I wasn't sure.

The knocking came again. Jim disappeared down the hallway. He opened the door. 'Oh, it's you,' he said. 'We were wondering whether you would show up.' Steps, then the door closing. More steps, heavy ones.

Then an old man with a thick white beard walked into the living room. He held up a bag in front of him. 'I brought you all something,' he said.

I blinked. 'Father . . . Christmas?'

Eamonn burst out, 'What? Father Christmas? What's wrong with you?' He walked up to the newcomer. 'William, you made it.'

'I brought you some fresh cheese, but it looks like you've already eaten.'

'This is William,' said Dora unnecessarily, still mortified by my invective. Other villagers were leaving silently. 'We thought of inviting him too, since you invited the whole village.'

'William?' I said, 'William, the shepherd?' I laughed with disbelief. The tears of dread that stood in my eyes fell down my cheeks and I wiped them away. 'Of course, I remember you from yesterday in church. I'm honoured to have you here. Yes, honoured. I was just telling everybody how nice everything is. How nice . . . all of this is. Please come in, sit down.'

He stood where he was, rotating his heavy body slowly, like a small planet, to take in the whole room.

'He knew Amber too,' said Dora to me.

'I see,' I said.

'And she's not here,' he said.

'No, she's not,' I said, 'but she'll be back soon, you know. Maybe tonight!'

He took a step closer to me. His large frame emitted the cold it had collected outside. 'Yes,' he said.

xii

William gazed at the people leaving and answered their farewells with a nod or a slow gesture of his hand. At one point he remembered his bag and gave it to me. I threw it on a sofa. William knew Amber, I thought, and knew her well, for surely he had spent a lot of time with her when he was making the sculpture. And that 'yes' had sounded so certain. It boomed inside me like a scream in a cave.

I looked past the leaving guests at Dora. I wanted her to disprove that 'yes', but I felt she was resigned to it. She nodded goodbye to William, then squeezed my hand warmly but with discomfort in her eyes, and left the room without a word. I followed her, starving for help, but I stopped at the threshold of the living room. Eamonn was waiting for her at the front door, and Tom was standing next to him. The subdued looks that had pleased me were gone from their faces, and their stares now kept me at a distance. I watched them leave, the two men strutting defiantly, Dora's curved back between them, until they disappeared into the darkness.

They were gone, but I couldn't stop looking at the night that had swallowed them, because I felt something advancing through it towards the brightly lit bed-and-breakfast. I felt such terror and despair! Yes, she was coming back tonight. And William knew why, I thought, and he knew from where.

I hurried back to the living room. William hadn't moved. 'They're gone,' I said, and hastened to turn off the lights.

'They are,' he answered. 'I arrived late.'

'Nobody else will come,' I stated, trying to sound confident.

'I think everybody was here.'

'And Amber?'

He placed a hand under his beard and stroked it upwards. 'Maybe I should go myself.'

'You can stay if you want.'

'You should eat the cheese while it's fresh.'

'You're not imposing.'

'Another time.'

'I'll walk you, then. I'll walk you home. I'd like to get some fresh air. You don't mind, do you?'

'I don't mind.'

He didn't wait for me. I turned off the last few lights, and for a second I thought of staying behind to hide in the darkness of the house. But how could I?

I ran after William. In a way, I could do nothing else but follow him: I knew he believed in Amber's return, and I was convinced he was taking me to her.

He had crossed the road and was walking in the direction of the village but heading inland. He didn't look annoyed by my presence. I had the feeling that he hardly noticed it. He seemed at ease, and only once did he look up at the sky, at the moon that kept pushing away the clouds that drifted in front of it.

I looked at it more than once. It was spying on us, I was sure. The ground felt treacherous under my feet, but William walked on without changing his pace during the landscape's silent plunges from colourless light to darkness. Nor did he notice anything strange each time the landscape re-emerged around us. Maybe he knew what those shadows were, those scattered shadows that the moon couldn't dispel.

No, I told myself, they were nothing. Just darker patches of grass, or irregularities of the ground. We passed close to a few and they proved to be no more than that, but the village looked menacing, pitch black at the foot of the hill. It was as if none of the villagers was at home. Nightmares flew into my head and clawed at my stomach, while rational thoughts struggled hopelessly against them. Maybe they were nothing more than nightmares, I tried to argue with myself, and I was in bed dreaming, and nothing had happened, no dinner, no victories, but no disasters either.

If it was a dream, though, everything felt horribly real. We walked on and the village moved to our right. Then I could see the empty cleavage of the main road and an unsteady reflection of the moon at the end, on the waters of the bay.

'There are no lights,' I said to William.

'They are all asleep,' he answered.

'But they left just before us. And there weren't any lights even as we were walking down.'

'It happens sometimes.'

'What happens?'

'The light goes. The power supply to this place is unreliable.'

I didn't believe him. Something was going on. Soon the village was behind us, but I kept turning round to make sure we weren't being followed. Larger clouds passed in front of the moon, and I couldn't help but feel there was something unnatural in this. I had begun to recognize the different shades of the landscape, but I was convinced that shadows darker than night were moving around us with deadened sounds, and each time light returned a wave of blond hair seemed to flash in the tall grass, lit by a stroke of moonlight.

'Where are you taking me?' I asked William.

'You said you wanted some fresh air.'

'I said I would walk you home.'

'We're close.'

I didn't want to go any further, but I had nowhere to run. Darkness descended thicker than ever, then after a while the moon shone again, and this time the shadows had grouped in front of me. They stood there, black and solid, nothing I could blink away, no dark patches of grass or irregularities of the ground, but real outlines, and William was leading me right into their midst.

He turned round when he reached the first shadows. 'You're going back?'

None of the shadows stretched past his shoulders. I moved closer. I could make them out better now, short stocky bodies, taller ones with arms outstretched and headless necks. Slabs and crosses.

William walked on. I lagged behind among the graves, touched the rough edges of the crosses, and I turned round to look for the village, but it was nowhere to be seen. I read the inscriptions on the graves, saw a few names I thought I recog-nized, looked for more, thinking feverishly that maybe nothing had been real, that the world of the living had eluded me once again and that I had been fooled by ghosts. The moon shone down on each grave to let me read the names, but there was no Dora and no Eamonn, no Tom, no Jim. And there was no Amber. I would have traded all I still had, all I could steal, for her grave and the safety it would grant me.

There was one last grave on the unmarked perimeter of the graveyard. I approached it slowly and hesitated before read-ing the name. It was Frank, my simple creation. He lay there dead, the understanding I had contrived between him and

Amber was beyond the inquisition of the villagers and I envied him for it.

William was almost out of sight and I ran after him. The ground descended into a hollow and the bulky outlines of a house and a barn stood at the bottom. When I was half-way down, a light went on inside and I saw William disappear past the front door.

I ran after him. The interior of the house was one single room, a fireplace at the end, a table in the middle, a bed and a low wardrobe on opposite walls. There was a rudimentary kitchen in a corner, and each wall had a long horizontal window. Small wooden sculptures of sheep were piled up under one, and a burning light-bulb hung over the table from a bent wire.

'There's light in your house,' I said.

'It must have come back.'

'The damage to the power supply was short-lived.'

'It can be.'

Was he making things up as he went along?

He picked up a pipe from a shelf over the kitchen stove and began to fill it. I looked around and out of the door, at the darkness.

'What about Amber, then?' I asked quickly.

'What about her?'

'You said she's coming back tonight.'

'I didn't say that,' he answered.

For a moment I stood there, like an idiot, as he walked outside. What had he meant? I rushed after him to a fence that enclosed the grounds in front of the barn. Past the fence, stirring, bleating puffs of white shone in the moonlight, then settled as they recognized him. I took a few steps, looked into the barn and found it empty. I saw an outdoor toilet between it and the house, the door swung open. The moon shone down, unchallenged by the clouds, conspiring with them, and grinned at showing me the emptiness it lit.

'She's not here,' I said.

'She doesn't come by that often.'

'She came for the statue.'

'Do you like it?'

'What do you mean you didn't say that she's coming back tonight?'

'I didn't say that. You did.'

I thought about it. Was that it? Had it all been a misunderstanding? 'But you were sure about what I said.'

'I was.'

'Why?'

'Because you were.'

'You trust me?'

'You're her boyfriend, aren't you? You should know.' He took a puff from his pipe and I felt he looked at me for the first time.

Was there anything besides his 'yes' that worried me? Maybe I was the one making him uncomfortable and he found refuge in those quick replies, in behaving as if I wasn't there.

'She told me a lot about you,' he said.

'The way I look?'

'No. The way you are. It's strange that you worry so much.' He leaned against a fence post. 'She's a nice girl,' he added. The air was cold and my breath produced wisps of steam. More resilient vapours lingered around his face when he exhaled pipesmoke.

I was dismayed. Had he simply believed the only lie I wished I hadn't told?

'And where's your wife?' I asked.

'I don't know.'

'What do you mean?'

'I don't have one.'

'Dead?'

'Never born.'

'You never got married.'

'Some people are not meant to.'

'Not even now?'

'Now I'm old. I have my work and I have my sheep.'

A low bleating came from the barn, as if to confirm his words.

'Amber and I make a good couple,' I said.

'I'm sure.'

'It's a rare thing.'

'So much the better.'

'It's the kind of relationship people can be envious of.'

'When you see her tell her to come and say hello. I'd like to talk to her.'

There was nothing left to say. I felt defeated. I looked at his sheep, I looked at his job, the solitude of these fields, in this house away from the eyes of all, with nothing to have and nothing to show. How could he stand there and smoke with such ease? His gaze was fixed on nothing. He seemed content, without the vaguest trace of doubt about the choices he had made and without regretting another life he might have had.

My own eyes found no peace in looking at all of this. I forced myself to leave and I didn't say goodbye. He didn't either, and I turned round repeatedly, hoping his composure would show signs of failure, but even his unbearable weight seemed feather-like against the slender fence post.

Surely I could forget him, I told myself as I ran away, and leave him alone at the bottom of that hollow. He was a small loss, and his contentment an even smaller worry for me. But no rational thought could prevail over how I felt. Not even

Frank's grave could give me the comfort I wanted, nor the peace of the cemetery, with its newly born grass growing on choices and regrets long gone, and bodies that must have stared with wonder at the roots that stretched down towards them.

I ran on without stopping till I reached the village. Jim's van was the only crushing presence on the road. It was parked in front of his house, under what I suspected to be his bedroom window. I circled it several times, not knowing what to do, unsure of where to go, of where I *could* go. Soon I found myself climbing on top of it to look into Jim's bedroom. I hoped desperately to find a peace there that was not as total as William's, some kind of conflict that could still comfort me.

The curtains were drawn but didn't meet. It took me a while to unravel what I saw beyond the gap, the complicated tangle of shades and folds on top of a bed. The edge of a quilt emerged from under another, then two arms overlapped above it. Round folds creased the sleeves of the pyjamas at the elbows, where the arms bent to converge in the hands. Above these was a face, and another leaned against it from behind. Mary and Jim, hugging in sleep.

I fell from the van and hit the ground with a dull thud. I got up in pain and managed to run away. The houses flashed past me, then the boats, and the beach opened up in front of me. I fell to my knees by the shore.

What was all this suffering I was undergoing? And for what did I suffer? I told myself that I didn't have to care about William and Jim. They were shipwrecks from an old-fashioned world of acceptance. That was all. Jim's clammy intimacy with his wife was nothing more than a variant of William's indifference, because he was as married to circumstance as William was.

This I told myself, as I ground handfuls of sand. And I had been a fool, I added. Jim and William were not my enemies, just nuisances, and their indifference was no secret plot against me: it could harm me only if I allowed myself close to it.

I found a small conch in the sand and held it to my ear. Its sound was nicer than the sea's. Yes. Amber's return was deferred. William and Jim were just nuisances. My problem was the imprudent invective I had voiced at the bed-and-breakfast, and my enemies were those who could exploit it against me.

I looked at the village and saw no faces in the windows, nobody searching for a glimpse of the house on the hill. I had wanted envy from the men and admiration from the women, but where were they? I felt dizzy and full of anger, and I was seized by a need for revenge.

I remember my desperate changes of mood during that strange night, how I slumped in fear and clung to desire, how I felt the moon burn down on me like a tropical sun. I knew I stood precariously on the edge between success and failure, and that I had to fall one way or the other.

I ran to the pub with the intention of teaching Tom a lesson. The door was unlocked. For a second I smiled at his attempts to behave like the villagers but, of course, there was no need to lock doors, because there were no strangers to protect ourselves against.

Blue light filtered into the pub from the windows facing the sea, and in the glow the new and old tables looked the same. Behind the bar and between two sets of shelves was the door that led to the flat above, and I had a smile on my face before I tried the handle.

Beyond the door, a steep staircase led upstairs. I walked up it slowly because its wood was old and dry. I was eager but I proceeded with the utmost caution, testing each step with the tip of my shoe, pressing down in different places till I found a spot that wouldn't squeak. I held myself against the flanking walls, to lift myself past the more ancient steps, or to ease my weight onto those I couldn't skip. After each I paused to hear if any sounds came from upstairs, and I thought I heard a low, troubled snoring.

When I had reached the last steps, I could see that the stair-case led to a short corridor perpendicular to it. The snoring helped me find Tom's room quickly, but I couldn't resist a tour of the rest of his flat.

Everywhere the furniture was old and worn-out. The kitchen was clean but spectral, and a modern plastic fruit basket seemed besieged by Frank's ancient furniture. In the living room other new objects scattered about tried to impose cheerfulness on it, but without success.

I was impatient. I glanced into the bathroom, then inched my way through the gap of the bedroom door. The air in the room was stale, and the curtains seemed to flow naturally into the quilt of the double bed placed under them. They had a filthy transparency that reminded me of a shroud and the rest of the furniture felt equally oppressive. I got used to the stale smell but the depressing atmosphere remained. This was Tom's reality, and I wanted to taste it for a while longer. I crossed my hands behind my back, and looked around as if I was in a museum. I could see again his failed attempts to counteract the flat's mood. I took my time to make out the posters he had put up, discovering dull landscapes and reproductions of famous paintings. I searched for signs of modernity, finding nothing more than a lamp with a flexible neck, sagging over an alarm clock on the bedside table. I felt a touch of pity for the head visible between quilt and curtains, buried in the middle of the double bed, but it was short-lived. Tom's mouth was slightly open, emitting that annoying snore.

As I moved closer I could see his eyes move below the lids. 'Dream, Tom, dream,' I whispered. The floorboards zigzagged my advance and slowed it down, but the sight of his eyes spurred me on. I was sure I knew about whom he was dreaming, and I knew how sometimes even the vaguest memory of a dream could upset a whole day.

I reached the bed. The quilt seemed like a copy of Amber's, and if I hadn't been sure that Tom had never visited her room before that night, I would have thought he had bought it to resemble hers. I lifted its edge slowly till I could see the length of him. He held his pillow parallel to his body, one arm on each side of it. I wanted to leap on him with clawed hands, and I stood there aware of the power I could wield against him, but instead I moved slowly, gently, a few inches each time he wheezed, intending to lie down in that bed too. Cautiously I stretched one of my legs next to his. I reclined on the bed propping myself on an elbow, the pillow marking a fat borderline between him and me. He didn't react to my presence until I pressed the top of the pillow gently against his face. His eyeballs slowed. His nose twitched, his mouth gaped wider, both seeking air. I allowed them some, but not enough. Soon his whole body was searching for a new position, and his eyes opened absently, only just, as if to look for it. They saw me and didn't connect, then I waved at them and they flung open.

'I didn't want to wake you so suddenly,' I said. 'I knew you were dreaming, you incorrigible boy.' He let out a feeble shriek and tried to get up. I threw a hand forward, caught him by the shoulder and pushed him down. 'No, don't bother getting up, I won't be here long.'

He trembled under my hand. 'What do you want?' he managed.

'Nothing in particular. I just couldn't sleep and I thought of paying you a visit. Is anything wrong?'

'But I . . .'

'You what? I was feeling a bit lonely in my big house on the hill, and you were here dreaming. About who, I'd like to know?' I pulled my other leg on to the bed and, with a swift move of my hand, flung the quilt over my body. We lay there facing each other across the top of the pillow, our heads and one of my arms emerging from under the covers. For a long moment he stared at me, smiling at him in the tomb-like silence of the room. Then he tried to get up again, but I held him down. He could have broken free had he wanted to, but he didn't. He seemed already subdued, as if afraid that he might provoke from me a vicious reaction.

'All right,' I said, 'you don't need to answer me. I think I know who you were dreaming about. I feel, though, that I can't blame you. I really can't.' He didn't seem reassured. I think he was busy trying to breathe. 'I can relate to you in a way,' I continued, 'but only in a way. You see, I'm here because I also felt lonely tonight. But I felt misunderstood too. I can accept being lonely since Amber is away, but misunderstood . . . Why do I feel misunderstood?' He said nothing. His movements were limited to a rapid blinking over eyes as big as eggs. 'Well?' I said. 'Once you were so talkative, and you seemed so friendly.' I stroked the pillow. 'But I think you were friendly because unconsciously you thought that friends share – don't they? – and you wanted me to share something with you. And when it dawned upon you that this was impossible you started to ask me unfriendly and distrustful questions.'

'I just wanted to ask . . .' he said, 'to make sure . . .'

I had no ears to listen. The hand that lay over the quilt dived under it and grabbed his flaccid genitals. I wondered whether they had been harder during his dreaming. He crumpled with a squeal, then patted my arm to make me let go. 'You listen here,' I said to him, through clenched teeth, 'and listen carefully. You might not like me, all these people in this filthy village might not like me, but none of you have to. As a matter of fact, your dislike pleases me. But distrust is altogether different.' I pushed up my chest, threw the pillow that separated us onto the floor, and pinned him down with my free hand. 'I'm Amber's boyfriend and only Amber can claim otherwise. Maybe you don't think I'm her boyfriend, maybe I don't behave as you would expect him to, but how do you know what makes me attractive in her eyes? Not my knowledge of her surname. You might know it, and know a lot of other things, but none of them brings you an inch closer to her. You like her, but she loves *me*, and I'm sure you understand the difference.'

My words sank into the silence around us. His body was still rigid, his mouth pressed tight in a short, straight line. He was pulling feebly at my arm to free himself from my grip. 'You can't dislodge me,' I said. 'I'm not giving her up for your little fancies. Because, you know,' I finished with a whisper, 'mine are much bigger than anybody's here, and nobody can tell me any more that they're untrue.'

I was done and he was quiet. I let him go, and crawled out of his bed without taking my eyes off him. His fright, his body, which had shrunk and gone moist at my touch, was enough tribute for now. I stood there, still bent over the bed, my hands resting on it, looking at him. He sat up, a hand over his crotch while the other was raised an inch from the bed, as if ready to protect him from another attack. We looked at each other for a long time, lit by a beam of moonlight that had crept between the curtains. I kept a tight-lipped smile on my face. His lips were trembling. I backed out of the room, and as the distance between us increased I thought I could hear his fright giving way to hot breaths of frustration. But what could he do? It was the increasing distance between us that made him brave. Maybe in a while he would think of something he could have done to defend himself, or to attack me, but it would be too late.

I flew down the stairs and out of the pub. I walked down the main road, in the middle, because if the moon wanted to watch, I would let it. I had nothing to hide and nobody to hide from. The air was clear and cold. The houses around me shone in the moonlight. Only Eamonn's house looked dark, rotten in some way.

I crept through its door. The darkness inside was almost total, and I had to wait for my eyes to adapt. I crawled up the stairs on all fours because they were even noisier than Tom's. I moved with meticulous care, with perfect clarity of mind, and even now I can only recall how sure I was of what I was doing, how I believed in these incursions into other people's houses.

Once I got upstairs I located the bedroom and took my time over a tour of the rest of the floor. The house was as miserable up there as I remembered it downstairs. The floor was uneven under my feet and felt fragile. The bathroom was neat but in a similar state of collapse, and there was a storage room with stuff practically shovelled into it. Only the last room, aside from Eamonn and Dora's, defied the rest of the house: it was furnished with slender closets and a bed kept neat and empty. The curtains were drawn, as though to hide the uselessness of the room.

I walked to their bedroom, slowly, very slowly, because the moment was precious and I was not going to rush it. The door stood ajar. My head snaked past the gap, my neck stretching to a previously unrealized length. The moon had found its way into that room too. Its light crept in from the window and lit the bed. There they were, Eamonn and Dora, turned in opposite directions for the comforting view of the inanimate wall. Maybe my evening had had the desired effect. The space on the bed between the two attracted me strangely. I wanted to lie there to feel again Dora's love for me and Eamonn's adversity.

The moon shone more intensely. It challenged me, I felt, and our meeting point could only be the bed.

Before I could move, Eamonn stirred. Slowly he sat up, facing the window, although he didn't look at it. On his bedside table there was an alarm clock like Tom's, and he looked at it briefly. He rested his elbows on his knees, and his head was a heavy load that arched his back. The vertebrae at the top stuck out from under a miserable, patched overall. He lifted a hand and ran it over his balding head, and I thought I could hear a rustling sound, rough skin against rough skin.

Dora seemed to notice it too. Her head turned, her body followed, and she sat up in bed behind him. She stretched out an arm and touched his back.

He didn't move. 'Go back to sleep,' he said.

'You're still angry with me.'

'I don't understand why you encourage him. He's not Charles. You heard him tonight.'

She turned her head and looked away. 'It's more than that, isn't it? You're still angry at me for the other thing. For Amber.' Her voice had grown darker, but I felt she was trying not to scold him. 'You know it was the thing to do.' Her hand stiffened on his back, and her arm, that narrow bridge between them, grew weak. 'Amber won't come back, Eamonn, you've got to accept it.'

'And you could only tell me all of this tonight? Why

did you keep reassuring that man up there that she will?'

'He mentioned a note . . .'

'But you don't believe him, do you?'

She said nothing. I waited, but she said nothing.

A great joy filled me, and I barely managed to retract my head out of the room without banging it against the door. So she wasn't coming back, she wasn't! What greater proof did I need than Dora telling her own husband? Of course, she could have told everybody that Amber was gone for good and her disappearance would have been a better barrier than I was, but she wanted me to be that barrier, she wanted me to serve as a punishment for Eamonn and the other men's lusts.

I was even beginning to imagine something unspeakable about Amber's disappearance, when I heard Eamonn say he was going to the toilet. I leaped into the empty bedroom just as he walked out of his. I heard him come down the corridor and shut himself into the bathroom. Soon after Dora left their room and seemed to stop in front of my hiding place, but if she did it was only for a second, and then I heard her walk down the stairs and tell Eamonn, her voice still tense, that she was going to prepare breakfast.

I sneaked past the bathroom and down the stairs, my feet touching the few noiseless spots I had discovered during my ascent. When I reached the ground floor, a toilet flushed upstairs and a jingling of cutlery came from the kitchen. Covered by the noise I reached the front door and in a moment I was out of the house.

Morning was close. The first feeble light of dawn promised to be more intense than the moon's strongest beam. In front of me was a narrow alley that led to the foot of the hill, and further on, the slope led to the bed-and-breakfast, a castle overlooking its fiefdom, and it was all mine. I took a deep breath before looking at it, before seeing its beauty in the light of a new dawn, but when I raised my eyes my insides tightened into a ball of lead.

A light was shining in Amber's room.

xiii

I thought of Amber, her soft features growing angular and unforgiving at the sight of the leftovers of my failed buffet, at her abused picture hidden under her bed, and at her belongings reduced to a pile of ashes in the fireplace. I saw myself through her eyes and felt shame and horror for what I had become.

I drifted down the alley, drawn by that terrible vision of her lit window. I kept in the ample shadows of a night not yet gone, but I realized there was no hiding place that could save me. Still I found myself hoping for some impossible solution, for the appearance of a devil or magician who could offer me a deal in exchange for making Amber disappear for good. In my head I was already renouncing the years of my life I still had to live, I was considering whether I could dispense with my soul – any deal left me richer than the nothingness Amber's return handed me.

I blinked and the light at the bed-and-breakfast was gone. Had *I* done it? I blinked again and the light was still gone. Yes, I thought, maybe I had. Maybe desires meant something after all, maybe fear and hate had their influence, and for a brief but lucid moment I was sure that we cannot be constrained to a reality shaped only by actions, when inside we have enough secret thoughts and desires for an entirely new world.

A light came on in the guest bedroom and I turned to stone. She had simply walked down the stairs and the new light was clearer and closer. A death rattle crawled out of my body like the last hiss of a deflating balloon.

'What was that?' I heard somebody say. I looked around for the origin of the voice, and I realized I was standing in front of Dora and Eamonn's living-room window. Inside two shadows sat at the table in the negligible light that came from the kitchen door. They were grey and curved, but I didn't feel condescending towards them as I would have done a little earlier. The tension I had felt between them was gone or hidden in expressions I couldn't see, and all I noticed was how they stooped over their meal like inseparable accomplices.

When Eamonn spotted me he coughed and spat out the food he was chewing. 'Look at that fool,' he shouted, and threw back his chair as he got up. He walked to the window and flung it open. 'What *is* it that you want from us?' he barked. We were at arm's length from each other. His voice rang disturbingly clear through the open window. 'Are you spying on us in our own houses now?'

'Don't be so aggressive,' said Dora approaching, but puzzled to see me there.

'Aggressive? What do you mean? Spying on me when I'm trying to have my breakfast.'

'Maybe he was having a walk.'

'At this time? Look at him. Look at his face. I bet you he hasn't stopped choking on his lies since last night.'

I paid no attention to them. On the first floor of the bed-and-breakfast lights were going on and off in a pyrotechnic display.

'Maybe he's tired and couldn't sleep.'

'I tell you what he is. He's frightened because I've called his bluff. Wait till Amber or the real Charles come back!'

'He's frightened because you're shouting at him!'

'Oh, so I'm the one . . . but I mean, look at him. What's he doing? He's just standing here to annoy us. He still thinks he can.'

'But he *is* a bit pale. Charles, are you well?'

'Answer her, boy!'

The question came to me late. I looked at them to say, 'No,' then my head snapped back to the lights dancing inside the bed-and-breakfast.

'Eamonn! Why did you slap him? Are you mad?'

'He's been asked a question.'

'Eamonn! Charles, I'm sorry.'

'Eamonn nothing! I'm tired of this. Do you really think Amber chose him? You must be joking. This man is . . . I don't know what he is. Maybe he's after her money. He could very well be a criminal hiding from the police, or something like that.'

'Eamonn, that's enough! Go now, go to work.'

When I became aware that the conversation had ended I looked back at the window and saw that Eamonn and Dora were gone. I found Dora standing next to me instead, and felt her arm slide round my waist. 'You cannot behave like this,' she said, with her face reaching up to mine. She didn't see the lights at the bed-and-breakfast – she was busy turning me round to face the main road. 'You need to be strong,' she said, 'you need to fight back. I'm sorry about what happened now. And I'm sorry you were mistreated last night. Your reaction was . . . it was understandable. I know my husband is tough to handle, but you have to do it for yourself and for me. For him too.' A door slammed shut and Eamonn walked heavily past the mouth of the alley. 'There he is now,' she whispered with her breakfast breath. 'Go after him. He's going to pull up his nets. Go with him. Convince him of who you are. You can't let him chase you away now. Amber will come back. Of course she will. I still believe in you.'

She tightened her hold on my waist with quick jerks, like electric shocks trying to revive me, but all the energy remained hers, and she had to find enough breath to drag me to the beach and speak encouraging words along the way that didn't, couldn't affect me any longer.

'Take Charles with you,' Dora said to Eamonn when we got to the beach.

He waved away her proposal.

I looked up at the hill. The front door of the bed-and-breakfast was open, and in the rectangle of light stood a black figure.

'Eamonn, you two have to make up if you are going to live in the same village. Charles, go with him.'

'No!' Eamonn protested. 'I'm going to work now. Why should he come with me?'

'Because you know why,' answered Dora, with clenched teeth. 'Charles?'

The figure up at the bed-and-breakfast had disappeared, maybe down the slope. I wasted no time checking. I leaped into Eamonn's boat. He protested and reached for me, but Dora held him by his jumper and snapped at him, then turned to me with a smile that I left unanswered.

I had no plans that might ensure her happiness. My only intention was to get as far away as possible from the bed-and-breakfast. Maybe I could convince Eamonn to let me off somewhere down the coast. I could even swim from the boat to shore if I had to. He would have no problem with that; on the contrary, I was sure he would enjoy it. I helped him push the boat into the water, then tried to get us moving with an oar, but he snatched it from my hands and began to row himself. I went to sit at the prow, looking at his angry gaze, but I was upset only by the slowness of his rowing.

After what felt like an endless period of time he pulled the oar on board and turned on the engine. The land bobbed further and further away in the morning mist. Dora watched us, immobile, and grew smaller as other fishermen appeared on the beach. On the hill a window was still shining. I looked for a slender figure walking down the slope, but I didn't see any, and soon we reached the headlands of the bay and everything disappeared past them.

We were far enough for me to feel some relief, but not safety. The distance we had covered was not enough, and I couldn't think of one that might rescue me from my failure and what it stood for.

Eamonn was impassive. The wind dug deep into his features and stuck his jumper to his body, flapping it at the edges. He looked past me as if I didn't exist. I shivered in the cold, and hated him because I knew the joy that would have brightened his face had he seen the lights at the bed-and-breakfast. He would have understood my distress at Amber's return, and would have had no further hesitation regarding my identity.

But he didn't deserve her! Nobody deserved Amber more than I did. Nobody had anything to offer her but a sordid relationship to be kept hidden in the shadows. I could give her much more than that, and for her sake I could sacrifice much more than anybody else. Hell, I thought, I was ready to live on my own at the bed-and-breakfast for the rest of my life, yes, the rest of my life, in order to be with her. But she had to spoil it all! What kind of sacrifice, what kind of commitment could be mine if she returned?

Eamonn veered right, moving slowly parallel to the coast. I looked in the other direction, at the open sea, a dark, creeping mass under an unpromising sky. A racing slab of leaden clouds had covered it almost completely. Hardly any light filtered from above; the day was reluctant, as if it saw no point in its own birth. The horizon was inevitably becoming sharper, though, a uniform straight line where sea and clouds pressed their distance into nothing.

'There's no island visible,' I said, almost to myself. A spark of something warm revived in me, but I didn't have the courage to turn and face Eamonn. 'Yes! The island where you picked her up. I can't see it. It's nowhere!'

Eamonn didn't answer.

I continued to scan the horizon and could see nothing more than a straight line. 'It doesn't exist, does it?'

'It's south,' he grunted, after a while. 'We're going north.'

I shuddered in the wind. What was this coming over me again? With dumb wonder I looked at my hands clinging on to the edge of the boat. I hardly noticed the two yellow buoys that had appeared on the water. Eamonn turned down the engine to a purr and veered in their direction. He stopped the boat at the first and pulled it on board. Empty squares of rope emerged with dripping locks of algae. The first fish looked exhausted already, gaping for water with unflinching eyes that spoke of bewilderment and pain, and a flipping tail that knew no hope but still could not accept defeat.

I looked up at Eamonn who didn't care, but I found myself staring at two dark shapes far behind him. At first I didn't understand what they were, but in a moment I knew.

They had crept up while I was looking away, and they hid behind Eamonn, playfully, because even at a distance of more than a mile he could not cover them completely. I knew right away that they had waited for my short-lived fantasies to pass, for me to see them again as the only answer to my problems, the real reason for my trip.

199

Eamonn moved to follow the net to the next buoy, and nothing stood between them and me. They tore from under a coast of grassy hills and jutted out into the water, rising vertiginously into two huge formations of brutal rock that kneed the sky and then sloped back to meet at the end of the cove they formed between them. Two massive twin headlands, spreading out from a darkness they sheltered. The enormity of it! I knew they were inanimate, but that rock seemed as alive as flesh, and waiting, demanding action. A wind blew invisibly between them and reached us like a whispered chant. All the waves under us, all the waves under the boats of the other fishermen who were somewhere picking up their own nets, were dragging us silently and patiently towards that dark cove. I felt a torment of guilt and fear inside me. Days earlier I had headed for the Cliffs to start a new life. I didn't know they looked like this, but it seemed to make sense now.

And just as I thought this, the Cliffs moved back behind Eamonn, who was pulling up his net and throwing it between us, fish hidden under mazes of ropes, and still the wet slapping of a frantic tail against the wood of the boat.

xiv

We travelled back to the beach, over waves as sharp as broken glass. The morning sun failed to produce anything more than a faint glow. All the lights were out at the bed-and-breakfast, but a window was open and flapping in the wind. I leaped out of the boat as soon as it touched the sand and left without saying goodbye. Eamonn yelled something after me, but I paid no attention to him. I should have asked him to drop me off down the coast, but I was overwhelmed by a sense of urgency that only the speed of my car could satisfy. I stumbled more than ran down the main road, but I was frightened by the idea of climbing the naked hillside to get to my car. I saw flashes of the slope at the end of the alleys, and I searched for the courage to turn into one. I ran past a house that was to be the last, then another, and then one more. All of a sudden a door was flung open as I passed it and an arm reached out and grabbed me.

'Did everything go well?'

'Dora!'

'It's me. Everything went well?'

'Let me go.'

'Where to? What did he tell you?'

'Nothing. We said nothing. Let me go now.' I pulled my arm but couldn't free it.

'You're not leaving, are you?'

I didn't answer.

'You have to come in here,' she said, and dragged me in before I could react. She shut the door behind us and pressed her back against it, her fingers crawling on the woodwork to find its edge. She stood there, hanging on to the door frame, and then spoke. 'Amber came here often.'

I looked around quickly. Door to the left. Stairs leading up. Empty. 'She's not here.'

'No, but she came here often.'

'She might come again.'

'Not while you're here.'

'So this is a safe place?'

'What?'

'Nothing,' I said. 'Nothing. I just need to go. I can't stay any longer.'

'Nonsense,' she almost growled, and her fingers tensed like claws. 'I know what you're like. I feel as if I know everything about you since my husband attacked you last night. You don't hide well enough who you are.' Her head unglued itself from the front door and hovered closer to me through the shadows. Her whole body followed, and I backed away from her.

'I know what you're like,' she repeated. 'You're so easy to read. You are . . . how can I put it? You're too honest.' She raised a reassuring hand. 'Mind you, it's not a fault. The other women of the village were as impressed with you as I was. We stopped dreaming so long ago, but last night . . . what you said . . . You're a dream come true for Amber, your love for her, the way you made everything between you two so romantic. Even too romantic. Your feelings honour you, but they also make you weak.'

She continued to follow me as I backed into the living room. The air was stuffy and the furniture loomed out of the shadows. I tripped against something, and saw I had knocked over a pile of books. Red and bright pink covers fanned out, pictures of stormy embraces between ladies and their lovers. Other piles dotted the room, I saw them now, towers of romances rising from the floor.

'My husband said you only talked dirty last night, but how can I believe him? The men of this village are not like you, Charles. We always wanted men like you, but we accepted who we had. Our husbands are not bad people, but they might be jealous, no, not jealous, but . . . unfrieṇ.dly, I should say. And with your honesty and good heart you don't know how to deal with them. That's why, last night, you reacted as you did, isn't it? Maybe you shouldn't even listen to my flattery or the other women's. It might make you too comfortable when you should learn how to defend yourself.'

An hour earlier I would have laughed with joy at what she was saying, but I could only despair at hearing about my success now that I had to give it up because of Amber's return. 'Why do you have to tell me this?' I said.

'I want to help,' she answered. 'I want you to see this house. It was my older sister's, the one you said Amber told you about. These books were hers,' she said, passing a finger tenderly over the cover of one. 'My sister spent a life dreaming. She thought she could live as if she was in one of her books, and she died alone. She waited for perfection, but what is there to wait for in a village like this?'

I wanted to shut her up, I wanted to leave, but I found myself standing there mute and frantic, incapable of dragging my eyes away from those horrid covers.

'I brought Amber here,' she said, speaking faster this time because she had become aware of my distress. 'When she used to eat at my house she told me she liked to read so I thought she might be interested in this stuff. And she was. She kept on borrowing books. I'm very protective about this house, but she was so sweet and so keen on reading that I gave her the key so she could come here any time she wanted to. Then a year ago she stopped coming down to the village, but she still came here at night. I know because I came here myself from time to time, and I saw books missing. Amber believed in the ideal man, like my sister did, but I thought *she* could find him, because with the bed-and-breakfast she would meet a lot of people, and hopefully one day the right one would come by and take her away with him. I thought she was young and she could wait. But when you're expecting something, you feel so much inside and you can't wait, and you need a release for all of it, or a substitute. You see the paintings?' Slowly I raised my eyes from the books, and I saw that the walls were covered with tacky pictures of Jesus with benevolent smiles and with bright, bleeding hearts hovering inside hollow chests. And there were crucifixes, a Virgin Mary under a glass bell jar, saints as candleholders, a flowerpot with Jesus's face in relief. 'My sister became more and more pious over the years,' said Dora. 'She found her substitute in religion. But Amber never went the same way, and what other options did she have in a town like this? You understand, don't you?'

I understood, I already knew, and now I also knew which lock would fit the key I had tried to destroy and that still lay under the ashes in the fireplace, but to what avail? I looked around at the towers of books, afraid to know that one was missing and that Amber was bringing it back now.

'I was getting worried,' Dora continued, 'and then rumours started to spread. Rumours about her. I thought she couldn't be allowed to stay. And I wasn't the only one who thought that. The other women . . . they thought the same. They were angry.

'But then you came that first time months ago. Not one

book was touched here after we heard about you. She didn't need to read this stuff any longer, she had found her prince, and all she felt inside she would now give to you.' She pointed a finger at me and shook it in a vague, reproachful manner. 'We all waited for your return,' she said. 'There were fewer rumours going about, and so many hopes, but I was so impatient, so anxious, and I wasn't the only one. The other women . . . again . . . Everybody was impatient. And Amber . . . After a few days I began to think you were just some bastard who had made promises he wouldn't keep. But everybody continued to wait. The tension—'

'You didn't believe in my return,' I shouted, 'and you still don't believe in hers. Are you trying to convince yourself? Why am I listening to you when I have to go?'

She held up her hands to prevent me moving, but I shook my head, standing there in that clutter of religious paraphernalia and romantic novels. 'Convince myself?' she said. 'No, no. You have to stay. She . . . she will be back one day. She will. She cannot just abandon her bed-and-breakfast, can she? Think about that. She needs to come back at least to settle the house, maybe to sell it. And she'll find you here, won't she? You're her hero, her dream come true. You can't leave.'

Was I her dream come true when she had to be mine? Yes, I thought, maybe I had fulfilled her dream in the eyes of all, but had raped it in hers. Maybe there could be forgiveness, but past it there could be no sunny solution. I remembered those lights on the hill, and I shuddered at the thought of her seeing me again.

The Cliffs, I had to get to the Cliffs.

I made for the door but Dora leaped to stop me. I tried to dodge her but she moved faster and grabbed my arm. I struggled, she held me tighter, I punched her fingers to weaken her grip. We wrestled, filled with desperation, and knocked something down that hit the floor with a crash and broke. 'Let me go, you old cow,' I shouted, blind with rage as I pushed her away from me. She flew backwards, tumbling against a cupboard. Plates and saints rattled violently inside. She looked at me with eyes I had never seen, and my image in them, I was sure, had changed forever. I didn't care. A second later I was out of the house.

Jim's van was a short way off with its back doors open. Eamonn was standing there with Jim, handing him an envelope. He turned round when he heard me, and tried to hide what he was doing. I paid no attention. I had no time for his letters, for whatever scheming he had devised to undo me, because nothing could make things any worse.

I had to get to the Cliffs, I told myself. There, everything would be all right. The Cliffs would heal me. The Cliffs were my only hope. I ran up the cold hillside to the bed-and-breakfast, trying to stay hidden by keeping low. The house was spectral, and now two windows were open and swinging in the wind, but I couldn't see if anybody was behind them watching my approach. The cracked boards of the walls grinned like fangs, and I felt the whole village hurrying silently after me with rapacious intent. My fears and the inclination of the hill set my heart racing in my throat, and I nearly choked on it when I saw the outline of an old, pale green car parked in front of the house.

At first I could only look at it with horror and bewilderment, and in a moment I knew whose car it was. It was Charles's car. I was sure it could only be his. My arrival at the bed-and-breakfast must have heightened Amber's desire to be with him again, and she had left to look for him. I had caused my own demise, but saw no irony in this because it was horribly in tune with the rest of my life.

I leaped into my car and started the engine. I backed onto

the road, jerked into first gear and pressed the accelerator flat. The wheels rotated on the spot, shooting up gravel. The door of the house opened. The wheels found their grip and I was off.

I didn't dare to look at the person who had opened the door. I could only look ahead now. At first I felt the fear of being hunted down by that green car, then a craving to get to my destination as fast as possible. The road felt familiar, the rutted surface, the hills coming one after another, the anxiety for the view the next ridge might reveal. It was terror more than anxiety, but I was desperate with the sense of waste and failure I felt inside, and I could see no other solution. It was an ashen morning, and it didn't rain, although the clouds were black and swollen, but I drove as if I had never left the steering-wheel since that first night. And when the road flowed into the larger, smoother one I had missed a few days earlier, the detour I had taken was fully behind me.

The Cliffs appeared soon after, past the hills still ahead. They grew larger as the landscape between them and me continued to change. I could barely take my eyes off them, and I only just managed to keep the road under me. The Cliffs continued to grow till I believed they would blot out all else, and suddenly the road eased itself down a valley shaped like a bowl from where the Cliffs rose, projecting up and out into the sea.

In the middle of the bowl, between the road and the low saddle of the Cliffs, the grass had been scraped out to produce a large car park. It had a semblance of a gate, with a cabin and two barriers for entering and leaving, but both were up and the cabin was empty. I drove in quickly and parked. With a ghastly sound the gravel ground to a halt beneath the car's wheels, and I was finally there.

I got out. A cold wind cut into me and brought the faint

sound of waves breaking against the coast. Nobody was around, not a soul. There was not even an abandoned car.

Past the end of the car park, towards the sea, slabs of rock stabbed the ground and formed the parapet of a path that led to the Cliffs' saddle. I walked down it, shooting frightened glances ahead. The sound of waves grew more insistent. I felt like crying and my legs were weak, but I walked on. A few feet from the edge the path lost the parapet and turned, fading as it rose, towards a small tower on top of the Cliff to the right. I left the path and continued straight towards the edge of the saddle. Two steps, and the grass under my feet had turned to stone, two more, and the stone disappeared and the Cliffs opened up in front of me. There was an immense gorge of grey and brown and red rock, inanimate but alive with the carvings of the past that had broken against it, dotted by unlikely patches of moss and grass that clung to the ancient surfaces, and with birds, like specks, that spiralled down or up before returning to a ledge, as if the tremendous height made them dizzy.

My fear of heights made me panic. At the bottom, waves crashed into the gorge, drifted out and regenerated. Foam exploded and formed again, and a stinging drizzle flew up. The wind pressed my clothes to me and they clung, glued by my cold sweat. I could have climbed to the top of one of the Cliffs instead of stopping here at the saddle, but having the rock on three sides filled me with a sense of enclosure I wouldn't have felt further up.

I swayed in the wind, and my panic became terror, but I couldn't turn back now, nor could I waste any more time. I sat down, my legs dangling over the edge. My hands were sweating and the rock felt slippery under them. It made me shudder, but I did not hesitate. I turned round and lay on my stomach, my feet projecting over the void. I looked at the ground beneath my face as I crawled backwards, and I sought comfort in it, as in the hug of an old friend. My knees rubbed and moved past the sharp edge. The rock crawled up my thighs, slowly, my body became lighter, and the ground started to move away from under my face. My hips became the fulcrum of my weight, the rock cut into them, and the wind made my body dangle like the beam of a scale.

Gravity pulled me, my hips scraped downwards, then my stomach, and my lower ribs anchored on the edge. I didn't move for a long time. I barely breathed, frightened to lose my grasp on the rock, but the smell of salt water seeped into me until I felt sick with it. My feet trembled as they searched for ledges. I made a wrong move and slipped.

I saw the ground in front of me, every detail, soil, imperfections in the rock, patches of lichen and moss too insubstantial to hang on to, and the earth was mapped, my hands racing for gripping points. I could feel my legs, my feet, their brief moments of contact with the Cliffs, every touch mapping a new area in my mind.

The clarity of it! After my delusions, this experience felt unreal, it ran through my arms and down my body with ripples of vertigo. I hung on. I tried to breathe, but for a long time I couldn't. My chin was pressed against the edge, my arms were still over it, my shoulders raised high on the sides of my head. This was more than enough, something inside me was saying, but I wouldn't listen.

I continued to lower myself. My body jerked as it moved further down, and my teeth clung to the edge. They scraped the rock with a deathly screeching. 'No, no,' I drooled onto the already damp ground, and suddenly I bit into the air. The open view ahead of me was gone.

My arms didn't resist for much longer. Soon they followed me past the edge. My nose rubbed downwards against the wet rock and stopped against a fetid patch of dead moss. Both my palms were flat against the vertical drop, my fingers hooked in two tiny crevices. My right foot had found a hole and was nailed in it, my left had found nothing but an imperceptible curve in the stone further up and stood flat over it, my leg raised like that of a dog about to urinate. I began to piss like one, a painful, hot trickle. I retched and an acid taste burned my throat, but nothing came out of my mouth. The sound of waves below continued to rise, echoing in the gorge, and a violent drizzle stung me like needles.

I was sobbing. I tried to control myself but I couldn't. My hands were growing weak, and I felt helpless. Slowly I got my head unstuck from the wall. I looked down under my left armpit, past my body to see what stood beyond.

There was nothing anywhere close, just the void. The rock disappeared and re-emerged much further down, rough and imperfect, growing darker as it raced towards the water. I imagined falling, and the wall of the gorge flashing past, moving closer and further away as I sped down, till I would touch it, gently at first, and then again and again, harder each time, and spin and tumble down till all my limbs were shattered and every organ of my body had exploded.

The vision overwhelmed me. I hung on with fingers and toes too cold and numb for me even to feel them. I giggled hysterically, I shouted, then the wind slapped me back against the Cliff and all the air was punched out of my lungs.

This was it. This panic, this situation. It was why I had come to the Cliffs. This was my revenge against my cowardly nature. I didn't lower myself past the edge to die, but to live or die trying. My mind turned in all directions and was baffled at finding that nothing it had done in the past would help now. I couldn't dodge this experience, it was action or death this time, and I wanted to see if I could give in to the latter as I had continuously in the past, because a concession to it now would have been total, not just another hour, another day, another year of wasted life.

Inside me I felt evolutions I didn't think possible. I was still scared stiff, but my blood was pumping with purpose and my limbs were tense. I focused on how to reach the edge. I moved a finger, secured a foot better, and suddenly I felt emotional and in awe of my efforts. I ignored a ledge too narrow for a foot, I laughed at the drops of ice-cold sweat itching down my cheeks, and I was filled with the desire not to have the dead moss pressed against my face.

I pushed myself up with an excess of confidence, and my shoes slipped on the wet rock. My fingers hung on to the edge, desperately, my nails scratching and breaking against the stone. For a moment I gave in to resignation, and imagined again my body hundreds of feet further down.

No. I was still there. Focus. Be calm. Calm and focused. Calm attention focused on where you are and on where you want to get to. Purpose. No resignation. I readjusted a hand at a time, looking for better holds. My fingers were frozen, but I could still feel them if I pressed them hard against the rock. I moved my legs carefully, searching for a sharp projection. I felt one and raised a foot to it. I tested the new position, then pushed myself up.

I felt regenerated, as if restored to a life of action and presence that had never been mine. I saw the rock move under my face and my arms bend as if pulling the edge down closer to me. I was almost there. I wasted no time in making my other foot search for another hold, but I couldn't find one. I had no other choice but to look for it with my eyes.

Far, far down I saw the water slamming against the walls of the gorge. My eyes shut instinctively. No. Another hold. Success breeds success. A good start is a job half done.

Sentences I had written down and learned by heart. They had been of no real use up to now. I opened my eyes again and saw only the rock close to me, and the ledge I was looking for was not far behind.

I pushed myself further up. Just above my face the edge was a thin line of light between rock and sky. One forearm slammed past it and my fingers crawled quickly in search of a new hold. The other arm came up, then a foot rose to a new projection of rock and pushed, and the gentle, horizontal ground I had left a few minutes earlier opened up in front of me again, but I saw it with new eyes. My chest pressed against the edge. One more foothold and I would be over. I took my time. I took more time than I needed, to be sure. I found the hold, I secured my foot, I put pressure on it to test it, then I took a deep breath and my upper body was over.

I crawled forward and stood up. I was frozen, I was aching and bruised, but I didn't care. My body shook with victory and success. I raised my arms, laughed and shouted. I was new.

XV

'What the hell are you doing?' said a voice. A young man was running up the path. 'You didn't slip, did you?'

The sound of waves was diffused and pleasant like a reward, and my blood was still pounding through my body. 'Something like that.'

'Jesus, you damn tourists, you . . .' He stopped and a finger rose to point at me. 'Charlie! What the fuck? It's you. I . . . I . . .'

'Hello, Chris,' I said.

He didn't know what to say. He walked up to me and, putting a hand on my arm, glanced into the gorge. 'Are you OK?' he asked. I nodded. He looked at me from head to foot. I did the same. My body was streaked with mud and wet patches. 'God, you're a mess,' he said. 'I mean, what's with the rock climbing?'

'I wasn't rock climbing.'

'Well, no. Flirting with death more like. To say the least.'

'Say I spat in its face.'

He looked at me quizzically, his hands on his hips. 'Well, somebody threw a bucket of shit at you in return,' he said. He seemed amused more than anything else. 'Here, I've got tissues. God, I'm happy to see you, but really, I didn't recognize you with all that muck you're wearing. Where's the usual respectable young man? You seem like a wild version of yourself.'

I smiled at that. 'Thanks,' I said.

'You're welcome.' There was genuine curiosity in his eyes, and for a while he looked as if he was trying to place me, recognize me, even. 'God, it *has* been a long time since I last saw you.' He slapped my shoulder. 'I'm sorry I reacted like that but, fuck, people have slipped before. We had this American guy a year ago and he fell down or threw himself over, I don't know which, and the police gave me a lot of hassle, because I was around, because I work here . . . shit like that. It's not my fault if the rocks get slippery and people get too close to the edge. Tourist safety is not my business.'

I thought of how he must have felt as he was falling, the infinite desire he must have had to go back just a few seconds, to be more careful. The way he would have blessed and filled every second of his life had he been offered the chance to continue living.

'Poor guy,' I said.

'Oh, yeah,' said Chris. 'Poor bastard.'

I laughed. 'Well, I'm happy I didn't slip as far as he did.'

'Hell, me too.'

'And I'm more than happy to be here,' I said. 'I have to thank you for that call.'

'For the . . . oh, sure. It's good you finally made it over.'

I have a vague recollection of the day when he called me before I made this fateful trip, a memory of a dark room with rain beating against the window. There was something condensed about my life in that moment, as if nothing had ever been different, as if nothing had existed before. I was prey to one of my increasingly frequent moments of despair and anger, for how I was, for how I could be. The phone's ringing tore past the darkness. I answered, and I listened to Chris as he told me how long it was since we had seen each other, about the town where he lived, about his new job and the place where he worked. I didn't say a word about my state, I barely spoke, but I listened to him as to an oracle speaking directly inside my head, and when I hung up, all his words fell off like flesh ripped from a bone, and all that was left was the image of the Cliffs, and my mind was obsessed with it.

And here I was, and it was done, and I was new.

'It really *has* been a while since we last met,' I said.

A smile grew on his face. 'Ages, man, ages. I would hug you but I'd rather give you my whole pack of tissues.'

I wiped my face some more, and then my clothes. My piss stain was disguised in the general dampness of my attire, so I didn't worry about it.

The day had finally dawned behind the clouds. In the distance a few cars dotted the car park and tourists were coming up the path. An old couple in bright rain-jackets had already reached us. The woman eagerly sought the view of the Cliffs, and then turned to us with a camera in her hand. I was closest to her. She gave me an uneasy look, and I felt she was put off more by my expression than by my dirty clothes. She hesitated, then turned to Chris and asked him to take a picture of her and her husband.

He took the camera from her and got them to stand close to the edge where I had lowered myself. From behind the camera he asked them to take a step back. 'And one more,' he said.

The woman was about to move when her husband stopped her. 'Marsha, be careful,' he said. 'We're on the edge.'

Chris took the picture as the man was still speaking. 'Here you go,' he said, and gave the camera to the woman, who took it with a trembling hand. The man looked angry. He took his wife's arm and they left without a word. 'Sorry about the edge,' Chris shouted after them. 'I didn't see it.' He turned to me and laughed. 'People are so stupid. I like to joke, but I expect them to understand that. A step back! Did she want to be in the picture or not? Jeez, Marsha. And that guy last year. What a total idiot.'

'You mean you . . .'

He looked at me with a smile. 'What? Do you think I'm a murderer?' He laughed. 'Nice opinion you have of your friends. Come on, let's go.' He pointed at the tower on top of the Cliff to the right. 'I told you about my castle, and now it's time for you to see it.'

I had known Chris since school, and for years we had lived in the same city. He had moved more than a year earlier, and we had lost contact before his fateful phone call. He considered me one of his best friends, and he never seemed to notice that I was his opposite. It was so disarming the way he looked for me every time he wanted to go out, that I began to think I was giving him the right signals, so maybe I *was* like him, deep down. More than once I went out with him hoping to stumble upon my true self, but I never did. I was always a pale, frustrated shadow next to him, but I owed him a lot. It was thanks to him that for years I had kept alive a feeble faith in my potential, and now I felt that maybe he was the only thing from my past that I still wanted to keep.

I looked at him as we walked up the Cliff, at how he approached every moment of life never stumbling forward, with plans aimed only at having fun, and without plots against the world. I felt I had no more reason to plot against the world either. There was a lack of morality in him, but during the last week I had lost that myself. He had so much confidence, and now I had that too, and I was happier than he was because I knew how life could be otherwise.

'We are alike,' I said to him. 'Almost the same, you and I.'

'You're right. I'm a bit cleaner, though. And I blame you for not having kept in touch. But, fucking hell, what a surprise to find you here.'

We walked the last stretch exchanging small-talk. The tower was a circular stone construction twenty feet high. Chris unlocked the iron gate that served as a door and we walked in. The interior was a single round room faintly lit by two small windows and filled with souvenirs and postcard stands. A cash desk stood on the right under one of the windows, and opposite the door was an iron spiral staircase that must have led to the roof. 'This is my domain,' he said, spanning it with a hand. He threw himself down on a chair and put his feet on the desk. 'Not much, but what can I ask for? I never did jack shit at uni so I shouldn't complain.'

'Do you ever feel the need to go home?'

'Does this place look that shit?'

'No, it's nice.'

'Don't worry,' he said, 'I'm just joking. Well, I suppose I do at times. I must say, I felt a bit like a deserter leaving. What made me come so far in the first place?'

'A woman,' I said.

'Being stupid, more like. I mean, I like where I live now, it's a nice town, but really I have no more reason to be here now that it's over with that . . . What should I call her? Especially since this is the only job I could find. Not very eventful, unless we have Americans skydiving.' He dropped his hand on to the table with a thump. 'Every man his own partner, that's what I say. Well, how's your job going? Still writing away? I see your stuff every night on TV. At least, I'm convinced I can still recognize your touch. I bet it was you who came up with that advertisement for a mobile where the girl snaps it shut against her cleavage.'

I nodded.

'I was right! I'm faced with the great puppeteer himself,' he rejoiced, pulling invisible strings and then bowing mockingly.

'And they wanted me as assistant director for that commercial,' I said.

'Oh, promotion as well – or is it?'

'Something like that.'

'They say the market has crossed the line of decency with these commercials, and I agree. But I'm your friend, and I stand up for your work. I think it's innovative. Pornography turning into socially accepted dinnertime sketches. Very nice, although it kind of makes you forget the food on your plate.'

A man with blue waterproof overalls and a black bag walked in. He saw us there, and he moved to the other end of the shop, where he inspected postcards from behind thick glasses. 'But you have to think about us too,' Chris said, pretending to be hurt, pointing at himself and then at the man. 'You have to think about us so far removed. You get to be assistant director, even. You're right there. But us common mortals . . . It's not nice of you to impose your fantasies on us.'

'Well, I quit. That should make you happy.'

'You what?' His feet dropped down from the counter. 'You're not letting me down, are you? I'm here in this oversized hole thinking what a ball you must have sitting in a room paid to think about what would trigger your erotic fantasies and you quit?'

'It took me a long time, but finally I managed it.'

'You managed? What do you mean "managed"?'

I didn't answer.

'What, did the director get all the credit? You helped him film your own work and he got your dream models? Or did you run out of ideas?'

'It doesn't really matter. It's the past.'

'Well, I suppose it is now. "Like scenes behind a glass. So close yet so far." I read it somewhere.' He crossed his hands behind his head. 'But wow, you walked out.' He stared blankly at the man in the overalls, who was wandering around aimlessly. 'Well, I suppose, never mind the past, you even had your present behind a lens, or a piece of paper, didn't you? Too long on the wrong side. I don't think you're enough of a voyeur to enjoy that.'

'I don't fantasize any more,' I said.

'Well, that's you,' he said, turning to me, 'but for us your commercials are still on the air. I'm still trying to figure out how to get those women you've invented. But first of all, are they virgins or whores? I must say you've got those two flavours well blended. It gives them an attitude I'd love to fuck out of them. Problem is, I don't think I could get anywhere close to them. I don't have a mobile, I don't drive the right car . . . I use the right aftershave, but maybe I don't drink enough beer. And now that you've quit I won't know what else I need to do.'

He laughed again. The man in the overalls came up to the desk. Chris looked at me with a smile and made him wait before turning to ask him what he wanted. The man spoke timid words I didn't catch. 'Upstairs,' said Chris, and turned back to me when the man's footsteps clanged up the iron staircase. 'A bird-watcher,' he told me. 'We've got binoculars upstairs. Have you ever observed a fucking bird? Watching paint dry is almost as entertaining. And I bet that guy's got some nifty camera in that bag of his. Won't get any nice pics of cleavages like you would, though. What I just don't under-stand is how their watching doesn't put some fire in their arses. Get hands-on business with real birds, if you know what I mean.'

'Are we going out tonight?' I asked.

'That's the way I want you,' he cheered. 'But what's the story? I mean, seriously. Are you on holiday or what?'

'I told you, I left.'

'So you're serious about that?'

'Why should I lie?'

'OK, OK, so what, you are . . .'

'Passing by.'

'Passing by. Where're you staying?'

'Your place?'

'Sounds good. You just have to be a bit patient. I close at six. Maybe you can help me handle the immensely small number of tourists that visit this shop.' He sighed. 'Luckily I don't get paid according to sales, which would improve considerably if I had some light in here and my clients could see what they could buy. But then again maybe they wouldn't. I mean, look at this,' he said, picking up a ceramic model of the Cliffs. 'Who'd want something like this on a shelf? It's tacky and it looks like a pair of legs spread open.' He held his chin between thumb and forefinger in a fake thoughtful posture. 'On the other hand, maybe a lot of people would want it.'

Silence filled the shop. Faint sounds came from upstairs. My body still ached. If I closed my eyes I could see my bruises pulse like traffic-lights in the night. I licked my lips and a vague taste of salt water was still there. 'I did it!' I whispered.

'What?'

'Nothing,' I answered, curbing my enthusiasm. 'Nothing, don't worry.' The shop was bleak and I felt it didn't deserve me. 'What about going now?' I asked.

'Go where?'

'Go out. Let's hit the town.'

'At ten in the morning?'

'What's wrong with that?'

He thought about it a bit. 'Yes, why not? We haven't met in years! I'll call in sick or something, and then I'll take you for a fucking spin, what do you say?' He rubbed his hands together. 'It's been a while since I started drinking this early.' He got up and walked to the bottom of the stairs. 'Hey, you, bird-watcher. The tower's closing.'

A pair of boots appeared at the top of the stairs, followed by a faint protest.

'Sorry,' said Chris. 'Special hours today. You've had your naughty little peek.'

The man in the overalls came down the stairs and trotted to the door under Chris's push. 'How rude,' he said.

'Yeah, well. This happens. We have some bird-watching to do ourselves. Birds of a different kind.' He winked at me. 'Let's go, Charlie.'

We walked outside. I welcomed the open air, the white, smeared glow that shone through the clouds ahead. A few tourists were coming up the slope and hesitated when they saw Chris locking the gate. 'Closed, closed,' he shouted, waving his arms.

'Well,' he said, turning to me, 'it looks like I was going to sell more than one postcard today. But tell me, what does this "passing by" you were talking about really mean? It sounds like you didn't come here just to see me.'

'It's a long story.'

'We have time,' he said, as we started walking down the slope.

I looked across the gorge at the other Cliff. Shivers of fear and pleasure ran through me, and the stability of the Cliff under my feet felt strange, almost impossible. 'I had a little fling,' I said.

'Oh, great. Better small than big. Which is also my policy on tits. Well, I want to hear all about it.'

'It's just some girl . . . in a village close by . . . It was all a bit odd.'

'I wouldn't expect you to get together with any type of girl,' said Chris smiling. 'Or with any type of village. I've seen on TV the magnitude of what turns you on.'

I didn't say anything. We walked on down the Cliff. The wind pressed my damp trousers against my legs. I looked at myself and saw that the wet patches were still there, although fading, and the mud was drying.

Chris put a hand on my arm. 'I'm waiting,' he said.

I hesitated. He insisted. He tugged at my arm jokingly, and soon I found myself telling him about Amber, her arrival from the island, her two years in the village, the men's interest and the women's jealousy. At first I spoke haltingly, frightened to remember, but the story came to me quickly and brought with it no emotion, as if I was as foreign to it as I should always have been.

'Randy old buggers,' said Chris, of the village men.

'I think even the priest went to look for her once, but from what I understood he didn't enjoy his visit.'

'Maybe she didn't like being lectured on morals. But where do you come into the picture?'

My days in the village were behind me. They had been mine, and in a strange, unconscious way. I wanted to bend down and caress the Cliffs with gratitude, but I smiled to myself, and I thought it no harm to remember my past in the village with the amusement of recalling a dream. 'Well,' I said, 'half-way during her year of solitude a rumour spread that she had fallen in love with one of her guests. A certain Charles.'

'You?'

I was not sure what to answer. I felt no emotion towards my past, but what past was I putting behind me? 'Yes,' I said eventually. 'All the village men were pretty upset. And then I came back about a week ago.'

'And?'

'And nothing. She left the day I arrived. I stayed on and had some fun with the villagers.'

'Fun?'

'Just fun. I was being silly.'

'Got some attention from what I can deduce.'

'Admiration, envy . . .' I said casually.

'The voyeur turns exhibitionist.'

'What?'

'Nothing. You were playing with people's feelings.'

'As I said, I was just being silly.'

'Well, so what happened? Sounds like you left for good.'

'She left before me. She left when I got there. That's not the way I want to be treated. I got more attention from the villagers than from her.'

'Because of her.'

'Whatever. I just couldn't be bothered to wait any longer.'

'The heat of the spotlights.'

'What?'

'Your makeup was starting to melt.'

I watched him smile at me. I had the impression he saw beyond my words, and it wasn't the first time I had felt that. Maybe it was me, maybe I was transparent. But I had changed. I *had* changed.

'So she left. And where did she go?'

'I don't know,' I said. I didn't want to talk about it any more. I began to feel that I had already talked about it too much.

He thought about it for a while. 'Ah, my little Amber!'

he said then. 'What uncaring behaviour towards my best friend!'

I was speechless. I was about to tumble forward, oblivious of where I was stepping. 'You know her name?' I asked.

'Oh, I know many things.'

'How do you know her name?'

'Hey, relax. Are you jealous? You said you left her, right?'

I controlled myself. I looked around for her, I looked at the tourists, trying to see if any familiar faces were grinning at me from under a cap or above the raised collar of a jacket.

Chris laughed. 'I know her very well,' he said. 'That barman you were talking about, Tom if I'm not mistaken, came to the Cliffs about a year ago. For some reason he introduced himself to me, said he would be around quite often for some surveys on the rocks, as if I cared. He used the binoculars up at the tower a couple of times with the other bird-watcher geeks. I think he told me he was writing his thesis on mineralogy or something like that, and that he was staying at the village down the country road. So one day I thought of paying him a visit.'

'You went to pay *him* a visit?'

'Well, not him. When he was here he couldn't stop talking about this girl who was running the bed-and-breakfast. I got the picture, so I went there one day after work. It was just after the American incident, and I was stressed out and needed a break, but I didn't find Tom or the girl there. I went down to the local pub and found him behind the bar. I don't think he was happy to see me. And the villagers! God, rough crowd. I'm impressed you stayed so long. A pack of hungry wolves drooling over their beer. OK, that village is isolated, but it was like visiting another world. I had at least a dozen pairs of eyes on me all the time. They kind of moved from me to her, to see if mine were on her too. She was serving – quite a woman, I must say.'

'So you know her?'

'Do I know her? I fucked her.'

I stopped. He took a couple more steps and then stopped too.

'You did what?'

'This was long before she met you,' he added.

'You fucked her?'

'There was nothing better to do in that place.'

'But weren't you with that woman you came here for?'

'So?'

'What do you mean "so"?'

He smiled.

'You fucked her!'

His smile burst into laughter. 'Not just that. I had to go back to kill her because she betrayed me with you. A year later, but still. It was easy and I didn't even have a hard time getting rid of her afterwards. You know, you can throw a body into the water here at a certain time of night, and the tide sucks it out into the open sea where it can't be found.' He laughed again. 'Well, hopefully none of your fishermen friends fished her out.'

I looked at him without saying anything. He laughed one more time. 'What?' he said. 'Do you really think I'm a murderer?' He continued to walk towards the car park. 'Nice opinion you have of your mates.'

I realized we had already passed the place where I had lowered myself. I looked back for traces of what I had done, but Chris kept on walking and I ran after him. 'And the rest?' I asked.

'What about it?'

'You had sex with her.'

225

'Yeah, while shouting, "You'll never get a piece of this" to all the village men I had invited over to watch.' He gave me a gentle shove. 'You're too gullible, Charlie. Don't believe everything you're told.'

'But you could have given her a lift home, and from there . . .'

'I did give her a lift home.'

'And then?'

'And then nothing. I went home by myself. I'm a realist, I knew I didn't have a chance. She didn't show any interest in me. Didn't invite me up. And that bed-and-breakfast looked a bit too creepy for my tastes. The whole village was much too weird.' He laughed. 'I don't want to have sex with a ghost or be chased about by her friends, you know. And for most of the evening I thought they were trying to lynch me. I got quite a kick from driving her home under everybody's noses, but I didn't want my luck to run out. Don't worry, I left her as pure as a virgin. For you to deflower.' He slapped an arm around me and hugged me to him. 'Ah, what I do for my friends, even unconsciously!'

I said nothing. We had reached the car park. I walked over to my car and Chris to his. Several others were now scattered about, just here and there, clusters of two or three. I turned to the Cliffs one last time, two heavy outlines against the clouds, with slender black figures moving along their edges. I still felt thrilled by what I had done, and I was glad I had done it. I looked at myself, at my clothes still marked, and told myself the experience had seeped into my body.

Then, as I was driving out of the car park after Chris, something new that I couldn't place began to disturb me. It wasn't until a minute later, when we were already on the road, that I realized what it was. The pale green car I had seen at the bed-and-breakfast had been in the car park too, and the more I thought about it the more I had the distinct memory of somebody inside it, watching me as I drove past.

XVI

I overtook Chris. I saw a surprised but pleased face in my rear-view mirror, but then I accelerated and his face grew puzzled and small, swallowed up in the frame of his car. He struggled to keep up with me. From time to time I slowed down a bit, but a car would appear far behind Chris's and I would accelerate again.

I couldn't tell whether it was the green car. The light was too feeble to bring out colours at a distance, but I was sure I saw a smudge of green on the road, even emerald at one stage, as an improbable ray of light fell on that car as it glided down a hill. I drove on fast and told myself that my pursuer was probably no pursuer but a tourist who had stopped at the bed-and-breakfast and moved on having found it empty. I told myself this, but in the back of my mind I knew it was Charles.

I drove on faster. The road continued to rise and fall over the hills, but after each rise it dipped a bit lower. A few cars began to stream from the opposite direction. I took it as a good sign.

A long time passed before houses began to appear, scattered and isolated, almost too white in the pale glow of the day. A few more miles and the houses were more frequent, the hills had gone and a huge bay opened up in front of me. The land that surrounded it was irregular, like a carpet not stretched out properly. The water of the bay was dotted with long shapes, boats of different kinds moving away or towards the geometric arms of a harbour located at the innermost point. The city touched the sea there like a gigantic animal that had crawled from inland for a drink of water. It had died, but its carcass had mouldered and outgrown itself. Ribs and bones had turned to buildings, modified and expanded, discoloured and riddled with holes. Its tail, which stretched back into the land from which it had come, had been cut open, and a flux of cars ran where its ancient blood once flowed.

I raced down the last slope and dived into the dull maze of buildings. I moved deeper and deeper towards the centre, and forgot to check whether Chris was still behind me. He had stopped honking, realizing that it served no purpose, and I paid little attention to what flashed in my rear-view mirror. I kept my eyes peeled for unexpected turnings, for narrow alleys, for newly blossomed red lights I could zip past, anything that would help me shake off anybody on my tail. When I finally stopped, though, I saw that Chris had followed me – but only just, judging from the way he stepped out of his car.

'Are you totally insane?' he shouted.

Surely I had shaken off anybody else.

'What was the point of driving like that? And I was supposed to show you my city. We've practically seen it all with your zigzagging.'

I looked around anyway. We were in a busy street. Pubs and restaurants flanked it, cosy places with glass walls that separated them from the cold day outside. People moved quickly on the pavement, wading past others. A man stood with a child in his arms in front of a billboard, pointing at it, apparently teaching the child to read. Traffic was stuck at a red light. I recognized nothing and nobody and was happy. I began to feel that the green car and its brooding driver would not find me.

I turned to Chris to apologize. I laughed, slapped him on the shoulder and told him it had been a joke.

'Hell of a crap joke. I nearly crashed.' He snorted. 'Anyway, we can't leave the cars here. They'll tow them if we do.'

I drove after him into a quiet side alley. I felt even safer there. Once I had parked, the silence inside the car invaded me, and I realized how tired I was. It was some thirty hours since I had got up. I closed my eyes for a second, then Chris knocked on my window and opened the door. He handed me a jumper. 'I always keep an extra one in my car. Take yours off and put this on. The stains on your trousers are not very fashionable but they've almost dried.'

The rest of the morning and the afternoon had a rarefied quality. I began to think of the green car as a materialization of my past not wanting to die. Chris wasn't of much help. He seemed to have a morbid interest in my life in the village, in the people there and in Amber's disappearance. I cut the conversation short each time he brought up the topic, and I dismissed Amber with a few quick insults. I didn't want anybody to help my past find me again. The Cliffs had left a physical sensation I felt on my skin, and I rejoiced in it.

We had lunch at around one, and the food gave me some energy but made me sleepy. Chris had never liked coffee culture but we stopped at a coffee-house after lunch because I told him I needed the caffeine. The three coffees I had served no purpose, and heavy-footed I followed Chris around town, in and out of shops and shopping centres, past historic buildings he gestured at more than described, past places where he had done this and that, and unlit faces of clubs where he had pulled women. He pointed at posters among the mass that plastered the city, frames from thirty-second stories I had invented myself what felt like a long time ago. At first I thought they were staring at me like promises, women I had failed to know, and yet they had been my creations. I turned away from them without trying to work out their expressions. Not that I cared, I told myself, because I was reborn, but I was tired and in need of rest, and the world of the city blared at me too loudly after the solitude of the village. I almost jumped back at an ambulance tearing by, I was disconcerted by honking and alarms, and tills, and music pouring out of smart shops. The disordered mass of people disturbed me, and the number of women was hard to accept. 'It's a small city,' said Chris, 'but it has all you need, and enough inhabitants so that you don't bump into people you know, or women you don't want to meet, if you know what I mean.'

It was reassuring to hear. Still, I looked around with the little energy I had left, with a vague apprehension. Amber seemed to have passed and smudged her own looks on other women, just a touch here and a stroke there. I looked more closely, and felt exposed in the wider streets.

Late in the afternoon I asked Chris to show me his flat. I needed a rest. He wasn't keen on the idea, he said it was almost time to go out, but we went back to our cars to drive to his place. He lived on the third floor of a five-storey building almost in the centre of town. The flat was small and messy, and I lay down on his living-room sofa as soon as I saw it.

I have a vague recollection of Chris sitting on an armchair in front of me, peering at me, a leg thrown over one of the arms, then darkness.

I woke from uneasy dreams to the thumping of music.

'Wake up, man,' said Chris, breezing past me with a clean smell flapping from his open shirt. 'I'm not going to let you sleep more than two hours. We have to get ready. Your request earlier today, remember?' He danced out of the room trailed by intense wafts of his aftershave.

I came to terms slowly with my newly awake existence. I looked at my body and almost didn't recognize it. What had happened to me? It took me a few seconds to remember that Chris had lent me his sweater. I embraced this novelty as a good sign. I was new, I remembered, and now I was rested too.

'Where are we going?' I asked.

'To pull women.'

'Where?'

He looked round the bathroom door. 'Mad Donkey,' he said. 'Good place. Never mind the name.' He disappeared again with a dance step. Both the TV and the stereo were on. The TV spoke softly from a corner, while the stereo provided samples of songs as one of Chris's hands appeared round the bathroom door, zapping at it with a remote-control. I ignored the TV and concentrated on the music. I closed my eyes and felt its effect on me. I felt looser in my limbs, and I thought they knew the tunes from long ago. Or maybe not so long ago.

'Are you asleep again?' said Chris, back in the living room. 'There's still enough hot water for four or five showers, which should be enough to clean you up. Then pick some clothes from my wardrobe. The trousers might be a bit short, but everything else should fit. Are you sure you don't have a change of clothes of your own? Not that I mind lending you stuff but, God, how can you travel without even a pair of clean underpants!'

I showered. The sound of water blocked out the music. I felt like I was shedding a layer of skin, and I looked blankly at the dirt and bubbles swirling into the drain. I felt a strange sensation, like that of coming home from holidays when I was a kid. Echoing silence in the still hot days. The feeling of being in between: the world of the holidays on one side, a new school year on the other, a step closer to the last.

I got out of the shower. No in-betweens, I told myself, I was new, and I looked for nice clothes in Chris's wardrobe to mark the occasion. I opted for a dark blue shirt and a grey V-neck jumper, but I struggled with Chris's trousers, trying to make them look long enough on me. The overall image remained imperfect. But it would do – it had to do. I tried to concentrate on the shirt and the jumper, and on my hair, which I could brush at last.

I found Chris in the kitchen playing with a butcher's knife. I watched the blade rotate in the air, fascinated. Chris caught the knife and lunged at me playfully. 'Ah!' he said. 'You're ready. Nice clothes by the way, where did you buy them? I thought we'd eat out but we have to get a head start on drinks at home, to save money. Whisky or beer?'

I asked for a beer.

He gave me two. 'Like in your commercials, eh?'

I told him I had done a commercial for whisky as well.

'Inescapable, then, isn't it?'

I didn't answer but turned my attention to my bottles. I tried to race Chris, but he was downing shots, so it was pointless. The blade of the butcher's knife smiled at me from the counter. I'm not sure what I saw in it. Maybe I already knew, unconsciously in those early hours of my new life, that soon I would be looking at it again.

We drank up and left. We weren't taking cars, said Chris, because we wouldn't be able to drive them back. I told him that was obvious, and that it was good like that. He said he was planning to barely make it home walking. I laughed. He laughed.

Once darkness had fallen his neighbourhood looked dingy.

I was not sure whether it had rained while we were inside, but the street looked wet and the buildings too. The streetlights and lit billboards filled every corner with imperfect areas of light and darkness. Chris found the filthiest shortcuts. In a dark alley I saw a rat and tried to kick it, but it scurried away too fast. Chris laughed. I laughed. All the shops were closed. My eyes ached looking into brightly lit windows at neat clothes and long trousers. Cars moved along at a more leisurely pace than during the day. People moved with less purpose, and with fewer clothes under their jackets. Handfuls of cleavage, bare legs sticking out, guys with shirts not buttoned all the way up. 'No need to eat just yet,' said Chris. 'A pint first will stimulate our appetites.'

The pub was crowded, but we found a table. The pint mixed well with the two beers I had drunk earlier. I had almost forgotten the green car, and I felt safe, as if I was in a bedroom with no windows. The city was too big for coincidences. Chris had said that. My tiredness had subsided, and a rapacious hunger grew inside me. We talked. I found myself looking around shamelessly. Nothing scared me. I glanced at women and men alike, pausing on what pleased me and on what tried to stare me down.

'Well, what do you think of my adoptive city so far?' asked Chris.

'Plenty of game around,' I said.

'Plenty, plenty,' he repeated.

'You don't mind living here?'

'Not really. But I'll move back. When they kick me out of my flat, which should be soon. Can't afford it since whatsername moved out. So expect me back in a few months' time.'

'Good. There's some catching up we need to do.'

'We can start tonight.'

I finished my pint quickly. I walked out of the pub with

heavy, long steps. It was my new, assured walk, and behind it I was cocky and calm.

We ate dinner in a restaurant nearby where I eyed a girl sitting at a table next to us. She looked back once, enjoying the attention. It angered me, but I continued to look. Our eyes met a few more times, but hers began to move away from mine quickly. A friend at her table, with a massive, black hairdo, made her stumble back into their conversation. My girl leaned forward and spoke to her. The friend looked at me over her shoulder and past the outskirts of her massive hair. My girl got up and went to the toilet. I was considering whether to follow her, but she came back quickly. She swapped places with her friend who sat down in her new seat and looked at me coldly. She wasn't as pretty as my girl. I gave her a dismissive smile and turned my attention back to my table. Chris was eating greedily. I stuffed my face with an equal lack of manners.

'You should never care about what people think,' he said at one stage, as some kind of principle. 'Look at me. I couldn't care less.'

'You should hold back from farting, though.'

'What? Did I fart?' he asked, innocently. He looked around at the people sitting next to us, who looked back at him. 'Mmm . . . it seems like I did. Well, it's no big deal, is it?'

We drank a bottle of good wine with our dinner. Chris liked jarring touches of sophistication to give quality to his life. A waitress was cleaning the glass surface of a table next to us. When she looked away I stole the bottle of detergent. She looked for it and Chris laughed. I gave it back to her. She smiled. Chris slapped me a five when she was gone. The friend with the hairdo looked at me with disgust but I ignored her.

We left the restaurant soon after. I felt good and the alcohol had kicked in. I felt a mixture of confidence and impatience. I imagined riches, fame, flattery and naked women waiting for me around the corner. There wasn't a day to be wasted, a moment to be lost, an opportunity to be missed. Achievement was going to separate me forever from my past.

I looked at girls, at those passing by. I commented on them with Chris. We saw quite a few we could have had sex with, but Chris promised many more at Mad Donkey. I told him we should get going, then. We walked on faster. On the way I kept turning my head at glimpses of bare flesh. I felt transported, but I ended up walking into a lit billboard.

'Love it so much?' asked Chris.

I took a step away. A crouching female body in lace underwear glowed out of the poster, her head cut out by its upper edge.

'One of your best,' commented Chris. 'I fell for it. Bought that lingerie for whatsername. I'm impressed at how you managed not to show this model's face in the TV commercial too. Shrimp woman. Rip the head off and eat the rest. Although I can't imagine how this girl could possibly have an ugly face.'

I blinked. I gulped. For a moment I felt like a criminal walking into a policeman. But that poster was not my past, it wasn't even my life. I could see it clearly now that I was rested, now that the poster was not like a face in the crowd but a beacon in the dark city. I felt that now I could walk through the picture and into the light that shone from behind it.

I slapped the poster with the flat of my hand. 'Let's go,' I said.

We walked on. The streets became narrower and darker. 'We're almost there,' said Chris.

A couple of minutes later we reached a queue and joined

the end. Chris wondered aloud how to bunk it. I looked at the girls in front, trying to find one I fancied. I didn't find any, but the queue was not that long, and I ended up watching a man who was passing by following a woman with a short tight skirt. She unlocked the front door of a building not far from us and they disappeared inside.

I turned to Chris, who had seen them too. 'They're going to have sex,' I said.

'Of course. She's a prostitute.'

I was surprised. 'Why do you say that?'

'Why are you so convinced they're going to have sex, then?'

'Well, you can see from the way she was dressed—'

'That she's a prostitute.'

'No, that she was out to impress.'

'To get customers.'

'You think?'

'I'm sure.'

I looked above the door they had gone through. A window lit up, but through it I could see only the ceiling of the room. I wondered what you could see from the building across the street. I hadn't liked the woman much – too puffy for my taste. I thought of the man, though, and of her in subordination. For a while I delved into the feeling. It was pleasant to be able to smile, after imagining, and then turn away. And turn back, if I liked. They might even have been a married couple, but it wouldn't have made a difference.

The things that happened behind other people's windows. The things I imagined happening. It was what I used to think about. I used to look across the street from my window into the windows of others, but none faced me directly, so I could never see more than thin slices of rooms. People appeared from time to time, like pearl divers, coming to the surface for a breath of air. It was even more special when the lights came on in the evening. I was in love with life after dinner, beyond windows that weren't mine, of people I didn't know. There were smells I could imagine, food and dish-washing, telephone calls I was sure I could hear, blue flashes of programmes I could have watched myself although it wouldn't have been the same. It was the perfection of life from without.

'What are you looking at?' asked Chris.

'I'm looking into my youthful past,' I said. 'I liked to look through windows, you know.'

'Right. Well, I want you less dreamy-eyed tonight and more on the ball. Look and touch, not just look.'

Yes, action. What was I thinking?

Chris was considering bribing the doorman so that we could skip the queue. He looked discreetly into his wallet, then decided it was better to wait. The queue was moving quickly anyway, and soon we were in. 'If we don't pull here,' Chris said, 'there's something wrong with us.'

The bar was our first stop. I practised the new, tough balance I was trying to master, trying to get as close to overdoing it as possible. Slow and steady, fuelled by the looks I received and uncaring of them. We crossed a still empty dance-floor. The bar stretched the length of the club. Facing it and against the far wall were sofas shaped like Cs, one against the other, so that they created little niches around tiny tables. There were more tables and chairs between the bar and the sofas, each table with a lone candle shining at its centre.

Chris bought drinks. We toasted the upcoming success of the evening. He drank merrily and scanned the crowd. I did the same. The place was filling up. An ugly girl came up to disturb us. She began to talk with Chris, but he wasn't interested. I wasn't either. I reached over to a table for a candle. Chris saw me and stretched out an arm on the counter without the girl noticing. She continued to talk. I poured some wax on to Chris's hand.

'Fucking whore bitch!' he shouted, as he pulled back his arm. The girl was shocked. Chris looked at her, quietly massaging his hand. 'I didn't mean you,' he said eventually. 'Look – my friend poured wax on me.'

She looked at me, then back at Chris, and left without a word. I tried to slap her arse but she had moved away too quickly. Chris and I laughed. 'Great,' he said, 'but for fuck's sake, you're supposed to pretend to pour the wax. Like last time.'

We drank and looked at those around us, ugly women, brash men. Both kinds trying it on with people they would never get. Imperfect individuals in search of perfect happiness. At the end of the bar, a young bearded guy with fluffy black hair even failed to attract the waitress's attention. He held a camera in one hand. A tourist looking for locals who wouldn't look at him. We laughed at that. Men in suits stood at the bar a bit closer to us, and we laughed at their clothes. A group of women in front of us was laughing aggressively, and we tried to imitate them. Our conversations were short, although the music wasn't too loud yet.

We began to make a selection of the women and soon discarded the majority. Too ugly, too fat, too thin, too dressed. We looked for exposed flesh then judged its quality, searching for the slim and beautiful. Smoke swirled around low necklines. Legs emerged from under tables, wrapped in short skirts with feet arched above high heels.

'You know why high heels are so erotic?' said Chris. 'Because they point upwards and direct your eyes up the legs – that might have been an idea for your next commercial, if you hadn't quit.' We were quiet for a while. We followed the directions of high heels up the curves of legs. 'To tell you the truth, though,' said Chris, 'all this flesh up for grabs puts me off sometimes.'

'You of all people!'

'What's so strange? Look, I haven't forgotten the aim of the evening, but sometimes I think I wouldn't mind having something stable.'

'Like whatsername.'

'That was a failed experiment. But I'd like to have another go at an old-fashioned relationship. Courting, get together, love, a bit of jealousy, and why not, even a break-up. Then back together. Something like that.' He took a gulp of his beer. 'I thought you felt the same.'

Two blonde girls had moved on to the empty dance-floor. They were putting on a lesbian act to attract the attention of some slick, hair-gelled guys standing under the DJ console.

'I've come to think that love just means first impressions,' I said. 'A man sees a woman and falls in love with her, but might never speak to her. And that's good. It shouldn't go any further.'

'Why not?'

'It tends to be a disappointment. You fall in love with a certain look and with the personality you think is behind it. You hang on to that vision, but the girl turns out to be different. People are not what they seem.'

'You're a misogynist.'

'I'm a what?'

'You hate women. Or you're scared of them.'

'They just don't live up to my standards.'

'How high are they?'

'Out of reach.'

Chris laughed.

At first I laughed with him. 'But come on,' I said 'No man wants to settle for less than the best. You see something nice and you don't see why you shouldn't have it. And nowadays we're even told to believe in perfection.'

'Like in one of the women in your commercials?'

'Sure. My job is simple. All I need to do is take a beautiful woman, and present her as a dream, in a spicy relationship, in an ideal life, and then I tell people they can take the dream and turn it back into reality. I'm not telling men to buy the product. I'm telling them to get the woman. Sales are a side-effect. I see it as a kind of impossible catharsis of frustration. Look at you. You bought that lingerie not because you wanted to put the lingerie on your girlfriend, but because you wanted to put your girlfriend's face on the body in my poster. You can try to live out your fantasies, but you can almost never fulfil them. It's frustration. You only need one woman to create the dreams of a thousand men, but that woman can only date one of them, and everybody else . . . It's all about being that one date, and laughing at the others once you are. But that's normal. Relationships aren't private. You boast with your friends if you have a nice woman. You want her to tell her friends how great you are. You kiss in public to show off. Today it's not enough to be first, you also have to crush the competition. You need a woman everybody wants. It upgrades your own pleasure.'

'Wow,' said Chris. He propped an elbow on the bar and looked around. 'That's deep, I suppose.' He sipped his beer, then raised a finger from the bottle and pointed at the tourist, who had finally got a drink. 'Wasn't that guy at our restaurant?'

'I don't remember,' I said.

'No, wait, he was at the pub. He sure likes corners.'

I took long gulps from my beer. The hair-gelled guys were dancing next to the blonde girls, who just smiled at each other and carried on with their lesbian act.

'OK,' said Chris, 'so say you're that one date. You still have a problem. The girl in your commercial is going to be different in real life from the way she is in the commercial.'

'That's what I was saying about first impressions.'

He tapped his head with a finger, trying to plop out a solution. 'Well, then, maybe you can brainwash her,' he said. 'No, even better, you kill her, stuff her, and hold her at your window, like a mannequin or something, but so that everybody else thinks she's still alive.'

'I don't want to talk about it,' I said.

'No, but really. All you need is a clean stab and make her bleed to death.' He lunged at me as he had in his kitchen, but with his beer bottle this time. Flashes of his knife's blade came back to me.

'Well, isn't it a good idea?' Chris persisted.

I reached for my beer and finished it.

'It seems to me that elimination is essential in one way or another,' he continued. 'What was that sentence you liked? "I will kill thee and love thee after."'

I ordered another round.

'But say you've got her and everybody knows that, and you've got her stuffed, but nobody knows that.' He spread out his arms. 'That's it!'

'That's not it!' I said. 'It's still not enough!'

'Why not?'

'Women are like TV channels. There are too many to flick through. You'll get distracted. The other men will be distracted from envying you.'

'Hell, have them all, why lower your sights?'

'I can't have them all,' I blurted out, 'I can't. But I can forget them, you understand? Shrink the world until all the beautiful girls but one have gone, and she'll be mine, and all other relationships will be impossible because . . . because . . .'

I couldn't go on. Chris was patting the hand I had placed on his shoulder to shake him. 'That's wonderful,' he said. 'I guess the idea excites you a bit too much. Now how about if we jump off your little world and get back to planet Earth?'

I let go of his shoulder. 'I just strive for pleasure like everybody else.'

'You have a complicated sense of pleasure. You think about it too much, that's your problem.'

'I just have immense erotic and emotional needs, but a disgust for reality. And I just don't see anybody fitting my bill.'

Chris didn't answer. He was nodding to the beat of the music. He raised his beer without looking at it, but when it was a few inches from his mouth he stopped. 'Hold on,' he said. 'That's what you've been doing in your village, isn't it? What a bastard! Just being silly, you said! Why take out the evils of the modern world on a bunch of fishermen? Maybe they just wanted to flirt a bit and feel young again. I doubt they really thought they could get the girl. And probably their wives envied her youth more than anything else.' He drank from his beer. 'Poor people, twisted by your mental wanks!' The music was getting louder. I finished my second beer quickly and then saw that Chris was looking at me with a serious face, although there was a hint of a smile at the corners of his mouth. 'But something still escapes me,' he said. 'How did you do away with your Amber?'

'Will you stop talking about her?' I almost shouted.

'Wow, calm down. Man, you really fell for her, but in a fucked-up way.'

I didn't reply. An image of Amber came back to me and I could only think of her as perfect.

'Look,' said Chris, 'the way I see it is this. When any type of masturbation becomes romantic, you've got a problem.'

I looked around and nobody was kissing anybody. Everybody looked, though, beyond themselves and I saw their thoughts like smoke below the music, thoughts and desires, but inhibitions I couldn't see . . .

'Ah, all these women!' Chris sighed. 'They don't know how much a single gesture of theirs can burn in us and grow huge!'

. . . the provocation, the prov—

'And we like that!' Chris added. 'And it's nothing a good lay can't cure. That's Dr. Chris's prescription for you. Look at those two girls on that sofa. There are two seats next to them and they've been looking at us. Charlie? What are you looking at?'

Had I been thinking about the past again? How had we slipped back to Amber? Where were the Cliffs?

'Charlie, wake up and listen to me. She left you there and didn't come back. You were there. Now you're here. There's no more there. Let's go over, and don't make me drag you like last time, or we'll look like a couple of poofs. I don't want my chances ruined.'

I walked after him. Momentum. It governed my life. I had gone beyond the edge and had climbed back up. But there's no momentum in climbing. Amber was like perfection and falling down towards her was easy and . . .

'Hi, I'm Chris and this is Charles.'

I realized I was drunk. I took comfort in it. I told myself that alcohol makes one all emotional about the wrong things. We were standing in front of one of the C-shaped sofas occupied by two girls. One was a dyed blonde, more sexy than beautiful. The other was dark-haired, with intense black eyes and a tanned, fluid body. She had on a long skirt with a slit up the side that revealed her whole left leg crossed over the right, with her shoe dangling off her toe. She pushed her foot back into her shoe and her legs uncrossed as she stood up. I was still living in my present. The girl had stood up so that I could sit between her and her friend. I wanted achievement and this was my chance. I sat down. The girl had beautifully inviting eyes, and all the rest was just as nice. She smiled and said her name, which I caught and forgot immediately. I shook hands with the other girl.

'I see your glasses are empty,' Chris said. 'What would you like?'

The girls ordered gin and tonics and I asked for one too. I wanted to ask Chris whether he needed help to bring the glasses over, but it was too late. I talked small-talk with the girls. I told them I was a photographer, that I could make them famous. They laughed. I laughed with them. I said I was joking. I said that actually I was a writer and could make them immortal. They laughed louder than before.

Chris came back. I took long gulps of my gin and tonic. Everybody else sipped theirs. We exchanged more small-talk. I imagined my girl was a model or an upcoming something. I didn't want to ask her, because I didn't want her to prove me wrong. She was beautiful, and that was enough for now, and I stared at her openly. Her black eyes gazed at me with interest, and at times her dark hair brushed my shoulders. I felt her thigh pressing against mine. I wanted to tell her what I had done earlier that day, but I preferred to stick to the small-talk. I gave that up as well when Chris started to crack his usual jokes. We all laughed. I couldn't hear him because the music was too loud, but I laughed anyway, thinking of the absurdity of the situation, at all these useless antics and pre-parations that nobody really cared about. They stretched things out for too long, they left too much time for thought, and action seemed unlikely.

I drank my gin and tonic and sucked an ice-cube. The music blared. Disco lights flashed insistently. After a while Chris dragged his girl to the dance-floor. Mine cringed at the thought of dancing. It was a pretty cringe. We were slowly getting somewhere. I finished my drink and smiled at my girl. She moved towards me and I towards her, and we both moved deeper into the sofa. People could still see us. I looked at them looking at us. The tourist was in his corner scanning for entertainment and seemed pleased with what we were providing. The men in suits had not moved from the bar and a couple were looking over at us.

I put an arm behind my girl along the edge of the sofa. She glanced at it, pleased, then she gave it a slow tap to let it fall. I moved my hand down deliberately, cupping her shoulder and slipping my thumb under the strap of her dress. I held her closer to me. She looked away for a while, at her friend, at the crowd, I wasn't sure. I looked at her legs, which were crossed in my direction. The cut in the skirt was on the side furthest from me, but I could still see a slice of bare flesh that pulsed darkly in the changing shadows of the disco lights. It roused my heartbeat into a parallel, excited rhythm. I kept on looking at her legs, at the darkness of her cleavage, her large breasts pressed against each other as her body was turned in my direction. She gave me an intense, teasing stare. I felt my hand on my lap move slowly. It reached her thigh. She didn't seem to notice, she just smiled and reached for my lips with hers.

I felt blessed by our contact. I kept my eyes closed and felt her mouth against mine, my hands on her body. I was feeling my way into achievement, into happiness, but still I would come away from her kissing with open eyes, and I would press my forehead against hers to watch my hand run over her body, over her legs and her breasts, pinching her nipples through her dress, then moving down again, past the cut of the skirt and between her legs, slightly parted under the table. Her hands were now running over me. One had stopped by my stomach and was pulling my shirt out of my trousers. I looked for Chris. Her hand reached inside, her fingers touched my stomach, ran up to my chest and I breathed in, almost with pride. I saw Chris. He was still dancing and I waited for him to look over. I made him notice my situation. He gave a sign of exaggerated admiration. My girl's head was between mine and my shoulder, her lips on my neck. Her fingers moved down teasingly as far as my belt allowed.

We trod along the edge of decency, until Chris and his girl came back. When my girl saw them she raised her head, as if out of sleep, and put her hair into place with a stroke of her hand. It took her longer to fix her dress. Chris and I smiled at each other. The girls smiled at each other. The fucking tourist was still looking over and smiling.

'Shall we go?' I proposed.

'Back to my place,' said Chris. 'Beat the crowd to the cloak-room.'

I went to the toilet first. The urinals were all occupied. A couple of well-groomed guys who were waiting were glancing at the unused sinks, but they managed to wait for the urinals, and I got one myself soon after. I stared at the wall as I pissed, and then at my face in the mirror over the sink while I washed my hands. The light shining directly above gave me a brood-ing look. A clear forehead and a face of shadows. I smiled to myself.

I caught up with the others at the queue for the cloakroom. Chris stood in front of me with his girl. I waited behind with mine, her hand round my waist, my shirt still hanging out of my trousers. I didn't care any longer that my trousers were too short. I looked at my girl and she smiled. Same smile as Chris's girl, but more developed, further down the line. She took her jacket and I helped her put it on. She thanked me and I bowed. I took mine and we were off.

Once outside I pointed out to Chris that since we had pulled there couldn't be anything wrong with us.

'Nothing at all,' he replied. 'But now *I* need to piss.'

We waited as he peed in a doorway, and then we continued. The girls walked a few paces in front of us, steered by Chris's directions. 'Talking about perfect women,' he said to me, 'I mean, this one is truly something. She's much better than your Amber.'

I gave him a shove. 'Why the fuck do you have to keep reminding me?'

'She's not as good!'

'I wasn't even thinking about her any more.'

'Well, that's great. You get in there nice and greasy tonight and you'll feel much better.'

'I'm not sick that I need to feel better.'

He didn't answer. We walked on to his block of flats. He couldn't find his keys. I pressed my girl against the wall of the building and kissed her, to bury Chris's words under my actions.

'Fucking hell, did you see that flash?' said Chris. 'Lightning.'

'Didn't look like it,' said his girl.

'Didn't look like what?'

'And there's no thunder.'

'So?' said Chris, his hands on his hips. 'Maybe we're too far away to hear it.'

His girl paid him no attention. She snatched his keys from him and opened the door.

Once we got in we all crashed into the living room. Chris brought out a bottle of whisky, but nobody wanted any. He put on some music then hesitated in front of the black screen of the TV, but decided not to turn it on. We sat there listening to the music for a while. Then I felt a hand on my shoulder.

Chris waved goodnight and wandered into his room with his girl.

I was almost there. This is what it all came down to. The sofa was spacious, but not big enough for two people. My girl took the cushions down from it and laid them on the floor. We got undressed and I felt troubled. I knew that if I finished this there would be no turning back, no more past. I reached over for the whisky and downed a shot, just in case. We collapsed onto each other and on to the cushions, and I tried to find, between the flesh of our bodies, a point at which my mind would stop nagging. I searched for poetry and some form of salvation in what we were doing, and I felt the alcohol was granting me a fraction of both. I reached over for another shot. I turned back to her, my throat refreshed, and I began again, putting more emphasis into my actions, but there was something about the girl's independence of movement that made my mind shudder with dumb surprise. But I kept on and held myself on top of her, and we fell through the cushions, kicked them away, and I kissed and grabbed and stroked, and then, when nothing else was left to do but one thing, I spread her legs, and lay above her with my dick in my hand and . . .

I remained there, hovering above her, hanging on to myself. 'Well?' she said.

I looked at her. My flesh grew soft in my hand. And then I was up, putting on my clothes, my thoughts focused on the bright, glittering smile of the butcher's knife Chris had been playing with earlier that night.

XVII

The road rolled under my headlights with its sickly grey colour. I was drunk, but although I was driving somewhat imprecisely, my mind was unnaturally clear. The butcher's knife lay on the passenger seat. When I had brandished it in Chris's flat, a deathly silence had choked the complaints of the girl I had been with. For a moment I looked at her and saw Amber, and I was caught by a sense of vertigo like a reverberation from the Cliffs, and it was not fear but a sense of purpose. I had raised the knife but I had stopped myself striking.

I drove on faster. Dawn had not yet begun to dig through the mass of clouds, and I raced past the Cliffs, barely noticing the car park. I slowed down in order not to miss the crossroads leading to the village. It was barely visible and must have looked unwelcoming to all eyes but mine, but without hesitation I left behind me the world of others and disappeared inside my own.

I felt no shame for the dreams I had left there. I saw no limits to what I could do to make them mine again. I had realized the Cliffs hadn't changed who I was: on the contrary, they had given me the courage I needed to be myself. I picked up the knife from the passenger seat and held it between my hand and the steering-wheel.

The bed-and-breakfast looked like an abandoned outpost.

Or a usurped one. Not a light was on. I stopped my car on the road and leaped out. Within moments I was standing in the hallway, holding my knife, feeling elation and greed. I took a few excited steps forward then stopped. Something wasn't right.

I walked back out. The green car was missing. Could that idiot Charles still be looking for me? Maybe for Amber's sake he was still driving aimlessly around the city. But if Charles had left, Amber was alone in the house. It only made things simpler for me.

It was almost six. The cold, humid darkness of dawn wafted in from behind me. Everything in the hallway was a patchwork of different shades of black. Something else was wrong. On the counter, where I had placed the villagers' coats two nights earlier, lay a shape I didn't remember. I took creaking steps forward. It was the register, open at the pages I had ripped out. I turned on a lamp and went into the dining room. The light seeped in from the hallway and clung to the white tablecloths and the plates that lay scattered around the room. The peacock hid in the shadows on top of the cupboard, but I wasn't sure from whom it was hiding. The smell of fish hung heavily in the air. I could see the food on the laid-out tables, the leftovers on the plates, but I thought of the smell as a remnant of the fishermen's passage rather than of the food I had prepared for them. What an evening it had been! And ruined at the last moment.

In the kitchen I took another knife, just to make sure.

I walked on. In the living room the smell of fish was milder. I couldn't help but think that my Amber would have cleaned up, and I wondered why the Amber I had to kill had not touched plates and glasses from the buffet, while clearly she had meddled with other stuff. There were slits of darkness under the sofa cushions as if they had been lifted up and not put back properly. I could only think that these signs pointed to the presence of somebody in the house.

I stopped by the piano and played a couple of notes and imagined them travelling up to rooms I still had to explore. Like a harbinger. I was coming.

The guest rooms were empty. Nobody was hiding under beds or inside cupboards, but there was a similar, subtle disorder here: a door of the wardrobe not closed, pillows thrown carelessly into place.

I ascended the last flight of stairs without trying to minimize the sound of my feet. I wanted to get this business over and done with, for I couldn't shake off a certain annoyance at the thought of the commotion that would take place if Amber was really there, the screams that would tear the peace and quiet.

The bathroom door was open. The white enamel of the sink collected the first, filthy light from outside. In the storage room boxes stood on the floor like gigantic flowers, and flaps I had closed were now open like petals.

I burst into the bedroom with raised knives. I saw the blades glimmer with a strange light as I screamed and stabbed the air, stabbed the quilt, stabbed the pillows, stabbed the quilt again. I was blinded by its colour as I plunged the knives into it, and for a moment I thought I saw blood squirting from the cuts I made, not the fluttering of white feathers. Then I turned to the rest of the room. Drawers hung open like arms reaching out for me. I kicked them in, then I kicked the door shut to see if somebody was hiding behind it, but my knives sliced through more immaterial blackness. I turned on the light. Nobody was under the bed. Nobody was anywhere. Amber's picture was missing. The moisturizer that had been under the bed stood on the window-sill. A pale, horrid drop had streaked the bottle and for a second I thought it was still moving.

I walked back to the bed. Carefully I lifted the pillow under which I had hidden Amber's note. It was still there, but it was unfolded, facing up, and I didn't remember leaving it like that. "'I've gone you know where'" I murmured, and I thought about where she could be, as if she had really written the note herself.

I looked out of the window. An untraceable dawn had revealed the blind, crawling shapes of the clouds. The hillside under them was cold and naked, as I had left it. Down by the beach the fishermen were pushing their boats into the water.

I lay down on the bed and stuck my knives into it. Somebody had been in the house, but I wasn't sure now that it had been Amber. I closed my eyes to think, but the darkness under my eyelids held me, and within moments I was asleep and dreaming of something indefinite that lived between the walls of the house and spied on me from gaps between the wooden boards.

I woke up feeling a stinging pain in my left forearm. I had cut myself on one of the knives that still stood erect on the bed. I pulled up my sleeve and the sight of my own blood upset me. I looked at my watch. It was half past four in the afternoon, and the room was lit by the sick light of another cloudy day. My dreams still fluttered thin as shrouds inside my head, and I had the taste of nausea in my mouth. I got up and looked out of the window. The boats lay quiet and abandoned down on the beach. I wanted to feel good, but something disturbed me even more than my blood and my dreams. The silence was unnatural, I felt it vibrate gently, like a flat horizon broken by an approaching, indistinct shadow. I walked downstairs and outside holding the knives. The road was deserted in both directions.

I was about to go in when I saw an envelope lying on the front step under a stone. I kicked away the stone, picked up the envelope and looked around again. Still nobody, only a cold, invisible wind. I walked back into the house and cut open the envelope with one of my knives. Inside I found a short note folded around some pictures. I was about to read the note when the first picture caught my eye.

I was in it. I wasn't facing the photographer, but looking at the woman sitting next to me on a C-shaped sofa. I flicked through the others, and I watched as I smeared myself on her, till both my hands had found a way under her dress. The last two were more sober. One portrayed me pressing the girl against the wall of Chris's building, and in the other we were disappearing inside. In a corner of each picture, little red digital numbers framed the sequence in time.

The green car, the lightning without thunder Chris had mentioned, the disorder at the bed-and-breakfast . . . Now I knew who had been behind them, and it wasn't Amber. I smiled to myself at the discovery, but as I looked at the pictures my eyes fell on my bloodstained arm and I felt a retch at the back of my throat, and the light around me became bleak and hard like the steel of the knives I held in my other hand.

I read the note knowing what to expect. It said: 'Meet me on the beach at 6.00 p.m. Don't be late or everybody will know.'

It was almost five. I drove down to the village and parked by the beach. Nobody was about, not a face in a window, just a wind that produced tenuous waves of sand that chased each other down the road. On the beach they formed a low haze that swirled around the boats' black hulls. The water in the bay was covered with a torn web of foam. The clouds were unnaturally low and, for a moment, I thought I could see, hidden in their long shapes, blind, sneering faces.

It was barely a moment, then the clouds changed in the wind, and the sky returned faceless. I was alone. I had left the butcher's knives at the bed-and-breakfast, but I had brought a smaller one with me. In my pocket I caressed its blade for comfort and encouragement. I didn't want to use it, but I didn't know how things would turn out. In slightly more than an hour, at six, all the fishermen would be on the beach and my blackmailer with them. It was a bad time to meet. A wrong move and I would give myself away. But I was not going to wait for six o'clock. I was going to settle everything beforehand.

I walked into the pub. It was empty. The wind hissed between the boards of the walls, but the air was stuffy. I stood still. Slowly a dome of red hair and two eyes emerged from behind the bar. I walked up to it and slammed down my hand. Tom jumped.

'Well?' I said.

'Well?' he asked, standing up slowly.

'Don't pretend,' I said. 'I have no intention of waiting till six. Let's settle this now.'

He remained impassive, then a smile broke on his face. 'So you know it's me.'

'I remember a tourist with a camera at that club. I must admit you disguised yourself well with that wig and the beard.' He looked pleased. 'I really pissed you off when I broke into your house two nights ago, didn't I?'

He tried to speak, but I didn't want to give him the satisfaction of telling his story. 'I had forgotten Jim had told me that you kept a car in one of the sheds, but in any case I wouldn't have thought you'd come after me. I guess it wasn't even that hard. You must have had Chris's address.'

'I did,' he said. 'It was a good idea to follow you. I was almost sure you'd end up pulling some compromising stunt with that friend of yours. And you did.'

'While you dressed up like a fool?' I said.

'You find this funny?' he spat out. 'Or maybe you think you're innocent. As long as Amber didn't see you, isn't that right? But now she can. Everybody can. She's lucky to have a friend who looks out for her.'

'A friend!' I repeated with scorn.

'Yes, a friend,' he said, and fixed his shirt collar with a quick tug. 'As for you . . . I looked around at the bed-and-breakfast and I saw no proof of who you claim to be. No luggage, as if you weren't intending to stay, no clothes, not even a toothbrush. I only found that note she left you . . .' He was quiet for a moment. 'But I don't believe it, or at least I don't believe it was intended for you. But come on,' he said, 'prove to me who you are. Tell me where she is.'

His fingers were raised above the edge of the bar, waiting.

'I wouldn't tell you,' I said.

He tried to stare me down but he couldn't. 'I know you don't know,' he said eventually, looking away and tapping the edge of the bar. 'You don't know anything. I really wonder how much you've made up since you got here, but I don't care any more because there's nothing you can do to cover up what happened last night. This is a backward village but the smell of infidelity can make people behave in a way you wouldn't imagine, especially when everybody seems to make Amber's business their own. And clearly they have a similar interest in yours.' His lips tightened. 'You can say what you want about the pictures, that they were taken a year ago, that the date on them is fake or whatever. After all, these people know nothing about technology. But let's put it this way: I'm not loved around here, but it's my proof against your word and I don't think anybody's going to believe you.' He picked up a cloth and spun it on one finger. 'And now I'm afraid you have to go.' He laughed. 'Now you're finally leaving.'

I watched the cloth spin and fly off on to the floor. He bent to pick it up then left it. In my pocket my finger gripped the knife, but I couldn't use it. Tom's rivalry pleased me, it was what I wanted, but this time it threatened to destroy me. He had two heavy, freckled bags under his eyes, he looked tired despite his happiness, but he *was* happy, and I couldn't accept that. When I had walked into the pub my sole objective had been to get whatever pictures and negatives he had, but now I was obsessed with the smile on his face and I wanted to smash it and all that was behind it.

'You like Amber, don't you?' I said.

'Shut up. Didn't you hear what I said?'

'But you do like her,' I insisted.

'You're leaving!'

'Come on, don't you?'

'Yes, yes, I do!' he burst out. 'Doesn't it show? I love her, if you must know. I expect you don't have a clue what that means. You just can't get enough, can you? One day one woman, the next another. As long as you have something new to brag about. Use, use, use. I lived in a city once myself and I know how it is. I'm happy I left because I couldn't stand it.'

'You left because nobody wanted you.'

'Whatever you say,' he answered.

'But nobody wants you here either.'

'Shut up!' His eyes were inflamed behind their glassy panes, and he was shaking all over. 'I was Amber's best friend here. I was the only one who saw her in these past months. I brought her food and all she needed every week. And we had plans, you know, we were going to go away the night you arrived.'

'You were going to leave together?' I asked, with genuine amazement.

'Laugh as much as you like,' he said. 'She told me to wait for her that night. She had packed her bags and I had packed mine. I was going to take her away from here, but I waited and she never came. I drove up to the bed-and-breakfast and knocked, but there was no answer.'

A knock. Yes, I remembered. And the sound of a car in the darkness. 'And then you drove back to the village with your lights out.'

'I didn't want to be seen,' he said. 'But that's the past, and you're leaving. Whoever you are. You say you're Amber's boyfriend, but you don't even know where she is.' He waited, hoping I would tell him, but I didn't flinch. 'Anyway, sooner or later she'll be back.'

'For you.'

He attempted a smirk. 'You're not funny,' he said.

We stood there in silence, rivals on opposite sides of the bar, each clinging to a different version of the same dream. I can't say how much time passed. I looked at his face twisted by a hatred he had never shown before but that I could only see as normal. His eyes fell on my sleeve, but the dark stain, whatever he thought it was, didn't surprise him. Nothing surprised us. Nothing could.

Then something behind me caught his attention. 'Well,' he said, 'it seems like you're leaving right now.'

I turned round. Shapes behind the frosted-glass windows were approaching slowly.

'Sometimes they come for a drink before setting off,' said Tom. 'They're not so stuck in routine after all.' He was smiling again. He could have written 'Leave' on his message and nothing else, but he wanted revenge, he wanted to see me defeated, and he wanted to enjoy undoing me on his own. I was sure he would tell nobody what he had done, but would almost burst with the anticipation of telling Amber how he had defended her while she was away. A little brave knight asking his lady for his reward.

I would have none of that. 'If I'm going down,' I said, 'I'm dragging you with me.'

His smile waned.

'You don't have the guts to show the pictures to everybody, do you? You'd be forced to explain what pushed you to follow me. You know they think you don't deserve her, and how can you say to them what you said to me, that Amber's yours? And what about your plan to leave with her? What if I tell everybody now?' The shadows had almost reached the door. 'And what about you searching the bed-and-breakfast? I thought I saw some bras and underwear missing from Amber's drawers. A fetish of yours, perhaps?'

The door opened. The first fishermen came in talking, something about the weather being strange. They must have seen my car outside and, from the fleeting looks that darted my way, it was clear that they were forcing themselves to ignore me. Their conversation died down, though. They sat at one of the old tables, hanging on to its rough edge. They were silent, as if they were about to discuss something of great importance, then one turned to Tom, and asked him why he hadn't been around the previous day. All the others turned to hear the answer, and a few evil looks fell on me. Tom took a step back, out of my reach, and pulled an envelope out of his pocket.

'Go ahead,' he whispered. 'Try to drag me down with you.' Slowly he pulled out a picture and kept it low, so that only I could see it. He turned to the fishermen. 'I've got something to show you that will explain why the pub was closed.'

I swallowed hard and bitter. 'OK, OK,' I said. 'You win. I'm going.'

I took a step back and waited for him to replace the picture inside the envelope.

The fishermen asked what he had to show them. 'Red tonsils,' he said. 'I was sick yesterday, and I drove to town for some medicine.'

I was walking towards the door, but I could imagine his triumphant smile. 'Have a safe trip,' he shouted after me.

I burst out of the pub. I heard a sudden commotion from within as the fishermen asked what that farewell had meant. I got into my car and drove off.

I had a vague sense that things were falling apart, but I couldn't leave. I had no intention of leaving. I had dealt with Tom once in the past and I could do so again. I would find the negatives, and I would destroy them together with his hopes.

I'd deal with Amber afterwards. I would find out everything about the night of her disappearance so I could track her down, but I dreaded that I would get to her when it was already too late.

It was because of this that I almost fainted when I saw a person standing on the bed-and-breakfast's front step. I regained some control when I saw it was a stocky young man with a suitcase in his hand. The bed-and-breakfast sign was still covered by the towel I had thrown over it.

'The bed-and-breakfast is closed,' I said, as I staggered out of my car.

'I'm looking for Amber,' he said. 'My name's Charles.'

XVIII

He had fair hair and a large face above a body as solid and heavy as a wardrobe. So this was Charles, in front of me, and I wondered whether he was another harbinger of Amber's imminent return.

'You're Charles,' I said.

'That's right,' he answered. He pushed the door with a finger. 'The door's open.'

'Yes, it's open.'

He didn't walk in, but looked at me and curled his fingers around the suitcase handle. He was big enough to make the suitcase look like a briefcase. I realized that my car's engine was still running. 'I have to park my car,' I said. I staggered back inside it and parked in the lay-by. His car was there too, old and blue, its sides streaked with oblique splashes of dry mud.

In the meantime he had walked into the bed-and-breakfast. I was expecting the building to regurgitate him, but the windows just stared indifferently at the landscape.

I looked around at the green land of my domain. I looked at the village, my village. I looked back at the bed-and-breakfast. Yes, it was up to me to take care of Charles. It was what I had intended to do from the beginning. I rolled up my sleeves. The bloodstain disappeared into the folds. The wound on my arm had dried up, but the murky red of the scab reinvigorated me. I felt the knife in my pocket. I would shove it inside Charles, so deep that not even the thickness of his body could save him. The bed-and-breakfast had no cellar, but I would dig one six feet deep just for him. And one for her when she got back.

I found him wandering around the living room with his nose twitching at the smell of bad food. I tried to see in him what Amber must have seen, but I couldn't. He was big and strong, but he wasn't good-looking, and there was something about his face that reminded me of a cow. 'It's very messy here,' he said.

'We had a buffet.'

'We? Who's we?'

'The villagers and I.'

'And you are?'

'I'm staying here at the moment,' I said.

He went to the piano and played a melodic succession of notes, casually. The piano keys sang with pleasure under his fingers, and their history was revealed. I knew then that Amber had played to dig out the notes he had buried there.

The man in front of me had become denser, more real, but my hand clung to the solidity of the knife I was pulling out of my pocket.

'And while Amber's away you give parties?' he asked.

My hand froze. 'How do you know she's away?'

'I know,' he said, looking at me with strange eyes. 'I was told a few things down at the village.'

The knife fell back into my pocket. I couldn't kill him if the villagers knew of his arrival. How would I explain his disappearance to them? I thought that maybe I could tell them he had been a tourist having a cheap laugh at their expense, but I wasn't sure they would believe me.

'I was also told who you claim to be,' he continued, taking

a step in my direction. I backed against the door jamb. 'The men I spoke to told me somebody lived up here, claiming to be me. It took me a while to prove to them who I was. I had to tell them things Amber had told me about the village, about her past here, her age, her surname . . .' He seemed to dislike my closeness as much as I disliked his. He drifted behind my red armchair and leaned on it with both hands. It creaked under his weight. 'You're not who you claim to be,' he said. '*I* am Amber's boyfriend.'

'And they believed you?'

He gave a hard nod.

'And you believe what they told you about me?'

'Why should I believe you rather than them?'

'I just told them my name,' I answered. 'It's not my fault if they got all paranoid and made things up about me. Maybe they wanted me to be Amber's boyfriend.'

'They wanted what?'

'You wouldn't understand,' I said.

He looked at me with eyes that didn't. He noticed my too-short trousers, the wound on my arm. I knew I was in a mess. I felt uneasy under his examination, but I was sure that each time our eyes met his retreated deeper into their sockets, and I had a growing desire to pluck them out with my knife to discover what they hid.

He walked around my red armchair and sat down, arms on the armrests as on a throne. 'I'm going to wait for her,' he said. 'As for you, I want you to go.'

I held the door jamb with both hands. The light was failing slowly in the room. The clock I still had to place chimed six times. We waited. The house waited for something to happen.

'Then you want Amber to kick you out herself,' he said. 'She's not going to be as nice as I am now.'

'Will she be back soon?' I asked, my heart thumping.

'I know that she goes off sometimes,' he said. 'I remember that when I left and promised to come back, she said to wait for her if she wasn't around. She told me where she would hide the keys for me, and that I should make myself at home.'

Why was he telling me all this? 'And where would she hide the keys?' I asked.

'Why should I tell you?'

'And where would she go when she's away?' I insisted.

'That's her business.'

'But you should know.'

'She will be back soon enough to tell you.'

I felt the sharp edge of the jamb against my spine. 'So she will be back soon.' I asked.

He had run out of patience. His face looked more squared than it already was. 'You'll be gone before she's back.'

'Wasn't she supposed to kick me out herself?'

With a hard jerk of his huge body he swung the armchair round. 'Listen here, pal,' he said looking straight at me, 'if you insist *I'll* throw you out myself now.'

'I can't go. I have a room to pay for.'

'You can leave the money with me and I'll make sure she gets it.'

'Really?' I said, with a burst of anger. 'And who are you to take my money?'

'I'm her boyfriend.'

His shrinking eyes looked away from mine. He considered moving his seat back to its original position, but left it where it was.

'I have to leave quite a sum,' I said slowly, 'and I don't want the first person that comes round to run away with it. You say you're Charles, but how can I be sure? She's got my name and details down, so she might chase after me if the money doesn't get to her.' I pushed myself away from the jamb. 'Can I see yours?'

'My what?'

'Any form of identification,' I said. 'If I see that you are who you claim to be I can leave you the money for the room and then I'll go.'

He looked angry now. His thick fingers had curled around the armrests and I was sure he was about to rip them from the armchair. 'You're being rude,' he said. 'I don't need to show you anything. Forget the money. Just leave.'

'And who are you to tell me I don't have to pay?'

'That's enough,' he said, springing to his feet. He towered over me. The day was fading, but I had the impression that it was he who was blocking out the light. 'Go. Now.'

I stood my ground and he stood his. I reached for the knife in my pocket, but I didn't feel the need to use it. I wasn't scared. He didn't seem capable of violence. He was relying on his size to intimidate me, but my appearance and attitude had him at a disadvantage. I saw nervousness in his face, wavering glints deep inside his cavernous eye sockets, and they gave me pleasure. There was something addictive in the problems I caused other people. The cracks and voids in their lives were like plaster for mine.

'You're going,' he insisted. 'One way or another.'

The darkness continued to pour into the room with unnatural speed. 'It's getting dark,' I said.

'You heard me.'

'All right,' I said. 'I suppose I'll have to trust you with my money. But it's nearly night and it looks like a storm is coming up. I'll go tomorrow morning when it's safer.'

He didn't move from where he was.

'I promise,' I lied. 'I just don't want to have an accident. I hope you understand.'

He backed into my red armchair, managing not to take his shrinking eyes off me. 'No later than tomorrow morning,' he said. He sat down, crossed his legs away from me then turned his eyes in the same direction. He seemed relieved.

I let some time pass. 'Why did you go to the village before coming here?' I asked.

'It's my business,' he answered, after a while.

'When did you go? I was there myself just now.'

'So?'

He said nothing else. I had doubts, and they were crawling all over him. He moved restlessly in his seat as if he felt them. He seemed disturbed by me, but he must have felt that the compromise he had achieved was the best he would get, and he was right.

I sat down on a sofa close to him, and he stood up immediately and walked out of the room with his suitcase. 'I'll unpack,' he said.

I followed him up the stairs. My head was at the height of his mud-stained shoes. I saw them hesitate on the first landing before continuing up to the second floor. They hesitated again on the threshold of Amber's room.

'You're not going to use a guest room, are you?' I asked.

'Stop following me,' he shouted, more exasperated than angry, 'or I'll make you leave now, no matter how dark and stormy it is.'

'I was just trying to be friendly,' I said, and walked after him into Amber's room. I waved a finger at his suitcase. 'There's plenty of room for your stuff in the drawers.'

'You should be more concerned with packing up your own.'

'Come on,' I said. 'I'm leaving tomorrow morning, so let's try to be civil to each other until then. I might not show it, but I do admire you. Amber told me a lot about you. She's a great

266

woman, really, so passionate. A bit out of place in a village like this. She had this strange light in her eyes when she spoke about you. And I know that you've slept here, don't deny it.' I waited for him to answer, but he didn't. He blushed instead and tried to ignore me. I was starting to view him as a nice, big, inoffensive ox. 'It's nothing to be ashamed of,' I said. 'You have no reason to blush just because she told me a few things about you. What was that about you jumping out of your window to prove your love to her?'

He didn't seem to hear. He had placed his suitcase on the bed and was inspecting the holes my knives had left in the quilt.

'Well?' I insisted.

'What happened here?'

'I don't know,' I said. I looked at the quilt, and for a second I was sad. It was like looking past years to a happier time that still retained its sharp lines, its bursts of joy, but that looked back at me with defiance, sure that I couldn't touch it anymore. But I knew I could. I would make it mine again.

The man by the bed must have seen something different in the quilt. He shrugged, apparently not wanting to think about what he was seeing.

'I know it was supposed to be your secret,' I continued, 'you jumping out of the window. But what's the problem with her telling me? I think it's nice that everybody knows what you can do for love. She even told me how much you liked her name, and how you even wrote a poem about it once.'

He either ignored my lies or he didn't know I was lying to him.

I strolled round the room, stopping here and there, looking out of the window. He fumbled with the stuff in his suitcase, without taking anything out. He walked to the chest of drawers, then back to his suitcase, but did little more than rearrange the clothes inside it.

'Well, never mind,' I said. 'I know I'm annoying you.'

'You are.'

'Yes. Like I said.' I looked out of the window again, my hands behind my back. 'But we did talk a lot in this room,' I said. 'Just long talks,' I repeated, in a voice as fake and distant as I could make it. He was still ignoring, or pretending to ignore me. 'But maybe I'm priding myself on knowing her better than I really do. If I knew her well I would know the kind of stuff you told the villagers today. And I don't. I mean, what's her surname? I don't even know that while you must.'

He looked at me and said it without hesitation. My eyes grew wide and his disappeared altogether, and he went back to his open suitcase. 'That's it,' he said. 'I don't want to talk to you any longer.'

'No more need to,' I said, and left the room.

xix

He was an impostor. He was too prepared in things I didn't know.

He stayed in Amber's room. He shouted something about being tired after the journey, and that he didn't want to be disturbed. I walked outside and round the house. After a while a dark shape, large and angular like a wardrobe, came to stand beyond Amber's window, and looked down at the village. A minute later it shrank out of view, and the window remained blank and cold. No light was turned on inside. It was better this way. If the newcomer had truly gone down to the village I was quite sure that by now Tom knew of his arrival, but I was afraid that he would interpret a light at the bed-and-breakfast as a sign of my own unwillingness to leave. I still feared the power he could wield with his pictures. I counted on his patience, and I started to count more and more on my ox-like friend's permanence. I was caught in their crossfire, but maybe I could duck and let them shoot at each other . . .

I sat on the grass and let my thoughts flow. The fishermen were coming back to the beach and the clouds had almost finished stifling the day. Lights began to shimmer at the base of the hill. A feeble one was shining inland, and I guessed it to be William's house, although I had never seen it. The wind seemed to rise from the village, and I imagined it was whipped up by talk about the newcomer. There was a lot of mending I would have to do, and not much time to do it. I felt that each wasted moment was like a further concession to Amber's return, and I feared that she would unmask me before I could get rid of her. I looked around repeatedly to make sure that I was alone. I was angry with myself for having left unexplained for so long the mystery of her disappearance, but I tried to remain calm. I walked back inside, and slowly, in the darkness, I cleared up the mess of the buffet.

I barely slept and dreamed too much. I dreamed of sounds in the darkness, the tapping of nails against the window-panes, a thumping at the door, even the petulant ring of a doorbell the bed-and-breakfast didn't have. And I dreamed of women's voices, muffled as if they were coming through a wall, and bricks grating against each other, pushed from behind, slowly falling from the fat frame of the chimney.

I woke when I heard the real sound of steps coming down the stairs. Everything else had been a dream I told myself, just a dream. I had fallen asleep in the living room, on my red armchair. The impostor appeared in the doorway and looked with surprise at the order I had restored, but he didn't greet me.

His rudeness angered me, but I kept cool. I had cleaned up for a last test of his identity. 'Amber put everything in order,' I said to him.

'Amber?' he said, bewildered.

'She's here. She's sleeping in one of the guest rooms. No, wait, is that her coming down the stairs?'

I unnerved myself in uttering the words I had prepared, but he was horrified. I no longer doubted that he was a fake. He stood immobile, like an animal scanning its surroundings for unusual sounds, but he heard only my laughter.

'It was just a joke,' I said. 'I'm sorry, I shouldn't play with your desire to see her again. I put everything in order myself. I wanted to apologize for what I had done in the past days. I admit I behaved badly, but I didn't mean any harm.'

'I don't care what you meant,' he said, wagging a shaky finger at me. 'You're leaving now.'

I stood up to show him my goodwill. 'And what are you going to do?'

'I'm going back to the village. I have to make sure everybody knows who the real Charles is. And that they won't let you come back.'

'You're going to town even if I leave right now?'

'Yes.'

'Wow, like a soldier on a mission.'

'What are you saying?'

'Nothing,' I said, walking past him. 'Just that I might as well have breakfast first.'

He looked at me with his hands on his hips. 'You're taking this very calmly.'

'How should I take it? I'm leaving. Look, I laid the table for two last night. I just have to prepare the coffee. Amber told me you like to eat a lot of breakfast.'

Slowly, seeing I wouldn't leave just yet, he made his way to the breakfast table. He sank into his seat and waited for me to bring the coffee. He looked annoyed, and he ate with little appetite. 'You know Amber will be back soon,' he said. 'Very soon.' I didn't like his words, but he didn't seem to like them either.

I was still eating when he got up. He said he was going to take a shower and that he wanted me gone by the time he came back down. I said I would be.

When he reappeared I was clearing the table. He looked exasperated. I asked when he was going into the village. He said he wouldn't leave until I did. I said we could leave together. He raised a finger to utter some new threat, but saw that my offer was his only choice.

We spied on each other like two cheats in a duel as we drove in opposite directions. I could see his head turned to his rear-view mirror as I drove slowly away from the bed-and-breakfast. He disappeared, equally slowly, down the slope that led to the village.

I was heading for the Cliffs, but not for any rite of passage this time, just to ask Chris for a small favour. The previous night the outline of a plan had formed in my head. I had realized that my enemies had left their desires so bare that I needed only to exploit them to get what I wanted. I would tickle them with plans and promises they couldn't fathom with their myopic minds, I would win their patience and their alliance, I would tempt their hopes and lusts, and with one clean sweep I would break them all.

On my way back from the Cliffs I parked my car a mile from the bed-and-breakfast and slashed one of its tyres with the knife I still carried with me. When I got back the house was deserted. The only presence was the impostor's suitcase in Amber's room, with all his stuff still inside it. I looked out of the window, and I thought I could see his car down at the village, a metallic glimmer that blinked irregularly between two houses, as if people were scurrying past it to come to see the real Charles. Yet, apart from those evanescent blinks, the village looked as quietly asleep as it did every morning, the same grey walls, the same roofs overrun by lichen. The world concealed behind that silence filled my heart with its greatness, and I felt I couldn't live without it.

I tried not to think about it too much, and I reassured myself that everything would work out fine in the end. I leaned out of the window to look for William's house far inland, where I had seen the light the previous night. When I found it I understood why I had never noticed it before. I could see only a slice of it beyond a low ridge, and its roof was green either with moss or grass, and its walls were of a light earth-brown. Its windows peered over the ridge, and I had the impression they were peering at me.

I hid behind the house when the ox returned. I waited a minute before I walked in. I found him on the first-floor landing, coming down with his suitcase. He started when he saw me, and the suitcase almost fell out of his hand. 'What the hell are you still doing here?' he asked.

'Please, don't be upset,' I implored. 'I got a flat tyre a couple of miles down the road and I don't have a spare.'

'A flat . . .'

'If you don't believe me you can check. I was lucky that somebody stopped. I used their mobile to call a friend of mine who doesn't live far from here. He's coming down tomorrow to pick me up.'

'Why didn't you call the recovery people?' he asked, not expecting an answer, seeing that the damage had already been done.

'It's a friend I haven't seen in ages,' I said. 'I thought of killing two birds with one stone. I thought it would be no big deal for me to stay here a day longer. I promise I won't disturb you.'

'But why? Why?' he asked, slapping his head. 'What did I do to deserve this? There must be a phone here you can use.'

'There's just an old payphone that never works.'

'OK, come on,' he said, grabbing my arm. 'I'll drive you to your friend.'

'He's away on business,' I said, resisting the pull of his beefy hand. 'That's why he's coming down tomorrow. And, anyway,

I had to come back because I forgot to leave you the money for my stay. I mean, I trust you.'

He shook on the spot, as if he was chained and sinking to the bottom of the sea.

'Please, be patient,' I said kindly. 'I'll be gone in less than a day's time. It's a small sacrifice for you, but a great favour you'll be doing me.'

He just stood there, incapable of answering.

'But where are you going with that suitcase?' I asked, with fake naïvete.

He looked down at it with surprise. He stuttered something, gasped a few half words before pointing at one of the guest rooms. 'There,' he said. 'In there. There's not enough space in the drawers upstairs.' He waited for his words to be believed, but I looked at him impassively. 'Well then, I'm going,' he said, and threw his heavy mass into the room.

I didn't see him again for hours. I spent the afternoon at a window facing the village. The clouds moved hypnotically from infinite stretches of water and disappeared over lands I imagined plain and empty, and I ached for the world, the whole world that was there in the middle.

I sneaked down to the village at six thirty when the fishermen were out at sea and the light was fading. I had to talk to Tom, but I didn't want to be seen by anybody else. The village, though, seemed more animated than usual. As I hurried down the slope I saw the priest pacing back and forth in front of the church. He seemed distressed, judging by his long strides, but his face was turned to the ground and I was sure he didn't see me. I was equally sure that a lot of women had. There was a general twitching of curtains, and it looked as if even the empty houses were inhabited. I only hoped nobody was considering chasing me away. Not yet at least. Not before I managed to talk to Tom.

I found him inside, slouching in a chair, his arms thrown over one of the new tables as if he was falling off it. He froze when he saw me, then jumped up and walked quickly towards me, pulling out the envelope with his pictures. 'That's it,' he shouted, trying to walk past me out of the pub. 'Everybody, come and see . . .'

I corked his mouth with a hand and held him to me. 'Shut up,' I said. 'I'm not here to cause trouble, but to talk about the other Charles.'

He wrestled free from my grip. 'Oh, the *other* Charles,' he whined, 'the other Charles, the other Charles! Why am I surrounded?'

'I'm here to help,' I said to him.

'Look, I'm not joking about these pictures,' he said, waving the envelope in my face. 'I'll show them if you don't leave. Not that it matters after what he told us.'

'Which is?'

'That you're a fraud! I had thought that myself, but I had hoped . . . And I put so much effort into trying to get rid of you! Now you just have to show your face here and you'll be – you'll be lynched or something.'

'OK,' I said, looking around, afraid that we weren't alone. 'I've betrayed Amber, and I know it's over, but I *am* Charles. As you hoped. I only ask you to believe me. It's this other Charles who's not who he claims to be.'

'He backs it up very well,' said Tom.

'Because he knows her surname and a lot of other petty details?' I slapped my driving licence on the table and pointed at it. 'Ask him to prove his name's Charles. He's nothing but an impostor and he's here on behalf of somebody else.'

He looked absently at my driving licence. 'What do you mean?'

'You're not the only one who wants to get rid of me,' I said. 'Somebody else is sure that I'm not the real Charles, and he thought that if he could get somebody to pretend to be the real Charles, I would disappear.'

Tom seemed pleased by my ordeal.

'You think this is funny,' I said to him, 'but if I go what do you think will happen? Amber knows who the real Charles is, and she'll hate you all for having chased me away. I'm sure you'll show her your pictures then, to prove she hasn't missed much. She might forget about me but as for you . . .'

His smile vanished. Somewhere in his head he must still have thought he had a chance with her and clung to the idea, but I was sure he was more desperate than hopeful. I told him that with his pictures he could get rid of me, but that the most he could expect in return was bitter gratitude. My words rang loud in the empty pub. He leaned with a hand against a table. 'Women don't like people who open their eyes for them,' I insisted. 'I'm sure you know that. As for the other Charles, you'll pave a highway in front of him. Because who will be closest to her, who will comfort her?'

'She'll kick him out,' Tom protested.

I laughed. 'And why should she? He's done nothing to hurt her. He came to the village to help her. It's not his fault that I've been mistaken for a fake. But he'll be more than happy to console her once I'm gone. And Amber's starving for affection. She'll be easy game for a guy as cunning and . . . hungry as he is. You should have seen the way he looked at her picture. He stared at it with this . . . this drooling look, and the way he just held it, as if he could undress her.'

'Stop,' he said, 'I understand, I understand.' He sat down, visibly upset. He thought about it for a while, then tried to argue that this other Charles surely couldn't stay for more than a few days, that he had a life to get back to, but he lost faith in this new hope as soon as I started to shake my head.

'He claimed to be in no rush to leave,' I said, 'once he saw her picture.'

Tom nodded as if he had suspected that. He remained pensive, running his hands along the jagged edge of the table. I was sure there wasn't an argument he could come up with that I couldn't counter, but I didn't want to indulge in a discussion. I looked out of the windows facing the sea. The beach was deserted, but it wouldn't remain so for long. The door of the pub was held ajar by the wind and I peered up the road. Nobody was about. Even the priest had gone.

When I turned back to him Tom was looking at me. 'You're doing this for yourself,' he said, trying for a cynical look. 'You think you can get rid of him then talk your way out of the pictures.'

'Damn it, I still care for Amber,' I said. 'Don't you understand that? And of course I couldn't talk my way out of your pictures. Look, Tom, I'll go, but not before I've made sure that she won't fall into the hands of that dreadful man. I know I can unmask him, and I know I can unmask who called him here. But I need you to help me do it. We'll unmask them in front of everybody. You love Amber, and you've got to do this for her.'

He tapped his fingers on the table and sighed. He was indecisive. I was quite sure that his chivalrous heart was ready and willing, but he still doubted my honesty and the benefit he could draw from my partnership. I pretended to be distressed then, I paced the pub, I told him Amber's need for help was desperate, and when he raised his eyes to mine I struck. 'I can promise you something else,' I said. 'You've read the note Amber left me. If you help me get rid of this impostor I'll tell you where you can find her.'

A fierce light bloomed in his eyes, and his face seemed to vibrate. 'Tell me your plan,' he said.

XX

I told him nothing. I said that I had to rush or our plan would be jeopardized, and that all he needed to know now was that I would return in secret that night after closing time, and that we would put our plan into action then. I ripped myself out of his pleading hands and ran out of the pub, back to the bed-and-breakfast. It was past seven and the day was dying.

The impostor was in the living room with a book on his lap. He asked me where I had been. I said I had gone for a walk and that I was going to make some dinner. 'Do you want anything?' I asked. He grunted a no and slapped through a few pages of his book without looking at them.

I assembled a frugal meal and ate in the dining room, looking out of the window that faced the village. The day was still struggling against its descent with an intensity I had never seen before. From the horizon sudden bursts of brightness like prolonged lightning pierced the clouds to burn the landscape. The fishermen returned from the sea and I thought I saw them pause to look up at the sky.

Finally it grew dark outside, the green fields turned black, and then all was gone as the window-pane reflected the image of my face. It reminded me of days earlier, and of how my desires had not changed, how I clung to them now even more. I felt everything depended on the night's success. I was sure I would come out on top, but I imagined failing and I saw a glimpse of how my remaining life would be, and there was much ahead of me, but it was all held in one cadaverous thought.

Behind me the impostor went to the kitchen. He returned to the dining room holding a plate beneath his chin and eating something from it. 'She should be back soon,' he muttered. I didn't reply. I didn't want to. I felt that all these words, even our thoughts, were slowly evoking her, and I began to fear her return independently from whether or not she would expose me. I got up and told the impostor I was going to bed in one of the guest rooms.

I used the same one I had been in on my first night. Memories flooded in from a few days back, from a distant world. The man downstairs began to play the piano. The notes sounded like a thousand doorbells. They were nervous, impatient, and they glittered through the floor, the bed and me with the cold cruelty of blades. I held the knife in my pocket and felt tempted to use it, but I waited, and waited, finding consolation in stabbing the mattress.

It was past nine o'clock when he stopped playing. I breathed deeply, and tried to calm down. I had to get ready. From my pocket I pulled out a crumpled envelope and some sheets of paper I had taken from Chris's souvenir store that morning, and I spread them out on the bedside table. There was a note I had to write, and I did so carefully, weighing each word before putting it down. By half past ten the note was in the envelope, and I tied it to the stone Tom had used to secure his envelope to the front step. Then, from under the bed, I pulled out a bag I had prepared earlier. Finally I undressed down to my underwear, as if I was about to go to bed, and everything was set.

I looked out of the window. The moon was somewhere

beyond the house. Torn clouds moved in a sky of a washed-out black. I checked my watch. Almost time.

After a few minutes two headlights approached from the distance, appearing and disappearing with the undulation of the road. I began to hear a car engine, but it died quickly, and the headlights were turned off. After a while a dark figure approached, moving straight through the wild rush of the clouds' shadows. It waved at me when it was close and did a stupid little dance.

I waved back at Chris. I threw him the envelope. He picked it up, untied it from the stone and, holding it high, he pointed at the front door of the bed-and-breakfast. I walked downstairs, making myself seen by the impostor who was still in the living room looking at his book. 'Just getting a glass of water,' I said to him. I walked to the kitchen and heard Chris rap at the front door. I waited a few moments before going back. When I did I found the impostor standing in the corridor with the envelope in his hand. 'Did somebody knock?' I asked.

'No,' he said.

'Well, I'm off to bed again,' I said, and returned upstairs.

Once back in the guest room I closed my door and waited a few minutes to make sure that the man was not considering talking to me, or checking whether I was really asleep. Minutes passed but all remained quiet. I got dressed quickly, I threw out of the window the bag I had prepared and then I climbed out. I lowered myself down as far as my stretched arms would allow. I knew I would have to let go, and a waft of remembered fear breezed through me, but I was hanging from the wooden frame of a window not a ledge of rock, and I wasn't sure whether this knowledge gave me pleasure or sorrow.

I didn't have time to find out. My fingers lost their grip. The façade of the building flashed past me, then the living room's lit window, then my feet made contact with the ground and one joint after the other bent as I crunched and tumbled.

I tried to ease the fall with a hand. Something cracked. I felt no pain at first, just amazement at the sound, then the pain hit me, and my heartbeat hiccuped. I rolled on the ground, choking a cry. The moon flashed past my eyes once, twice, and I thought it was inside my head. I crawled in the grass, pant-ing. Blood hammered inside my hand. I had the dreadful feeling that the wrong fantasies were becoming reality.

I forced myself to resume control. I stood up, holding my injured hand away fromi my body. I picked up my bag, and made my way towards the spot where I had seen the head-lights disappear.

'What's the matter?' Chris asked, when I reached him.

'Nothing,' I said.

'Why are you walking like that?'

'Did you bring the stuff I asked for?'

'It's all here,' he said, holding out a bag.

'And you're sure he didn't see you when you left the en-velope?'

'Letter delivered without fail,' he answered, 'and I'm ready to serve.'

I made him cram his bag into mine. 'Let's go, then,' I said. The pain in my hand was making me dizzy. Luckily Chris didn't say any more. We circled the bed-and-breakfast at a good distance and walked down to the village. The moon came and went, capriciously splashing with light the land in front of us before letting it sink back into darkness. I worked from memory. Chris was right behind me. I looked back at him a few times, and I saw two rows of teeth, grinning at me.

We stopped behind the pub. From round the corner we watched the fishermen leave. Chris pointed at the first. 'Are you going to take care of him tonight?' he asked, then asked the same about all the others. At first I didn't answer, but he wouldn't stop teasing me.

'I'm going to take care of all of them,' I burst out eventually.

'And once you've conquered your village . . . what next?'

At first I didn't know what to say. 'What's . . . Find her,' I said then. 'Find her, of course, even if I have to swim to her island.'

'Oh, there's an island here?'

Soon all the fishermen were gone and the lights of the pub went off.

'You know what to do?' I asked Chris.

He nodded. 'You're going with that man Tom upstairs into his flat. I'll wait for you to come down and leave with him, then I'll sneak inside and look for the pictures and the negatives.'

'I count on you,' I said.

'What if I don't find them?'

'Improvise something,' I said to him.

'I'll burn down his house,' he said, and laughed. He grabbed my injured hand and shook it. 'Partners, like in the old days.'

I contained a scream and tried to pull my hand free, but he was already looking at it. 'Fucking hell,' he said, 'what have you done to yourself?' I glanced at my hand for the first time since the injury. It was badly bruised and swollen along its side. I tried to move my little finger but it was too painful.

'Nothing,' I said, freeing it from his grip. 'I hurt myself when I jumped out of the window.'

'Well, Jesus, we can do this another night. I think you should have it checked.'

'Rubbish,' I hissed. 'I don't want any delay. I'm tired of people trying to stop me.'

He blinked, and the fun in his eyes was gone. 'Your wanking hand,' he said, almost seriously.

I hurried down the alley that separated the pub from the first house of the village. Behind me, Chris was a blue, clear-cut shadow, while I was dizzy with pain. I felt that the grin that had disappeared from his face was now eating its way into me and laughing at what it found there.

I jumped when I reached the pub door. Tom was standing there in the darkness, silent, almost reproachful, as if he had overheard my conversation with Chris.

'You're late,' he remarked. He pulled me into the pub and rushed ahead of me. We went upstairs and into his living room. He turned on a lamp, one of his modern additions to the place, but even its light seemed besieged by Frank's old furniture and, for a moment, I felt we were too.

The bags under Tom's eyes had swollen and he was nervous. 'Well, you can tell me your plan now, can't you?' he said, flapping a hand between himself and me.

'That's why I'm here,' I said, showing him my bag.

'What's in it?' he asked.

'It's what you need for tonight.'

'What do I have to do?'

'Dress up.'

I pulled out the contents of the bag almost with anger, and bolts of agony shot through me when I had to use my injured hand.

Tom stood where he was, not moving. 'What kind of farce is this?' he said. 'You want me to wear that stuff?'

'Trust me.'

'A skirt?'

'I told you to trust me.'

'A wig? I'm not wearing a wig. And lipstick? Are you mad?'

'I don't want to repeat myself a third time.'

'Oh, no, you're trying to trick me,' he said.

I grabbed his collar with my injured hand. The pain left me on the threshold of fainting, but my mind was clear. 'You have to trust me,' I said. 'I don't expect you to like what we have to do, but this is the only way to bring down that man up at the bed-and-breakfast and whoever called him here. We're doing this for Amber, remember? And for you too. I could just leave and let you sort out all this shit yourself.'

He looked down and his eyes disappeared into those huge flaccid bags beneath them. 'Well,' he said, 'explain to me what you've come up with.'

'I don't want to waste any more time,' I said.

'Explain the plan, then,' he insisted. He pried open my fingers to free himself, but suddenly his hands let go of mine. 'What the hell happened to your hand?'

I hid it behind my back. 'Nothing that should worry you,' I said. I returned my attention to the clothes I had pulled out of the bag, hoping he would too, but he just stood there looking at me. 'Look,' I told him, 'I had to jump from the window not to be seen by that man. I fell on my hand, all right? I mean, damn it, can't you see I'm serious about this?'

He still seemed worried. He flicked a finger at my bag. 'Your plan then . . . I want to hear it.'

'All right, listen,' I said. 'I left a note on the doorstep of the bed-and-breakfast for the impostor. I know he's read it. I made a rough draft so you could read it too.'

He took the crumpled piece of paper I handed to him and held it to the light. '"Dear friend,"' he read, '"I don't have much time. I know you have been called here to get rid of the man who pretends to be my Charles, and I'm grateful. It makes me feel I can trust you, and that I can ask for your help. I have to. You're the only person who can help me. I need to see you tonight. Everything depends on it. Meet me at one o'clock at the fifth house after the pub. I'll leave the door open. I'm counting on you. Amber."' Tom looked up from the paper. 'That's Dora's sister's house.'

'That's right,' I said, and I showed him the key I had dug out from under the ashes of the fireplace. 'That's where we'll set our trap.'

'Why would he come? Don't you think he'll suspect something?'

'He'll come,' I said. 'I imitated Amber's handwriting, I made sure he wouldn't think I wrote the note myself, and I made sure that he thinks I'm in bed asleep now. I don't reckon he's intelligent enough to realize what we're up to. Plus he's keen to meet her.'

'And what happens when he comes?' he asked.

'He just needs to see Amber. He might be stupid, but he's going to want proof before he falls into our trap. And you're going to be our perfect replica of Amber.' I lifted the blonde wig from the table. 'We'll disconnect the lights, so that he won't be able to see that he's dealing with a double. All you have to do then is to tell him to call whoever brought him here. Say something terrible will happen if you don't talk to his contact immediately. All you need to do is pitch your voice a bit higher, but I'm sure you'll have no problems with that. Just for a few words. He doesn't know Amber's voice. If he shows reluctance, promise him you'll go out with him or something. Can you manage that?'

'This is a schoolboy's prank,' he said, lifting the edge of the skirt, which lay on the table.

'This is impeccable,' I barked. 'He'll reveal his own falseness and the identity of whoever is scheming behind him. And we'll do all of this under the eyes of a special witness, just one, somebody who won't keep his mouth shut about what he sees, somebody who's concerned with the sinful life of this village and who will punish those who need to be punished.'

'Father Terence?'

'Exactly. There's a window in Dora's sister's living room that we'll keep open. I'll get Father Terence to stand there with me, and I'll make sure he doesn't miss a thing.'

'But I'm going to be dressed as a woman!'

'It's for the sake of our plan. I'll explain it to him and he'll understand.'

'I don't know. And I've heard Father Terence isn't feeling too good.'

'Why not?'

'Something about this new Charles coming.'

'An even better reason for him to help us.'

He looked over at the table and his nervousness faded. I think he almost forgot I was there. He studied Amber's clothes as if he was about to propose to them. My plan must have faded into an excuse for him to get closer to her. Briefly, the intensity of what he felt for those clothes excited me too, but then he climbed out of his own and his eager flesh showed, and I felt disgusted at the idea of his body, more colourless than mine, craving to conquer Amber's perfection.

He put on the bra and then, without having to think about it, he filled it with the socks I had brought. He struggled into the tight white top, but his alacrity soon got the better of him. He stepped into the skirt and I fastened it at the waist for him, hard and tight, which made him moan almost with pleasure, and I noticed the way he looked down at himself, the way he fixed the folds of the skirt, caressing them.

I gave him a hostile shove and told him it was time to put

on the makeup. He said, 'OK,' shrilly, then looked at me with surprise as if it wasn't he who had just spoken. 'Is . . . is this OK?' he stuttered, in the same tone. 'Is it OK if I speak like this to the other Charles?'

I should have been pleased, but it disturbed me to stare at this complacent, happy creature of mine. Sure, I said. It was fine if he spoke like that.

He sat down in a chair, legs together, hands on his lap. I started to pile makeup on his face, and added more and more in search of a face I remembered only too well. Tom's eyes began to look worried as the cage grew around them, and the pleasure they had shown earlier was gone. Slowly Amber's face appeared, a thin, imperfect mask, her gentle features strained over Tom's more pronounced ones. I piled on more makeup, trying to minimize the distortion, but I made it too brassy, and his face was always under hers, and her eyes were his.

I stood up and took a step back. I looked at Tom, his red hair sprouting over the hybrid face I had crafted. I told myself I needn't worry. It would do. It would fool the impostor, and that was all that mattered. With the wig and in the dark he could almost be Amber.

Tom asked whether we shouldn't start moving. Absently I looked at my watch and said it was still early.

I put away the makeup, fastened the wig on to his head then backed into a chair. His appearance was disconcerting. I was still feeling dizzy because of my hand, but I had the vivid impression that the figure seated in front of me had mush-roomed out of something, the floorboards maybe, fed by the bad light of the room. It was Tom, it was Amber, I wasn't sure. It sat still and its lips moved. At first I couldn't make out what it was saying, then the voice reached me, faint but vibrating inside my head, as if I was hearing myself speak while wearing earplugs.

'I have hopes,' it said. 'I've had them since I got here. I don't know. I came here for work, and here I stayed . . . but where did I live? I've asked myself this. Not here, I had dreams . . . I've asked myself why not leave, but where would I go? Because here is . . . you know. The promise . . . nothing can ever happen, and everything already had . . . I would leave and come back. Nobody can leave. Nobody. Before coming here I used to put my alarm clock on the other side of the room, and I would put things in between, so I would trip when I went to turn it off. Otherwise I wouldn't wake up. Here I've got an alarm clock that rings more gently, by my bedside. I don't want to wake up quickly. I wouldn't remember my dreams . . . Like this I believe them for a few minutes, when I'm still not sure whether I'm awake or not. I don't know . . . I dream of . . . Doesn't matter . . . but not this morning. This morning I dreamed of a distant city, of cellars there.'

The figure before me was quiet. I sensed sadness, almost resignation. Whatever it was I was looking at, I felt that everything was as it should be. And still, I don't know if it was the pain in my hand or the light, but I continued almost to disbelieve its presence. We looked at each other, waiting – I had almost forgotten for what.

The figure got up, and seeing it move was even worse, but it was Tom's voice that spoke. 'I don't know,' he said. 'I heard that his name really is Charles. The impostor's. Somebody has seen his driving licence or something.'

'It's a common name,' I said. 'That's what Eamonn told me when I had lunch in his house. He said he has a nephew called Charles. I think the man is Eamonn's nephew.'

'I don't care who he is. I want you both out of this village.'

He stood at the window looking out. Her blonde hair shone in the moonlight.

We had to get going.

'The time is close,' I said, as I stood up. We walked down-stairs and outside. I made him hurry to prevent him locking the door in case he had that in mind. Chris had better be ready. The moon was still out, and Tom walked in front of me at first, but I felt unable to look at him dressed as he was, and I overtook him and led the way. We reached Dora's sister's house, and I unlocked the door. I rushed into the living room and opened the window. 'The priest and I will look in from here,' I said. 'You can stand by the kitchen door. You'll be far enough away for the man to see you clearly, but not clearly enough. I'll take out this light-bulb so that he can't turn on the light.'

Tom waded past the piles of books. He reached the kitchen door and stood there. 'Is it OK, then?' he asked. 'You can't tell it's me?'

In the darkness he looked like a scarecrow, or something worse. I was frightened, terrorized as if on our way into the house Tom had disappeared again and Amber, or a brutal, half-dead version of her, had walked in and she was now, finally, confronting me. And still I couldn't take my eyes away from the vision; it awoke in me shudders of horror and deep desires I feared I could never resolve.

I told Tom he looked like Amber, and I ran out of the house. I headed blindly for the church, and felt something behind, chasing me. Curtains were drawn at most windows, but more than once I imagined one move to reveal a dark shape I thought I had left behind in a dead woman's house.

I found myself clinging to the church door, but it was locked. I felt this meant something, but I didn't want to think about it. I hurried to the door of the presbytery but it wouldn't open either. I knocked but there was no answer. I knocked louder, again and again. I saw my injured hand crawling in its agony towards the one knocking as if it could provide some last, desperate help. A sound came from inside. A chair screeching against the floor, then footsteps.

The door opened and I burst in.

'It's you,' the priest said.

'I'm here to tell you about the other Charles.'

'The other . . . Charles,' he repeated, and staggered to the table. A strong smell of alcohol hung in the air. 'I think I was dreaming,' he said.

'I'm the real Charles,' I said to him loud and clear, 'not that impostor who showed up yesterday, and I have proof to get rid of him and to show that somebody in the village brought him here. And whoever it was, I believe they're plotting with Tom. I've seen him now, walking up the road in Amber's clothes.'

His eyes opened wide.

'I need your help. We can unmask them all.'

'What a disaster,' he said.

'It's no disaster. Can't you see? This is a chance to set things straight.'

'You keep on coming,' he said, as if he hadn't heard me, 'Amber, and George, and you . . . I had faith in you but . . . And now another Charles . . .'

'You're not listening to me,' I said, growing desperate. 'You're still dreaming. I'm here to prove who I am. We could even redeem Amber from all the rumours.'

'Redeem Amber!' he spat out. 'Are you a priest as well now? That girl . . . She told me once that communion was everything, and that there was no sin, no need to confess, anything, ever. You could participate but you couldn't be pushed away. And this is what she brought upon us.' He spanned the room with a hand, but I could see only an empty whisky bottle lying on the table.

It all happened in a few seconds. I tried to catch him. I was going to drag him out, and I was going to make sure he remembered what he saw. He looked at my swollen hand reaching for him as if it was the claw of the Devil. He ran away into the church, quickly, as if animated by supernatural speed. I ran after him. The church resounded with our steps, and with the screeching of the pews along the floor as I chased him past them. He ran towards the altar, dashed a few inches from the statue he had commissioned, and I leaped then, my arms outstretched.

I saw him disappear behind the statue, and in mid-air I caught her with an arm. For a moment we flew together, wingless in the hub of the church, and then we hit him. We fell to the ground together, priest, statue and I, one after the other. There was a sound of something breaking after each of the last two falls. Father Terence screamed.

'Shut up,' I hissed, and covered his mouth with a hand. He moved his limbs helplessly under the statue, like a pinned insect. He looked at the statue and she looked back at him. I held both under me, pressing her against him. I felt something wet under my hand. I lifted it and saw liquid on the priest's mouth, like a mass of smeared lipstick. A dark horror filled me. He chuckled or maybe he was coughing up blood. My plan was ruined. In his face was my own destruction.

'The way she upset the life in this village,' he gurgled, 'the way she upset it . . .'

'She's here to remember the old days with you,' I said, without remorse. 'Can't you see?'

He chuckled again. Weak fingers had reached the halo he had nailed to her head. I wasn't sure whether he was clinging to it or trying to rip it off. He had no energy for either. His hand lost its grip but it caressed the statue briefly before collapsing against the floor. 'The perfect model . . . the way I thought she was . . .' His voice was little more than a whisper, and his eyes couldn't turn away from the hollow ones of the statue. He tried to breathe deeply but he couldn't, and I thought the weight on his chest would stifle his words, but instead it was uncannily squeezing them out of him. 'But the confessions started almost immediately after her arrival,' he said. 'Eamonn first . . . upset and repentant about things he said he didn't do . . . dreams he had that he didn't understand . . . And Dora asking forgiveness for her anger, because suspicious . . . And then, when they stopped, the rest began . . . The same repentance from the men . . . about dreams, fantasies . . . But no fantasy is ever only a fantasy . . . And the anger of the women who suspected . . . like me . . . who suspected . . .'

He coughed again. His head fell back on to the floor, and he looked at the statue from under closing eyelids. 'I even thought this statue could make her change . . .' he whispered, 'if she saw herself like this. But she never came to church . . . hiding up there in that house for those who wanted to find her.'

'And you climbed up there yourself, didn't you?'

His eyes flared at me. 'I went to put that bitch back in line,' he croaked, 'and she kicked me out.' He lifted his head, but he couldn't hold it up. Veins had appeared on his forehead under a cold sweat. A ray of moonlight from a window was advancing on the pale floor, moving closer to his face. He blinked slowly, and he looked at the statue again. I saw guilt or sadness in his eyes, but I thought a smile had touched his lips. 'She kicked me out . . . but a week later a certain Charles arrived. And the confessions . . . they became milder. I thought peace would return with you . . . You could even take her away from here . . .'

'You're a fool,' I said, with desperation. 'We could have settled this tonight, without anybody having to leave.'

'. . . but you want to stay,' he continued, as if he hadn't heard me, 'and the confessions this week . . . All the evil you caused . . . and now with that other newcomer . . . there's no going back to our original peace . . . and my flock . . .'

His words had faded into silence. His mouth continued to move, feebly, as if he was still talking. Then nothing. For a moment I deluded myself that he was asleep. I staggered up and stood there, above the bodies. 'I've had enough of your talk,' I said. 'You're like the others, trying to get rid of me, but I'm staying. You can just lie here if you want. You can just lie . . .'

My words faded away as well. The beam of moonlight had crawled up the priest's cheek. He blinked slowly, and I thought he smiled. 'She woke me in the middle of the night, the night you arrived. To confess. God knows the truth, but I only know what I was told . . . She asked me if I was satisfied . . . and ran off to Eamonn's house . . .'

He said no more. His eyes closed, and they wouldn't open again. The moonlight had reached his open mouth and it reflected over the bloody surface of his teeth. His face was like wax, carved by the lost struggle of years.

I turned and walked away. The double tap of each step on the marble floor sounded like the pulse of a giant heart-beat. Then his voice crept upon me like the hand of a skeleton: ' . . . and she will be back.'

When silence fell again, his words continued to ring in my head like a threat. I saw the statue move and fall off him, and I felt it did so with intention. It landed with a thud, and rolled, thundering, to the pew I had occupied just a few days earlier. Her impassive eyes were turned to me now, and the sight was worse than the priest's bloody face.

I ran out seeing nothing but those wooden, hollow eyes, and once outside I was hit by the feverish light of the moon. I leaned against the church to catch my breath but I couldn't. The Black Mirror screamed out of the wall just a foot from my face.

I think that unconsciously I had wanted to stop in front of it. I searched it, but there was nothing, just a void looking back inside me.

I ran from the church. I told myself nothing was beyond repair yet. I could use a couple of villagers instead of the priest. They would do, they had to do. I burst into the closest house and up the stairs four at a time. Two figures leaped up in bed in a commotion of sheets as I broke into their bedroom.

'Don't be afraid,' I said, flashing my driving licence at both of them. 'This is Charles. The real Charles. Believe me, I'm here to help you. Things are going on behind your backs right now, and I can prove it, and I can prove that the other Charles is an impostor.'

The fisherman tried to chase me away, but I would have none of it. I drowned both him and his wife in a flood of words. 'And if what I say isn't true,' I kept repeating, 'I'll leave this village and I'll never bother you ever again.'

I dragged them out of their home into the cold street helped by my promise and by the confusion I had forced upon them. They fluttered in their white nightclothes as I urged and directed them in front of me, down the main road and into the alley that led to the lookout window. I glanced behind me as I was about to turn the corner myself, and realized we were just in time. Black shadows were gathering at a doorstep further up the road. Maybe the impostor had smelt the stench of my plan, I thought. Maybe he didn't want to meet Amber alone and was already calling on whoever had brought him to the village. It would do anyway. Almost anything would do now.

Past the window I saw a figure by the kitchen door reading a book, its face in the shadows, the blonde hair falling about it. It held the book close under its face because the light was feeble, but it looked as if it was inhaling fumes emanating from the open pages.

I think I gasped or croaked, and the face looked up. It could only be Tom, I assured myself, only Tom. Secretly I pointed at the fisherman, who must have looked like the priest in the darkness, while I held his wife out of view. I whispered some excuse to her for being so rude, and I rammed her in front of the window only when I heard people enter the house.

Into the room stepped the impostor. Across the semi-darkness and the towers of romances, a fake Amber and a fake Charles looked at each other. It was just a short, simple, grotesque moment, but during its brief life I felt something that was both revulsion and delight.

The impostor looked behind him. Dora and Eamonn walked into the room.

The figure by the kitchen door froze, taken aback. 'I'm Amber,' it managed to say.

'And I'm not your saviour,' said the impostor. 'I don't want to take part in this any longer. I'm not your boyfriend, and I'm not your friend either. Here are those who sent for me. If you have a problem talk to them about it.'

I felt disbelief and tremendous joy at how neatly the ox had favoured my plan. 'Did you hear what he said?' I shouted into the ear of the fisherman next to me. 'Did you hear?' I repeated in the ear of his wife. 'He's not Amber's boyfriend, he was called here by Eamonn and Dora. He's a fake, and I'm the only real Charles!' Inside the house the shadows looked our way, petrified. 'And that is not Amber,' I continued. 'Can't you see it's that pervert Tom dressed up like her?'

Tom ran to the window, but I was already pushing the

fisherman and his wife down the alley. 'Don't let them force you into silence,' I said to them. 'This is something everybody must know. You're my witnesses.' When we reached the main road I ran ahead of them, from door to door, knocking, shouting and screaming I don't know what, to wake everybody. Lights turned on up the road in quick succession. People appeared. I continued to shout, to exhort the fisherman and his wife to share with everybody what they had seen. They were bewildered and I saw myself suddenly through their eyes, but I couldn't stop. The villagers poured out of their houses, overcoats thrown over their nightclothes, and I felt even more galvanized.

Tom had run out and was trying to get hold of me, imploring an explanation or deliverance. He clung to my arm, he tried to cover my mouth with his hands, he wept some plea, but I pushed him away again and again. He gave up. He looked around, considering whether to run away, but people were approaching from all directions.

The impostor, Eamonn and Dora had come out onto the road. Dora was tugging at Eamonn's arm, while he was trying to calm her.

'Look, everybody,' I declared, 'today you thought you were calling my bluff and here in front of your eyes you see who was truly lying. Ask your friends here who have witnessed what this impostor, this liar, is doing with Eamonn and Dora.' Already the news was spreading of its own accord. 'And Tom here, this pervert dressing like Amber to meet them, to scheme with them.'

Tom's eyes were about to pop out. He gasped like a fish and he couldn't speak. The other accused were just as mute, while around them grew the whisper that explained what had happened. The impostor seemed the most scared. With horror he watched his involvement increase and degenerate, and to the approaching villagers he blurted out his cowardly defence. 'I have nothing to do with this,' he said. 'I came here to help. I thought I was going to help.'

'Oh, sure,' I said, 'you've been called here to help. I know that. I saw Eamonn give Jim a letter two days ago.' I looked around for Jim, but he was nowhere. 'A letter probably asking a relative or a friend to oust me from the bed-and-breakfast. Oust *me*! Amber's legitimate boyfriend! This is the help you had to provide! How honourable! And even you, Dora, my friend . . . I feel stabbed in the back at seeing you here. I didn't think you hated me, but clearly you must hate me as much as Eamonn does. As for you, Tom, dressing up like this . . .'

The windows and open doors were like primitive flood-lights on the scene. By this time almost all the villagers had arrived, and they had formed a circle around me and my victims, casting long shadows towards its centre.

Tom broke his silence, but with little eloquence. 'You tricked me,' he shouted. 'This is all your plan, you told me to dress like this!'

'I did what?'

'You made me dress up like this,' he insisted, raising his voice even more. 'It was you!' He tried to pull off his wig, but I had fastened it too well, and it slanted over his face. He tried to rub off some of the makeup, but only smudged it.

'And you,' he shouted at Eamonn and Dora, pushing them, 'look what you've done. Look what you've done!' Everybody was quiet now and watching, immobile as menhirs around a sacrificial stone.

'Will you stop it?' Eamonn shouted back. 'You're making things worse!'

Tom wasn't listening. He ran round the circle, the wig slapping his smudged features, the fake breasts out of place, begging sympathy from people who had never liked him.

'I'm Amber's only legitimate boyfriend!' I shouted.

Tom stopped. He tapped his skirt where his trouser pockets used to be. 'The pictures,' he whispered, 'yes, the pictures!' He moved round the circle again and pointed at me. 'This man claims to be her boyfriend, but what kind of boyfriend is he? I have proof that he's been with other women. I have pictures that prove it!' He looked at me, his face streaked with ghastly smears of lipstick. For a moment it was blood to my eyes, and I was horrified. 'I have pictures,' he croaked. 'Have you forgotten? *I* am going to be the one taking *you* down with me.'

He dashed towards the pub. Cold sweat slid down my temples and the pain in my hand returned in waves. I was hoping that Chris had done his job. In the short yet unbearable moment of anticipation, I hated him as if he had failed.

Tom disappeared inside the pub. 'Locked!' I heard him shout. 'Locked! Locked! Why is my flat locked?'

Yes, Chris had failed. He had locked Tom's flat, hoping it would be enough. I heard heavy thuds. Tom must have been throwing his weight against the door behind the bar. I didn't know how much time I had, how much strength his madness could produce. Any time less than forever would not do.

The end was close, I could feel it now. I didn't even consider talking my way out of the pictures. I looked at the grim faces staring at me, at the wall of men and women, the outer perimeter of the world that had to be mine, and I knew the pictures were the least of my worries. Everybody stood still but they appeared to flicker in front of me like that first day in church, but with the anger and disappointment they had shown after my invective at the bed-and-breakfast. I felt that something had gone terribly wrong with me, something had got lost, but I told myself that victory was the same in sanity and madness, and I romanticized about making that moment last forever before my demise.

'You all thought me false,' I shouted, 'but who's real here? Who's not false? You can't hide what happened any more. You men can't hide what you did with Amber!' A stir ran through the circle. Some men took an instinctive step forward, then stopped. By their sides the women were petrified. Not a word came from them, and I knew they realized they couldn't keep the past hidden from me any longer. Slowly, a few fixed their overcoats around their shoulders or clasped them at their throats. They had lived on the edge of their dream, like the men on the edge of theirs, but it was all over now.

'I am Charles,' I insisted, and I took out my driving licence and held it high, as if it was a luminous badge that everybody could see, 'and I want to know what happened to Amber the night she disappeared. I want to know!' I turned to Eamonn and Dora. 'I found out she came to your house that night. I want to know what happened then. I want to know what you did to her!'

Eamonn said nothing. He looked at Dora.

'I told her to leave the village,' she said.

Tom shouted something, but everybody stared at Dora in surprise. I turned briefly to the pub. An orange light shone unsteadily in the windows of Tom's flat. Chris had set the place on fire. I tried to see it as good news, but I couldn't.

'I bet you told her to go,' I said, turning back to Dora. 'You were sick about what was happening between her and your husband. The affair he had with my girlfriend!' I turned to look at everybody. 'He, along with all the other men in this village!'

I was sure the men were about to attack me, but Dora spoke first. 'He never laid a finger on her!' she yelled. The men froze. I saw surprise on their faces, and I thought I saw anger on those of their wives.

Tom continued to shout at the pub. Something about pictures rather than about his flat. The sound he made ramming the door and the blood pulsing in my hand were making me crazy.

'He never laid a finger on her,' Dora said again. 'Did you, Eamonn?'

'Not a finger,' he repeated.

'He loved her like a daughter. I'm sorry I ever thought otherwise. It was only my blindness that made us fall out with her . . . but that was only at the beginning . . . only then. I cared for her, I really cared for her like a daughter. And I was happy to hear about Charles. Weren't we happy, Eamonn?'

'We were happy,' he said, looking at me with ice-cold eyes, 'when we heard about Charles.'

'But I started to think she'd been fooled,' Dora continued. 'You said you'd be back . . . but would you be back? I couldn't bear to have her crushed by a place like this. I found her in my sister's house, a few days before you arrived . . . crying . . . crying like a child . . . She said she had taken rides with Jim, just to see how the next village looked, how the rest of the world looked . . . I told her she had to go. I had to. I told her to stop dreaming of Charles's return, I told her that he had been playing with her. I told her you were nobody, and that life is not like books even when it looks like it. I didn't want her to become like my sister. I didn't want other things to happen to her. It was the thing to do.' She looked up at Eamonn and he took her hand, but he kept his eyes far from hers.

'That day,' said Dora, looking at me again, 'I didn't let her

301

go until she promised me that she'd leave the village. There was nothing here for her, and it's so full of opportunities for young women out there . . .'

She gestured into the blackness beyond the village, but didn't look that way. A lot of other heads turned instead. I was sure that the women were looking for a figure disappearing into it, the men for the same figure to come back, but there was nothing, just blackness.

'I thought you wanted me to stay,' I said, 'to keep your husbands off Amber.'

'We wanted you to stay,' said Dora, 'but *I* wanted you to stay for Amber's sake. The night you arrived she came to me with a backpack. She looked distressed. She tried to say something, probably that you had returned, but I thought she was just looking for the courage to leave, so I didn't let her speak. I urged her to go. She said she wanted to say goodbye to Eamonn and William, but I knew Eamonn didn't want to see her leave, and I feared he would make her reconsider. I told her to just go.'

Eamonn stood there and barely blinked. The anger I had overheard two nights earlier in their bedroom was nowhere on his face. I thought he made an effort, because of Dora, or me or everybody who stood around him, to keep all his movements to a minimum.

'But you had arrived,' Dora continued, 'and I believed you were who you claimed to be. But I had sent her away . . . I had already convinced her that you were just playing with her, that she was nobody to you. I wanted you to stay because I was sure she would realize it wasn't true. I was sure she would forget what I said. And you seemed like such a nice man.' She began to cry. 'I wanted you to stay for her good, only for hers. I loved her like a daughter . . . I wanted her to be like a daughter.'

'But where did she go?' I pressed.

'I don't know . . . I don't know what's beyond this village.' She looked at Eamonn and at the impostor. 'But tonight I found out about the letter Eamonn had given to Jim, and about a message found on the doorstep of the bed-and-breakfast . . . I was sure she had returned. I had to come too, to see her . . .'

'To apologize to her,' I said.

'To tell her to go again.' Her cheeks were wet with tears, but her eyes were fierce. I realized there was a type of hatred I couldn't feed on. 'I believed in you,' she said. 'You seemed perfect, but that's because I was blind for having sent her away. But I finally saw what kind of person you really are. I don't care if you're the real Charles or not. There's still nothing for Amber in this village.'

A door burst open. Darting tongues of fire appeared in Tom's windows. A strong wind carried the stench of smoke. The villagers stirred, and I thought they were happy to look away from me, from what had been revealed to them. But nothing had changed. Their past hadn't died, nor had it been clarified. It would never return and still it lived in them, scorching and unpleasant.

The circle of villagers broke and I was left at the centre of nothing. For a moment I thought I had never been, that since the beginning I had only been somebody to humour. Everybody was moving towards the pub now, talking loudly and waving their hands in the air. The impostor had run ahead. He was helping a couple of fishermen to shuttle the petrol tanks out of Tom's shop. Eamonn had disappeared in the crowd of the other fishermen. Only Dora stayed behind for just a moment, to give me a last look of loathing as if she wanted to catch up with those her husband had always given me, and then she was gone.

A sudden long scream came from inside the pub, and everybody froze. Above, past the wafts of smoke that rushed by, the moon looked down at me.

I ran up the road, past each house, the open doors, the windows that pierced the darkness with frightening lights. Halfway up it I saw Jim and his wife coming down, looking at the pub, not even seeing me, as if I didn't exist. She placed a hand on his chest, and his arm was around her shoulders.

I ran past the village and into the fields. Behind me, on the hill, the bed-and-breakfast was dark, but its windows, for brief, terrible moments, reflected the moonlight like glimpses of Amber's return.

But it didn't matter if she returned. It didn't matter if she was still away. I would find her wherever she was.

I looked away from the bed-and-breakfast as I tumbled down the slope that led to the cemetery. I tried to run faster among the graves, but I tripped and fell. I felt I had no energy left in me, but somehow I got up and ran on.

I rushed down the hollow to where William's house was. A light shone ahead in his windows, a faint, orange light that came and went. It made my knees go weak reminding me of another fire, but I didn't stop. I saw a shadow move past and around the house and I thought it was her. I ran round the corner – I felt as if my body might shatter like glass. I looked into the barn, through and under the stirring sheep, and into that open toilet. Then the shadow emerged from behind it, its arms crossed, holding a few logs against its chest.

'It's you,' I panted.

William looked at me as if my presence there was normal. 'Getting some logs for the fire.'

'Anybody here with you?'

'Nobody,' he said. 'Just you.'

I stood there as he walked into his house. I just stood there with my hand in pain, the scar on my arm hurting, my sweater and trousers covered with mud. I ran a hand over my face as if I could erase it, but I felt only sweat and nerves.

I forced myself on. I walked into William's house. The only light in the room came from the fireplace. William was feeding the flames with a few new logs, while the old ones crumbled and spat. 'I thought I heard shouting coming from the village,' he said.

'You heard that from here?'

'Sound travels far at night.' He sat down at the table. The fire burned right behind him. He was a black figure with burning edges.

'It was me,' I said. 'I'm tired of being treated like a fool. This time I've made it clear who I am and the kind of respect I deserve.'

'I see.'

'You – you know where Amber is,' I stuttered. 'I know she wanted to say goodbye to you the night she left.' I touched the table with weak fingers and leaned towards him. He was calm as he surveyed my dilapidated appearance. 'All right, I know I'm like this,' I said, 'but it's because I'm treated for what I'm not. Look what they've done to me. Look at how they've reduced me. I'm here begging to know . . .'

'Didn't she leave you a note?' he asked.

I didn't answer. I paced the room and stumbled over the pile of carved sheep under the window. A few fell on their sides. I looked up from them, and opened the window so that I could not see my reflection. Outside, on top of the hill, the outline of the bed-and-breakfast was glossed by the light of the moon, which had climbed right above it.

'All right, I lied!' I burst out. I was on the edge of tears. It was the moonlight, I thought, its incandescence that seemed to burn even past my eyelids. 'I lied,' I said again. 'And I'm sorry. She never left me a note. She left. Just like that.'

'Do you have any other confessions?' he asked.

'Any other . . . So you're like all the others, you don't believe I'm Charles. Well, here,' I said, slapping my driving licence on the table, 'read my name.' I wanted to tell him I was Amber's boyfriend, but I could only point to my driving licence and push it closer to him. 'Read, read.'

He leaned forward and glanced at it, not interested.

'You probably think you know Amber better than anybody else,' I said. 'Like everybody here.'

'I liked the girl,' he said. 'We got along well when I carved her statue.'

'I'm sure. Well, what would you know? It doesn't even look like her.'

'I'm used to carving sheep,' he said calmly. 'And I couldn't carve her face. She talked all the time, she frowned . . .' He looked at the fire and stretched a hand towards it to check the heat. 'She kept on telling me what she felt about everybody and the way they treated her.'

'And you were jealous, weren't you?'

'I sensed that something was going to happen,' he said, 'but I thought she could take care of herself.'

'And?'

He rubbed the hand he had stretched towards the fire with his other. 'And time passed, the statue was finished, and I didn't see her much after that. Months later she started coming here again. She said she went for walks, and hardly ever visited the village any more. She had been the barmaid, she said, but she didn't like it. She was quieter than before. She wasn't like she used to be. I felt that maybe I had to do something.'

'You kidnapped her,' I said, hearing the absurdity of my own words.

He got up and fed another log to the fire.

'You killed her,' I said, more as a hope than as a question, and I realized that I was not afraid of Amber, but terrified, and I didn't know whether I could get close enough to her to kill her myself.

William chuckled as if I had been joking. He reached for the iron poker. 'So you want to know?' he asked, as he thrust the poker into the fire to break a few logs and move others.

'I have to know!' I shrieked. 'I'm Charles! Everybody knows it now! Why would you think differently?'

'Because Charles doesn't exist.'

He was serious. Impassive as before.

'I don't exist.'

The fire was crackling, lively. William hung the poker on its hook and I watched it dangle. He walked back to the table and eased himself down in his seat. 'One night Father Terence paid Amber a visit,' he said. 'She came here afterwards, crying, and said she had been accused of horrible things. She had denied them to Father Terence, and she denied them to me. But then she said that the more she thought about them the more possible it seemed that she was guilty. Or something like that. She was afraid, she said, of what was happening.' He caressed the rough surface of the table with a hand. 'That night I told her to make up the story of a man who had stayed at the bed-and-breakfast and who had promised to return for her. She would have to make it clear to everybody how much she loved him and how she was going to be his and only his forever. It would keep everybody at bay, and it would keep her safe. A couple of weeks later I found out about Charles. She had gone down to the village and had spoken about him in such detail that I thought he was real, that a real man had come before she could make up a fantasy one. When I saw her I asked her whether he was invented. She smiled, and she told me stuff about him.' He paused. 'I've thought about it a lot. I think she spent too much time alone.'

'So you thought I was a fake.'

For a while he said nothing, stroking his beard upwards. 'It doesn't matter what I thought. What matters is that she met you and she decided to leave.' He leaned back in his chair. 'She looked sad whe she left, but I'm sure she's fine now.' His hands reached for a bottle on the table and for a couple of glasses next to it. He filled a glass and held the mouth of the bottle suspended over the other. 'Would you like some whisky?' he asked.

I didn't answer. Amber had gone crazy with her own invention, but what kind of creation had I tried to achieve once she was gone but a failed copy of what she had accomplished? I looked at my hand and it stared back at me, swollen, in agony, yet the only thing that felt real was the pain.

William was drinking. He placed his glass on the table and squeezed his lips tight under his beard. A dull explosion lifted a puff of ash in the fireplace.

I walked towards it. My trembling fingers curled around the shaft of the poker. 'You're trying to trick me,' I said. 'Like all the others. You're all trying to trick me out of my place because you want it. I've seen that chisel you gave her. Trying to win her over with your sad gifts.'

'She asked me if she could have it,' he said unperturbed. 'She said it was important for her. For what it had done.' He drank a gulp of whisky. 'I have others,' he added.

'Say what you like. I don't believe you. I don't believe you told Amber to make up stories. And none of it matters now. I want to know what she told you the night she left.'

'She said goodbye.'

'I know that. Where did she go?'

'I walked her to the next village. She was going to stay there at a bed-and-breakfast, or at a hotel, for a day or two while she planned where to go. She had inherited enough money to go where she liked. She said we would see each other again one day.'

'So she *is* coming back. When?'

'One day. She'll come back to sell the bed-and-breakfast.'

'I asked you when!'

'She didn't say.'

I slammed the poker flat on the table in front of William. He didn't look scared. I moved it closer to him, till his indifference broke.

'When?' I asked.

'You heard me,' he answered, with a touch of anger that towered over his previous calm.

I paced the room with the poker in my hand and stopped in front of the window facing the hill. 'Well, I'm not worried,' I said. 'Not at all. If nobody knows when she's coming back why should I worry? On the contrary, I'm glad she's coming back. It's not as if she'll pass by here before coming to me. And I can wait for her. I'll be glad to wait forever if I have to.'

Outside the moon hadn't moved an inch from over the house. I turned back to William. He hadn't moved either. In the depth of the fireplace I thought I saw one of his sculptures, but a log broke in front of it and the fire crackled with renewed intensity. Then I heard something else, coming from outside, a car engine, growing distant and faint, and a humming of gravel. William moved just slightly as if to look behind me out of the window.

I froze. I couldn't turn round. I managed to walk to the table and stood next to William.

'I was unknown here,' I resumed with a trembling voice,

'and I had to fight for my position, for a position that was already mine.' I looked at William, who wasn't looking at me. I turned round and thought I could see headlights, two bright dragon eyes in the distance, where the bed-and-breakfast was. I blinked and they were gone. I told myself I couldn't have seen them. Maybe they had been reflections of the moon.

I looked back at William. His white beard seemed to be burning along its edge with the reflection from the fire, and his eyes looked more alert than before. He turned his head slowly towards me. 'Well?' he said.

'I . . . I had to fight,' I said. 'They tried to insinuate things, tried to tell me that Amber, my Amber, had done things with them that went beyond simple friendship. As if she was their pretty toy. Even the women, looking at her as if they could see right through her to her cheapness. Preying on me and on her and on our love. A whole village living their sick fantasies at our expense! But I did away with all of that.' I had to raise my voice to concentrate on my words. 'I did away with all of that! Nothing stands between me and what I've always wanted. And Amber wanted me. She wanted me and I'm here now!'

A loud clanging filled the room. I started, half demented, my bones reverberating with the sound. The poker had fallen from my hand. I felt that no energy had backed my words. I felt my last words had pierced through me.

William seemed to have ignored my speech. He filled his glass. 'I'm happy for you,' he said, and turned to the window again. 'You have what you want.'

Slowly I followed his gaze. The moon was unchallenged in the sky, and there was a light below it. A light there where the bed-and-breakfast was. A warm glow, despite the distance. 'It's my friend!' I shouted. 'It's him! I told him to go back home, but he stayed to wait for me.' I looked at William and

I thought he was amused, but I wasn't sure. I searched his expression while the logs crumbled in the fireplace and the flames flickered off his features, but I couldn't pin it down. He nodded, I shook my head to say that I had not understood what that meant, but he didn't move again. I looked out and the light was still there.

I ran out of William's house. The village glowing blood-red, the house, my car and the Cliffs were laid out in front of me like the tips of a huge fan. I ran, and my thoughts went back to that first night, to tentative touches, dreams and expectations forming and breaking inside heads hardened and ruined, and to the loneliness before and after, the cavernous expanses of a mind that nothing from the outside could reach. And that hopeless hunger had been there, for another time gone and lost when fantasy and truth were joined, and love tasted of both death and eternity. And so I ran, my fists clenched hard, the healthy and the sick, bursting with fast, repetitive swings through the air, a smell of spring or falling leaves in it.